Under Indifferent Skies

Under Indifferent Skies

Vasken Berberian

THESPRING

Washington, DC

THESPRING is an imprint of New Academia Publishing

New Academia Publishing
4401-A Connecticut Ave. NW #236, Washington DC 20008
info@newacademia.com - www.newacademia.com

For Novàrt, whose smile I shall never forget.

Contents

viii

Premonition

You and me, as children. Playing together. Surrounded by enchanting scenery, in a spot I wouldn't be able to place yet so familiar to me, shying stones on the shore of a bay. The pebbles skim weightlessly, bouncing over the waves. Each of us pitches his own, as far away as he can. We stand side by side, our feet ankle-deep in the soft wet sand. We study our throws, serious as can be, but nobody wins. This is evident right from the start. Even if the haze prevents us from seeing clearly, we are dead sure that out there, on the deep, our flying stones, thanks to some strange optical illusion converge and join, becoming one. We look at each other, spellbound, as if watching a magician at work, then we throw two more, follow them, until they reach the point where they come together again, a veritable miracle. We smile, pleased with ourselves and throw several more, with childish doggedness, challenging the bay's spell, which never fails, anyway. I turn around to look at you, to capture your image so like my own, then, all of a sudden, I'm afraid because you're walking away from me. You're wading into the waves, fully dressed, your hand clutching one last stone. You want to get the better of it, break the spell that ties our pebbles together and, heedless of the icy water, you advance bravely.

I'd like to call you, only I don't know your name and then, suddenly, you disappear, as if swallowed into empty nothingness. I don't want to lose you, dear friend, so I dive in too, in your wake, looking for you everywhere. Finally, I find you, but only because, at a certain point, I look around: and there you are standing stock-still on the shore, right there where I had been a moment before, guilt all over your face for having made me run such a risk. And yet, I feel more surprised than angry, though I'm mad at myself for having been so naive, for falling for your hoax and following you. But then I realize that I'm holding the stone you had in your fist before and I find myself in the water instead of you, as if I were you and you were me. I swear I don't understand what we're playing at anymore, the sense of what's happening, so I just remain still for a while, thinking, suspended, like a particle of vapor in the fog all around us. In the end — and this is the absurd thing — somehow, I know what you know, but above all, I feel what you feel. It's not that I'm guessing and I'm certain of this now, it's because we are made of the same stuff, are a single being, split in two.

I see, that you, on the shore, are upset and worried, because you can see I'm not able to stay afloat. Don't do that, please don't! It wasn't you who made up the rules of this game.

Shhh, look!

The bay is turning into a river. A strong rushing stream. Easy does it, I give in to the current. Let it carry me away, wherever it wants. I don't feel a grudge anymore, only a little sadness, maybe, a strong longing for the happy moments we spent together.

You and me.

Torment

1

Patras, Greece, 1937

«My love, I'm away», whispered Seròp to his wife.

Satèn turned in the bed with a soft sigh. The oil lamp burning on the table lit up her eyes, and, as always, Seròp was spellbound by their color; amber, golden and transparent, unlike anything he had ever seen.

«I'll get up now», she murmured, as if fearing, though they were alone, she might wake someone.

«No, no, go on sleeping», said her husband lovingly, caringly. It was the dead of night, and he wanted Satèn to rest another little while, but she, already seated on the edge of the bed, was rummaging for her slippers.

Satèn was young, even though she did not know precisely how old she was. According to the stories she had been told, she supposed she was born in the spring of 1919, three years before the Smyrna catastrophe, when a dreadful fire lit on purpose by the Young Turks had destroyed that beautiful city on the Turkish coast. On that same day of hell fire and smoke, little Satèn had lost her entire family and was left alone in the world. That is why nobody would tell exactly when she was born.

«I'll give you some fresh bread, Lussià-dudù brought it», said the woman, putting on a worn-out dressing gown and tying it gently at the waist. She was tall and slender, her bearing proud, her hair raven-black with a blueish sheen. Seròp was always awestruck when he looked at his wife and told himself over and over again that God had blessed him, undeserving as he was, by giving her to him. He lowered his eyes and they came to rest on her taut swollen belly which grew bigger and bigger every day: Satèn was pregnant.

«You eat it, you're the one who needs to grow strong», he urged, his head bent. Satèn's pregnancy filled him with pride yet it worried him too. Seròp was poor, like all the Armenian refugees in that camp, and the idea of a child — in these conditions — held his stomach in a vise and robbed him of his sleep.

A bed, a table and a chair could barely fit into the room where they lived. On the rare occasions when the couple ate together one of them had to sit on the bed. They had no wardrobe so they hung their clothes on a line stretched between two of the walls. Beside the door, below a tiny window which opened upward, high in the wall close to the ceiling, stood a tin sink which drained into a large basin. Satèn, like all the other women in the camp, had to empty it in the yard, several times a day. Above the sink, was a small metal tank, with a miniscule tap. Satèn used to fill it with water from the village pumps. On the front of it you could read the Greek word *kalimera*, good morning, surrounded by a garland of flowers, and whenever Satèn used it, her eyes would fall inevitably on the greeting and this used to cheer her up a bit. Nearby, lined on a wooden shelf that Seròp had nailed to the wall, were their dishes and two pots, one small, the other slightly bigger. On the floor, to the left of the sink, on a pile of bricks stood a kerosene stove, which required a certain skill and lots of patience to get it working, so much so, that Seròp often wondered how his wife managed to cook such tasty meals in a modest, pokey kitchen like this.

«Here you are», she said to him putting the bundle he was to take with him to the factory on the table. It contained bread, olives and goat's cheese. She moved about with some difficulty, slightly out of breath.

«Promise me you'll go back to bed», her husband pleaded gently: Satèn had had one miscarriage already.

The young woman smiled, revealing her two front teeth with the gap between them; Seròp had fallen in love with her when he had noticed that intriguing little flaw and how her pink tongue moved behind that split as she spoke. «I want to help you sew the uppers of those slippers», she announced.

He shook his head. «You've plenty to do as it is. Tidy up, wash, cook and all the rest».

«It's no trouble to me. I want to give you a hand; the more you make, the more you earn», she replied, firmly.

Since he had been told that the family was growing, Seròp had decided to get a second job. He was still young and strong and in no way afraid to work hard. Like the majority of the men in the camp, he worked at the Marangopoulos textile factory, but to boost his meagre wages, he had decided to put his skill as a slipper maker to good use. He had learnt the trade from his father Toròs-agà, who, in Adabazàr, in Turkey, had owned one of the fanciest shoemaker's shops in the city, the famous *Altìn Cicèk*, the Golden Flower. In his spare time, between one shift at the factory and another, Seròp would sew beautiful soft slippers in felt, like the ones his father, God rest his soul, used to make. He was convinced he would be able to sell them and get a good price for them too. For that reason, he had bought a sewing machine at the Aghià Varvàra Sunday market; a bit of a wreck, really, but he had patiently taken it asunder and put it all back together again until it was in working order.

«Heed to what I say, remember you're not supposed to lift weights», he warned, recalling the miscarriage she had had.

The sewing machine was under the bed and more than once he had come home to find it on the table, with Satèn sewing uppers in an impeccable fashion, like the excellent apprentice that she had become.

«You get it out then before you leave, what are you waiting for?» she answered, bursting out laughing.

Seròp thought himself the luckiest man in the world.

He left the house and hurried through the rows of hovels, all like his own, comprising the camp where he had been living now for fifteen years.

The Armenians had arrived in Greece from Turkey, at the end of 1922, like thousands of other refugees, on board ships belonging to the French, English and Italian allies who had saved them from certain death, in the disastrous aftermath of the Greco-Turkish war. They had landed on the Aegean islands, many had reached Athens, others the country's larger cities. They had come to Patras by boat and train, wearily carrying with them the few belongings they had salvaged from their *memlekèt*, mother country. Seròp was only twelve at the time, but he never forgot his father's reaction when they first got off at Patras railway station. «This is a fine city, my son», he had said softly as he stared at the sea and the greening hills, «but no place will ever be like our dear Adabazàr. You're young, you'll get used to it, but my life ends here», he had concluded bitterly.

The municipal authorities had assembled them all in a clearing near the Cathedral of Saint Andrew, patron saint of Patras. Here, there were some dragomans — interpreters — who did their best to communicate with these poor souls. They had to be registered — names, dates of birth, places of origin — but, above all, it was their human dignity, torn from them so brutally, which needed to be restored to them. Alongside these, there were several officials from the Red Cross and other humanitarian associations, who invited the refugees to fill in forms so they could help them find relatives they had lost sight of during their flight. Toròs-agà, Seròp's father, had asked his son to see if they could trace his beloved niece Miriam, his dead sister's daughter, who had been studying at the time in the American College in Istanbul, but of whom they had heard no more after the breakout of hostilities.

After that, they had been transferred to an abandoned, derelict factory, the *govoush*, the oubliette as they soon baptized it: a squalid place, but the only one available in a similar emergency. Greece was a poor country and the war with Turkey — which had ended so catastrophically — had brought it to its knees. There was a continuous influx of Greeks to the home country as they fled Smyrna, Eastern Thrace and Pontos, all areas they had been forced to leave when the war was over. If the Armenians were hosted, this was because of the Greeks' genuine sense of hospitality and to the undeniable bond existing between the two peoples.

The *armènides*, as they were called here, had rolled up their sleeves and set down to work at once. Each man had set a claim on a small part of the factory, not only inside the building but also outside in the yard, and with sheets of metal, wood and bricks made of mud, had done his utmost to create a place of his own. Every day they had only one goal in mind: to survive. To get by, it was necessary to learn a new language, find a job, take care of the ailing and, worse still, look after those suffering from that incurable malady called homesickness. Every so often, someone would wake up in the dead of night, howling in Turkish: «*Bèn memlekèt ghidiorùm*! I'm going back to the homeland!»

It certainly sounded bizarre to hear them call homeland the very Country that had persecuted and tortured them.

As the years went by, the refugees adapted to their new situation: the children grew up, many of the young people married and several children were born in this new fatherland. The Red Cross worked miracles, reuniting many families or, at least, tracing countless of those believed to be lost. Toròs-agà was overjoyed when he was told that his sister's child, Miriam, was thriving and living on the other side of the ocean, in Los Angeles. Miriam submerged them with letters, each one entreating them to move to the States. She was going to marry a very influential American diplomat, so, it would be very easy to get them visas and documents so they could emigrate.

«Let me pay you back, at least in part, for your generosity, dear uncle. Had it not been for you, I wouldn't have been allowed even 'to walk in the quad' of that prestigious Istanbul college», she had insisted in one of her letters, alluding to the economic support she had received from Toròs-agà over the years. But he, then an old man, had always refused her invitation.

«May God bless you and endow you with great happiness, dear niece», he used to answer, «but if the Lord has chosen to separate us, we must bow to His will», he would add.

It was the old people, actually, who suffered the pain of exile and the diaspora most: many were unable to bear the sudden loss of everything they had created in a lifetime. Toròs-agà was one of these. Barely a year after his arrival in Patras, the night before he died, he had called Seròp to his deathbed and, clasping his hand as hard as he could, had murmured: «Son, I have lived out the years the good Lord has seen fit to grant me. I have no regrets, only one: I'm sorry I had to bring you up all alone, without your mother».

On hearing these words, Seròp had grown distraught. That thorny issue had been addressed by the two of them only once before, when Seròp, still a child, arriving home from school one day in floods of tears had burst out, «They all say my mother was a whore, why have you always hidden this from me?» Toròs-agà had struck him hard in the face saying, «Don't you ever call your mother that again!» Having reprimanded him soundly, he had then gone up to his room, closed the door and failed to come down to dinner.

But that night, before he breathed his last, Toròs-agà had felt the need to reveal the family secret which had weighed on his conscience for so long.

«Your mother», he began, «was the most beautiful woman in Adabazàr…»

«Papa, I beg you…» said Seròp in an attempt to silence him.

But he had waved his lean hand in the air, a sign that he did not want to be interrupted.

«She was not only the most beautiful, but also the most sought after. Maybe only the angelic hosts could have rivalled the light in her eyes, her sprightly step, her stupendous body. And God had made a gift of her to me. I worked day and night in my workshop, to make more and more money. It's true I had to think of your aunt Miriam's college fees, the shop's rent and pay for the upkeep of the beautiful home where we lived. But I had grown excessively greedy, insatiable. How stupid of me! Stupid and blind. And so, I lost her», he continued. «She was very young, much younger than me, and you'd just been born. I used to come home late and there she'd be, waiting for me; looking her very best for my sake, enticing me with delicious dishes, caressing me and I, idiot that I was, paid no heed to her. She used to plead with me, wanted me to love her, wanted us to spend more time together; but I made a burnt offering of her love on the altar of Mammon…»

«But you used to come back home exhausted, papa!» Seròp said, trying to justify him although he blushed for shame.

«No, that's not true, I was the only one to blame!» the old man exclaimed, shaking his head. «Then, one evening I came home, and she was gone. You were sleeping peacefully in your cradle, but she was gone. She'd left everything behind her, taken nothing for herself, disappeared just like that. I never saw her ever again». Then he paused and gazed at his son, his eyes full of wisdom. «You're old enough now, you might even get married soon», he had continued, «therefore, if I'm no longer around, remember to love your wife, look after her, cherish her as if she were the most precious, delicate flower in the world.»

At this point Toròs-agà just wept and Seròp bent down to dry his tears.

«You were always asking me what she was called…»

Seròp stiffened. For years he had asked his father to tell him her name, the only thing about her he would be able to keep in his memory. But Toròs-agà had never wanted to tell him, lest he himself collapse as he pronounced it.

«*Siranush*, Sweet Love», he had whispered in his son's ear, his last dying words.

When the girls in the camp reached the marriageable age, *the ciopcatàn*, matchmakers, got down to business. They visited the homes of potential suitors, and, sitting down to a cup of coffee or a glass of fruit compote, they began weaving their webs. They would advance bizarre claims and make the most outrageous predictions: «She has the fingers of a fairy, everything she touches turns to gold», or, «Her teeth are so white she'll surely bear male children» or, again, «She was born on a Saturday, so, the man who marries her will be blessed by fortune», and similar nonsense, all aimed at enthralling the listeners, making them believe their future bride or daughter-in-law was truly rare and precious.

But no ciopcatàn had ever taken it upon herself to act on Satèn's behalf although she was old enough to marry. When the girl walked across the camp, on her way to the water pumps, the jar balanced on her shoulder, the men just could not take their eyes off her. They would admire her shapely thighs, her full breasts, her amber eyes, nudging each other, making comments in hushed tones, blushing even, but none of them had ever plucked up the courage to approach her. And certainly not because she was an orphan without a large dowry. After all, upon her arrival in Patras, Satèn had been adopted by Rosacùr, an elderly childless refugee, who had brought her up and educated her. Rosacùr, a language teacher, was the *oriòrt*, the school mistress appointed by the community. In a little room behind the church of Aghià Varvàra, furnished by the refugees with a few tables and chairs, one of the walls painted black to act as a blackboard, had been set up the *tebròz*, the first school for the Armenians of Patras. It was a primary school where you could learn to read Armenian, Greek and English and Rosacùr was in charge of it.

«I'll leave you my *burmà*», she used to tell Satèn as she made the row of gold bracelets she wore on her arm jingle, «they'll do as your dowry», she would add to cheer the girl up.

Rosacùr did not believe that marriage was the only pathway to a woman's happiness, there were several more, but she did not want her daughter to be unhappy.

«Look, there are sixteen of them», she would insist, counting them, «you know what that means, don't you? You'll be married before you're sixteen». But that birthday was only a few months away, and no man had asked for the girl's hand so far.

The gossips said she was «strange», that deep inside her something ugly and evil lurked. This because Satèn, especially when she was a child, would wake up sometimes in the middle of the night screaming, thrashing and tossing in her bed as if in the throes of an epileptic fit. Those who had seen her in that state, and many had, as the camp was so promiscuous, used to describe her spine-chilling screeches, like those of pigs being dragged to the slaughterhouse and the horrified expression that appeared on her face, as if she had seen the devil.

«*Yazìk*, what a pity, such a beautiful girl. It's better that God deprive your body rather than your soul of health», they would remark knowingly, whenever they discussed her. «No fault of hers, these illnesses are passed down from mother to child!» And with a verdict like this, what mother would choose Satèn as a bride for her son?

«Get up, child, we're going to the doctor's», said Rosacùr after one of these crises. It was time to find a cure.

«No, grandma, there's no need», Satèn had replied. It was the first time she had spoken immediately after one of her attacks. She had usually remained speechless at length before succeeding to formulate a coherent sentence again. «I'll get better on my own», she had explained, decided and determined.

«And how will you do that?» the incredulous Rosacùr had asked with a sigh.

«All I have to do is not heed the ghosts, I'll free my mind of the images that torment me.»

Rosacùr had taken her hand and kissed it tenderly.

«What are you talking about, my love?»

Satèn was snuggling in her arms, trembling like a frightened puppy. «I'm burning, grandma, burning all over. I'm surrounded by flames, big red tongues trying to devour me. I try to escape, but I can't, so I scream, I cry and then I wake up …»

The woman listened with a lump in her throat because she realized that Satèn's soul had been deeply wounded. She supposed it was due to a traumatic, painful experience she had undergone in early childhood.

That Wednesday, the 13th of September 1922, little Satèn was in the garden of a house in the *Ermenì mehelé*, the wealthy Armenian district on the slopes of the lush Smyrna hills. She had just finished having lunch with her mother, her nursemaid and her brother, who was only a little older than herself. As the weather was still warm they ate in the open, under a gazebo from where they could enjoy a spectacular view of the port. She knew that her mother was about to bring her up to her room, read her a story before putting her to bed for her afternoon nap. Papa was still at work, in the famous jeweler's shop near the port he had inherited from his grandfather and would not be back home before dusk.

All of a sudden, the blue sky went black and a bitter, dense burning cloud crashed down on the entire area. Her mother and nursemaid were petrified. Satèn always remembered her hand being held tightly, herself and her brother, standing there frozen for what seemed like ages, her mother undecided what to do, where to go. The house was ablaze, devoured by fire, the flames, like gigantic infernal tongues, spewing from the windows and doors. Then, there had been a deafening blast, something had exploded. The garden was filled with a thick, dark, suffocating cloud. Everyone was coughing; mamma, her brother, the nursemaid, and herself.

«I can't see…» she had whimpered lost in the smoke.

A cornice had collapsed, and immediately after it the pillars of the lovely nineteenth-century hallway caved in. Her mother had heaved a ghastly rattling sigh and her grasp had fallen limp.

«Mayrìg, where are you?» The child had cried as she groped around, her eyes shut, her feet tripping over pieces of masonry.

«Where's my little sister? Come here!» she had heard Hampìg, her brother, call.

«Where are you?» she had barely managed to ask when a second explosion sent bricks, tiles and chunks of wood hurtling all over the place. «Hampìg!» she had shouted in despair, but no answer came and none ever would.

At this point, she recalled bursting into floods of tears, sobbing with terror. The garden was on fire: the fan-like palm trees, the red roses, the white agapanthus; the plants were all alight like torches at the mercy of the greedy blaze. Then, when from the thousand-branched pine tree the cones began falling like red-hot grenades, Satèn had managed to escape through the gate and run into the street where she found herself surrounded by a throng of people from the neighborhood, now one gigantic pyre. All around shouts and laments, every now and then a gunshot. They were all running downhill, towards the port, the sea, and little Satèn followed the flow, coughing and spluttering, her eyes all watery because of the smoke; as she fled, she kept stumbling over the things cluttering the road, sometimes over dead bodies, even.

«Give me your hand, little girl», said a distinguished-looking man at one point. At least that is what she thought he said, because he spoke a language she did not understand, but she guessed what he meant because his arms were reaching out to her.

«Your mamma, your papa?» he had asked, but she had just shaken her head and continued to cry.

Her hand held firmly in the stranger's, she had arrived down at the port, where a crushing, shouting, frantic crowd was assembling. Many people's faces were so black that their features could not be made out, yet their horror, bewilderment and despair could be read in every eye as they fled the flames which advanced threateningly, fanned by an easterly wind. The ships in the port were blowing their sirens, and the sound rang out through the air with an excruciating shrill, like some heart-rending mournful chant. Satèn had glanced hopefully in the direction of her father's jeweler's shop, but the fire had devoured that too already. Just then, someone had pushed her roughly and she had found herself sprawling on the ground, having been separated from the stranger. Summoning up all her meagre strength, she had managed to avoid being trampled on and crawl through the crowd which pushed its way in the direction of the water and the ships, their flags flying on the masts. There were lifeboats and kayaks, but they could never have held the swarms of people thronging the piers, waving their arms wildly, all shouting the same desperate plea in a variety of languages, «Help us, for the love of God, we're burning alive!»

When the tongues of fire began to lick her body, Satèn, yielding to pure instinct, had thrown herself into the blue water of the bay, doing her best to stay afloat as papa had shown her when teaching her to swim. But as soon as she realized that his strong fond arms were not there to support her, she felt herself being dragged down, her throat choking with the saltwater that prevented her from breathing.

"This is what must have happened to Little Red Riding Hood when the big bad wolf gobbled her up", she reckoned as she surrendered to her fate.

The first time Seròp had spoken to Satèn it had been to provide her with some information. He was returning home from his morning shift at the factory. His head was a muddle, his body one big ache, his shoulders bent after hours of pressing the reed on the loom.

«Excuse me, fellow countryman», she had addressed him, recurring to the formula they all used in the community, «do you know, by any chance, if they hire women where you work?»

Seròp had raised his eyes to look at the girl he considered the most beautiful in the whole camp. She was only fifteen, but her body had nothing to envy the voluptuous curves of an older woman. She was sweeping the little yard where, on fine days, she sat out in front of the house with Rosacùr, enjoying a breath of fresh air.

«Why don't you ask me?» butted in the interfering Noemì, known as Fitìl, the *Fuse*, because her slurs and tittle-tattle regularly sparked off furious rows among those living in the camp. She was a nasty spinster who lived in the shack facing Satèn's. She had no job, so she sponged on her neighbors who would give her a bowl of soup or a bite of stew. In exchange, she used to offer to tell them their fortunes. She claimed being a palm reader endowed with extraordinary powers. «Let me see your hand», she would insist, more out of inquisitiveness than anything else and driven by a morbid craving for other people's business, surely not by any special talent. She knew everything about everybody, but relayed the information she gleaned in a distorted, slanderous manner. She sat all day outside her hovel, on a stool, chewing heaps of sunflower seed which she ably cracked open with her teeth before spitting the hulls on the ground.

«Because you don't work in the factory», Satèn had retorted promptly.

Seròp had felt awfully uncomfortable. He had glanced at the two women, proffering them a timid conciliatory grin, red as a beetroot with embarrassment.

His appearance was not great; he was wearing a short-sleeved smock, his bare muscular arms, out of proportion with his extremely lean body, his over-loose trousers making him look really skinny; his face long and gaunt, his hair — kept combed back — a reddish golden hue, his skin milk white. He was often referred to as the «blond» to distinguish him from the other men in the camp, most of whom had dark hair and swarthy complexions. Although he was not yet twenty-five, he bore the signs of the hard life that had been his lot till then. After his father's death, he had lived all alone in a remote corner of the camp near the community latrines. Most of his peers were already married and had children, but he seemed destined to remain a bachelor.

«I'm sorry, Satèn-cùr, sister Satèn», he had answered at last, avoiding the amber eyes that held him in their gaze. «But mine is not women's work, it requires too much strength. Maybe you should look for something at the packing department», he had suggested.

«But I am strong», she had replied, her tongue flipping behind the gap in her front teeth. Then she had straightened her shoulders to prove she was as tall as him.

«Excuse me, but why not marry him? Look at those arms? He can go out to work for you and you can stay at home», Fitìl had taunted spitting out yet another hull.

«B-but what are you s-saying, N-n-oemì-cùr?» Seròp, had stammered, overcome with shyness and embarrassment.

«Don't tell me you don't like her?» Fitìl had teased.

«Stop it!» Satèn had exclaimed, brandishing the broom she still held in her hands.

Fitìl had burst out laughing. «Just listen to her! That one's a real *erìk zezò-gh*, a husband-beater», she had yelled, turning to Seròp, in full view of the inquisitive neighbors, who had all come out to relish the scene.

Seròp had felt the ground give way beneath his feet.

But only a few months later, accompanied by Lussià-dudù, his next-door neighbor, he was sitting in Rosacùr's place, sipping coffee and, stammering as usual, asking for Satèn's hand.

Marangopoulos, where Seròp worked, was Patras's most prestigious textile firm. Rumor had it that the owner's huge fortune was the fruit of a bizarre stroke of luck. In 1912, a merchant ship full of costly French cloth had sunk in the port. None of the town's merchants was prepared to risk buying the cargo, fearing it might be damaged, rotted by the saltwater. The only businessman who had dared make an offer and negotiate, acquiring the lot for a song, had been the young Marangopoulos. Then he had simply washed the material carefully and sold it afterwards at an enormous profit, making enough money to set up his first small textile factory.

Thanks to his business acumen, his firm determination, his curiosity and the will to innovate, he became successful by leaps and bounds. In 1925, he had visited a cloth-making factory near Bologna and, impressed by the invention of the use of the «flying shuttle», a device used to speed up the slower traditional system, he had ordered thirty or so of these machines.

«Just think of labor, only one worker per loom, that will make productivity soar», he had said to his son, who, although still a child, always accompanied his father on his business trips.

The machinery had been shipped from Ancona and after three days sailing across the Adriatic, had reached the port of Patras.

The factory comprised three big sheds made of mudbricks, arranged around a yard, at the center of which stood a century-old olive tree with a huge trunk and an immense verdant crown. During their breaks, the workers would sit out here in the open, under its majestic silver-green foliage which scintillated splendidly, filtering the sunbeams.

To enter the place, the workers had to pass through an iron gateway, under the watchful gaze of the custodian, who, seated in his little hut, jotted down their names and respective shifts. The majority of them were Armenian refugees, because, it was rumored, Marangopoulos had a particular preference for that persecuted people, so akin to his own. The factory never stopped, but, night and day, it spun its prized table and bed linen, celebrated throughout the Country. The ceaseless noise of the reeds as they drummed on the looms could be heard clearly outside, at a distance of several yards from the building. At the end of each shift, that din continued to resonate inside the workers' heads as they made their way home and well after that.

As time went by, however, the Marangopoulos company lost the luster and fame it had enjoyed for decades. A new, fully-fledged textile plant had been built only a few kilometers from the port: the *Peraica-Patraica*. Two large firms had merged, giving rise to the Country's largest and most modern textile industry. Avant-garde looms had been imported from England with the blessing and the enormous financial backing of the National Bank of Greece. Compared to it, the Marangopoulos factory seemed outdated, obsolete.

«Hard times!» Marangopoulos had admitted, speaking at the end of a meeting of workers where he too was present.

Little Sahàk was running, panting, scudding like a hare across the green fields on the outskirts of the city. Every now and then he stopped to catch his breath and study his route. It was not far, but he needed to fly.

«Listen carefully to what I ask you, …run», Satèn had recommended, «run as quickly as you can, down to the factory and fetch my husband.» The woman at the door was barely able to stand.

When he arrived at the factory gate, the boy, gasping, turned to the custodian, «I have to speak to Seròp Gazarian; it's really urgent!»

Seròp came out into the yard and saw Sahak sitting under the olive tree. The boy sprang to his feet at once and ran straight over to him. «Baròn Seròp, it's your wife, she's not well…» he shouted so his voice could be heard above the noise of the machinery.

«She's not well?»

«No.» And he stretched his arms in a circle, miming a belly. He would never have dreamed, out of shyness and respect, to speak explicitly of a birth or of a woman's birth pangs.

Seròp rushed towards the gate, but before he left, the custodian made him take off the white gloves he always wore to avoid soiling the snow-white cloth he wove.

As he drew back the heavy curtain that acted as a door to their home, he found Satèn crouching on the bed, holding her belly and moaning with pain.

«My love…» he said bending over her.

Satèn was naked, wrapped only in a sheet. It was nearly November, but that autumn was particularly mild. The young woman forced a smile.

«I sent for you because I'm in great pain», she murmured stroking her husband's face. She was wearing the gold bracelets which had belonged to Rosacùr, who had died suddenly only a few months previously. After that, Satèn had never taken those *burmà* off again.

«I'll call Lussià-dudù? Do you think it's time?» asked Seròp lowering his eyes to her belly which seemed to be on the point of bursting open. Then he saw the sewing machine on the table, uppers strewn all over the place, even on the ground.

«Why did you insist on working on your own? I asked you not to!»

Satèn groaned and collapsed onto the bed. Seròp noticed that the sheet was smeared with a yellowish fluid, hot and damp to the touch. He straightened up, unable to hide his fear.

«I'll be back at once», he said, as he rushed out the door.

His heart throbbing in his temples, his vision blurred, he turned right and hurried away. This camp, the place where he had grown up, where he had lived practically the whole of his life, now seemed cold and hostile. He ran past the boys, including Sahàk, kicking a ball of wool, he saluted old Legòs lost in his armchair smoking his *hookah*; he avoided looking in the direction of Fitìl who was about to rise to her feet, a sunflower seed between her teeth, all ready to quiz him.

Finally, he started running, head down, staring at his boots, the same ones he had worn for years and which he had begun to patch. «You're soon to be a father», said a voice in his head, feeble at first before it spiraled loudly becoming a roar. He felt as if he were trapped in a tangled skein of contrasting emotions. The prospect of having a child had always pleased him, but now that it was about to be born, fear was beginning to prevail, and he doubted he would be up to the challenge.

At times he asked himself whether he had married for love, or for what he had thought love might be. He had been extremely hesitant about proposing to the beautiful Satèn, wondering whether Rosacùr would ever give her to someone like him, a poor, uneducated man, an untimely orphan, without either prospects or a future. He had been dumbfounded when the woman had risen to congratulate him and Lussià-dudù, the neighbor who had accompanied him.

They were married a few months later in the church of Aghià-Varvàra in the Armenian rite, celebrated by the parish priest of Surp Hagòp, who had come especially for the occasion from the large Armenian community of Piraeus. Seròp had bought a pair of rings in red gold with the dollars Miriam had sent from the States and inside he had them engraved with two letters and a date: S-S 1935.

Rosacùr had been right: Satèn was not yet sixteen.

«Why did you marry me?» she had asked him on their wedding night as she lay by his side, naked, just after they had finished making love.

«Because it was written in my *kismèt*, my destiny.»

Satèn was displeased: it was clear she would have preferred hearing something else.

«But also because», Seròp had continued, «in my eyes you've always been the most beautiful of women, the most tenacious and intelligent too; I'd often thought of you, but I was afraid you wouldn't even look at me.»

Satèn had laughed so hard that her breasts shook. A drop of blood had stained the sheet, undeniable proof of her virginity.

«And I thought you'd done it to shut Fitìl's mouth up!»

«No.»

«And the rumors about me?»

«We all have some failing or other. But I've never paid much heed to what others say», he had lied.

Satèn had fondled his shoulder. Then, in turn, he had asked: «And you, why did you accept?»

«Because I feel for the child that is in you, which moves me so deeply. I want to embrace you as if I were your mother, hug you tight, console you, telling you that everything will be all right», she had whispered fixing him with her hypnotic, amber eyes. «Besides, I wanted a family.»

Seròp was amazed at how profound and sensitive she was, though she was ten years his junior.

«Don't wash the sheet. Hang it outside, in full view», he said shortly afterwards as he rose from the bed.

«Lussià-dudù!» he shouted outside a rusty tin shack.

Gasping for breath, he was nauseated by the pong of the latrines mingled with the aroma of frying food wafting in the air. He knew that smell only too well: Lussià-dudù was surely cooking. He approached the little window and peeked inside. «Lussià-dudù», he called again. The woman stood only a few meters away, fork in hand. «Ah, my son, I was just frying some meatballs, I didn't hear you coming because of the sizzling pan…» she excused herself as she turned the little stove off. She leaned out of the window and read the fear in Seròp's eyes. «But, can it be her time already?» she asked him, incredulous.

He nodded.

«Please, oh, please, let's hurry», he entreated her, anxiously passing his fingers through his hair.

No one could guess just how old Lussià-dudù was. When asked how old she was, she always said sixty. She was tall and stout, with a round face and protruding eyes, like people who have problems with their thyroid. She had landed here with all the other refugees in '22, fleeing from Erzerum, in Anatolia. And when Seròp had been orphaned, she had helped him overcome that awful period. They lived in neighboring shacks, so Lussià-dudù used to cook for him too, wash his things, keep him company and, when he was ill, cure him with medicinal herbs whose properties she knew well. They said she had been a nurse in the old country, besides being the lover of a famous surgeon who had never married her, however. She had learnt a lot about medicine from him but, above all, she was an excellent midwife, and, in the camp, her strong capable hands had helped bring most of the children born there into the world. «So much for the Turks!» she would exult after every delivery, referring to the ferocity with which they had massacred her people. Then, having examined the infant, she used to give it a sound slap on the buttocks to make it cry, obliging it to fill its tiny lungs with air.

The first breath of life.

«Push, my child, breathe deep and push...»

Lussià-dudù had placed two cushions under Satèn's thighs and covered her groin with a sheet. She believed no husband should ever see that part of his wife's body dilated by childbirth.

«How are you feeling, my love?» Seròp asked. With one hand he caressed her face, flushed with heat and distorted by pain; in his other, he held a piece of cloth which he dipped into a basin of cold water to bathe her forehead, murmuring soothing, loving words to her.

«*Megà Asdvàtz*, God forgive me, but I've never seen a belly as big as this one», the midwife muttered to herself as she massaged Satèn's abdomen, from top to bottom.

«Push, now!» she ordered. She clenched her teeth as she put her fingers between the woman's thighs. Satèn groaned and gasped with pain. «Seròp, help her to bend, now...»

Finally, covered in blood and mucus, the child's head made its timid appearance.

«Here it is!» the midwife exulted.

«Where?» asked Seròp, totally confused.

«You tend to her», Lussià-dudù said, shaking him. «It's a fine little boy, by God!» she exclaimed pulling the rest of the body out.

When Seròp laid his eyes on the baby for the first time, his heart skipped a beat. It was the tiny, kicking, mewling creature the midwife was holding up and slapping to make him breathe; his face was purple, his eyes closed, his teeny mouth toothless. A tuft of copper hair was pasted across his forehead. He was covered in blood and still tied to his mother by the umbilical cord. "That's my son", he thought, making a great effort to hold back his tears.

«I want to see him too», demanded Satèn, impatiently. She smiled as she tried to lift herself up, but a lacerating pain made her drop back down immediately. She freed herself from Seròp's arms and began to scream and thrash about, bent back by the pain in her belly.

«Keep her still, hurry!» the woman ordered Seròp.

This was an extremely critical moment. Lussià-dudù had seen so many births, she was familiar with all the risks and the accidents that could present themselves.

«My God, she's bleeding», she whispered to herself. «Now you be good, my little man», she told the newborn placing him on the bed and she started to clean the blood from Satèn's thighs. The girl was as motionless as if she were unconscious.

«What's happening?» Seròp asked her, alarmed, guessing from her nervous, frantic behavior that something was amiss.

But Lussià-dudù, however, was too engrossed to answer him. She continued to feel Satèn's belly which had remained full and hard. Then she put her hand up into the vagina to explore the womb with extreme caution. Eventually, she sprang to her feet, an amazed, astonished expression on her face.

«Well, I never! By all that's good and holy, there's something else in here!» she announced, her bulging eyes piercing Seròp.

«What?» asked Seròp in a low whisper.

«There's another little rascal waiting in there», the midwife explained indicating Satèn's abdomen.

In that miserable little shack for refugees, life was kicking its way into the light.

«Another?» gasped Seròp, stunned. On impulse he turned to look at Satèn to see her reaction, but she lay motionless, her head on the pillow behind her, unconscious because of the atrocious pangs.

«Wake her up», commanded Lussià-dudù.

«How?»

« Hit her face.»

«*Gierìm*, my love, there's a second child», Seròp said, slapping her softly on the cheek, but all she did was to mutter disjointed, incomprehensible sentences.

«We need to get a move on!» urged the midwife.

Seròp shook his wife by the shoulder, this time energetically.

Satèn surfaced again and began at once to moan as her husband bathed her lips with the wet cloth.

«Just a little more patience», he implored her. He was close to tears seeing her in this state. She was drenched in perspiration and, although Lussià-dudù had tried to staunch her blood with several rags, the bed was soaking. Satèn was dreadfully pale, but the child had to have the precedence.

«Darling, can you hear me? You need to push again!»

Lussià-dudù began to feel weary and anxious because of the huge responsibility weighing her down. Bringing twins into the world was a difficult and delicate task, needing far more skill and experience than that required for an ordinary birth. It had happened to her only once before. She had done her very best. It had taken her all day, but, unfortunately only one of the babies had survived. The mother and the other child had not made it, although she had fought to the bitter end. For ages afterwards, blaming herself for what had happened, she had not left the house. Not only, but she had not attended the deliveries of any more babies, despite the insistence of the families. «I can't do it anymore», she used to say when they came knocking on her door. However, one day, after a few months had passed, as she leaned out of her little window, she had watched the children she had brought into the world pass by. «Hello, Lussià-dudù», they had greeted her sincerely, fondly. Bedròs and Lussarpì, Matheòs and Agavnì, and many, many more, big and small, all her children. Looking at them she had recovered pride in what she had accomplished, as well as awareness of the social and patriotic significance of her work. «I'm here, if you still need me», she had announced one morning in spring, arriving on tiptoe at the house of a woman about to give birth.

«Push, now», she told Satèn, plucking up courage once more. Exhausted, the young woman exhaled without contracting her muscles. «Help her to bend over», she shouted at Seròp, who was just standing there stunned and confused, only too aware of the risk his wife was running.

Lussià-dudù rolled her sleeves up and once again put her hand into her womb. As she felt around for the second fetus, she realized that he was coming feet first. She heaved a sigh, took hold of its ankles and pulled them gently downwards. Satèn felt an excruciating pain and let out a terrible scream.

«Shake her, she mustn't lose consciousness», said the midwife to Seròp. «The other one's coming.» Her voice was firm again, steady.

The sole of one tiny foot appeared.

«Thanks be to God!» she exclaimed. «Now get her to bite on that cloth, put it between her teeth.»

She then expanded the lips of the vagina with one hand as she held the two tiny ankles with the other and, rotating the child, she pulled it straight out.

«No!» yelled Satèn when the baby's shoulders forced their way into the world.

«Welcome!» said Lussià-dudù greeting it with a smile which died on her lips at once. The first baby's umbilical cord was wound around the neck of the second, choking it, practically. The infant was cyanotic and the eyes under its little lids looked as if they were about to pop out of their orbits.

«Damnation!» yelled the woman. «Give me the scissors!» she ordered Seròp.

«What's happening?» cried Satèn. Seròp shook his head.

«Now», said the midwife trying to unravel the cord; this boa constrictor was strangling its little victim with its coils. Seròp let go of his wife and sprung to his feet. He stared at the scene, saw the midwife's hands and felt faint, petrified at what he beheld.

«What's the matter?» Satèn kept asking, her voice growing weaker and weaker.

«Something to cut with, anything, quick, for the love of God», Lussià-dudù howled.

Seròp rushed over to the sink, picked up a knife and handed it to her.

Satèn tried to sit up in the bed to find out what was happening.

«Keep her still, Seròp», ordered Lussià-dudù and, holding the cord between her fingers, she cut it in several places with clean, decided stokes. Then, skillfully and quickly, she began to undo the cord circling the baby's neck. As soon as she had freed the little boy, she held him up by the legs, head downwards, and slapped his bottom once, twice, three times.

«Breathe, little man, breathe!» she urged, through clenched teeth.

After several interminable moments, the baby yelled at the top of his voice, waking his brother who seemed to have fallen asleep at his mother's side. Seròp and Satèn embraced each other, tears in their eyes.

«So much for the Turks, two for the price of one!» the midwife exulted, lying the second infant down beside his brother.

Then, with calm competence, she carried out the tasks of cleaning, cutting, swabbing and binding. With a damp towel she washed the two little bodies, hands, feet and faces, so strikingly alike, before placing them on either side of their young mother, one on the right, the other on the left.

«May God protect them», she prayed softly, making the sign of the cross on their foreheads.

The news of the birth of the twins was received and remarked on in the camp in discordant fashion. Some were delighted that the community had been reinforced by the addition of two new male children, others expressed their doubts, saying their father would be hard put to provide for two extra mouths, while other members of the community wondered, with allusive grins, how a body as skinny as Seròp's could contain so much virility. Only a few commented on Satèn, and that only to recall her attacks of the falling sickness, which now seemed a thing of the past, defeated by the miracle of motherhood.

«Who'd have thought the Gazarians would have produced such a lovely little family?» the majority concluded.

The babies were welcomed into the world with a shower of gifts, according to the community's tradition. Each one was twofold: two jars of aromatic basil, two pairs of handmade bootees, two cinnamon and honey waffles, two pillowcases embroidered with two identical ducklings, and other presents that cost little but of great value because offered full-heartedly. Sahàk, the boy who had run so quickly that day, brought a bunch of wildflowers he picked in the fields.

The compatriots presented the gifts to the mother, radiant, the two babies in her arms, as Seròp poured out glasses of *moschùdi*, the famous wine from Acaia.

«May they grow up strong and healthy», they all wished the children as they toasted them merrily.

Lussià-dudù, the midwife, the woman who had also mothered Seròp, brought them a pair of gold coins, the so-called *kurùsh* of the Ottoman Empire, which she rubbed on the soles of their feet, the palms of their hands, their foreheads and, finally, their hearts.

«Gold wherever you walk, gold whatever you touch, gold in your thoughts and gold in whomever you may love», she recited, her voice breaking with emotion. Then she embraced the parents fondly and let the two *kurùsh* fall into Satèn's lap.

«Lussià-dudù, you shouldn't have», objected Seròp.

«We can't accept them», protested Satèn.

«I haven't had any children; these are my grandchildren», the woman retorted, simply.

Fitìl dropped by one evening, but her hands were empty. «I'm poor, I have nothing to bring», she said, to justify herself.

«You're more than welcome, anyway», Seròp responded, greeting her.

«But I wish you all the very best», she added, approaching the sleeping babies. She sat down beside them and began to caress them with fake tenderness as Satèn watched her with great suspicion. Then, slowly, she brought their hands to her lips and began covering them with sweet kisses.

«They are really lovely», she said, turning over their hands to read their destinies there, in the name of the powers she claimed she possessed as a palm reader.

«No!» she cried after a moment so loudly she risked waking the twins.

Satèn gasped, startled.

«There's a curse on them», she proclaimed, covering her mouth in horror, as she dropped their two little arms. «I see so much suffering», she prophesized like a true Cassandra, through the long curls that curtained her face.

«What the dickens are you saying!?» snapped Seròp springing to his feet, the glass of moschùdi he was pouring out for her still in his hands. The woman was already slinking out of the house, but he blocked her on the threshold.

«Get out of my way», Fitìl challenged him.

Seròp held his ground, his eyes flashing with anger, while Satèn gaped at the scene, dumbfounded.

«You», said Fitìl pointing her finger at Seròp, «you are a serpent which devours its own eggs.» And she fixed him at length with her piercing eyes to make sure he grasped the true weight of her words.

Seròp backed away, staggering, so she was able to leave, but before she vanished in the dark, she broke into a loud, harsh cackle.

It was a deep-throated ominous laughter which echoed in Satèn's head for the whole of that endless night.

Patras, 2nd of November 1937

Dear Miriam
I am well as I trust you are too.
It is with great joy that I announce the birth of my sons. Yes, you got it right, there are two of them. It was God's will that on Saturday the 22nd of October I should become the father of two baby boys. Only you can understand how proud your uncle would be, were he still with us. In any case, it was a difficult birth. Satèn had a long and painful delivery as you can imagine. But the children are well, and she is recovering quickly. May God be praised. As soon as they are a little bigger, I'll take them to the photographer's and send you a picture, so you can see how beautiful they are.

There are ups and down at work at the moment. Rumors are going around that they want to lay some people off. Yesterday, I took part in a demonstration in defense of workers' rights. The very thought of losing my job makes my blood chill, especially now that we have two infants to bring up. But God is good, and I hope, He'll take care of us...

But now, what about you? How are things with you? Let me have all your news. I know you're very busy, but every letter we get from you brings great joy to all of us here. It's too bad we have we to live so far apart, isn't it? I hope providence will permit us to meet at least once more in this life. I have a faint recollection of you and your smile but to refresh my memory I often look at the photograph of your wedding. How good-looking you and Gerry are! Give him my kindest regards.

Now I must sign off, the babies have just woken up. Satèn sends all her love.

Hear from you soon, I hope.
Big hugs from your cousin, Seròp.

The arrival of the twins had changed Satèn's and Seròp's everyday lives completely. The babies cried and were restless all the time. Maybe they were trying to tell their parents something they did not have the foggiest idea what it was. But the joy at having received these two heaven-sent gifts made ample amends for the discomfort and sacrifice involved.

The Gazarians' little shack was so full that you could not swing a cat. Every inch of the place was cluttered. Besides, the bed had to hold a multitude of things and perform several functions. Seròp had built a cradle, nailing a few planks together, but it could hold only one child at a time, being far too narrow for two. Not only, but the infants had made it quite clear from day one that they would not permit anyone to separate them. As soon as their mother picked one up, they both began to sob desperately, obliging her to put them back side by side again. Then and only then — after they had made close physical contact, one baby's arm around his brother's stomach, his nose nuzzled against the other's cheek, his foot between his twin's legs — would they calm down, smiling, sweet as pie and falling into a deep sleep.

«Which is the firstborn?» Seròp had asked one day, seeing that he could not distinguish one from the other. He had just arrived home, jaded, after a night shift and, without changing his clothes, he had sat on the bed with Satèn to look at his sleeping offspring.

«The one with the thinner lips», she answered.

«This one?»

«No, no, the other one!»

«We should find names for them.»

«You wouldn't be able to tell one from the other just the same», said his wife laughing gently.

«I'll find a way! I'll put some kind of label on them»

«All right, what names, then?»

«We'll call the first Toròs, after my father.»

«And the second?»

«After yours.»

Satèn shook her head, disappointed.

«That won't do at all, we should give them names that single them out.»

«Meaning?»

«That they were born together, belong together and resemble each other like peas in a pod.»

«And where shall we find these names?»

Satèn sighed. «I don't know; two names that when you call them, it can only be them, nobody else.»

«Complicated...» murmured Seròp springing to his feet.

She followed him with her eyes: he looked thinner than ever, his shoulders visibly stooped, his face terribly drawn. Seròp, who really needed his rest after those strenuous shifts at the factory, had been unable to get one night's sound sleep because of the babies.

«Shall I serve your soup?» Satèn asked, rising from the bed.

One of the twins woke up and began to wail only to be followed a second later by his brother. Their mother lifted her eyes to the heavens in resignation, and turning towards her husband who was already seated at the table waiting for her, said, «Well, it seems to be feeding time already», and sat down again on the bed from which she had just risen.

The man moaned feebly.

Satèn bared her breasts and lifting up the twins, put them to her nipples. «There, there, my lovely little angels», she whispered.

Seròp lowered his eyes, visibly embarrassed. He felt a little awkward at the sight of his wife's bare breasts, but he was also deeply moved by the scene: the most natural representation of motherhood you could imagine. Satèn was like a lioness, strong and proud, her cubs sucking at her nipples. The hovel was a haven of tenderness and love.

«I've got it!» she exclaimed at a certain moment abeam with satisfaction.

Seròp lifted his head and looked at her inquisitively.

«Their names, I've found their names!»

He continued to fix her, a puzzled expression on his face as he slowly continued to chew a mouthful of bread.

«We'll call one of them Mikael», said Satèn nodding to the right, «the other Gabriel», she added, indicating the baby on her left.

Her husband remained composed, he simply raised his eyebrows slightly.

Satèn looked suddenly displeased. «Don't you like them? They're the names of the two archangels, see?», she objected.

He shook his head and kneaded some breadcrumbs between his fingers.

«Yes, yes. Call them whatever you like. In any case, we won't be able to baptize them for a year at least», he replied, thinking of the cost of the ceremony. Then, he suddenly rose to his feet and, drawing the heavy curtain aside, left the room.

«Take a seat, Mr. Gazarian.»

Seròp looked at the chair standing in front of the enormous mahogany desk. He was in the office of Marangopoulos, the master. He had been summoned there rather suddenly.

«You speak Greek, I presume», the master began.

«I grew up in Patras», answered Seròp, fixing the boss's double-breasted pinstripe suit.

«Fine», the factory owner said as he steepled his fingers and brought them to his lips. He wore a grave and thoughtful expression, like that of a person about to say something really serious. He was old now, tall and gaunt, an emaciated air about him, and, had it not been for the expensive suit he wore, you could scarcely have guessed he was the richest man in town.

«I am aware of your family circumstances, the birth of the twins, of how hard it is for you to bring them up and all that. But listen carefully to what I have to say. I cannot allow these to become an excuse for negligence on the job», he insisted, drumming on the top of the desk with his fingers covered in rings, including one with an enormous sapphire sparkling on his index finger.

Seròp reddened immediately.

«Your foreman tells me you have been arriving late and worse still, that he has found you napping at work. Is that true?»

«It... it...» Seròp stammered.

«It what?»

«It happened only once», he managed to utter, finally, to justify himself.

Marangopoulos sighed. «Hmm. You are aware that once is enough to get you the sack? But let it be perfectly clear that this is the first and last time», he concluded, dismissing him with a histrionic gesture.

Seròp rose and moved silently towards the door, crab fashion, to avoid turning his back on the master.

«Gazarian!» the boss called out, just as he was about to open the door.

Seròp froze.

«I was forgetting», Marangopoulos announced, as he set down on the desk two little coins which would not suffice for a week's supply of bread, «this is our gift to your sons.»

Seròp turned around, his head bent, startled, afraid almost. He stretched out his arm and as he was about to pick up the coins, the master's hand came down on his, pinning it to the desk.

«It's not out of sympathy or pity», he explained, nodding at the two copper coins, «but a matter of pure duty», he ended, crushing Seròp's little finger with his sapphire ring.

«Thanks», he replied in a low voice, though he felt like screaming to relieve the pain.

Sitting facing Lussià-dudù, Satèn was enjoying a moment's respite, sipping coffee and nibbling a biscuit. The midwife had popped in for her usual little visit. She was one of the few women in the camp who came to give the young Satèn a hand and, every time she came, she brought a little treat for the family: a loaf of bread, a piece of cheese, some of the meatballs she made, even biscuits. That day too, they had performed their customary ritual: first Satèn had fed the babies, then the women had heated up some water and together, they had given the twins their bath in the little tin tub. After that, they had dried them off thoroughly, brushed their copper-red curls, put them into their pajamas and, singing their favorite lullabies, had laid them down to sleep, side by side, as always.

Satèn had still to clean the house, cook and wash the dishes and the clothes. Lussià-dudù had promised to help her, providing they relaxed with a nice cup of coffee first.

«Are you eating properly, my child?» the midwife asked her, genuinely concerned, noticing how thin she had become after the birth of the babies. «You need to, you know, otherwise your milk will run thin and then stop coming altogether...»

«Yes, I know. I do my best, but I'm exhausted.»

«It's early days yet, things will soon get better, you'll see.»

Satèn put her cup down on the table.

«I wanted to ask you something, only I'm ashamed...» she murmured.

«My child, you can confide in me, you know...»

The girl, seated on the bed, fidgeted nervously.

«It's my husband, you see; the thing is, that, well, he insists on making love, but I...» And she blushed, almost choking with embarrassment.

Her friend listened, blowing on her boiling-hot coffee.

«Well, you know, the babies sleep with us, but now he's making a double cradle to put over there», she said, indicating a space between the bed and the wall of the mud cabin. «The other night we quarreled. He said that since the arrival of the twins, I've had no time for him.»

«The scoundrel!» remarked Lussià-dudù, indignant as a mother listening to a daughter's complaint about her husband.

«You know the pain and toil it cost me to bring these two into the world», added Satèn, looking tenderly at the twins. «The last time he tried, he really hurt me, but I bore it without complaining...»

The midwife shook her head, to express total solidarity with her friend.

«I'm really fond of him», the girl continued. «And I realize he's so very tired, with the factory and the slippers and all. I wouldn't want to deny him the little pleasure a wife can offer her husband», she sighed.

Lussià-dudù took one of the girl's hands and brought it to her heart. «You're young, but God has blessed you with so much sensitivity and wisdom. You needn't feel downhearted. When you're in bed», she whispered as if about to disclose some amazing secret, «you must try to make him see you're close to him ... in a different way. Tell him about your dreams, your fantasies, what you would like to do with him. Charm him by whispering sweet nothings in his ear. 'That thing' is not what it's all about; on the contrary, it's worth very little between a couple where there's no true understanding.»

Satèn's amber eyes beamed again.

«Meanwhile», the midwife continued, «I'll make you up an ointment to apply down there so you'll be as good as new — and that will be soon. Trust me», she added smiling, knowingly.

«My dear Lussià-dudù, I sought you in Heaven, but found you on earth!» exclaimed Satèn hugging her tight, in an impetus of genuine affection.

«My little pasha», cooed Seròp, leaning over the baby and covering his stomach in kisses from his bellybutton to his willy. The child chuckled, revealing his toothless mouth, full of milk-veined dribble. Beside him, his little brother, stared up at his father, as if expectantly awaiting the same cuddles.

«Which one is he?» asked Seròp pointing at him.

«Gabriel», Satèn replied.

«The firstborn?»

His wife shook her head and smiled. It amused her that her husband just could not distinguish between them. It was true that, physically at least, they were identical. But Satèn had taken up on those tiny minutiae, those insignificant details that only a mother is able to notice: a certain twitch on his face when he cries, a vaguely off-key shrill when he laughs, that slightly longer hair in one of his eyebrows.

At that point Seròp straightened up and opened the drawer in the table.

«What are you doing? The other child will be disappointed and will surely cry», his wife scolded.

«Coming», he called, rummaging in a tin box, where he kept the colored yarn, he used to sew the slippers. Then he returned to the babies holding two spools. «Red for Mikael, Green for Gabriel, or whatever we'll call them!» he exclaimed, satisfied with himself.

He tore off a length from each spool, took one of the baby's hands and winding the thread yarn twice around his wrist, he tied a double knot before biting off the remaining thread. The infant smiled, finding daddy's little game really funny, it seemed.

«There we are!» said Seròp having done the same for the other twin.

«But does that seem normal to you?» Just as Satèn had barely finished complaining when she heard someone calling outside.

«Who is it?» asked Seròp hushing his wife.

«The postman.»

Seròp drew the curtain aside and looked out.

A boy in uniform carrying a brown parcel in his arms, nodded at him and asked «Are you Mr. Seròp Gazarian?»

«Yes», he answered, holding his breath with surprise.

«A parcel from America, sir.»

Seròp prepared to take the box, but the postman stopped him in his tracks: «One moment, sir. You need to sign first.»

«Come inside, then. It's cold out here», invited Seròp. «Have a drink of *moschùdi*, that should warm you up», he added, pouring out a glass without even waiting for an answer.

«What beautiful babies», remarked the postman, raising his glass to toast them.

As soon as he left, husband and wife ripped the wrapping off the parcel, which was really big. As soon as it was open, the air was filled with a delicious fragrance, a mixture of vanilla and chocolate. Seròp glanced over at Satèn who was smiling, beside herself with joy. Then she began to open the box, pulling out the contents, and placing them, one by one, on the table. First, two elegant, warm, blue and brown woolen coats, two different colored pairs of toweling rompers, then — wrapped in tissue paper — two sets of tiny underwear in finest cambric, one for each twin. But that was not all, because the parcel also contained a casket in red velvet with the inscription: *Barney's de luxe chocolates*. Seròp shook it gently so they could hear the dull rattle of the chocolates inside.

«What a stupendous aroma!» murmured Satèn, fascinated by the velvet chocolate box. «Wait, there's more!» cried Seròp, taking out two tins of condensed milk and two of powdered egg. Then rummaging around, checking to see if the parcel was empty, he fished out a book.

«*The Daring Young Man on the Flying Trapeze*», he read pronouncing the title badly, «by William Saroyan.» He examined the sleeve of the book— the profile of a man flying through the air holding a trapeze — and flicked through the pages for a few moments before putting it down, disappointment written all over his face: he did not understand one word it said.

He turned the box upside-down, and a sealed envelope fluttered down onto the pile of baby clothes lying on the table. "For Seròp", proclaimed the round, elegant handwriting. He ripped it open and read the letter:

Pasadena, LA, 7th December 1937

Dear Seròp,
what happiness to learn of the birth of your two sons! Gerry and I send you and your dear wife our very best wishes.

Please accept these gifts as an expression of our sincerest affection for you all. I hope you like them. I got the coats big enough so that my little manciuk *may be able to wear them next winter.*

Dear Seròp, included you will also find a book. It is by an author of Armenian origin, William Saroyan, whose parents moved to the States many years ago. This collection of his short stories is meeting with enormous success over here: the Americans appreciate his humanity and sensitivity, very much. I have looked everywhere for an English-Greek dictionary for you, but, unfortunately, I haven't found one as yet. I hope to be able to send it to you with the next present. I would love you and your children to learn English, because it might prove very useful.

I trust you still have work. If I were you, I'd attend those workers' meetings with a certain caution; there might always be spies who go back and refer all to the masters.

Before signing off, I wish to send you and your family our sincerest Christmas greetings. Gerry says he considers himself lucky for having married me, because it means he can celebrate Christmas twice, once on the 25th of December and again on the 6th of January, the day of the Armenian Tznùnt.

I miss you all very much, as always, lots of hugs and kisses
Miriam.

«It's true, it's nearly Christmas», said Satèn as if awakening from a delightful dream.

«Yes, my love», answered Seròp embracing her and planting a tiny kiss on the tip of her nose.

«Merry Christmas.»

2

Venice, 1952

The orderly line of students made its way swiftly along the embankments, their heads held high. A dark-colored crocodile, or rather a centipede whose legs all moved at the same pace, in the same direction. It went up and down bridges, advanced and turned, all its parts in unison, without ever altering its shape. Nobody was allowed to change tempo, become distracted.

«Mamma, look!» remarked a little girl pointing at them.

Her mother stopped. The line overtook her swiftly, marching on soundless shoes.

«*Xe armeni*», the woman said softly to herself. She scrutinized them carefully as they filed past, two abreast, with their slicked-back hair shining in the pale afternoon sun. Their shirts were starched and snow white, their grey trousers perfectly ironed, with knife-sharp creases. They all wore navy-blue, tailor-made blazers with a golden insignia on their breast pockets.

«What does it say on the crest?» the little girl asked.

The woman bent down and looked into those green eyes, so impatient to know everything. She, in turn, smiled up at her mother, revealing her baby teeth and the gap left by the missing upper incisors.

«The name of their school, love, Moorat-Raphael.»

«Muratafael, Muratafael...» chanted the child.

The woman looked up and pointed in the direction of the man at the head of the crocodile who was finding it really hard to keep up. «That priest, the man with the hat, see? He's one of their teachers.»

The girl frowned and wrinkled her nose as if to say he was not to her liking.

An icy gust of wind rucked the water of the canal which was turning the color of old silver. A boat creaked, straining against its moorings. To the north, one corner of the sky was filling up with black clouds.

The woman hastened to wrap the scarf more tightly around her daughter's neck. «Come on, we'd better be going!» she exclaimed. «It'll soon be dark.» And she hurried her away, holding her by the hand.

«Bakunìn!»

Mikael turned to face his classmate who had called him by the nickname he had been labelled with in college. He liked it because it was the name of his favorite philosopher; he was well used to it by now, besides, everyone had one in there. For example, the boy who had just addressed him was known as «Aznavour», though not by way of his voice. It was because Aznavour, whose real name was Emil Megoyan, was the son of a wealthy restauranteur in Marseille, the French city where the famous *chansonnier* was from. They were coming back from the cinema in campo Santa Margherita where they usually spent their Sunday afternoons. They were accompanied as usual by Father Keshishian, their literature and religion teacher, who also taught them Armenian, the tongue imposed by the college, as well as Italian, English and French. Thanks to him the majority of the students spoke several languages fluently.

«'The thief' is back in action…» whispered Aznavour to Mikael, nodding towards a boy called Dick, one of the classmates walking right in front of them. Dick was a long-limbed, lanky lad, with the agile muscular, physique of an athlete. He was the son of an Armenian industrialist from Detroit. The college boys were all Armenians, scions of families who wanted them brought up with a strong patriotic sense and in observance of their native traditions.

«Want to bet?» insisted Aznavour.

Mikael winced.

«Watch out! Now!» he alerted his friend in a low voice.

A little further on there was a greengrocer's shop, with two stalls on the pavement outside, laden with fresh fruit and vegetables all carefully arranged in pyramids to render them enticing to passers-by. The students were just filing past the doorway where the owner stood busy attending to a customer, when Dick stretched out a hand and, quick as lightning, grabbed an apple and thrust it furtively into his pocket.

«See? I told you», murmured Aznavour, elbowing Mikael in the ribs.

Dikràn «the thief» walked swiftly back to keep his place in the line. He puffed away the lock of blond hair which was always falling down onto his forehead, straightened his jacket, then turned around and winked at his two classmates seeking their approval. He had been so quick that none of the other boys had seen a thing.

«You are such a jerk», Mikael rebuked him, as he checked out of the corner of his eye that the shopkeeper had not noticed anything and was not chasing after them.

«*Fuck you*», snapped «the thief», recurring to his favorite oath. He used it often, especially when his friends failed to give him the support he expected.

«This time, I'm not going to cover up for you, I'm warning you», cautioned Aznavour, tall and stout, his face pitted with acne, He was renowned for his easy-going ways and sense of loyalty, so, Dick knew he would never snitch on him.

Father Keshishian stopped walking all of a sudden. His sixth sense told him that there was something going on back there at the end of the line. He waved his arms around threateningly in the air and all the boys bent their heads, resumed their march, not a peep out of them.

«One of these days, I swear, I'm going to kill that Dick», hissed Aznavour as they neared the college gates.

At number 2596 Dorsoduro, the line came to a halt in front of an imposing Baroque building with its austere off-white façade. Beneath the chipped plaster one could catch a glimpse of pale pink bricks. The large windows overlooking the street had marble mullions adorned with wrought-iron railings. Four columns supported the central balcony beneath which was riveted a plate proclaiming that this was the *Collegio Armeno Moorat-Raphael*. The main door, painted ink black, was always closed, except on very special occasions so, normally, everyone used the secondary entrance to the left of the building.

«Anybody missing?» father Keshishian asked himself with a sigh, as he inspected the line of students, making absolutely sure all were present. He had just finished counting them when Dick removed the apple from his pocket and took such a loud bite out of it that the teacher sprung round. Dick froze, his jaws motionless, holding the fruit behind his back.

The bell of the Chiesa dei Carmini struck five.

«Inside», the glum-faced teacher ordered the boys who obeyed him instantly.

A flash of lightning ripped through the dark cloud-filled sky. «The thief» played for time, looked up into the air and waited to be the last to enter. Just then, Mikael saw him rid himself of the apple, hurling it with amazing ability into the canal. At first the fruit sank, then re-emerged and, bobbing like a tiny boat, it was carried away by the current as the first drops of rain beat a tattoo on the surface of the water.

«I'll buy a hotel and two houses.»

«One hundred and fifty more… so, now you owe me two hundred and thirty thousand dollars.»

In the recreation hall the students were playing *Monopoli*. These premises were on the ground floor, beyond the atrium, which opened onto a rose garden. At the center of the room stood a ping-pong table, while under the windows squatted a row of large comfortable-looking, worn-out sofas. Next to the door towered a mahogany bookcase, its shelves teeming with books in all languages and on all subjects: religion, history, classical novels, poetry, Greek tragedy, philosophical treatises, as well as rows of magazines dealing with geography and architecture. Beside the bookcase there was a piano which Mikael played, now and then, having first tuned it carefully. On the walls hung several nineteenth-century etchings of Venice and some pictures of Armenian history: «the glorious history of Armenia», as the fathers always made a point of emphasizing.

«Hey, I saw you, you cheat!» said Keropé, a small slip of a lad with spikey hair, attacking Dick, «the thief».

Padre Keshishian, seated nearby, raised his eyes and peered over his reading glasses.

«You're dreaming, my friend!» replied Dick.

«You're a liar, you stole a hotel. Bakunìn saw you too! You did, didn't you?»

The boy turned to Mikael, imploring him to tell the truth.

Dick stared at his friend forcing him to lower his gaze.

«I didn't see anything», muttered Mikael.

«The thief» smirked mockingly and Keropé gave him a kick in the shins, of which he took no notice.

«Silence, here comes the Wolf!»

Aznavour had noticed that father Keshishian had risen from the sofa and was coming in their direction. «Wolf» was the nickname his students had given the priest because of his keen intuition and infallible 'scent'.

«Dick, what are you up to now?» he asked placidly.

«But why are you always picking on me?» the boy protested. He was a master of dissimulation and those who did not know him well could be taken in and believe he was as good as gold. He had barely finished complaining when Peppe, the college caretaker, appeared at the door of the recreation hall.

«Father Keshishian», he informed the priest, «there's a gentleman here who wants to see you.»

Wolf turned around and saw a distinguished-looking man, with well-groomed grey hair walking towards him. Around his waist he wore a bottle-green apron which he continued to rumple with one hand, most likely because he felt ill at ease and tense. The turnups of his trousers under the apron were soaking wet. The Wolf looked at him in astonishment, wondering what on earth he might want at the college.

«That boy, that blond one, stole an apple from my shop», he burst out after a moment of surpassed indecision.

Father Keshishian felt he needed to convince the fellow that he must be mistaken. But the greengrocer insisted and, without backing down, kept pointing at Dick «the thief».

«This evening there won't be any meat like any other Sunday evening. You are being punished for covering up for your schoolmate

Dikràn», proclaimed the rector, father Ayvazian. He was an elderly man, his face always impassive whatever the circumstances. «Now, sit down and let us pray.»

He waited for an instant, so that the students might all take their places on the benches, and then he began:

«Blessed art thou oh Lord, God of Creation, by whose bounty we are about to receive this food...» His hoarse, nasal voice ricocheted off the unadorned walls of the refectory. The boys were all immersed in obsequious devotion, their hair damp from the pouring rain and some even dared sneeze. To come to the refectory, it was necessary to cross a quad, so, getting wet in bad weather was perfectly normal.

«Amen», the rector concluded in the meantime.

At a mere gesture of his hand, three nuns began moving between the tables and ladling out bowls of potato soup. At the pungent smell of onion Mikael felt his stomach lurch, and, for a second or two, the urge to retch, but he managed to control himself.

«Sister Valentina, only a little for me», he pleaded, thanking her with a labored smile.

The bell rang out through the mumbling dining hall to announce that the ritual of silence was about to begin.

Father Sirapian, known as *Gabìg*, the monkey, because of his hirsute appearance, stood up. «Mikael, please, it's your turn to read a passage from *Purgatory*», he said thrusting the big black volume lying in front of himself. During supper, in fact, the boys were required to take turns at reading passages from carefully chosen texts.

Mikael rose hesitating, glancing at the big table where the fathers sat for supper. Their dark habits, stark against the white walls of the refectory, made them look like bats or creatures from some other world. Aznavour looked furtively at his friend who was clambering awkwardly over the bench. Bakunìn's expression was glum and unfathomable, but it was clear he did not like performing this task. The French boy followed his friend with his eyes as he walked down the hall and noticed that he was staggering slightly, so much so, that he feared he might actually collapse all of a sudden.

«So», father Sirapian explained, «we have chosen a salm called *Miserere*. It seemed appropriate after this evening's deplorable events.»

Mikael was tempted to say something in defense of Dick. He would have liked to explain to the fathers that the boy's intention was not, actually, to steal, but simply to show off his dexterity, his innate talents of an illusionist. After all, it had merely been a boyish prank, not an act of authentic shoplifting. But the impassive face of the rector, that bored, aloof expression of his, made the boy change his mind. Wolf, who sat next to the rector, scrutinized his student with the air of an inquisitor. Mikael picked up the volume and walked over to the short spiral stairway leading up to the wooden pulpit. Making sure he would not lose his place in the text, he mounted the steps and dropped the book clumsily down on the lectern, with such a loud thud which seemed to respond to the booming thunder raging outside. Then he cleared his throat and began to read:

«Pity me, oh God, in your mercy…»

The soup in the bowls was growing cold. Nobody dared eat, because that excerpt aroused too much nervous tension. Only the rector plunged his spoon into the pottage and slurped it up, in no way worried about the awful noise he was making.

«…with your infinite bounty wipe out my sin…»

«Honorable fathers!»

The door suddenly flew open without any warning and Peppe stood there more flustered than usual. Rivulets of rain were streaming down his cheeks and he had to make an enormous effort to keep his eyes open. The rector stopped eating, his spoon suspended in mid-air.

«Honorable fathers, something awfully serious has happened. The student Dikràn is nowhere to be found… he's disappeared», he stammered.

A flash of lightning lit up the rose garden and Mikael startled, while his lips continued to move of their own accord, as if he were no longer in charge of them.

«Behold, I was begotten in sin, conceived in the throes of my mother's passion…»

«Mikael, that will do for now», the rector ordered, springing to his feet. «Signor Peppe, I beg you; please try to explain more clearly what you have just said», he asked the caretaker while doing his utmost to remain calm.

Images throng my mind, so lifelike they take my very breath away. I know they are the fruit of the symbiotic bond we share. It's as if one of my eyes continues to take stock of the everyday scenes here in the college: the long refectory trestles, my schoolmates sitting at their old worn-out desks, the blackboards with Latin words scribbled all over them, the boys' bodies sleeping in their iron bunks in the dormitories. This eye is obedient and well-trained, while the other, rebellious and practically schizophrenic, perceives some reality beyond my ken and to which I think I can never belong. I'm terribly frightened, I feel something awful is about to happen. But I hold my peace, because, were I to speak out, no one would ever believe me; they'd take me for a madman to say the very least.

«You can come down now, can't you see there's nobody left in here?» boomed Wolf bringing him back to his senses.

Mikael, who had remained stock-still on the pulpit for several minutes, staring blankly into empty space, his face white as a sheet, jumped at the sound of his teacher's voice and lowered his eyes.

Padre Keshishian was quite disturbed by the boy's strange behavior.

The padlock, open, its hook through the ring in the little door's lintel, swung loose. Why on earth had Dick left it there? To show everyone how quick and able he had been, maybe, or as a mocking memento to leave behind before he took flight.

Earlier that evening, the fathers had decided to lock the boy into the cubbyhole of the second-floor dormitories. Only once before had it been used to punish a student, under whose mattress they had found a pornographic magazine. It was a narrow, windowless room, full of cleaning materials, and once closed it was pitch dark inside.

«Why did you lock him in here?» the police inspector asked the rector.

«For bad behavior.»

The officer, pot-bellied and bald, shook his head as he rummaged among the brooms and pails, as if Dick could be hiding amidst the floor cloths.

A crowd of students had invaded the corridor while the fathers searched for the boy, making a superhuman effort to keep them all at bay. Their curiosity was far too keen: how had Dick managed to beat it so easily?

«You, on the contrary, claim you saw him as he made his escape...» said the policeman turning to the caretaker.

Signor Peppe sought the eye of the rector.

«Hmm, well, yes, I saw him from behind, through the window. He was running like mad in the pouring rain, towards the library,» he mumbled indicating the building beyond the little bridge in the garden. «I called out to him, 'Mikael', I shouted, because I though he was one of the other boys, seeing that he was wearing Mikael's trench coat.»

Padre Ayvazian moved his lips as if about to say something but decided not to speak.

The policeman nodded to the caretaker to continue.

«Well... I decided to follow and stop him but, then, as I was passing by the cubbyhole, I saw that the door was wide open, the padlock undone, I realized at once that the boy in the yard was Dikràn. Then I began looking for him all over the place. It was raining cats and dogs; well, I rushed off down to the low boundary wall, the one there, behind the college...»

There was a moment's silence as everyone drew his own conclusions.

«Take me downstairs» the policeman grunted.

Padre Ayvazian and Wolf led the way to the marble staircase, that all three of them descended in perplexed silence. Crossing the Hall of Mirrors, the agent slowed his pace a moment to gaze up admiringly at the frescoed ceiling. From there, they entered a dark narrow corridor with no windows.

The rector stopped in front of a door. «This is my room», he said putting his hand to the knob. «The lock has been tampered with.»

It was a modest though decorous room with very little furniture and only a few objects: the bed was up against one of the walls, there were two chairs, a wardrobe, a writing desk and heaps of books. A small window looked out onto the courtyard, and there was a pot of geraniums on the sill.

The police took the room in, in one sweeping glance. Then his eyes rested on a tin box, which lay open on the bedspread. He walked over and examined the contents, touching it gently with one finger.

«You said that there was nothing missing except the boy's passport and a sum of money?»

The college regulations foresaw that the students, upon their arrival, should hand over their documents and the money they brought with them. This policy was believed to discourage the boys from running away from school.

«How much?» continued the inspector.

«Thirty thousand, four hundred Liras: all my students' pocket money», answered Ayvazian.

The three men remained in the room just a few minutes longer. Then the policeman donned his hat again and said: «We have already informed all the ports and the railway authorities and provided them with a description of the fugitive. But, as I was saying, no sign as yet of Dikràn Same...»

«Samuelian. There's no use in telling you how we are all feeling, inspector», said father Ayvazian. «If we receive no news by tomorrow morning, we shall be obliged to inform his parents in the United States...»

«We'll do all we can», reassured the other as he took his leave.

The rector turned to father Keshishian: «Bring Mikael to my office. I'm sure he knows something. If he doesn't tell us, he'll regret it bitterly».

«May I have a drink of water, please?» asked Mikael red-eyed and sleepy.

Wolf picked up the carafe standing on the desk and poured a glass of water for the boy, noticing how pale he was. At times like this the priest sorely repented having ever become a teacher.

«Are you feeling all right?»

The adolescent nodded.

Father Keshishian and the rector had spent the whole night insisting that Mikael provide them with information about Dick, making him repeat the same story over and over again. The boy had sworn he knew absolutely nothing about his classmate's flight, though he did admit having seen him steal the apple.

«What about the trench coat, then? How can you account for that?» father Ayvazian had asked him curtly.

Mikael did not know how to explain the raincoat and this made his self-confidence wobble all of a sudden, a sure sign, according to the rector, that he was in cahoots with Dick.

In reality, Mikael was at a loss and wondered why his friend had taken his coat. Who knows, perhaps he had put it on trusting it might bring him luck or, maybe, because in the rush he had taken the first thing he could lay his hands on.

«Tell us, then, why you didn't report the theft at once?» father Ayvazian persevered. «Tell me, father, am I right or am I wrong?» he had asked, turning to the Wolf to seek his complicity.

«Yes, you should have come to me», Wolf admitted, reading signs of deep resentment in the boy's eyes.

At that point, the telephone rang making them all jump; there had been developments the police needed to discuss with the rector personally. Ayvazian had left in all haste, throwing his hooded cape over his shoulders, and without proffering any explanation whatsoever.

Wolf glanced anxiously at Mikael who was shivering, growing paler and paler, as if he were about to faint.

«Lie down for a while», he suggested, indicating the little divan with the cherry-wood arms. «You'll go upstairs to the dormitory as soon as the rector gets back», he reassured him.

The boy shifted his exhausted body onto the couch which seemed anything but comfortable.

«Here, take this…» offered father Keshishian handing him one of the cushions from the armchair.

Mikael lay down. He was long-limbed, although not very tall, his skin was fair — a characteristic rare in an Armenian — his hair had a copper sheen which gave him the air of an *odàr*, a foreigner. When Wolf had seen him enter the classroom the very first time, he thought he looked a little like lord Byron, an etching of whom hung in the library on the island of San Lazzaro. His erect bearing, the clear, sweet timbre of his voice were markers of his careful upbringing and his social class. Despite his years of experience with boys and their problems, father Keshishian used to tell himself over and over again that there was something impenetrable about Mikael. He seemed to hide within his innermost self a world all his own, of which he betrayed little or nothing.

Meanwhile, the boy, exhausted, had fallen asleep embracing the cushion, but Wolf, seeing he was sweating copiously, rose and went over to feel his forehead. Mikael did not move.

You're in bed and then you wake up all of a sudden, earlier than usual. In the hushed silence, you're listening for the sounds of the house

Mikael's breathing had grown labored. His face was twisted in a grimace, his chest heaving frantically as he gasped for air.

Wolf, alarmed, shook him by the shoulders.

«Don't touch me, don't touch me», yelled the boy, his legs thrashing wildly.

3

Patras, 1938

That afternoon, Martiròs — known to some as the *wheeler-dealer* had called in at the factory as was his wont whenever he returned to Patras. He was a big man who always sported a straw Panama hat, set at an angle. He wore an elegant brown suit, a white poplin shirt and a silk necktie. His trousers, baggy as was the fashion back then, were held by a belt so high on the waist that the legs looked just that little bit too short for a man of his height.

The son of Armenian refugees himself, he had grown up in the camp with all the others but, at a certain point, he had decided to move to Athens and there he had made his fortune having got in with some rather influential people, Greeks and Armenians, who had given him a helping hand. His field was business. For Martiròs all and anything could be bought and sold, were mere commodities, potential sources of profit. It was rumored that he had no scruples, nor was he squeamish when it came to the legitimacy or otherwise of a transaction. The backbiters even went on to say that he was involved in dubious, dodgy deals, regardless of that well-groomed Hollywood-movie-star attitude of his.

«What brings you back here?» the caretaker asked, welcoming him with a broad smile. Once, Martiròs had done him a favor; he had found him a pair of silk stockings for his girlfriend.

«Just popped by to say hello t'ye all», he replied winking at him through the smoke spiraling up from the cigarette dangling between his lips.

Then, he strode over and sat under the olive tree where he waited for his childhood friend, Seròp, to finish his shift. Meanwhile, he continued chatting with the custodian speaking loudly to make his voice heard over the clatter of the looms, trying to amaze him with tales from the capital. He paused now and then to salute some old acquaintances of his, laborers leaving the factory, jaded and weary after their long shift.

«Gov', you wouldn't have a fag to spare by any chance, would you?» asked one of them, hoping he might actually get a full packet from him.

«You're the image of Rodolfo Valentino», cajoled another who was particularly fond of cinema, admiring his impeccably tailored suit.

Studying these men's miserable appearance, Martiròs thanked God for having meted him out a better lot than theirs. Had he remained in Patras he would certainly have ended up like them. But what really bowled him over was how awful Seròp looked as he came out into the yard. He had not seen him for six months but in that brief span of time his friend had changed utterly. The clothes on his back were virtually in tatters: his shirt, though carefully mended, was threadbare and practically see-through from too much washing; his trousers were tatty and shiny, patched harlequin-style all over. When he took a closer look at him, Martiròs was shocked to see the deep wrinkles that scored his friend's face giving him an air of perennial, unbearable sadness.

«Hey, what's wrong, Stakhanovist?» he addressed him jokingly and patted him on the shoulder in an attempt to conceal his embarrassment.

This quip barely won a melancholy smile from Seròp.

«Let's go where we can talk», he added, looking about him with a touch of suspicion in his eyes.

The two men walked through the gate and down the dusty road leading to the town.

«Let's cut across the fields», suggested Martiròs with childish enthusiasm.

«Why?»

«Because! Just to do what we used to as kids.»

When they were children they loved to race through the fields full of sunflowers, hiding among the tall stalks, smelling the sickly-sweet scent, chewing the seeds that tasted of milk. And when it rained, they knew exactly what to use as an umbrella.

Seròp burst out laughing as he looked down at his companion's two-tone, laced shoes gleaming immaculately beneath the turnups of his custom-made trousers.

«Yes, but then you were barefoot», he mocked as he entered the field.

«What the heck!», exclaimed Martiròs, throwing his cigarette butt to the ground and crushing it with his heel before following his friend in among the stalks.

«How are the children?» asked Martiròs lighting up again.

«Fine», answered Seròp with a shrug. «But the first-born is really bad news.»

«Come on! He's only a baby!» exclaimed his friend.

«So, what's that supposed to mean? The fact is, that his brother is an angel and he's a veritable demon…»

«How do you tell them apart?»

«The first has a piece of red cord tied around his wrist; the second a green one», he explained with a frown.

The two men advanced among the tall flowers elbowing their way, especially Seròp who was the shorter of the two, the only dark splotch against the yellow background.

«Hey, look at that! Isn't it just beautiful?!» Martiròs cried out at a given point, spinning around and holding on to his hat lest the wind carry it away.

They had reached a clearing on a small plateau from which they could admire a breathtaking view of the bay. The setting sun, an amazing ball of fire, was brushing the crests of the waves, turning the sea to molten gold. Having been baked by the heat all day long, the earth now exhaled a shimmering vapor which caused the contours of everything to tremble. The tall yellow flowers, little suns in their own right, all turned towards their god to pay their last respects to him and the dying day.

«Count up to twenty and it'll be gone.»

Seròp looked at his friend baffled.

«The sun, *yeghbaìr*, brother», Martiròs explained. «Today is already yesterday, and d'ye know something?» He paused briefly for theatrical effect. «Tomorrow's another day!» he boomed in that well-modulated voice of his, experienced thespian that he was.

Seròp was standing there, his gaze fixed on the horizon when, all of a sudden, a shudder rippled through his body making him quake from head to toe.

«Are you feeling all right?» Martiròs asked him anxiously, noticing this singular spasm.

«Let's get a move on», murmured Seròp, swatting at a buzzing insect before moving on again.

«Trouble at work?» asked his friend, making an educated guess only to receive no reply.

«Jivan told me you wanted to see me», he insisted, referring to a mutual friend, the lorry driver who brought goods from the factory to Athens.

«Yes.»

«How can I help you?»

Seròp stopped in his tracks. «The other day the foreman called me and let me know that there's a problem of redundancy...»

«What?»

«That in September, after the holidays, I'm going to be laid off.» He pronounced this sentence in detached tones, as if talking about someone else's hard luck.

«Does your wife know?»

«No.»

«What do you think you'll do?»

«Talk to the unions, they know me well. The owners can't be let get away easily with this» Seròp declared, convinced, violently tearing a sunflower to shreds; it was as if he wanted to vent on the plant all the anger he had bottled up for so long. «It's about time those people there understood once and for all that they have to respect workers' rights.»

Martiròs knit his brows: he had never heard his friend speak like this before.

«Don't tell me you've become a Communist!» he exclaimed, flabbergasted.

Seròp threw away the remains of the flower and changed the subject. «You know I make slippers, lovely soft kundure. They're really beautiful...»

«Yes, I've been told.»

«You must help me sell them.»

Martiròs looked at him bemused.

«You know so many people over in Athens; all over the place», added Seròp. «I'm willing to give you a cut...»

The other burst out laughing.

«What's so funny?»

«You won't get rich selling slippers, my friend...»

«I don't want to get rich...» Seròp turned abruptly to face the bay where the sun was being drawn down beneath the waves. «All I want is to have enough to bring my children up», he explained candidly, as the last ray of sunshine swept over his face before fading away completely.

«I understand», replied the carpetbagger respectfully, «but how many pairs would you be able to sell in a week? No, let me put it another way, how many could you make? Two, three?»

Seròp tilted his head from side to side, expressing his uncertainty.

«I'm sorry, but there's nothing I can do to help you; I can give you some advice, though...» Martiròs suggested throwing the end of his cigarette away. «You know the Italian quarter, don't you?»

«Aha, the other side of the port, no? At San Dionisio?»

«Yep. Go over there and talk to Caputo, he owns a really fine shop. The Italians know how to appreciate beautiful things. If Caputo likes the slippers, he'll pay you a pretty penny for them. Just tell him I sent you.»

«Caputo?»

«Yep.»

They were almost at the city gates.

«Where are you going now?» Seròp asked him as he mopped beads of sweat from his brow.

«Back to Athens, there's a train at nine.»

Seròp nodded. «Take this, clean them up», he said handing him a handkerchief and indicating the two-tone brogues.

«Ah, thanks.» said Martiròs bending down and rubbing some dirt off the toes. «Well», he concluded. «I'll go this way, it'll be quicker.»

«Bye then. Be seeing you.»

«If there's anything you ever need...»

«Sure…»

Martiròs saluted him raising the brim of his hat slightly before setting off in the direction of the lights that were beginning to wink through the dusk. Seròp remained motionless as he watched his friend disappear amid the warren of narrow dirt tracks. He thought how wonderful it must be to be free to catch a train to somewhere else, anywhere else and take a short break from everyday cares and worries.

«What if I didn't go home?» he asked the evening star which had just made its appearance in the darkening sky.

«I was waiting for you», said Satèn with an edge of a scold in her voice as she tried to make herself heard above the bedlam filling the room.

Seròp had just pulled the cabin's curtain aside when he was swamped by the din of his children crying. On the bed sat his wife doing her best to calm down one of the twins who was wailing desperately, while Lussià-dudù held the other who emitted short vexed staccato howls.

«What's going on?» he asked coming closer.

«You stink of *moschùdi*; you've been drinking, haven't you?» Satèn reproached him, fanning the air to dispel the stench of his breath.

«What's going on?» he reiterated, raising his voice.

«Kids' stuff», the midwife butted in. «One of them hurt the other», she added trying to play things down.

«Who?»

The two women looked knowingly at each other.

«Mikael», Lussià-dudù admitted, nodding towards the child in her lap. Seròp took note of the red cord.

«Now what's he done?»

«He's pricked his brother with a needle», answered Satèn with simulated aplomb.

«A needle?»

«Yes, I was finishing off some of the uppers…» And she gestured towards the sewing machine on the table.

«You will insist on doing things on your own!» shouted Seròp, louder than the racket the howling twins were making.

Satèn jumped, frightened.

«The idea was mine, I wanted to help her», Lussià-dudù said lowering her gaze.

«Shut up! Shut up all of you!»

It was the first time that Seròp had ever shown any lack of respect for the woman who had brought him up. But now he had just lost control. So much so that in an impetus of rage he had torn Mikael from her arms and had shaken him violently in mid-air.

«You're a bad boy! Bad!» he yelled, his eyes bulging with sheer anger, without noticing that the clothesline stretched across the room was right under the chin of the baby he was shaking so furiously back and forth.

«You'll choke him that way!» screamed Satèn in alarm as she sprang to her feet having thrown the other baby roughly down on the bed.

«Stay where you are, woman», Seròp bellowed, pushing her back.

«For God's sake, stop it!» Lussià-dudù cried out. «Shame on you both!» And without adding another word, she picked up her canvas shopping bag, the one she used to fill up with food for them all, and simply left.

The twins were asleep at last in their cradle.

Satèn and Seròp, as they lay in bed, were staring in silence at the corrugated metal ceiling.

«I'm sorry about this evening», Satèn murmured.

Seròp snorted.

«You work too hard, your nerves are in shatters...» she added, turning towards her husband who persisted in his obstinate silence.

«Why won't you speak to me? I'm your wife, you should confide in me...»

Seròp stifled a laugh. «Well, if you really must know; let's see what you can do to help me?»

Satèn sat upright in the bed, an expression of satisfaction on her face, she fixed the shoulder of her nightdress, folded her hands in her lap and waited.

«They've sacked me; so, what do you think you can do about that? Eh?» Seròp burst out tersely, raising himself up on one elbow, his face just a few inches from that of his wife, staring at her defiantly, «So let's hear what you have to say, now!» he added to rub it in more viciously.

Satèn sat there, speechless, still as a statue, in a state of utter shock.

«Is that all you have to say for yourself? Eh?» he mocked, grabbing her by the arm as if he wanted to shake some kind of reaction from her.

«And, you know whose fault it is, don't you?» he yelled. «That cursed child's, Mikael's; he's jinxed, brings us all bad luck.»

Satèn began to shake her head, first slowly, then faster and faster, as if having an epileptic seizure.

«The other morning when they sent me packing, it was he who had woken me up… he'd even scratched my hand… See?» he roared showing his wife the tell-tale red mark, by no means worried about the pain he might be causing her.

«I beg you…» Satèn entreated him, as she fell back limply on the bed sobbing her heart out.

Seròp was rather ignorant; he was inclined to heed the beliefs and superstitions that went around among poor devils like himself, brought up in dire straits without any education worth mentioning.

From the moment of the birth of the twins, when he had seen Mikael's umbilical cord choking the other baby, he had been convinced that his firstborn was evil, that he would bring bad luck, as if the poor child acted of his own volition. From then on, this notion had grown stronger and stronger, thanks also to a number of banal coincidences which Seròp attributed to his son's nefarious influence over the family's destiny.

Despite this, he had never thrown this terrible accusation in his wife's face before. Satèn was visibly upset, distraught, so Seròp, now that his rage had simmered down, began to realize he had gone too far. To see his wife in such a state pained him, because his sole desire had always been that of protecting and cherishing her.

«Calm down, please do. I just lost it. Now all I have to do is look for another job, no?», he whispered in an attempt to appease her, but she went on sobbing, her face lost in the bolster. So, he began to stroke her long hair fanned out all over the rough linen pillow.

«There, there! Stop crying», he murmured.

Satèn flinched as he began to sidle over to her in the bed, overpowered by a sudden upsurge of passion. For weeks now, because of the shifts at the factory, they had not made love.

Remember to love your wife, look after her, cherish her as if she were the most precious, delicate flower in the world, the advice his dear departed father had given him echoed in his mind. But, in vain.

He straddled her clumsily, lifted up her nightdress and penetrated her in a single rough thrust, pinning her down by the shoulders and sliding effortlessly inside her, thanks to the sweat oozing between her thighs.

«No!» Satèn groaned with pleasure mingled with resignation towards this brutal approach she was unused to.

«Tell me you love me», Seròp ordered.

She remained silent, immobile under his weight.

«Tell me you love me», he insisted.

Nothing.

Seròp unlatched himself from her, as if saying he would concede no further intercourse unless she reassured him first of her feelings. He waited a few moments but, seeing no response was forthcoming, he caught hold of her and turned her around on her side to face him.

In the dark, he gazed into her eyes that sparkled like two amber pearls, shinier than ever.

«So, you do love me, don't you?» he asked once more, this time pleading with her.

«I can't love you unless…»

Satèn was unable to continue because Seròp had taken hold of her and was kissing her in an impulse of unbridled desire. He nibbled her tongue and her lips, then spread her thighs, lifted her legs up to place her feet on his shoulders. Her inebriating woman's scent stunned him. He caressed her damp vagina, a ripe sap-drenched pod. Without further ado, he bent over to savor it as she bent back rocking with bliss and pressing his head to her groin.

It was she who heard first the soft whistling sound. She turned her head around and was able to make out the silhouette of one of the boys, who, clasping the edge of the cradle was staring at her motionless.

«May God forgive me!» she exclaimed.

She pushed her husband away, sat up in bed and wrapped the crumpled, damp sheet around her.

«But what the devil is happening?» protested Seròp, bewildered. He was wiping the drops of Satèn's pleasure from his lips when, with the corner of one eye, he caught sight of a tiny arm with its wristlet of frayed red cord.

Patras, 27th July 1938

> *Dear Miriam,*
> *we are all well as we trust you are too.*
> *I have finally managed to have a photo of the family taken. See how beautiful the babies are? Everyone says they look like me. The girl on the chair is Satèn. She has eyes of a wonderful color, only here you can't see them. The one standing behind her is myself of course. A friend loaned me the suit and the Panama for the occasion.*
> *Thanks for the five dollars you sent in your last letter. You're spoiling us. Unfortunately, we can't baptize the children this summer. I'd like to hold a nice party for them. You know how important this rite is in our tradition, only I haven't got the money. I'm in trouble as far as work's concerned because for the moment, I've been made redundant. What can I do? I don't know yet.*
> *I really appreciate all your invitations to move over to America but, my dear cousin, that really scares me. I don't speak the language and I don't know anybody, not even you in that I've never met you. I remember how difficult it was for me to get used to living here in Greece, to learning the language, making new friends… I think that if I were ever to leave again, it would be to go back home to our beloved Armenia, the country of my great-grandparents, where everyone speaks my language, prays in the same way, understands me before I even open my mouth. They say it's part of the Soviet Union now, that it's good to live there, everyone equal, no owners, no workers. All together for a better future, so they say. Maybe I should have left in thirty-six, with the refugee caravan. But I trust in God and wait patiently.*
> *Best wishes to you and your husband.*
> *Thanks again,*
> *your cousin Seròp.*
> *P.S. Satèn and the babies send you lots of hugs and kisses.*

The young woman who came to the Gazarians' door made Fitìl turn her head, a seed caught between her teeth. She was slim, wore European dress and had a sophisticated, distinct air about her. The girl waited a few seconds. Receiving no response, she drew the heavy curtain aside.

«Mrs. Gazarian?» she called out in a voice with a slight foreign accent.

Fitìl strained as forward as she could but could not hear a word because, as soon as Satèn appeared in the doorway, the girl spoke in soft undertones. The two women stood for a few seconds on the threshold before Satèn invited the other inside.

«Please, be seated, Lusiné», she said indicating the only chair in the place.

«Lucy», the girl pointed out. She smiled embarrassed, looking quickly about her before sitting down and smoothing out her silk dress.

«As you can see there isn't much space here; we're lucky you came at nap time!» Sate'n exclaimed indicating the cradle. Lucy stood up. «But they're twins, aren't they?» she inquired, taking a step forward.

The two children were fast asleep wrapped in each other's arms; one of them had thrown his leg over his brother's as if seeking to keep him joined to himself, the way they had been in their mother's womb.

«They are absolutely gorgeous!» the girl remarked enraptured.

«Thanks.»

«How old are they?»

«Eight months... Would you like one? They've just been picked...» Satèn said pushing a dish of fresh figs across the table towards her.

«Not one, thanks, later maybe.»

«You were saying you knew Rosacùr»

«She and my mother went to school together in Adabazàr.»

«But you were born in London?»

«Yes. My parents met and married in England.»

Satèn nodded, without understanding the real reason for this unexpected visit.

«Look», Lucy continued, seeing she was perplexed, «I'm about to take up a post here in town. The AGBU, the Armenian General Benevolent Union — set up in the United States of America — they asked me to come over to Patras as a teacher, beginning next September. Have you heard about the funds they've made available to enhance and enlarge the community school, here?»

Satèn shook her head.

«It's been months since I met anyone, I hardly ever leave the house», she explained. «When Rosacùr, the lady who adopted me taught there, she used to tell me everything. She was such a well-educated and learned woman», she added with a hint of pride.

She felt a lump in her throat at the mention of Rosacùr's name. Since becoming a mother, she had come to realize, hands-on, how difficult it was to bring up a child and often recalled the woman who had taken her under her wing, bringing her up with the same care and attention as a natural parent.

«Do you see these?» she added, indicating the bracelets she wore. «They were hers. There used to be sixteen of them, but now there are only ten left because we've had to sell a few of them...»

Lucy, noticing Satèn's bitter smile, changed the subject. «Everyone blesses and appreciates Rosacùr for what she did for the community, for the children of refugees newly arrived here», she remarked. «Without her classes many would have remained illiterate.»

«But will you teach Armenian too?» Satèn asked interrupting the girl.

Lucy chuckled a little. «No. Can you imagine that!»

«Let's do away with formality, after all, I'm younger than you are.»

«As you wish. I was telling you that I'll be teaching English; my Armenian is not great.»

They stood there in silence for a while, one in front of the other. Satèn could catch the perfume of roses and cinnamon that Lucy diffused around the room.

«I was wondering», the girl resumed with a little cough, «if, by any chance, you'd put aside the books Rosacùr used. I'd love to have a look at them; I'd like to follow the same approach to teach English, so the pupils may learn the same concepts and words in both languages simultaneously...»

«If I'm not mistaken, I still have something of hers», Satèn responded, «I put all her things in a box.»

She rose and bending down, rummaged beneath the bed. «Our life in a casket...» she murmured as she drew out the red velvet case. She blew off the dust, placed the box on the table beside the figs.

«Barney's De Luxe Chocolates», read Lucy.

«There, all that's left is in here», said Satèn removing the lid. «You can look inside», she invited.

The girl hesitated for a moment, then began to take out some of the documents, including Rosacùr's death certificate and that of Satèn's wedding, a few tests pupils never collected, and, at the very bottom, a volume of Armenian language and grammar.

«Here it is!» she exclaimed, leafing through the book avidly, lingering over some of the notes in the margins that the teacher had jotted down. «Wonderful...» she whispered more or less to herself.

«There should be some photos too», Satèn added. «Take a good look.»

«Don't tell me Rosacùr read Saroyan in English!» Lucy cried in amazement a moment later, waving a book.

«No, that was a present from America. My husband's cousin sent it to us. She said it was great, do you know it?»

«Fantastic, you really must read it», answered the girl; then she blushed deeply when she became aware of her tactless blunder. «Sorry, I didn't mean...»

«No harm done... tell me, rather, what it's about?»

Lucy sighed. «Nothing special. Short stories, but it's the writing that's sublime.»

«But there must be a story!» Satèn insisted.

«Well, yes. Let's say that the title story is about a young author during the Great Recession that hit the United States roughly ten years ago. Do you remember?» she asked, again in too much of a hurry. «It's moving, engrossing. You just can't put it down before the end.»

«And the title?» asked Satèn pointing at the sleeve.

«The Daring Young Man on the Flying Trapeze?»

«What's a trapeze?»

«The swing acrobats use in the circus, a bar held up by two

cables suspended from the top of the tent», she tried to explain miming shapes in the air.

«What's that got to do with the story?»

Lucy was obliged to ponder an instant. She raised her eyes and saw a wet vest dripping on the clothesline stretched across the room.

«In the end, the young writer dies of hunger...»

«Dies?»

«Yes.»

«What's that got to do with it?»

«I think the writer, Saroyan, compared the thrill, the magic of the flying trapeze to the delirium that immediately precedes death...»

Satèn listened holding her breath. «It's a sad story», she murmured.

«Yes, but very poetic.»

«How lucky you are to have been able to read it... read the beginning to me!» she asked unexpectedly.

«Now?» ventured Lucy unable to hold back a chuckle.

«Oh please, pretty please.»

«But I'll have to translate it on the spot...»

«But you teach English, don't you?» Satèn challenged her.

The girl shifted uneasily on the chair and opened the book. The odor of ink mingled with Lucy's rose and cinnamon perfume.

«The first paragraph», said Satèn.

«Agreed, just the first one.»

The teacher cleared her throat and read the opening in silence, then, having reflected for a moment or two, began speaking in Armenian: «Sleep. Awake and in a horizontal position, amid universal spaces, at the prey of laughter and hilarity, satire, the end of all...» She lay the book down suddenly on her knees and shook her head angrily. «No, it isn't possible that way, I'm murdering the text, I'll have to think it out better», she complained.

One of the babies stirred in his sleep so she took advantage of this and sprang to her feet.

«It's late, I don't wish to disturb you any longer», she said. «May I take this with me? I swear I'll bring it back to you», she asked indicating Rosacùr's old primer.

Satèn reflected for a moment. «Yes», she consented «providing that...»

Lucy raised her head and looked at her inquisitively.

«...providing you tell me the story of the trapeze, translating it for me word by word. Do you think you could do that for me?»

The girl took in Satèn's miserable home; it took only a sole glance around the place: the intertwined twins lying on four planks nailed together, the vest and trousers dripping on the clothes line, the water tank with *kalimera* written on it, the half-sewn slippers lying on the bed, the chocolate box on the table beside the dish of figs, the fly buzzing around it.

«Why not? It sounds like a good idea to me», she answered with apparent levity.

Then she picked up the two books and with a wave of her tapering hand, bid goodbye.

«I'll be back soon», she promised before pushing the tarpaulin curtain aside.

4

A particularly hot day for that time of year was dawning on the western outskirts of Yerevan. Although the sun had not risen yet, the impatient roosters were in a great hurry to herald its arrival. The bulk of Mount Ararat, somber and imposing, was silhouetted against the dark blue sky. The shimmering light of the stars was ebbing fast to the rhythm of the golden tresses of the trees, tossing in the morning breeze. The red and yellow trams screeched as they struggled along their shiny, brand new tracks. This was Nova Sebastia, a district in the making, earmarked to host the returning emigres: *the aghbèr*, the brothers, as they were called sarcastically by the locals. Over time they had arrived in their thousands from Europe, from America, from the rest of the world, persuaded by an astute re-entry campaign, conducted for years by the church with the approval of Stalin himself, that there was no future for Armenians except in their homeland, their «sweet, battered» Armenia.

Tall, high-rise cement buildings towered all around, dwarfing the few pumice-stone houses still standing. Soon there would be no more gardens, barns or henhouses left. In the valley beyond the hill, a cluster of chimneys belched smoke and vapor up into the air.

The streets were already thronged with people, most of them laborers, hurrying off to work. The tips of their cigarettes—red embers betraying the torment of their souls—glowed in the semi-darkness as they flooded the sidewalks of Ohanov avenue, moments before the next tram snatched them away.

They did not exchange glances: it was forbidden to look another straight in the face.

The lights were still off in the apartment where the Gazarians lived.

Gabriel had woken up earlier than usual and lying awake in bed, was listening for the sounds of the house. On the living-room sideboard the obsidian clock ticked to the rise and fall of papa's snores. Gabriel loved Mondays, the only day when they all had breakfast together. His sister Novàrt and himself seated at the table like a princess and prince, while papa who did not work the morning shift, got their milk ready and mamma heated the bread and cut the cheese.

Novàrt, in the bed next to his, let out a soft sigh in her sleep. Gabriel lifted his head and looked over at her fondly. She was what he cherished most in the whole world, his mite of a little wren aged only four, her shock of black curls peeping out from under the blankets.

The Gazarians were newcomers to Armenia and, however absurd it might seem, they had no friends in the city. The few people with whom they had any ties had all decided to remain in Greece, because they had no faith in the promises the propagandists had waved under their noses. He had eavesdropped once at the door of his parents' room and had heard them quarrelling, their voices low: mamma said she missed home, that coming to Armenia had been an awful mistake...

The noise of a car braking outside startled him. An infernal screeching, followed by the dull thud of car doors slamming violently. Gabriel held his breath, sprung from the bed and looked out the window. He squinted, blinded by a ray of sunlight coming from behind the building across the way. A cream-colored car was parked sideways across the doorway and three men, of whom he barely managed to catch sight, were entering the house. He remained motionless for a few seconds, barefoot on the icy tiles, his ears straining to hear the feet scrambling along the floors below. Whoever they were, these three had not called the lift because they were mounting the stairs two at a time. Just like he did when he got home from school.

He rushed back to bed and buried himself under the blankets, his heart pounding in his ears, faster and faster as the footfalls approached. Petrified with fear, he could not breathe and he thought he was going to smother. He looked over at his sleeping sister, unaware of the looming danger, and could smell her rose-scented breath, like the flower she was named after: Novàrt, 'rosebud' in Armenian. He reached for her hand, and when they knocked on the door, he clasped it tightly in his own.

Without even waiting for someone to open the door, the three simply kicked it wide open. The stench of filthy uniforms wafted through the house.

«Novàrt giàn», said Gabriel to his little sister as one of the veins on his neck began to throb frantically.

He could hear the muffled voices of his parents in the next room.

«Seròp Gazarian, get up», an unknown voice ordered in Russian.

«Wh… what's going on?» his father babbled by way of reply, before the loud thud of a falling body shook the floor.

Gabriel's mother protested feebly entreating, «Please, let me wake the children at least».

Meanwhile, her husband was shoved roughly into the living room.

With bated breath, Gabriel did not budge until someone entered the room.

«*Màlchiki*, kids, out of bed!» yelled the voice of a shadow, its hand on the switch. It was a tall, stout young man wearing a mud-colored beret with a red star on it.

Gabriel let go of his sister's hand and stood up on the bed.

The man tried to catch him.

«Don't touch me, don't touch me!» the boy screamed, kicking the intruder away from him as Novàrt awoke with a start and burst into floods of tears as if she were having a nightmare. She jumped up onto Gabriel's bed and hid behind him.

«*Aghbarìk*, dear brother», she implored, her face flushed, her eyes aghast with shock.

Gabriel shielded her with his body as he continued kicking wildly trying to keep the man at bay. Fed up with these ridiculous attempts, the man went around to the other side of the bed and, lifting the child up with both hands, began to shake her violently. Novàrt let out an ear-splitting shriek and dug her nails into her brother's back, terrified lest she be separated from him. Gabriel simply saw red: he could not bear anyone to lay hands on Novàrt. He was eleven years her senior and had always stood up for her in every way. He lifted the cast-iron lamp from the night table and hit the aggressor over the head with it. The man grimaced with pain, the blood oozing from his nose, and, after a moment's astonishment, jumped right up onto the mattress, his beret almost brushing the ceiling. Gabriel noticed his dirty combat boots and the muddy footprints on his mother's clean white sheets as the man caught hold of him and lifted him up.

«*Zhopa*, asshole!» he shouted, throwing him down off the bed.

Novàrt backed away. For an instant she thought her brother was dead.

«You may call me Dimitri», said the man with the salt-and-pepper hair, a cigarette clamped between his teeth.

The old man he addressed was wearing a frayed shawl-necked, red and black checked bathrobe, its front all spattered with dried out shaving-cream stains.

He was over ninety.

«*Tovarisch* Aganian, do take a seat», continued Dimitri, having accompanied him into the Gazarians' apartment. «All you need do is sit here and observe. Nothing more, is that clear?» From his accent it was evident that he was from Yerevan.

Aganian sat down wearily on one of the living-room chairs, his eyes moist with tears and gazed over at his neighbors. All four of them were huddled together on the little sofa under the window in a beam of sunlight which, mockingly, lit up that corner of the room, leaving the rest in semi-darkness.

Dimitri was the only one in civilian clothes, the other two, younger and certainly not Armenian, wore the uniform of the Commissariat for Internal Affairs, the notorious NKVD.

«Name?» he barked, addressing the head of the family.

«Seròp.»

Dimitri jotted it down in his grey-paged notebook.

«Surname?»

«Gazarian.»

«Born?»

Seròp frowned as if he had forgotten the date. «August 1910.»

«Date?»

«I don't know.»

«Place?»

«Adabazàr, Turkey.»

«Father's name?»

«Toròs.»

«Mother's name?»

«I don't know», he said after a moment's hesitation. *Siranùsh*, sweet love, too lovely a name to defile in similar circumstances.

The other fulminated him with one look.

«No-one ever told me», lied Seròp.

Dimitri tap-tapped on the table with his pen. Too many uncertain data. «What does it say on your papers?»

«Unknown.»

Dimitri inhaled his cigarette and made smoke rings before continuing.

«Wife's name?»

«Satèn.»

It took half an hour to fill in the form. When they had finished, Dimitri turned to Aganian

«Comrade, do you know these people?»

The old man stared at the divan. He realized that lovely little Novàrt, who was now buried in her mother's arms, was whimpering and, despite his cataracts, he could make out the bruises on Gabriel's face and read the terror in Satèn's eyes. Of course, he knew them. Aganian lived in the apartment across the landing from theirs. Satèn was the only person in the whole block who ever knocked on his door. «Dadìg, granddad, I'm going out, is there anything you need?» she would ask. Gabriel, on the other hand, used to pick up his medication on his way home from school. Novàrt, his little 'rosebud', cheered him up by bringing him drawings with which he covered the walls of his home. As for Seròp, he used to invite him in often on cold winter evenings to share a bowl of soup with the family. The Gazarians had looked after him and helped him bear his sorrow, when he—a widower and a repatriate from Romania—was left all alone after his only son had been deported to Siberia He did know them, and well!

The Gazarians were his family, in a certain sense.

He took them in in a glance. Seròp nodded to him fleetingly and he responded likewise.

«Yes, I know them», the old man said at last.

Dimitri gestured to the two officers who stormed into the other rooms. They emptied all the drawers, cupboards and wardrobes. They upturned boxes and tins. They ripped open mattresses and quilts. They even ransacked the bathroom, bending pipes and tearing off loose tiles. Then, they returned to the living room and dashed everything they found on the shelves to the ground. They went through the bookcase and fine-combed the letters from Greece. They dismantled Satèn's sewing machine completely. Thuds, bangs and crashes echoed throughout the apartment, making the child in her mother's lap tremble. Gabriel looked at his father hoping he would speak out to protest against similar mindless, destructive frenzy. He was only deluding himself. Seròp did not even open his mouth.

Every so often, the two officers brought Dimitri what they thought might be their prey: Novàrt's doll, Gabriel's accordion, Satèn's satin slippers, Seròp's imported aftershave.

«This?» they asked.

But Dimitri shook his head. «Again, look more thoroughly», he ordered.

At noon, he stretched himself and turned to Aganian with a jeering smirk, «*Enkèr*, comrade, don't you worry. It'll soon be over, just you wait and see».

His agents looked at him baffled, mopping the sweat from their brows.

«May I have a glass of water?» Gabriel was thirsty; up until then they had not allowed him to eat or drink. That was to punish him for what he had done. He had a bump on his forehead, the blood from the cut on his upper lip had clotted.

Dimitri looked at him complacently.

«Help yourself, make yourself at home», he jibed, while his agents burst out laughing. «You go back into the kitchen», he thundered at them, quenching his cigarette in the ashtray too full of butts already. «What are you waiting for?»

Then he yawned barefacedly, opening his mouth so wide that his eyes began to water. It was evident he was bored to tears. When Gabriel had resumed his place, Dimitri rose suddenly and stepped into the middle of the room, to stretch his legs, maybe. He was not tall and, though no longer young, he was muscular and fit.

«I get it, I have to do it myself», he groaned.

Joining the other two men in the kitchen, with brisk, clean moves he began to smash the dishes and pull down the shelves. Then he threw the cutlery and table linen all over the place. He opened a cupboard and, rummaging inside, found three colored glasses and two tins of food. He opened these, smelled the contents and began to frisk the covering paper. He removed the bottom panel of the cupboard and pulled something out, his face beaming.

«Now, this is what we were looking for!» he gloated.

They all looked at him inquiringly. Even Aganian leaned forward to see what he had found.

It was a piece of cardboard.

«The Daring Young Man...» he read in labored English. «Literature, and by an American writer, too. Bravo!» he commented sarcastically, indicating the words on the cardboard to Seròp, his two henchmen close upon his heels. «How do you explain this, eh?» he inquired, shoving the cover of the book under his nose.

Seròp reddened.

«Have I got to ask again? What's this crap?» Dimitri suddenly raised his voice.

Gabriel saw his father bow his head like a scolded child. He could not bear it that papa had not the courage to name the author they had always admired so much. How many times had he read those stories to him after dinner, before bedtime, as they sat side by side on the divan where they were sitting now? Gabriel knew some of it by heart, the more, intense beautiful passages: «*He would fly though the air with the greatest of ease, that daring young man on the flying trapeze*».

«It's the cover of a book», Gabriel blurted out impulsively, unable to hold his tongue. Satèn shot him a piercing glance while Novàrt thought her brother was a hero.

Dimitri knelt in front of the boy, biting his lips and shaking his head. «Well, thank you for having informed me. I bet you've read it, eh?»

«Of course he's read it», butted in the agent whom Gabriel had struck before with the clock, a wad of cottonwood stuffed up one of his nostrils to stop the bleeding.

«My son has nothing to do with it», said Seròp who had decided to speak at last. «It's a book I brought with me from Greece.»

«They're only stories, for goodness' sake...» pleaded Satèn as she shifted nervously on the sofa.

«Don't you try to fool me, madam», snapped Dimitri. «I know William Saroyan. I am perfectly aware of what he writes. We keep ourselves up-to-date so that we know how to appraise anything that might corrupt our people and jeopardize the values in which we believe.» Having heaved a deep sigh, he added: «So, you keep the cover of this book with the flour and rice; food for thought I dare say. But the inside of the book? Where is it?»

«Thrown out. It was in tatters, ruined...» responded Seròp.

Dimitri stiffened, straightened his shoulders and took a step in his direction and clouted him across the face so hard that his head was knocked backwards. Novàrt, terrified, dug deeper into the ample folds of her mother's dressing gown. Gabriel felt all his father's pain and quivered with anger. He would have reacted had Satèn not stopped him in time with a telling glance.

«This so you know you must never, never lie to the homeland, to our Holy Mother Russia», pontificated Dimitri, his face red with fury.

«I entreat you, comrade», Aganian intervened in a tiny feeble voice. «That book used to belong to my son, it was I who loaned it to them; you see, I had nothing else to give them to thank them for the kindness and attention they have always shown me», the old man volunteered coughing and wheezing.

«Shut up, you wretch», Dimitri shouted at him in scorn. «Remember, your son is moldering in the icebox and you, for all I care, you may croak tomorrow!», he concluded, spitting on the ground.

It was almost dark when the cream-colored car, which had been parked all day in front of the entrance, carried Seròp and Gabriel off.

They had spent all those hours answering all sorts of questions as Dimitri filled in form after form. They had not had a bite to eat, but neither of them felt hungry anymore. When the investigation had come to an end, old Aganian had signed a declaration saying he had been present while the Gazarians' home was being searched, that all the procedures had been executed according to the book, that there had been no violence, no intimidation, and no abuse whatsoever.

«Forgive me», he mumbled when he had finished, with the pen still in his hand.

Then, the officers, having handcuffed father and son and seizing the felonious material — the worn-out cover of William Saroyan's book — had left the apartment banging the door which now hung swinging on a single hinge.

«Where are you taking them?» Satèn called down from the landing. «When will I be able to see them?» she called after them, in vain, while their neighbors, their doors a bare sliver ajar, squinted out to see what was going on.

«Get in» ordered the agent who had been injured as he opened the rear door of the vehicle.

Seròp complied. The temperature had fallen considerably, and murky grey clouds were assembling in the sky. Gabriel lingered a moment to fill his lungs with fresh, bracing air. In that brief lapse of time, he managed to take in a great number of images. Scenes of everyday life, which suddenly assumed extraordinary significance for him. Like the glum-faced girl getting off the tram, the lady in the hallway across the road putting her hand into the letterbox, the children playing tag amid the rubble at the nearby building site, the elderly couple crossing the driveway who pretended not to see him. Finally, the black mop of Novàrt's hair, which was sticking out like a dark blob from their apartment window. Then he lowered his head and got into the car.

As Dimitri slammed on the accelerator and the car skidded off down the avenue, Gabriel turned back to catch one last fleeting glimpse. He felt he had to impress on his mind, indelibly, the life he was leaving behind.

They spent the night in one of the cells reserved for political prisoners in the basement of the Commissariat for Internal Affairs, in Nalbandyan avenue, in the heart of Yerevan. It was a three-storey building with a stairway leading up to the entrance. A place Gabriel recognized instantly as soon as they pulled up at the foot of the steps. During their Sunday walks they had often passed in front of this building and he remembered having noticed the cream-colored cars parked outside and people being pushed and shoved towards the steps. He recalled how papa, when they came across scenes like these, simply hastened his step and mamma peered down at the tips of her shoes while he, holding Novàrt by the hand, never mustered up the courage to ask what place it was.

At dawn, a light drizzle spattered against the panes of the building's windows. Seròp and Gabriel were led into the commissar's office.

Gaunt, his complexion cadaveric, the officer sat behind a wooden desk. Father and son waited in silence, while he arranged the papers in front of him and lit one cigarette after another, only to leave them there to burn out in the crystal ashtray. A framed photograph of the «Father of the People», Comrade Stalin, dominated the wall behind him.

«Sit down», he told them at a certain point without even lifting his head. «I have read everything and am disconcerted to learn that amongst us there are individuals who seek to corrupt the conscience of our people», he began.

«But…» began Seròp trying to justify himself.

The other stopped him with a gesture of the hand.

«Listen to me, comrade…» he interrupted searching for the surname on a paper in front of him, «Gazarian, I have drawn up a declaration in which you admit your guilt and…»

«But I didn't do anything, you simply found the cover of a book of stories.»

«And does that seem a light matter to you? That book is garbage, venom for the health of the party! You have young children», he said pointing at Gabriel who never stopped staring him straight in the eye, «it is your bounden duty to bring them up in observance of our sacred values and ideals.» His tone was placid, but it was plain that he would admit no objections.

Seròp remained silent.

«Therefore, as I was saying, you have to sign this declaration.»

He pushed the sheet of paper and the pen before Seròp and invited him to read it.

«I, Seròp Gazarian, admit before the Soviet People that I have read and diffused books and articles of anti-Communist content, aimed, therefore, at damaging the Soviet Union and its sovereign people. I declare, furthermore, that I repent bitterly for having behaved as an enemy of the people and declare, therefore, that it is my desire to make amends to my fatherland for the harm I have caused.»

«What do you think?»

Seròp shook his head without knowing how to answer.

«After you sign this document, it will be attached to another which we shall draw up here together, that is, the report of the perquisition carried out at your home. As you can see, we are giving you the opportunity, even if you don't deserve it, to clarify, in black and white, how such a deplorable thing can possibly have occurred.»

Seròp was shaken by a fit of sobbing so sudden that Gabriel looked at him in utter astonishment.

«Papa...» he said.

The commissar was unable to work out whether the boy wanted to express his compassion or call his father to order.

«And you, young comrade, how old are you, fifteen, sixteen? I trust you can thoroughly grasp the gravity of the situation», he said lighting the umpteenth cigarette.

Gabriel scrutinized the man carefully, summing him up in a few seconds: an executive draped in a uniform far too big for him, sitting behind a desk on a leather armchair wielding the power he had obtained thanks to who knows what compromise, atrocity and cowardly baseness. He noticed his trembling nicotine-stained fingers and for an instant feared the cigarette might fall from his hand. He took in his emaciated face, his waxen skin, his thin lips, half-open to reveal a number of gold teeth.

«All the worse for you», the commissar said at last, as if aware of the disgust he was arousing in Gabriel. He pressed a button and a sharp buzz rang through the corridor outside the office door. Shortly afterwards a young officer appeared on the threshold.

«You must type his confession», he ordered pointing at the text he had prepared for Seròp.

The young man hesitated. «We can't comrade», he responded at last.

«Why not?»

«Our typewriter is out of order, they should repair it by this evening.»

«Borrow the one on the second floor.»

«No, impossible.»

The commissar rose, his jacked weighed down by the decorations on the epaulettes. «I don't understand», he said.

«Comrade commissar, it's got no tape.»

«So? Use the tape from yours.»

The young officer shook his head.

«I am so sorry, I'm afraid it's not compatible; a different model altogether, comrade commissar.»

5

Venice, 1952

«Soap up!»

His hand tightly grasping the levers of the iron taps, signor Peppe, with the impetus of a condottiere, dispensed the water the students needed to wash themselves. He alone and nobody else was allowed to operate the plumbing apparatus situated in the corridor just outside the men's baths. A line of fixed showerheads was arranged along the wall at a height beyond the boys' reach. From these the water spurted out in all directions but, worst of all, it was freezing cold. It was late November and taking a shower in the morning was startlingly akin to torture. They all rubbed the suds over their bodies with great energy in hopes of producing a little heat.

«Rinse off!» came the prompt, imperious order of the caretaker who seemed to derive amusement from seeing the boys shivering under the jet of gelid water. Some hopped and jigged, some yelled and tried dodging it, while others drew back thus giving up the idea of washing properly.

«Brrr… it's like being in Siberia, only worse», Aznavour joked, rinsing himself with surprising speed. «But what on earth are you doing? Why don't you get a move on?»

Mikael stood motionless in the shower, his face turned towards the wall, his head bent as the water ran over him carrying away patches of lather from his shoulders and back.

«Hello there, I'm talking to you! Sleeping on your feet or what?» Aznavour remarked as he shook him by an arm. At last Mikael turned around.

«But aren't you freezing? Just standing there like a statue!» continued his friend.

«I am so very sad…» mumbled Mikael.

The water gurgled like a monster trapped in the old rusty pipes.

«What are you on about?»

«My heart is in bits.»

«Dry off and away with you! It's seven o'clock already», boomed signor Peppe turning the water off all of a sudden. Huge lumps of foam floating like icebergs, accumulated around the plugholes. It was time to be going back to the dormitories, getting dressed and rushing down to breakfast and class.

«We're all in bits», responded Aznavour. «Dick was dead right to cut and run and, who knows, he's probably kicking back in the ham-mam in his lovely mansion.» He picked up the flaccid bar of soap and placed it in its metal box.

He had not been listening nor looking carefully, otherwise, amid the streams of water running down Mikael's face he would have noticed the tears, which, despite his best efforts, his friend was unable to hold in check.

They students were having their religion lesson, taught by father Keshishian with his usual passion and his communicative skills which always managed to capture the boys' attention, even if the topics were often tricky and complex. Though he was awfully strict, they all acknowledged his vast learning and remarkable charisma. Mikael, who was particularly interested in theological matters, admired the priest for his teaching which went far beyond his subject and could sense that he was anxious and thirsty for knowledge. Yes, Wolf was certainly a very particular person. At the moment he was discussing the Council of Calcedonia and the dispute over the nature of Christ availing himself of ancient Greek terminology.

As he listened to the sound of these words, Mikael looked out through the windows which overlooked the college garden. His eyes wandered beyond the wrought-iron gate, the little romantic bridge linking two verdant mounds, to sweep down over the gravel pathway and linger on the neoclassical façade of the Casin which hosted the school's library.

Mikael remembered the first time he had seen this building. He had just arrived from Greece after a long journey across the Adriatic. Having come in through the door, he had put his cases down for a moment and caught sight of it from the atrium. The elegance of the construction brought his own country to mind. For an instant, it was as if the Casin were the Parthenon and he was back at the window of his own room enjoying that splendid view of the Acropolis. For the rest of the day he had been overwhelmed by homesickness, so strong that it even caused him physical pain. He had felt like running away, taking his luggage and hurrying down to the docks to await the return of the Kanaris, the Greek ship with its red funnel and its thousand portholes, get on board and sail back to Piraeus.

One Monday morning of the previous spring, a few weeks before the end of the school year, the parish priest of the Armenian community of Fix, father Petrossian, had rung the bell at the home of the Delalians.

«Dighìn Delalian, have you half an hour to spare for me?» he had asked Mikael's mother Veronìk. «There is an important issue I would like to discuss with you.»

Dighìn Veronìk was not surprised by this visit as the priest was a frequent guest. Although Petrossian spoke with a certain urgency, she had sat down in an armchair only having first made some coffee and served it on a silver tray alongside a glass of cold water.

«I'm listening», she told him with a cordial smile. She was dressed in black, as she always was since her husband had died and she tied her grey hair, with its blue highlights, up in a traditional bun.

«I knew your husband, doctor Harutiùn, God rest his soul, well», the priest had begun. Veronìk had fiddled with her hairpins to cover up the emotion she always felt when someone mentioned her husband, although a year had already passed since his death. «I also know how active he was in the community, a pillar of our society», he had continued. «His premature passing pained us all, left an unfillable void.»

Veronìk had turned her eyes towards the window. The sky was a blazing turquoise color.

«Thank you, father Petrossian», she had murmured.

«But life goes on, and one cannot give up… Therefore, it's no use reminding you how vital it is to our community that the new generations thrive and make their mark in the countries of the diaspora. We find ourselves in Greece, which isn't bad at all, we should be grateful, actually, to this country for having welcomed and fed us. But only if our children become learned and well-educated, and only then, I say, will there be a future for us.»

It was a serious statement, which reiterated the principles and convictions pronounced over and over again during celebrations and anniversaries. God-given concepts often difficult to put into practice, alas.

«How can I help you?» Veronìk had asked at that point thinking it was yet another alms gathering campaign in favor of the poorer families, or in support of the Zavarian primary school, in the rundown Palia Kokkinia district. «I'll have to see how much money I have in the house.»

Padre Petrossian smiled. «It's not a question of money; it's much more important. It's about Mikael.»

Veronìk reacted, covering her mouth with her hand on hearing her son's name.

«I know you've only got him, that he's your only company, your source of comfort. But the foremost families, like yours, have set an example so that others may follow. Look, the Armenian college in Venice has reopened and is willing to take in our boys, guaranteeing them an excellent secondary education and preparing them for a life of success, while also instilling in them true awareness of being Armenian.»

The woman had sat up straight in her chair, biting her lips, overcome by emotion.

«Mikael is a boy endowed with rare intelligence, I myself noticed his brilliant mind when I taught him at primary school. In the college he will be able to cultivate his numerous talents, music for example», Petrossian had added, as he pointed towards the piano with several family photographs on the lid. One photo of doctor Delalian wearing his white coat stood out amongst all the others. «I prayed at length before coming here and I can say without a shadow of doubt, that I am sure the dear doctor would have been proud to see his son graduate from the prestigious Moorat-Raphael college.»

Veronìk, her head bent, had managed to dry her tears carefully with her embroidered handkerchief, but she was unable to conceal her heaving sobs.

So, father Petrossian had risen and gone over to pat her paternally on the shoulder.

«Dear child», he had said, «I know it is hard, but one day you'll be grateful to me, you'll see. Reflect upon it, reflect upon it well.»

Then he went over to the door, somewhat amazed that Veronìk had remained seated.

That day Mikael had arrived home early from school. «What's for lunch?» he had called out from the hallway.

On receiving no answer, he had gone into the kitchen where his mother was busy at the cooker. The aroma of *mantè*, little meat parcels, were making his mouth water.

«Didn't you hear me?» he asked offering his cheek for the usual kiss.

As Veronìk brushed it with her lips, he became aware of her misty eyes. «What's the matter?» It was not often that Mikael failed to guess how his mother was feeling, as his bond with her was really strong.

«We'll talk about it later, my son», she answered spreading the check tablecloth. She cared about setting the table properly, as she had always done when her husband was alive. She wished to keep everything as before.

«Would you like some *sumak*?»

Mikael had nodded and she had passed him the little bowl with the maroon-colored spice. Both had begun to eat in silence, but Veronìk just pushed the mantè around her plate.

«Your hair's too long», was all she managed to say looking at her son's thick head of dark copper hair.

They had remained a long time at the table after lunch, waiting for something which found it hard to materialize.

«Mikael, you know how much I love you», Veronìk began reluctantly.

The boy's attention had been alerted. He had just folded his napkin and laid it down beside the dish which still contained the last two mantè in yogurt sauce.

«I was thinking that for the sake of your future it would be a good thing that...» Unable to continue the woman had broken down in sobs.

«Mamma, what's wrong? What were you trying to tell me?» asked Mikael, seeking her hand and clasping it tightly.

«Nothing, I was thinking... father Petrossian and I were thinking that you should continue your education in Venice, at the Mekhitarist college», she blurted out at last all in one breath.

Mikael remained silent, his expression perplexed and stunned at the same time.

«In Venice?» was all he managed to say after a while.

«Your Excellency, Mr Delalian.» Wolf's ironic words made Mikael jump. «Will you be so kind as to honor us with an answer. You, who are so competent in ancient Greek, please translate and explain the term *logos*.» The boy, suddenly brought back down to earth, folded his hands on his desk and with a serious expression that amused Aznavour, responded:

«Logos, from the verb *legein*, means sense, spirit, word but also teaching. According to Christianity the logos is the verb, the word made flesh in Christ, the Son of God».

Wolf's eyes lit up. He was pleased and satisfied, because Mikael had given yet another demonstration of his brilliant mind. Without doubt a very promising boy.

«Yes, not bad at all», he commented, containing his satisfaction. «So, let's continue.»

Padre Keshishian with a little cough he always gave when seeking to concentrate, proceeded, «Those who have suffered are well aware of the enormous cost of communion with Christ on the Cross.» He righted his spectacles a little with a twitch of his nose. «Those who have suffered know how long, hard and fraught with peril is the pathway leading to this awareness...»

«And if...» Mikael's voice interrupted the teacher and the whole class turned around to stare at him. So, he sprang to his feet and continued without a moment's hesitation: «And if, and this is a question I ask everyone, this long and hard pathway led to nothing?»

«Illustrate your doubts to us...» invited the teacher who, meanwhile, had risen to his feet and was walking towards his pupil.

«If we were to discover, instead, that religion simply annihilates humanity in favor of the divinity? Impoverishing, enslaving people in favor of Christ and the Church?»

Wolf was only two paces away, his expression taut, his gaze penetrating, «This thought is not your own, you are simply repeating parrot-like the theories of Bakunìn whom, we know, you like so much», he taunted.

Derisive comments and titters went around the classroom.

«I, we, would like to know, instead, what you, Mikael Delalian, think», added the teacher.

Mikael swallowed and gripped his fountain pen so hard that he stained the palm of his hand with ink.

«Well», he answered in a voice lower than before. «I think that it is only through faith that one can redeem oneself in life, and that only faith can give one the strength to carry on, but...»

In the classroom, everyone awaited with bated breath.

Mikael bent his head and, when he raised it again, his eyes shone. «Sometimes I have serious changes of heart; then, I ponder upon things, but the more I reflect, the less I understand, and everything becomes confused and I lose the thread and...»

«And?»

«I don't know, I read, I look for the answers in Sacred Scripture, in the philosophers, in everything that may enlighten me, even if the theses, the schools of thought are so many. Then I lose myself once again...»

Aznavour stared at him, gaping, amazed and impressed by his courage.

«I ask myself, I confess», continued Mikael, «because I think it's right to be convinced, without doubts or repentance», he concluded.

He had just finished his sentence when three rings on the bell announced that it was time for lunch.

Seated on the wooden bench, his body bent over the keyboard, Mikael was playing the piano, his nimble fingers flying over the keys with surprising speed, while his voice, intense and a little hoarse, sang Jezebel, the hit of the moment.

In the recreation hall, some of the students were reading, others playing, while Mikael's numerous fans had formed a circle around the instrument, swaying to the rhythm of the tune. If anyone dared join in the singing, he was immediately hushed poked in the ribs by his companions' elbows. Nobody was allowed to spoil the interpretation because, when Mikael sang, he was the college's undisputed star. His accent was perfect Yankee, his mellow voice akin to that of Frankie Laine, Gene Kelly, even Frank Sinatra. Aznavour, fired by enthusiasm, rocked his head while two other lads improvised a dance step or two.

Mikael ended his song on a treble note of his own invention, a touch of creativity which received a thundering applause from his fans. The young musician sprang to his feet and thanked his audience with a slight bow, just like a real crooner.

The little group broke up slowly, but this brief concession to merriment made it easier for the boys to get through their heavy daily schedule.

«Attention, please; attention please!»

Some of the boys were still lingering in the room, others wandering about the atrium and the rose garden, when the voice of Gabìg, the science teacher, demanded their silence above the clatter of the dishes being removed from the refectory.

«Closer, I cannot be expected to shout», said the priest waving a red- and-blue-bordered envelope in the air; it was slit open on one side and sported a stamp of the USA Postal Service. The boys crowded into the hall and surrounded the teacher.

«Here is a lovely letter from Dikràn Samuelian, you all remember him, don't you?»

Most of the students commented beneath their breaths, someone even tittered. The Dick affair was a distant memory by now. The boy had managed to cross the border in the nick of time, before the police might stop him and then he had made his way to Vienna. From there he had called his father beseeching him to allow him to return home. He said he would do anything to avoid being sent back to the college. Mr Samuelian, persuaded, had sent his son the where-with-all to return to Detroit.

«Guess who the recipient of this missive is?» asked Gabìg, carefully unfolding the pages.

Mikael startled, knew what the answer would be, and, therefore, felt uneasy. Reading private correspondence in public, whenever the priests deemed it necessary, was one of the college's most loathsome habits. But in there, everything was supposed to be shared, even secrets.

«I'll read it for you», Gabìg continued. «"Dear Bakunìn, hope you are well. Here it's damned cold, fucking freezing, man, and in Venice?"» The priest stopped for a moment and waving his hand theatrically in mid-air, added, «Magnificent literature, don't you agree?» he quipped sarcastically. «I shall proceed, therefore: "Sorry if I got you lads into trouble with my escape, but I just couldn't bear it in there anymore. I'll hold onto your trench coat as a souvenir. It was raining cats and dogs that evening and I had no raincoat to put on.

P.S. I won't say another word, because I'm dead certain they'll open this letter. However, even if the college was a horrible place, I miss it at times. Regards to Aznavour, Bedròs, Keropé and the others. You're the best pals I've ever had. Dick 'the thief'."»

When the reading ended, the boys all stood in embarrassed silence, as if Dick's sincerity had made an impression on them, profoundly, intimately. The teacher approached Mikael to hand the letter over to him. The boy snatched it so brusquely that he made the priest stagger. Then he made a run for it up the stairs leading to the dormitories, anger making his temples throb, while humiliation gnawed at his very innards.

Where are you? Where are you to be found? I cannot see a thing.
They have humiliated you, trampled your honor into the dirt.
Locked you up in the dark. Dragged you there like a lamb to the slaughter.

6

Soviet Union, 1952

They were all crammed tight inside a boxcar, destination who knew where. Somebody had mentioned in passing that they were being taken to Siberia, nothing more.

The train made its way clanking rhythmically down the tracks, its regular beat was broken only every now and then by the shrill whistle of the locomotive. In the silence of the wagon, Gabriel listened to these sounds and imagined composing a song to that very accompaniment. The lyrics would be lively and cheerful, in strident contrast with his present frame of mind. At a certain point, he closed his eyes in an attempt to catch a wink of sleep.

His father had signed the confession. The cadaveric commissar had persuaded him by tormenting, bating, insulting, threatening him, so that, in the end, he had given in, admitting that he was an enemy of the people. However, as soon as he had endorsed the declaration, he had made a stand, telling the torturer to his face that, «I am nobody's enemy. I came to this country because I share your ideological convictions. I love Armenia. I had to fight to get hold of tickets so that my family and I might be allowed on board the ship and the trains, that brought us here. I have always believed and continue to believe; you are making a terrible mistake, I entreat you », he had concluded in an almost inaudible voice.

Then, Dimitri had entered the scene. First, he had got them to write up — on the typewriter, now repaired — his report of the inspection carried out at the Gazarians' home. He began by foregrounding the furious hostility with which he and his men had been received. Then, he had described the violent way Gabriel had attacked and injured one of his officers with a cast-iron lamp and went on to claim that the boy had hidden the cover of the book in the kitchen when, on the pretext of getting himself a drink of water, he had gone there. Then he had declared, fixing a tuft of his grey hair as a sign of his evident disapproval, that the father had always covered up for his son in the most shameful and despicable manner. With subversive individuals like Seròp and his young son it was difficult to guarantee the progress of the Union...

«What have you got to say? Speak up now in your own defense, you can still save yourself!» the talking corpse had bellowed.

«Comrade Commissar, you see, that book was a present from a cousin of mine, Miriam, who has been living in America for quite some time. She sent it to me in a parcel with other gifts several years ago. We were still living in Greece and when we left, well, I didn't feel like leaving it behind me and...» Seròp in his attempt to clarify matters, had actually got himself into such a twist that, in the end, he had fallen silent.

At this stage, Gabriel had spoken up, his voice loud and clear: «It was my favorite book. My aunt sent it to me, and I would read it using the little English I know ».

Dimitri and the young assistant eyed each other. The commissar had even managed a faint smile, while his subordinate, awestruck for an instant, had to shake himself back to reality by quickening the speed of his typing.

«Take them down to the station», was the last sentence uttered by the senior officer, who then stamped the document drawn up by his secretary and, with a crease between his brows, had scanned it briefly to make sure everything was in order.

Finally, he had lit yet another cigarette, and laid it down to burn itself out amongst the others in the crystal ashtray.

«Papa!» shouted Gabriel in the gloom of the boxcar.

«Yes», he heard him answer in the distance.

He had caught sight of him when they were being loaded onto the train. He had been the last to climb aboard, literally shoved into the wagon before the policeman had rolled the wagon's heavy iron door shut, leaving them in the pitch dark.

The boy began to crawl, rocked from side to side by the swaying train. The darkness prevented him from seeing anything, but he had to reach his father. As he advanced, he scrambled over the bodies of several strangers, digging into them with his hands and knees. There were about a hundred people in this cattle wagon. The stink of the manure which impregnated it mingled with the reek of filthy bodies. This human merchandise had to be shipped to its destination, wherever that might be, quickly and without waste of either time or means.

«Papa!» Gabriel repeated.

«Shut up», snarled a nasty voice.

Someone sighed in his sleep, someone else muttered feebly.

Everyone was bent over with cold and fatigue.

They had been travelling non-stop for days. It was a journey that seemed to be devoid of both an end and a destination. It was not even possible to distinguish between night and day. At times, the odd ray of light, tenuous and deceptive, trickled in through the cracks in the boards: maybe a sunbeam, maybe a gleam from one of the lamps on the side of the tracks.

«I can't breathe, I need air», complained a man somewhere further down the wagon. Now and then, amid the wagon's generalized torpor, one heard the sound of a lament, strong at first, then fainter and fainter. This time, Gabriel read in the man's voice the terror of someone afraid of dying alone and abandoned. Nobody would have come to his aid, nobody would have been close to him. The boy tried to imagine the man's features, where he came from, what he used to do before. That stranger slumped in a heap, a few yards further down, near yet far, had encountered a fate identical to his own. He felt compassion for him and so he began to beat his fists against the wall of the wagon.

«Open up, open up!» he shouted.

The prolonged whistle of the locomotive was the only answer he received. «If he dies, we'll all die. Can't you see? We'll be travelling in the company of a corpse.» He tried to get to his feet so they might hear his voice better. The stranger was choking, gasping. Gabriel pounded on the side of the train again, this time with his feet, kicking with all his might.

«Open up!» he yelled with all the breath in his lungs.

Someone else joined in. Another man began hammering on the wall too.

«Help!» now two of them were shouting.

Soon a small chorus of men was banging on the sides of the boxcar and shouting: «Open up!»

They opened up too late and certainly not because they had heeded them. With an abrupt jolt the train screeched to a halt in order to stoke up. As soon as it stopped, a soldier slid back the enormous heavy door. Light flooded the wagon and bitterly cold air rushed in, reducing the terrible stench a little.

«There's a dead man, here», said Gabriel, for the first time able to take stock of what surrounded him: bodies huddled up together, jam-packed like sardines, excrement, urine.

The soldier hoisted himself up onto the edge of the wagon.

«Here.» said a man with a white beard indicating his neighbor who seemed simply to be sleeping, his head thrown back. Gabriel studied the dead face, completely unlike the image he had previously conjured up. A boy, scarcely two or so years older than himself. In death he resembled a wax statue.

«Move aside!» the soldier ordered, covering his nose and making his way down through the wagon.

He seized the corpse by the collar of the jacket and dragged it over to the door. Then, with the heel of his top boot he shoved it, making it roll out and fall with a dull thud onto the snow heaped up on the tracks below.

Gabriel looked around in search of Seròp, knowing that they would soon be plunged back into darkness. He saw him down on his hunkers next to the door, only a few yards away. His head between his knees, he just sat there, squatting, a vacant expression on his face. Gabriel began to move towards him, but the door suddenly clanged shut and the train resumed its journey. Groping his way in the dark, he managed to reach his father.

«I'm here», he whispered shaking Seròp gently.

Seròp mumbled.

«I'm so sorry papa, it's all my fault», he said. «We should have burnt that book, the cover too. You were right.» He paused a moment before adding, «Only Novàrt didn't want me to, she made me promise». Sighing, he put his arm round his father's shoulders.

Seròp sought his hand and clasped it in his own.

The KSA, the shoe factory in Yerevan where Seròp had found work, was a building in tufa which had once housed a primary school. By size and production-rate it was considered of medium-to-low status, of little or no importance, seeing that at that time the USSR aimed at boosting its heavy industry. It was situated on the southern outskirts of Yerevan and could not be reached by urban public transport but only by means of a shuttle train which left every thirty minutes from a secondary station.

Seròp had always calculated far more time than was actually necessary to get there in order to allow for possible hitches that might make him late for work. He had always striven to show his comrade supervisors his goodwill, how keen his sense of duty and regard for the rules were, how faithful he was to the values he had embraced when choosing to return to Armenia.

In the morning he often arrived at the factory far earlier than his workmates. It was his choice. He would put on his steel-grey apron with meticulous care, sit at his bench and turn on the lamp above it. First of all, he would check that none of the tools were missing: awls, needles, cobbler's knives, thread and rasps. Then, he would glance up at the factory clock and, making sure he had several minutes to spare, would put on his glasses, open the newspaper and read it with the greatest of interest.

«Enkèr Seròp, you're always reading, you should have been a professor», Hampò Sellian, a returned emigre from New York used to say when he greeted him. Hampò was usually the second to arrive. Tall and stout, with a plump face, his eyes magnified by his thick spectacles, his American comrade had the air of a comedian from a silent movie. Seròp, would then fold up his newspaper and have a friendly chat with his workmate. Hampò spoke Armenian with such a bizarre accent that he seemed to have a pebble in his mouth he was unable to spit out. The two men would talk about their wives, their children, the everyday life of a perfect Soviet family. Naturally, they never mentioned the United States where Hampò had been born and where he had grown up; nor did he ever say why he had come to live in Yerevan.

They broke off their conversation, whatever the topic, as soon as comrade Raffik appeared on the scene. Raffik, the foreman responsible for production, never arrived either early or late. But precisely on the dot. Before he even had his jacket off, he would register the presence of the workers. Still quite young, he had a slight limp, but what one noticed most about him was his hooked nose which practically dipped into his mouth. During the men's short breaks, all their eyes fell involuntarily on his elephant's trunk, because, as he sipped his tea, his nose got dunked, practically. Although it was such a comical scene, nobody dared pass remarks, let alone laugh. Comrade Raffik was greatly feared, also because he was an honored member of the Party.

«We need to produce sixteen pairs of shoes before the end of the shift», he often declared in the guttural accent typical of the Yerevan dialect, to which Seròp had not as yet grown accustomed.

«What size?» the man in charge of leather would ask.

«A woman's, size thirty-eight», Raffik would answer.

«We can't manage that, too short of hide and brown leather.»

«Haven't you reported this shortage to the central office, comrade?»

«A month ago, comrade.»

«It's unthinkable not to be able to meet our quota», Raffik would complain, raising his voice as he blushed at the mere idea.

«I don't know what to do, comrade.»

Raffik would turn towards the window, as if the solution were to be found written somewhere up there in the sky. «We shall make shoes for children, sizes thirty-two and thirty-three. We should have enough for that», he would suggest at that point.

«Let's not forget that one time we changed the sizes without informing them, we were reprimanded...» the man in charge of the leather would remind him.

«We might, however, optimize the way we cut and save material that way», Seròp butted in one morning as he listened to the umpteenth endless discussion which had failed to reach any practical conclusion. «We need to redesign the pattern. We waste so much hide and leather!» he had burst out no longer able to contain himself.

Raffik had frozen him in one scornful glance. «Nobody asked for your opinion, brother», he had dismissed him with contempt.

Seròp had learnt the noble art of shoemaking from his father Toròs-agà, the most famous cobbler in the whole of Adabazàr, in Turkey. The man had owned the city's most prestigious workshop, in the center of town, with its elegant stained-glass windows. On the wooden shop-sign was painted the name *Altin Cicek*, Flower of Gold. In there, Toròs-agà created his footwear, veritable works of art. Having finished those ordered by his customers, he would make others of all shades which he would place in the window on a bed of purple velvet, arranging the different models and colors with the utmost taste and sublime aesthetic sense. He often went outside and hid behind a tree to observe the effect his creations had on window-shoppers. If nobody came into the shop for some time, Toròs-agà would go back and rearrange his merchandise with a view to making it more attractive to passersby.

«Toròs-agà, you're an artist, your shoes are as beautiful as roses», Esmé-hanùm, the wife of a wealthy property-owner, had exclaimed one day. «Not only but they are also softer than e peacock's feather», she had added as she tried on a golden-healed *passùm*.

Seròp, who had witnessed the scene from behind the counter, had flushed with pride. To be praised by a Turkish woman was the best possible compliment.

Seròp had begun helping his father in the shop when he was still a child. In the afternoon after school, he used to pop in to bring his father some fruit and cheese and then would stay on to learn how to make shoes. He had actually become his father's apprentice and Toròs-agà used to treat him as if he were a grown-up, demanding utmost attention and discipline.

«These are things that I have learnt in long years of hard work, my son», he used to say. «Therefore, you must consider yourself lucky. Keep your eyes wide open, your ears too, because, when I won't be around anymore, you'll have to carry on, without me, on your own!»

Seròp always felt like crying at the mere idea that one day his father might die and would duck under the counter pretending he was searching for something, to hide his tear-filled eyes. Down there, he would breathe in the scent of the leather and of the German glue which made his head swim. After a while, however, he would re-emerge to observe Toròs-agà closely as he worked, his skillful hands pulling, cutting, cluing, nailing, sewing and lining. As if by miracle, a shoe came into being out of practically nothing: a length of leather, a handful of nails, a few drops of glue. Then, having concluded, came that closing gesture which had never ceased to fascinate Seròp: Toròs-agà would place the shoe in the palm of his hand and stroke it gently like a father caressing his new-born child.

«You must love what you do, love is the motor, the driving force. »

Although Seròp did not fully understand what this was supposed to mean, he listened just the same, perfectly serious.

«Love and respect. Respect of nature, for those poor animals sacrificed to provide the leather without which none of this would be possible.» Toròs-agà would look into his son's eyes. «*Anadìn me*, do you understand?» he would ask in Turkish, as if seeking to underline the importance of what he was saying. Then he would get up and smoke his hookah.

«Above all, never waste anything. Waste not, want not. Waste is a sin that God himself punishes», he would affirm twirling his black moustache.

«Did you see how he treated you yesterday? That Raffik is a snake in the grass, he thinks he's someone only because he has friends in high places.»

Seròp had looked behind him with great caution. They were alone as yet in the factory.

«This Country is shit», complained Hampò.

Seròp did not utter a word.

«I can't wait to go back to the States. Air, freedom!» Hampò had moved his chair closer to Seròp's and begun to whisper in his ear: «I'd give anything for an emigration visa. Those swine are scared stiff lest we go back and tell Harry how utterly hare-brained they are».

«Tell who?» muttered Seròp, lowering his voice even more.

«Harry Truman, my friend, president of the United States of America»

Hampò knew how to be ironic when he wanted.

«I'd just love to take part in the 'witch hunt'» as he gestured towards the exit, and towards the communist «witches» out there.

Seròp had nodded, drumming nervously on his newspaper with his fingers as a red flush flooded his face and his heart began to pound harder and faster.

«Satèn says to thank your wife Diruì for the apple tart. She says it's your turn now, you really must come to dinner at our place.»

Seròp did not want, was unable to continue the conversation on politics that Hampò had got him into. So, he had changed the subject to focus on something more innocuous. His companion had straightened up and looked at him with a certain air of contempt.

«Satèn insists, she wants you to dinner on Sunday. Bring Edi, that will make Gabriel happy», he had almost shouted so he might be heard clearly by their mates who were just arriving at the factory.

Whispering, in that Country, was forbidden. And suspect.

That Sunday Satèn had risen early. She had cleaned and dusted every corner of the house with Gabriel's help. Novàrt too, duster in hand, had gone over all the knickknacks on the living-room shelves.

Then Satèn had started to get the food ready for their guests. Her specialties, the dishes in which she was sure she excelled, were *ishli koefté*, little dumplings of meat and spelt, and *hunghèr beiendì*, eggplants in ragout. Luckily, Seròp had managed to buy some mutton on the black market, without which it would have been impossible to cook these dishes.

That afternoon she had laid the table using the lace cloth which she had washed and ironed with the greatest care. The plates and glasses were of the ordinary common or garden variety because they possessed neither a good set of china nor crystal goblets. But Satèn trusted that her delicious food would compensate amply for any lack of elegant tableware.

The Sellians had arrived five minutes ahead of time, when Seròp was still in his bedroom slippers. As soon as he opened the door, Hampò guffawed pointing at the tell-tale footwear peeping out from beneath his trouser bottoms and because, apart from this, the man of the house was done up to the nines, tie and all.

So, that Sunday, dinner had taken off to a brilliantly good-humored start. Everyone had savored and appreciated Satèn's cuisine and drunk the red Arenì wine.

«You are a lucky man, indeed», exclaimed Hampò at a certain point. «You have a wife who is not only beautiful, but also highly capable. What a table, everything truly exceptional».

Satèn had thanked their friend and, after dinner, had tactically linked arms with Diruì accompanying her over to the sofa where they sat down together to discuss clothes.

«I would like you to make a frock for me, I trust only you, there isn't a decent dressmaker in this place», Diruì had complained.

Hampò was staring at her from the opposite side of the room through a screen of smoke which rose from the cigarette Seròp had offered him from his precious packet of Astra, reserved only for important guests.

«If you manage to find the material, it would give me great pleasure to make it for you», Satèn had assured her, exchanging glances with her husband and noticing his smile of contentment.

Meanwhile, Gabriel had taken Edi to his room to show him his accordion. It was his latest gift from papa and, although second-hand, it shone as if brand new. The grey bellows blended in perfectly with the shiny ebony-black casing.

«It's really beautiful.» said Edi running his fingers gently over the surface without even trying to hide his envy. «But are you sure you know how to play it?»

«Choose a tune», Gabriel challenged him, handing him a book of scores.

Edi had chosen Glinka, the most difficult mazurka of the repertoire.

Novàrt felt she was being excluded as, unlike her brother, she had no friend to play with, so she wandered about among the guests in search of attention

«Do you like my doll?» she had asked passing from one to another.

They all caressed and cuddled her, but she felt neglected just the same.

«So, do you like her? I sewed her skirt myself», she insisted.

It was as if she had no part to play in a group; as if she did not count, so she tried her very best to attract some kind of attention.

When Novàrt appeared with the book in her hand, Satèn's

expression changed at once, revealing her dismay. It was as if she had the sensation that something terrible was going to happen. Seròp, instead, had begun to cough violently, without stopping even after the child had put William Saroyan's book into Hampò's huge hand.

«Mr Sellian, you know English. Can you read some of these stories for us?» she had asked in that gentle, innocent voice of hers.

The scene was to be stamped in Seròp's memory forever after: that glint in Hampò's eyes, Diruì's wink, the tiniest detail, the smallest particular; he was never to forget any of them.

And now, as he travelled with Gabriel on that goods train going, allegedly, to Siberia, he could even recall the response of comrade Hampò, to whom the coveted visa needed to return to the United States had finally been granted, a few days later: «Dear child, this is certainly no book for you», he had told Novàrt, chilling Seròp with an icy look, while Gabriel in the adjoining room kept fudging on his accordion some of the joyous notes of Glinka's mazurka.

7

Patras, 1938

«Mr Kapetanaki.»

«Just call me comrade.»

«Comrade, I've been given the sack, they've done exactly what I feared most.»

«I know, the same has happened to many others.»

«Yes, but I still have two babies to bring up!»

The trade-unionist nodded.

«I was hoping you might have a word with the owner, explain our situation.»

«I will», the other promised, «though we all know him too well», he added twisting the end of his goatee.

Murmurs of malcontent rang out through the hall. Somebody even swore.

«I'd hoped you'd done so already.»

«We are experiencing a period of great uncertainty», continued the union man trying to make himself heard above the babble of voices. Then he used an ample sweep of his arm to catch the workers' attention «The situation is looking very bleak indeed at present, not only in Greece but in the whole of Europe.»

«People are being laid off at Vesso's and Ladopoulos's too», growled a man even thinner than Seròp.

«Comrades!» called the trade unionist, raising his voice more and banging his fist on the table, trying to make the men pay attention.

«Hard times face us, looming on the horizon! This brother of ours is a living example of what we need to expect.» he announced, pointing at Seròp who stood there in the midst of a small group of men.

«Down with capitalism, long live Marxism!» shouted a few of the men. About twenty laborers had come — as they always did every last Friday of the month — to the meeting held in the factory basement, a long, narrow, bleak place, that reeked of mold and rat killer. Seròp took a good look around him and wondered how on earth he had ended up in this place. He had been approached at the factory gates one day about two years before. «United we win», they had promised, adding, «You won't be left alone, we'll tackle all these labor issues together». Handsome promises, oodles of persuasive words. And so, he had given up part of his precious time to attend assemblies, marches and rallies, asking nothing in exchange. More often than not, he had stood there in silence on the margins, listening to how the world was going to be changed. He had been told about wonderful concepts like Equality and Justice and agreed that, when all came to all, what they said was not so unlike what Toròs-agà had always taught him. But today, amid this boisterous, vulgar din he realized that it had all been for nothing. He failed to grasp the sense of the slogans, the catchphrases, the insults hurled through the air.

All he needed was to be able to feed his family and all he wanted to know was how this might be achieved, but right now...

«Excuse me», he yelled, making his voice heard for the very first time. «I believed you'd defend and protect me. The other workers laid off were all a certain age, their children all grown up. But I am only twenty-eight!» he objected.

«Masters monsters!», shouted the man standing next to him, a fellow sporting a paunch and a beard yellowed by nicotine. Soon a chorus of voices joined his, ranting, hurling abuse and insults at the factory owner and the managers. They were free to do so at this hour: at three in the morning. The bosses were all fast asleep at home.

After the voices had subsided, Seròp, disheartened, just recovered his rucksack which he had hung on the back of a chair, put it on his shoulders and, begging pardon of those closest to him, walked off in the direction of the exit.

«But where are you going, comrade?» called the trade unionist when Seròp had already reached the door.

«I need a job, work, Mr Kapetanaki», he responded, turning around for a moment, «as for the rest, what's right and what's wrong, I know already.»

He took the road down to the sea silver lined by the light of a full moon.

He crossed an ancient olive grove, its trees all twisted and tangled, at times bent so low that seemed to be prone; in the trunk of one of these, he noticed a cavity resembling a Dionysian mask.

He rested for a moment under a fruit-laden branch, plucked two olives and popped them into his mouth: they were still green and, therefore, made his palate fizz.

"Earth and sun", he thought as he tried to define the aftertaste of the fruit. He kept the pits in his mouth, playing around with them now and then with his tongue. He then walked by a kitchen garden full of tomatoes and eggplants, then alongside an orchard full of fig, almond and orange trees.

«God is great, his gifts are plentiful», he said, crossing himself. Then he lifted up his head and beyond the crowns of the trees caught sight of the dome of Saint Andrew's cathedral shimmering in the moonlight. That church was the gem of the city, the most beautiful and sumptuous of its kind, second only to Constantinople's Hagia Sophia. Seròp knew Saint Andrew's well. He used to go there sometimes to pray, kneeling before the icon of the white-bearded saint who had been crucified tied to a wooden cross. He used to shiver at the thought that he was actually kneeling on the very spot where the saint had been martyred. He would remain there at length contemplating the votive offerings left by members of the faithful who believed they had been saved thanks to the intervention of the saint: the effigy of a foot, of an eye, of a body.

«Dear Saint Andrew», he prayed, addressing the heavens, «help me!»

He was tempted to enter the church courtyard and wait for the doors to be opened for the pilgrims, including foreigners, who came to the city and often slept in the cloister. But the night air had bewitched him and with its bracing freshness it had urged him forward. So, he turned right and, walking along the seashore, headed in the direction of the ships whose silhouettes appeared blurry in the early morning mist.

At that hour the neighborhood was teeming with people.

Seròp was amazed that they were all up already: the truth was that they had not gone to bed as yet. Two launches and a tall-masted sailing ship were moored at the central pier. A chain of work-weary, dirty-looking dockers were unloading a cargo of wooden crates. Some were singing to cadence and coordinate their work.

«*Eia molla eia lessa*», the whole port rang.

Seròp stood there watching. A very young man, little more than a child, performed his task with remarkable strength and diligence. As they passed through his sturdy arms the crates seemed so light, almost weightless, but then when they moved on to the next in line, a wizened, bent old man, they seemed to acquire all the weight of Atlas's globe. One of the cases slipped from his hands and tumbled into the sea. The poor fellow began to howl like a cur. The chain halted, the boss cursed, and approaching the old man, beat him with the rod swinging from his belt. The elderly longshoreman, who might well have been Saint Andrew by his looks, tottered and fell to the ground.

«Equality and justice!» Seròp muttered sarcastically.

Outraged but disheartened too, he walked on, unsure of where he should go. He had no particular destination in mind. He just wandered through the city prompted by an impelling desire to meander. It had been years since he had simply gone for a walk. He ventured into the alleyways of the old town with a bold swagger he had long forgotten. Ambiguous shadows lingered in corners, loitered in archways, muttered shockingly dirty words which though they aroused his disgust also led him into temptation. Brazen-faced men and women, laying all restraint aside, groped and petted in a way that made him blush with shame. Unable to feign indifference or aloofness, Seròp slipped into the first joint he came across. The strains of a buzuki struck him with its wistful sound. The place was crammed with customers, crowded around the tavern's few rough-hewn tables. They slapped each other on the backs, smoked, laughed raucously and addressed the women with foul language. At the back of the room stood a small platform where the young buzuki player sat, next to him stood the singer, a good-looking, buxom girl, sheathed in a taffeta dress which left very little to the imagination, warbling in a clear, strong voice.

«My darling little canary, you drive me crazy», she sang, keeping time with a tambourine she slapped against her shapely thighs, abundantly highlighted by her tight dress.

«*Manoula mou esy*, my pretty little titbit!» shouted a man dashing a plate at her feet, already surrounded by a heap of broken crockery: a Greek custom used as a sign of appreciation for an artiste.

Seròp was brought back to his senses again when a waiter, bearing a tray laden with orders, elbowed him aside shouting «Out of my way!».

He stood there stock-still and dumbfounded in the middle of the premises savoring the aroma of the *mussakà* that still lingered in the air after the waiter had pushed his way through. He was beginning to feel exhausted and pangs of hunger gnawed at his gut: he had neither slept nor eaten for an entire day.

«Hey! Seròp!» a voice called to him above the din.

He looked around, astonished and squinting through the cloud of smoke he recognized the wrinkled face of Jivan, the Marangopoulos company's truck driver.

«What are you doing here? Come and sit with us a while», he invited.

«Just one more for the road», said Jivan later on, pouring him another shot of *rakì*.

«No, brother, I've downed too much *moschùdi* as it is», slurred Seròp.

«What the hell, this is far better than a dose of medicine, it disinfests the veins», the other insisted, picking up the glass and putting it right under his nose. Seròp grabbed the shot, gazed at Jivan's shiny bald head for a second, then guzzled the alcohol in one mouthful.

«Doesn't that feel better?»

Seròp nodded.

«Yes, but it's the last one; I haven't enough money to pay for another …» he managed to say between one hiccup and another.

«By the way», said Jivan suddenly lowering his voice, and dragging his chair closer to Seròp's as if about to let him into some awfully important secret. «What did Martiròs say? Will he help you?»

«Nothing much», answered Seròp. After their stroll through the field of sunflowers field, he had seen him only once, when the carpetbagger had loaned him one of his best suits so he could have the family photo taken.

«The rogue!» grumbled Jivan, enveloping Seròp in a cloud of smoke. «He may act the hard man, but he's a sissy beneath it all. He told me he'd talk to you about a certain deal.»

«Yes, he did give me the name of an Italian I might sell my *kundure* to.»

Jivan guffawed so loudly that customers at the neighboring tables turned around to stare.

«No, not *kundure*»

Seròp tried to sit up straight on his chair and look his friend into his turbid, bloodshot eyes.

«Did he say nothing to you about the baby?»

Seròp, completely baffled, tried to make some sense of what was being said.

«That now, is what you might really call a deal!» whispered Jivan sinking into the collar of his jacket, «Three thousand Drachmas, a fortune! You could live on that for five years without doing a day's work».

«What the hell are you raving about, brother?»

«You have two. Just give one of them away; he's too young, you just can't have grown that fond of him yet. Besides», he added smiling inanely «you're capable of producing a pair at every foul swoop.»

Seròp felt his stomach lurch as if a hand had grappled his gut. He barely managed to remain conscious.

«Shut your cakehole, you bollox», he just barely managed to slur, feeling he was going to collapse.

«Call me a bollox?» the other retorted spitting on the ground. «When you're all dying of hunger, you, your beautiful wife and your precious twins, it'll hot you that I am a true friend. I'm offering you a way out, because you're fucked up, you know, you don't stand a chance, they're sacking people all over the place.»

Seròp moaned in utter despair.

«You'll come crawling back to me on your hands and knees!» were the last words Seròp heard before passing out on the table among the carafes and glasses.

«It is only in sleep that we may know we live. There only, in that living death, do we meet ourselves and the far earth, God and the saints, the names of our fathers, the substance of remote moments.»

Lucy put the book down on the table and looked Satèn in the eye. She was unable to tell if her gaze was absent because she had been impressed by Saroyan's haunting words, or because she was chasing thoughts of her own. She had known Satèn for a few weeks now, had spent time with her, had translated nearly the whole of the story for her — only a few pages, after all — and yet she was unable to make the girl out or guess what she was thinking. Certainly, she was always polite, cordial and affectionate, but often a pall of sudden sadness would cover her eyes as she sank into a quagmire of dejection, as if overwhelmed by some unbearable thought.

«Is everything all right? Do you want me to go on?» she asked her that day.

Satèn barely managed a hint of a smile. «Yes, even if...»

Lucy patted the hand lying on the table. «Speak to me, please», she implored with sincere concern.

Satèn freed her hand and brought it to her mouth as if seeking to prevent herself from breathing a word.

«At times, speaking out, sharing a problem can be good for you», her friend insisted.

«I'm not happy», Satèn exclaimed shaking her head, «I'm not happy!», and she broke into convulsions of despair.

Lucy was overwhelmed by this dramatic and unexpected emotional reaction. She really wanted to say something to her, only she could not find the words, so she simply leaned over and embraced Satèn like a sister. She wished to console her, let her know she was not alone. But Satèn stiffened suddenly: no woman had ever embraced her before and this kind of physical contact disturbed her, created embarrassment. Rosacùr, who had been like a mother to her and loved her dearly, had never been generous with hugs or kisses.

She drew back from Lucy, dried up her tears quickly, sprung to her feet and went over to stand in front of the sink. Realizing she had nothing to do there, she turned around and pretended to check if the children were sleeping soundly in their cradle.

«I think it's just that I am a bit tired», she ventured by way of apology and sat down again at the table.

«Yes.»

«Tired and lonely», she added. «If I could talk to my husband at least… I'm sure it would do him good too; you see, he's lost his job and feels even worse than I do.»

«I am so sorry to hear that», whispered Lucy, amazed both by the outburst and the trust Satèn seemed to have in her all of a sudden. Satèn shook her head and with a bitter sigh said, «The other day he didn't even come home. He stayed out all night. I waited up for him, out of my mind with worry. I couldn't even go out to look for him. How could I have left the babies here all on their own?» She struggled to hold back the tears that were filling her eyes.

«And when he did manage to get back home eventually», she continued shaking her head again, «he stank to high heaven like a pig and his clothes were covered in mud. He must have fallen in the street, because he was so drunk, he couldn't even stand up». Then she broke off, upset as she recalled the scene. «And as soon as I asked where he had been, he insulted me 'You miserable little whore!', he said and slapped me across the face. 'Who do you think you are that you can meddle in my affairs?' he yelled and continued hurling the foulest language at me until he woke the children up.»

Her voice broke. She lowered her head and, finally allowed the tears she could no longer hold back, to roll freely down her cheeks.

«And what did you say?»

«Nothing. I would have liked to say something but because I respect him, I held my tongue.»

«But had you spoken, what would you have said?»

Satèn looked over at the little water tank with *kalimera* on it and then, distractedly, patted the bed where she was sitting.

«I'd have said: I fall to sleep and wake up by your side, I share your dreams and worries, I watch over your every breath, we become one when we embrace. You're my husband and I'm your wife.»

Lucy listened to her in respectful silence.

«You know», added Satèn licking the tears that had trickled onto her lips, «when I decided to marry Seròp, I thought life would be very different. I fooled myself that I'd find true companionship. I've always been on my own, no siblings, no family. Poverty doesn't trouble me, but loneliness, isol...isola...», she faltered.

«Isolation», her friend suggested promptly.

«Yes, isolation. We are both young, we can work, face life together. God has rewarded us with two lovely, healthy sons. This is the gift He has made us, and we ought to be happy and thank Him».

She sat up on the bed and with new-found energy went on,

«As soon as they are big, I dream of a future for them. I would like them to study, be respected. Above all, I would like them to grow up together, to be fond of each other, look out for one another. They are really special, each one in his own peculiar way. When you look at them, they seem to be identical. But I who brought them into the world know they are very different. In a certain sense it's as if they completed each other». Having said all this in one breath, she fell silent again.

Lucy was struck by her words. Although uttered in a simple and naïve manner, that speech of hers was extraordinarily profound.

«Do you believe that a man and a woman are equal?» she asked, point-blank.

Satèn frowned. «What do you mean?»

«I mean, do you believe that a woman should bow to a man's will?»

Satèn remained silent, permitting her gaze to wander as she reflected on questions she had never taken into consideration before, ideas that had never even crossed her mind.

«For example,», Lucy tried to explain, «if your husband did something you didn't approve of, would you oppose him? Tell him how you saw things?»

«Well...» Satèn began but then stopped: she wanted to find the right words to express a difficult concept.

«Rosacùr used to tell me», she said, resuming, her face the picture of sad nostalgia, «that there are neither men nor women, but only God's creatures. When Seròp came with Lussià-dudù to ask for my hand, Rosacùr asked me what I wanted to do. 'The choice is yours, you need to be aware that he is not a strong man, that he is uneducated and may not be intelligent either', she said, 'therefore you will have to make up for his failings, compensate, that's the very word she used.»

She smiled at Lucy and Lucy smiled back.

«I often miss Rosacùr, her wisdom, her advice. I always had the impression that she was very different from every other woman in the camp.»

«She was a teacher, a very well-educated lady.»

«Yes, she was.»

They remained in silence looking at each other. Lucy wore a dark-brown pleated skirt and a cream-colored blouse with padded shoulders. Her auburn hair was curled on the forehead and gathered into a bun at the nape of her neck. She had a slender, oval face highlighted by large sky-blue eyes.

Suddenly, Satèn picked up Saroyan's book and flicked through the pages. «Do you know the part that struck me most?» she asked her friend, a catch in her throat as she pointed at the text.

«Which one?»

«The one where he says that of all the things the writer was obliged to sell in order to eat, what he missed most were his books. Selling them caused him real pain.»

Lucy nodded gently encouraging her to continue. Then, Satèn's expression changed as did her tone which now seemed more self-assured, audacious even: «When the writer dies, his death is different. His thoughts and ideas are all very important. He's sorry for the reality he is about to leave…»

The young mother glanced gratefully up at her friend. «He knows he must die like anybody else, but, at least, during his short life he has managed to understand the world around him. There's nothing worse than dying in ignorance. I am so grateful to you», she whispered finally, lowering her eyes.

Lucy looked at her watch and excused herself: she had an appointment-at least that's what she said- which had escaped her mind completely, something she absolutely had to do. She jumped up and saluted her friend leaving behind the distinctive waft of her roses-and-cinnamon scent.

Fitil, sitting in front of her shack as usual, wondered what on earth the two young women had been saying to make that lovely English girl burst into tears right in front of her, there, in the middle of the dirt-track.

«First you need to prepare the *afleki*.»

«What's that?»

«This string is too thick to sew uppers with; it won't pass through the eye of the needle, see?»

Satèn nodded.

«So, first you need to pass some thread, which is finer, through the eye, then wind that tightly around the string and graft the two», said Seròp rubbing his hands together, eagerly. «Look, they also need to be spliced, otherwise they won't join. Now, you do it.»

Seròp was showing Satèn how to sew uppers, the hardest and most complicated part of the job. Husband and wife had been working together making slippers, and by now she had gained enough experience to help him concretely and increase their small cottage-industry production.

The twins, sitting beside them on the bed, looked on in religious silence, as if trying to understand what their parents were up to with all these threads, needles, awls and those other thingamabobs scattered all over the place.

«These slippers need to be sturdy…» he said, passing the needle through the holes in the sole.

«Most of all, I think, we need them to be beautiful», Satèn remarked earnestly.

Her husband raised his head and looked at her in wonderment.

«Why, aren't they beautiful?»

«They could be more so.»

Seròp stared at his wife as she simply poked a finger at the center of a toe-cap.

«We must make them unique, particular" she said, lifting it up. "For example, I thought of embroidering a flower like that one over there» indicating the border surrounding the word *kalimera* on the water tank. «I could do it with colored thread, I might even embroider the words good morning. Just think how nice it would be to read this greeting every morning as you slipped them on!»

Seròp scratched his head perplexed. He simply wanted to sew slippers, his very own soft, comfortable *kundure*, like those his father had taught him to make.

«But I have to take them down to the Italian quarter», he groused as an excuse.

«Better still, I'm sure they will appreciate them. Let me get a sample collection together and see what they say», she insisted.

From the bed, one of the twins leant forward with the air of a grown-up, to inspect one of the slippers.

«What are you looking at my little man?» Seròp asked him tenderly, happy at the chance of changing the subject. He fondled his son's head. It was Gabriel, his favorite, the one with the green wristlet. Immediately, the other baby, pouting, crawled over trying to wriggle in between the two and get his share of the cuddles. Seròp pushed him away in a watchful way hoping Satèn would not notice.

But she did.

«I'll go and get the *bulgùr* ready», she said with a heavy heart, bending down to pick up the child who had been spurned.

«Come here to your mamma!» she exclaimed.

Then, as she poured the grain, a fistful in all, into the pot, she decided she would put an end to this travesty. She was going to cut those bands off her children's wrists. She had put up with this outrage long enough.

The Gambetta district surrounding the church of Saint Dionisio, inhabited mainly by Italian emigrants, was at the city's eastern gateway from which the road to Athens departed. The community, comprising several thousand emigrants from Puglia, Campania and Calabria, had established itself in Patras at the end of the nineteenth century. Trade and fishing, in a place not too far from their native land, had urged them to move there. Not only, but many of these people descended from the ancient settlements of Italy's Magna Grecia, considered themselves veritable *griki* and proudly spoke an ancient Doric dialect, reminiscent of a tongue several millennia old.

The Italians of Patras were admired by the local population. They were reputed to be excellent artisans, able businesspeople, talented scientists and architects, who also smacked of Europe, that enticing continent the object of the dreams of the Greeks who had been freed from the yoke of the Turks only recently.

«Good morning, how can I help you?» a shop assistant asked Seròp, coming out from behind a counter. He was young and wore an exquisitely tailored suit.

Seròp stood there admiring the shop he had just entered. As soon as he had arrived in the Italian neighborhood he had asked where he could find the shop belonging to signor Caputo and had little trouble in finding it. It was the city's most luxurious shoe emporium.

«Mister?» inquired the assistant, without taking his eyes of that thin man, bent under the weight of a sack slung over his shoulders. He could not possibly have been a customer.

Seròp froze. The very idea that he might be in the wrong place petrified him. He had taken a fleeting look at the shoes on the shelves and in the shop's windows: classy stuff for wealthy people. What had his *kundure* to do with a place like this?

«Is… is signor Caputo here?» he stuttered.

The salesclerk stared at this miserable creature who actually had the nerve to ask to speak to the boss.

«Signor Caputo?» he repeated, unable to conceal his astonished disapproval.

«Yes», answered Seròp, self-consciously, «Martiròs sends me.»

«Pardon?»

«Mar-ti-ròs», he said again, pronouncing the three syllables slowly and with deliberate clarity.

«Wait here», ordered the young man imperiously and walked to the end of the shop and to a door with a long mirror where Seròp caught sight of his own reflection. He could not remember when it was that he had last seen a full-length image of himself. When he shaved, he used a tiny mirror where he could see only one small part — chin, cheek, jaw — of his face at a time. He had some idea what he looked like, because now and then he would examine himself in shop windows, but on seeing himself so clearly was a totally different matter and he was shocked at what he saw; he hardly recognized himself. He shifted his gaze from the door and looked around the shop. On a velvet divan sat a blond lady with a tiny hat and veil perched precariously on the top of her head which managed to remain there by some kind of miracle. At her feet knelt another shop assistant, a girl, who helped her to try on a brown bootee. Both women sized him up with ill-concealed contempt and he blushed.

«Signor Caputo will receive you now», said the other assistant indicating the half-closed door.

«Thank you.» Seròp adjusted the sack and walked towards the office.

Caputo was a slim middle-aged man, his hair still completely raven black. He was on the phone as Seròp entered. The room was decorous but in no way in keeping with the luxury of the shop and this brought some relief to Seròp.

From behind his desk, the owner beckoned to him to sit down as he finished the phone call.

Seròp hesitated, then timidly placed the sack down on the floor and sat down on the small armchair, all hunched up. Caputo's voice fascinated him: it was light, well-modulated and had a sing-song quality about it.

«What can be done in these cases?» he was asking, sincerely worried.

He waited a moment, then scribbled a word down on a piece of paper. «Quin-ine, right?» he sounded out the word.

He listened again, then shook his head conveying his indignation.

«And where can I get it?» he asked. «All right, thank you very much», he replied heartened again.

Then he frowned gravely. They were certainly informing him of something really serious.

«Don't think it's any better here», he burst out, «it has wiped out an entire village near Kounoupeli; they aren't saying anything, but it's becoming a veritable epidemic.»

Seròp was amazed as he listened to Caputo speaking so excitedly about matters that clearly had no bearing on his line of business. Ingenuously, he imagined that an astute entrepreneur like him would be interested only in matters strictly connected with his field of business: new models, hides, manufacturing systems.

Instead, it seemed to be an urgent problem of a completely different nature that was worrying signor Caputo considerably.

«What can I do for you? A friend of Martiròs's I understand?», he began, having hung up.

«Yessir.»

«You have something to show me, I suppose.»

«Yessir.»

With a gesture Caputo invited him to empty the sack. Seròp untied the cord and pulled out two pairs of his kundure, the ones he believed had turned out best and was about to place them on the desk.

«No, don't put anything down here», said Caputo stopping him abruptly.

Seròp started and stood there like an idiot with the slippers in his hands.

«Show them to me from a distance», said the shopkeeper.

Seròp, with a sweep of the arm, tried to show him his *kundure*, and have him take note of the double row of stitching on the uppers.

«Soft and sturdy», he stuttered, blushing.

«Nothing else?» Caputo asked

«Another twelve pairs like these».

«Anything different?»

«Yes, an embroidered pair...»

Caputo gave him to understand that he should get a move on, that he had no further time to waste on him.

«Here you are, these», Seròp said, showing them to him.

«Nice. How much the pair?»

Seròp shrugged undecided. «Well, I don't know really.»

Caputo sprang to his feet: «All right, I'll buy thirty pairs of the embroidered *kundure*, sizes thirty-six to thirty-eight, mister...»

«Seròp.»

«Bring them to me as soon as they're ready, fifty cents the pair.»

«But...»

«Fifty, not a penny more.»

Seròp did not dare to utter another word.

«Do you live in the Armenian refugee camp? Have you a wife, children?»

Seròp nodded.

«Beware of the mosquitos», Caputo warned him as the telephone rang again.

As Seròp left they were closing up. He caught the whiff of rotten eggs and was astounded to see the young shop assistant spray something all over the shop. He used a metal cylinder with a tube and nozzle producing a cloud of vapor which caught him in the throat and made him splutter.

8

«What's your name?»

«Francesca, and yours?»

«Mikael»

«Mikael?»

«Yes, Mikael», said he, stressing the last vowel of his name. He was clambering over the boundary wall, his feet resting on the stone jutting out, hidden from the eyes of the others by the girth of a huge laurel bush. Behind the library, the wall had crumbled a little and this made it easier to climb on top of it and peer out at the world beyond the college.

The girl on the other side of the wall to whom he was chatting must have been about fifteen. She was slim but, in surprising contrast with her appearance, her voice was strong and assertive. She was wrapped in a blue duffle coat with a large hood lined with tartan flannel draped over her shoulders like a shawl. She held a stick in her hand, like a fairy, and was using it to tap on all the cracks in the wall.

«What are you doing?»

«The Countess sent me», she answered indicating the palace opposite. «She's afraid there may be a nest of rats here. The other morning, she began screaming like a lunatic and woke us all up.»

«And what have you got to do?»

«Well, I'm not sure; just see if it's true»

«Aren't you afraid?»

«Not in the least! After all they're only little field mice»

They stared at each other for a moment.

She was just a girl like any other, but her eyes were beautiful, brilliant and full of little twinkling golden flecks.

«Is this a school then?» she asked, indicating the building behind Mikael.

«A boarding school.»

«You're not Italians, are you?»

«Armenians.»

«My mother told me about you. She says you've been here forever.»

Mikael nodded.

«What's the book?» Francesca asked indicating the leather-bound volume he was hugging to his chest.

«A novel. Crime and Punishment. Have you read it?»

«No.»

«It's by Fedor Dostoevskij.»

«The Idiot.»

«What?»

«I've only read The Idiot by him»

«Well, this is a very different story.»

«What's it about?»

«Crime and punishment» replied Mikael, bursting out laughing, enjoying his own witty remark.

Francesca volunteered a faint smile.

«Read me the most beautiful passage.»

«There are so many, I wouldn't know which to pick»

«Read me any one you like, then.»

«Let's do this, I'll open just any page and read that.»

«Fine», Francesca answered.

The boy tried to assume a more comfortable position and so he hoisted himself up onto the wall and lay down on one side on top of it.

«One, two, three.» He shut his eyes and opened the book, then glanced at the text and winked at the girl who was waiting there patiently. Finally, he drew in a deep breath and began: «For a moment he thought he was going mad. A dreadful cold overpowered him; but the chill was from the fever that had begun long before in his sleep. Now ...» he jumped, startled.

A rustling sound among the trees had made Mikael spin around suddenly, afraid that a schoolmate or, worse still, a teacher was spying on him. This brusque movement made him lose his balance.

To prevent himself from falling, he had to hold on to the wall, but the book went flying downwards. Francesca caught it with amazing dexterity.

«Now what shall we do?» Mikael asked, disheartened.

«I'll read it», said she, chuckling.

«But it's not mine. I took it from the library. If they find out…»

«I'll bring it to the door of the college, then.»

«No, no, for goodness' sake!»

Francesca smiled. «Now what are we going to do?»

«Do you like the cinema?» Mikael asked her, turning on all his proverbial charm.

Afterwards when he jumped down off the wall, a sweet taste filled his mouth, as if he had been sucking on a butterscotch toffee.

The meeting with the gold-eyed «fairy» had exalted him and he started walking around the garden, as if wandering through a wood, the ideal place to meet that kind of imaginary being. He brushed the laurel bushes flanking the pathway, breathing in the fragrance which filled the air; further on, he encountered the enigmatic smiles of two marble cupids who stood there guarding the enchanted Garden of Eden. In front of him towered a cedar of the Lebanon and, impulsively, he leaned up against the trunk and tried to embrace it. He could smell the scent of distant lands, glorious battles, fecund brides, and stood there motionless, pondering on the precariousness of human life, fooling himself for an instant that he was omnipotent and immortal. Finally, he crossed the bridge under which flowed a gurgling stream. He mirrored himself in the water, love-besotted Narcissus, the child of cosmic dust.

«Who are you, really?» he asked himself, examining the emerald-green water.

A tadpole swam between the mossy stones. Mikael noticed its gills pulsing to the syncopated rhythm of his breath, a creature just come into the world and already so bold, swimming around propelled by its tail.

Just then, a crow swooped down quick as lightning onto the water, creating a spray of freezing droplets. Mikael screwed up his eyes and when he opened them again, he saw the tadpole wriggling in the bird's clamped beak. The crow, feeling himself observed maybe, fixed Mikael with his implacable, ruthless black eyes and with a flick of his beak, swallowed his prey in a jiffy. Mikael stood there still as a stone. A puff of wind ruffled the feathers of the bird, who rose up on his chipped claws. He took flight immediately, spreading his wings and brushing the boy who, startled, backed away.

«Kraaah!»

There's a «Kraaah!» and you wake up.

The crow screech of the train's brakes makes your heart pound wildly in your breast. A soldier, all wrapped up against the cold, slides the huge heavy door open, fanning the air in an effort to chase away the stench within.

«Get out!» he orders.

Nobody moves except you. You get to your feet urging papa to do likewise. Outside there's a snowstorm raging, but you jump down with all the nimbleness of your sixteen summers. Papa follows, then soon all the others. You huddle close together, rubbing against each other in an effort to obtain some solace from the gusts of icy wind that nearly sweep you away.

Mikael leaned on the bridge's wooden railing, his gaze wandering all about the garden. A few dozen yards away, he could hear the hum of his school fellows' voices. Had one of the fathers noticed him that would not have caused any alarm. Mikael was inclined to be withdrawn.

I am greatly pained, I confess, but I have to master myself, learn to deal with this feeling as you carry me away with you.

Someone is driving you, and you, like a flock of sheep in the footsteps of a cruel shepherd, trod in the direction of the lights glinting in the silvery sky, beyond a curtain of spiraling flakes. Your feet sink down into the deep snow and you squint, your eyes now only two slits, because you insist on looking ahead, through the storm that lashes your face. At a certain point, you notice a rainbow and rejoice; you take it as an auspicious omen regardless of your tremendous plight. But then, you lift your eyes as you near the gate they herd you through, and you realize it is only a strip of gaudy colored paper badly glued to a sheet of plywood.

«With my work I will pay my debt to the fatherland», the block capitals above the gateway announce. You are too weary to comment. One by one, you file past the guardhouse, as two soldiers aim machine guns at you, prepared to fire. You arrive at a clearing, where an officer orders you to get into groups of fives before walking off and disappearing into a billet. You wait, motionless, like stakes stuck in the snow which slowly covers you over.

Papa no longer speaks to you not even when you address him directly. He responds only with nods of the head. His eyelids are heavy, swollen, his expression leaden and, when you take a closer look, he even looks funny, with his eyebrows and beard all white, his nose and cheeks a purple hue. A stocky officer, his fur hat falling down over his eyes, is counting you: «Odìn, dvà, trì» and writing assiduously in his roll book. Then, not satisfied, he counts you all, over and over again. Now he decides to shout out your names, Azerbaijan, Belarusian, Uzbek, Kalmyck and, finally, Armenian names. Papa jumps when he hears his name, he would like to reply, make some kind of answer, but he remains still, mute, paralyzed. The officer calls the roll again, twice, three times over. Lift up your father's hand, I beg you, don't tarry, let him say something. The soldier comes striding, determined, over to you, gripping the rifle slung over his shoulder, and stops right in front of you. All look on with bated breath, waiting. Papa steps back and loses his balance. You reach out to steady him, but you don't manage it in time because the soldier strikes him on the head with the butt of his weapon, a resounding blow which knocks him to the ground. You are astonished and watch him writhe in the snow which is now being stained bright red. You want to bend down and help him, embrace him more than anything, but the soldier warns you he will fire, so you stay still, anguish painted on your face, hate tearing your soul to shreds.

From the depths of the forest, the voice of a wolf howls revenge.

Gabriel fixed his gaze beyond the wooden fence smothered in mounds of shoveled snow. Two lines of man-high barbed wire bordered the camp which stretched out into the distance, as far as the eye could see. A cluster of huts, like some ugly nativity scene, occupied the center of the compound. Beyond the barbed wire the black-green tips of fir trees marked the blurry horizon. The sky, the color of liquid mercury, was edged with fiery red.

Had Gabriel been able to rise above the ground up to a certain altitude he would have been able to admire a vast mountainous area, full of lakes, rivers and valleys. To the south, he would have seen the bulk of Mount Belukha, watchful sentinel of the Mongolian-Chinese frontier and, to the east, Lake Teleckoe, the «golden lake», as it used to be called, in lethargy under a thick coating of ice, waiting for the spring thaw.

To the west, on sunny days he might have watched the flowing waters of the Katun river and the recently constructed roadway, winding its snake-like way between the various work camps to end its course in the region's only inhabited settlement: the town of Barnaùl, about two hundred kilometers away.

Beyond Barnaùl, empty nothingness.

These were the bearings of Altaj camp n.11, its number carved into a rock on the roadside. This gulag was destined above all to political prisoners, the so-called *kontrìk*, citizens who opposed the regime and were sentenced to make amends by the sweat of their brow for the harm they had caused the people.

«Right, left», shouted a soldier dividing the prisoners into two long lines.

«Right», he said to Seròp.

«Left», to Gabriel.

The boy was obliged to let go of his father's hand. Seròp looked up and shook his head. «*Hachoghutiùn*, good luck», he wished his son, as he dragged his feet in the direction of the line indicated by the soldier.

Trickles of clotted blood stained his forehead and temples.

A terrible stink overwhelmed Gabriel as soon as the soldier made him go inside. The place stank of stale air, filth and the smoke of *machorka*.[1] It was full of men who were changing out of their damp overalls after a day's hard work, before going to supper. Their clothes were hung out to dry on a line stretched above a wood-burning stove. Some of the prisoners, worn out, were lying on wooden boards arranged in two-tiered bunks. On seeing the new arrivals, twenty or so in all, they groaned and grumped, in sounds somewhere between a lament and scorn.

«Beasts!», the soldier called out by way of warning.

Gabriel, observing them, noticed that they were of all ages. They were thin, often gaunt. One in particular, who paced relentlessly back and forward between the stove and the door, was all skin and bone, a stray specter.

«I, on the contrary, bid you welcome!»

This voice belonged to a huge man who, despite the cold, wore only a vest, making a display of his powerful tattooed biceps. Lying one of the top bunks, he allowed his legs to dangle while the little boy in the bed below massaged them with slow, careful movements. Gabriel noticed that the ugly brute had such long, curved nails that they made him think of the talons of a falcon.

The soldier spat on the ground.

«Find a place for yourselves», he told the new prisoners, banging the door as he left.

The men rushed to bag the best places for themselves and a fight broke out between them which amused the billet's veteran inmates considerably.

«Have you booked?» they asked with sarcasm as they engaged in a kicking match.

Gabriel was the last to move. He noticed a bunk at the back of the hut, a cold, damp spot, far from the stove.

«Hey, you!»

The boy turned around.

«You, come over here.»

The fellow with the tattoos lifted his foot out of the hands of the boy who was massaging it and sat up on his pallet. Gabriel remained motionless.

«I told you to come here!» he ordered.

He moved closer.

«What are you able to do?»

At close quarters, the man seemed less threatening. His eyes drooped downwards, he was completely bald and had a blond goatee.

Gabriel said nothing, uncertain what he ought to say.

«What are you able to do? Talk! He, for example», he said indicating the boy, «is good at massages, that other fellow over there at cleaning toilets, while that bloke down there…» He made a vulgar gesture with his hand, stuck out his tongue and pretended to lick. They all howled with laughter. The fellow referred to, made a face, and then joined in with the others, smirking. Although he was very young, Gabriel noticed he had no teeth and his gums were black and rotten.

«You can see why Maggot is so good at what he does? Toothless as his namesake.»

The laughter continued.

«That will do», ordered the giant with a wave of his hand. «So, what are you able to do? If you don't answer, I'll get you something to do in here.» His expression changed all of a sudden.

Gabriel shrugged. «I play the *bayan* and sing», he said at last.

The man leapt down from his bunk. He was so tall that Gabriel had to take a few steps backwards to look up at his face.

«Where are you from? Your accent's strange…» And he sized Gabriel up carefully. «Georgian, Armenian maybe», he proclaimed.

«I come from Yerevan.»

«*Yés kés siroùm ém*, I love you», the big man said, at last.

Gabriel did not even bat an eyelid.

«Just call me Gara, Mountain. And you are?»

«Gabriel.»

«So you can play the bayan?» And off he set in the direction of a bunk, cleared away some of the stuff piled underneath it, shifted a pair of boots with no soles, a heap of filthy rags, a tin plate and, eventually, found a large cardboard box. He blew the dust off the lid and drew out an accordion.

«Shurik was the best», he told Gabriel, «God rest his soul! You all remember him, don't you? He certainly knew how to charm us when he took this contraption into his arms.»

Gara stopped in front of Gabriel and handed him the instrument. «Take it. Play whatever you like.»

The boy felt everyone's eyes upon him. The prisoners had stopped chatting and gathered round him. He examined their suffering faces, their eyes sunken with hunger and fatigue that were tacitly imploring him. They needed entertainment, a ray of hope. He put the straps on his shoulders and ran his fingers gently over the keys wondering what tune he might play. Something easy and popular, suitable for this audience.

«*Oci ciornie, oci strastnye…* Black eyes, passionate eyes», he sang before beginning to play the instrument. Gara stiffened as if the song had opened a wound that had never healed completely, but then yielded to the notes of the accordion as they blended with the lyrics:

«… *burning eyes, beautiful eyes,*
How I love you, how I fear you,
I seem to have met you at an unfortunate time.»

He turned his back to him and, approaching the window, he stared out thoughtfully into the black Siberian night.

The other prisoners, moved by this unexpected performance, stood there like statues, their eyes wide open, each one probably going back over his luckless life.

«But I am not sad, I am not pained, my fate brings me comfort», whispered Gara, singing along.

And then, Gabriel noticed, even though Gara tried to hide it, that his shoulders were heaving: Mountain was weeping, his hands gripping the windowsill firmly.

At half past four in the morning they had to line up in the clearing next to the camp entrance.

They had been woken up by the yells of the chain-gang supervisor. They had dressed in the dark, coughing and grouching and had then gulped down a meagre breakfast of tea and stale bread. Each one had been given another piece of the same bread to take with him for lunch — a short midday break in the forest where they worked.

Escorted by two guards with machine guns, the prisoners had been led to a billet where pickaxes and hatchets, shovels and spades, hammers and trowels, saws and wheelbarrows were all jumbled in a heap. Each man, like an automaton, chose his own tool.

«Get a spade, that way we can be close to each other», Gara whispered to Gabriel, heaving his pickaxe onto his shoulder.

The boy did not get the message.

«I split, you shovel», he explained elbowing him in the ribs so hard that it made him bend over double. «Have I hurt you, little chicken?» he mocked.

Gabriel was about to react when he caught sight of a figure on the other side of the fence. Another group of prisoners was lining up in the clearing to receive their orders for the day. His gaze fell on the familiar outline of a skinny man with bent shoulders.

«Papa!» he whispered to himself.

Despite the dim light, Gabriel recognized him and was horrified to see that Seròp was barely able to remain erect.

«Well then,» began Sergej, the chain-gang boss, advancing down the line, his hand raised to demand everyone's attention. Reluctantly, Gabriel had to take his eyes off his father.

«For those who have just arrived, today we'll be going to our usual construction site. We are digging a road, a shortcut to be exact, to connect camps 11 and 27. It is absolutely mandatory that we finish by spring. There's a swamp in this area so working with mosquitos is out of the question. Therefore, seeing that mathematics is not a matter of opinion, we need to dig twenty-one meters of road today and every other day. Therefore, I'll be breathing down your necks, I'll be totally ruthless. You know what the punishment for slackers is, don't you Maggot?»

The toothless young man jumped. He had been almost sleeping on his feet.

«Certainly», he replied promptly, «no bread for those who don't work.» And then he broke out into a nervous cackle, a cloud of vapor pluming from of his mouth, hiding his rotting gums.

«Let's go then», ordered Sergej.

Gabriel turned around, hoping to catch sight of his father again, but there was nobody left in the clearing across the fence.

They marched, under the surveillance of an armed guard, through the fog that was beginning to lift and the sky was growing a little brighter.

«What happened to you back there?» Gara asked Gabriel who was walking by his side. «You looked as if you'd seen a ghost?»

The boy did not reply.

«Well?» the other insisted.

They were now skirting a copse having turned into a dirt track. An icy wind was whistling through the branches of the trees.

«Drop dead!» muttered Gara.

«I saw my father.»

The man stifled a laugh.

«So there's a whole family of you in here; where's your granddad?»

Gabriel chilled him with one foul glance.

«Come on now, tell me; what awful mess have you people got yourselves into? Something really serious, eh?»

The boy shook his head.

«They found a book in the house. Only the cover, actually.»

«Only? And the rest of it?»

«My little sister has it. Wherever she hid it, she did a great job, they don't seem to have found it; maybe…»

A flash, like a rainbow exploding high up in the sky above their heads made him stop talking. Out of the blue, three veils of light appeared in the sky fluttering like net curtains in a breeze. They were bright green, almost fluorescent in color, bordered with pink specks. At the center glowed a huge purple heart.

«The Aurora Borealis», someone remarked.

The chain slowed down, and, spellbound, everyone looked up.

«The Lord is speaking to us», said someone else.

Gabriel stood gaping. The phenomenon stirred a mixture of wonder and fear in his breast, but, above all, he considered it a sign, proof of the greatness of God. His heart filled with hope and he recalled Novàrt again, as he had done day after day. He regretted not sharing this wonderful experience with her. Novàrt had been his fond little pupil and he had always done his very best to teach her all he knew, to instill the noblest of feelings in her, as well as a deep love for the beautiful, the good and the just.

Besides, his dear little sister was not only intelligent, but cunning and perspicacious as well, always succeeding in reaching her goals without revealing her hand too much. That ability of hers — typical of many females —amused Gabriel who pretended not to notice it. He simply let her have things her way, forgiving her wiles, because he found her childlike candor irresistible.

«What language is that?» Novàrt had asked her brother one afternoon while he was reading Saroyan's book.

«English.»

«But Saroyan is Armenian.»

«Yes, but he was born in the States, like I was born in Greece.»

«Do you know how to read English?»

«I began learning it in Patras. We had a brilliant teacher back there»

«Will you teach me to read English?» the child had entreated him, passing her fingers gently over the pages as if they were something really precious.

Gabriel had smiled. «I can tell you one of the stories, if you like.»

Novàrt had opened her eyes wide with delight.

«Which one?»

«*The Daring young man on the flying trapeze.*»

«What's it about?»

«It's the story of a jobless young man during the American recession.»

«Recession?»

«The economic crisis. Well, you see, when business is bad people get poorer and poorer.»

Novàrt had nodded and curled up on the sofa beside her brother. Paraphrasing to make the text more comprehensible for her, Gabriel had narrated the sad story of a few days in the life of a young writer as he tried to survive in a world that was falling apart. He had told her about the young man's vain attempt to find work, of how he had been obliged to sell all he owned — books, clothes, everything — so that he might eat. And how, in the end, he had been left with nothing, or rather with only one bright new penny, which glinted on the table in his poor lodgings under the roof.

«Wait, wait!» Novàrt had ordered her brother, her face all a wrinkle as she prepared to sneeze. She did not want to miss even one word.

«What did he do with the coin?» she asked, bright-eyed because she had stifled the sneeze.

«Well, he realized that he wouldn't make it. He hadn't eaten for days; he knew he was dying and…»

«And?»

Gabriel had put the book down and held her close to him, listening to her little fluttering heartbeat.

«And fearing that the penny might be wasted, he thought he should give it to some little girl before departing this life.»

He had finished the sentence looking into her eyes which shone brighter than before.

«Where does it say that? Let me see», she had demanded.

«Here.» he said pointing at the word *child*.

«Does that mean little girl? Why a little girl and not a little boy?»

Gabriel had cleared his throat. «Because boys are not as good as girls; a girl knows better than a boy how to spend a penny», he had lied.

An innocent white lie to gratify the little sister of whom he was so awfully fond.

They had arrived at the construction site after an hour-long march as the sun gilded the tops of the trees. They had set down to work with all the strength they possessed, splitting rocks, sawing tree trunks, shoveling and clearing, overseen by the armed guards while the head of the chain-gang egged them on, heaping insults and curses on their heads.

Gabriel had shoveled alongside Gara. His companion had split those stones with surprising strength while he had scooped up the shards which he then loaded carefully into the cart which Maggot hastened to empty at the side of the road. All proceeded at a repetitive, mechanical pace, with no time for anything but inhumane fatigue.

At noon they paused for lunch.

Gara spread a rag out on the ground and sat down on it, grumbling.

«Come, sit down here, or else you'll freeze your arse off», he said to Gabriel.

The prisoners took out their morsel of bread and ate in silence. Eating bread was akin to a religious rite. First of all they smelled it, breathed in its aroma, then nibbled at little pieces of it allowing then to dissolve very slowly in their mouths in order to savor the taste thoroughly.

«The more you lick it, the sweeter it gets», remarked Maggot, who stood a few paces away from them as he brushed the crumbs into his mouth while an expression of bliss lit his face up.

«You're talking about the bread?» mocked Sergej, but his quip fell on deaf ears. Everyone was too intent on eating.

Gabriel looked at Maggot's hands and saw that his fingers were bent and deformed.

Their gazes crossed.

«They make you pity me, don't they?» he commented, waving them in the air.

Gabriel blushed to the gills.

«Twelve years of hard labor, that's what it takes», he stated growing suddenly serious.

«I was a fine-looking lad when they brought me here, much more handsome than you. And just look at me now!»

He sprang to his feet and moved away from the others.

«Shit!» he cursed as he wandered off.

He stopped under a tree, his back to his mates and began punching and kicking the trunk. From the branches a shower of snow fell on his head and shoulders. Then as calm as can be, he opened his fly, let his trousers down and defecated right in front of them all.

«Shit, utter shit, that's what it is», he grumbled.

9

«Papa!» exclaimed Gabriel, overjoyed.

«Son!»

«Are you all right?»

«Yes, I'm managing all right.»

Their paths had crossed by fluke on the doorstep of the billet that acted as the prison-camp canteen. The air was full of the strong, acrid smell of kale. Gabriel was about to enter just as his father was leaving. They clung to each other, embracing with such warmth and passion that they totally disregarded the hostile looks they were receiving from the armed guards.

Seròp proudly informed his son about the little cobbler's shop inside the camp where he was working now and where he made those clodhopping boots known as *zagruzki*, especially suitable for the wet, snowy weather of Siberia. The doctor had declared him unfit for outdoor work. This he believed had been a remarkable stroke of luck, because had they assigned him to a job in the bitterly cold air of the taiga it would surely have cost him his life.

«But you, my boy, how are you feeling? You've lost weight…» he remarked with some concern.

«I'm fine, papa.»

They stood to one side to avoid blocking the other prisoners as they came and went. They kept looking at one another as if they had not seen each other for years.

«The workshop overseer congratulated me recently», Seròp announced with pride, «good behavior is so very important; who knows, maybe they'll soon…»

Gabriel's heart plummeted. His simple-minded father was

fooling himself if he believed that their henchmen might change their minds and send them home. He nodded just the same, though he smiled bitterly.

«*Aràch Asdvàtz*, God is mighty», he added raising his eyes to the heavens.

«But what have you done to yourself here? You hadn't got that before», said Gabriel, pointing at a cut on his father's right eyelid.

«Oh, fiddlesticks! I slipped…»

«Where?»

Seròp hesitated.

«Where?» Gabriel insisted.

«In the showers, he slipped in the showers», said a voice in gruff, vulgar tones.

Gabriel noticed a man standing behind his father. He was in the company of another far taller fellow who had lost one of his eyes. Together they caught Seròp under the arms and prevented him from moving.

Gabriel, though frightened, protested. «Leave my father alone!» he shouted.

«Well, well only listen to the little cockerel!» said the one-eyed brute.

«Looking for trouble?» Gara's unmistakable voice was heard even before his bulk loomed to fill up the intervening space.

From a distance one of the guards bristled.

«What's going on here?» the giant asked Gabriel.

«Nothing», volunteered the smaller of the two bullies, letting go of Seròp.

«We've had our din-dins and now off to beddy-bye's, isn't that so, *tovarich?*»

Seròp nodded. His two mates pushed him outside into the cold evening air.

«That shorty bloke and his one-eyed buddy are authentic pieces of shit», declared Maggot.

«Do you know them?» Gabriel asked.

Gara grinned sarcastically. «Maggot knows everybody.»

He was downing his lukewarm swill. The tables and benches were distributed around the place higgledy-piggledy. The prisoners busied themselves to gobble down their rations because they had to take turns and because those who finished first had enough time to enjoy a *machorka*.

«He shared a billet with them before being moved over to ours», Gara told him. «They had to transfer him because those two had beaten him to a pulp.»

Maggot shivered and fixed his gaze on the dirty, blurry window. When he started speaking again his face was as red as a beetroot, «If they've picked on your dad, well, you'd better prepare yourself for a funeral». Then he broke out in an equivocal, maniacal cackle.

Gabriel lowered his eyes.

«But we can make sure that doesn't happen», said Gara.

«Meaning?» asked Gabriel hopefully.

«We can reach some kind of an agreement», he whispered, as Maggot stared at him knowingly.

Gabriel laid down his spoon in the bowl where a stray leaf of cabbage was floating in a pool of grey slop.

«What kind of an agreement?»

«What are you prepared to do for your father?»

«Anything, everything.»

«Anything, everything?»

«Yes.»

Maggot began cackling again.

Sergej, the head of the chain gang, was walking about among the tables, carrying a basket and handing out the rations of bread to the prisoners. He gave Gara a slice, Gabriel another, but nothing to Maggot.

«Hey, my bread!» protested the toothless man.

«This evening nada, you haven't earned it», he retorted gruffly.

«Fuck off! Give me my bread!» said Maggot, springing to his feet and pouncing on the biggest slice of the batch. Caught completely off guard, the overseer, in an effort to react just managed to send the basket sailing through the air. One or two of the prisoners took advantage of the incident to corner some extra slices for themselves before the bread fell to the floor.

«You faggot!» he yelled, pushing Maggot down onto one of the tables and banging his head off its hard surface. The bowls and spoons began to hop while Maggot's blood spouted all over the tabletop. None of the guards batted an eyelid but simply stood there, sadistically enjoying the scene.

«That'll do!» shouted Gara rising to his feet and drying the broth off his chin. Sergej threw him a sidelong glance but did not dare breathe a word. That man, true to his name, was a veritable mountain.

«Put that bread back in there, or I'll beat the shit out of you!», yelled the foreman.

Meanwhile, Maggot had slipped down onto the floor like a ragdoll, leaving a trail of blood on the table.

Gabriel rose to help him.

«Stop!» said Gara holding him back. «Sit down. It's none of your business.»

«Beating people up is the only form of entertainment in here.» Gara lit his *machorka*, his back to the wind. They were walking around their billet and had stopped for a moment in a dark corner.

«Want a pull?»

Gabriel took the fag in his hand and inhaled deeply. The smoke burnt his throat.

«What have those two got against my father?» he asked, the smoke choking him.

«Nothing really; it's just that in here the herd has the knack of ferreting out the weak.»

«Do you think they beat him?»

«Positive!»

Gabriel sank into his jacket, his heart racing like mad as Gara took his chin between two of his fingers and turned his face up towards the light. The boy was crying

«You just leave things to me», he said to him in gentle, reassuring tones, one would not expect from a giant like him. His eyes lit up with a sudden flash of desire. He took Gabriel by his slim waist and clasped him tightly to himself as he hungrily sought his lips.

«Kiss me…» he begged.

«No, what the hell's got into you?»

«Only one kiss, now.»

Gabriel broke free and stepped back disgusted as he cleaned the other's saliva from his cheek and mouth with his sleeve

«Fuck off!» he shouted.

Gara pierced him with an ice-cold glare. In the half-light his goatee gave him an absolutely diabolical air. Gabriel held the other's stare for some time before dashing to the billet as fast as his legs could take him.

«Run then, you little trollop!»

Gabriel did not look back at him.

«You're a looser, just like your old man.» he heard him yelling as he opened the door and, as usual, was overpowered by the sickening pong.

«Your dad's a goner, boy!», were Gara's last words as he slammed the ramshackle door.

Gabriel groped his way cautiously in the dark. It was the dead of night and the only sound to be heard in the billet was that of the prisoners snoring.

The boy made his way around on tiptoe. He brushed against a pallet; the one belonging to Maggot who was groaning with pain: his eyes were swollen, his head covered in cuts and bruises, his nose blocked by clotted blood which obliged to breathe laboriously through his gaping mouth.

When he heard someone coughing Gabriel dropped down on his hands and knees. One prisoner turned in his bunk and spat on the floor. As soon as the man began to snore again, the boy stood up, squinted in the dark and peered around in search of Gara's bed. He recognized it because of the man's bulk. He hoisted himself up carefully to the giant's bed, placing his toes on the edge of the planks below and pushing himself up. Then he lay down beside the big man.

«Welcome», whispered the mountain.

«We'll do whatever you want», murmured Gabriel in a toneless voice.

Gara pulled the blanket over their heads and the stink of dirty underwear grew stronger.

«Touch my dick», Gara told him.

Gabriel complied.

«Did you like that?»

«What else have I got to do.»

«Take off your clothes

Gabriel undressed quickly.

«Turn around!»

The boy shut his eyes and waited his muscles all tense. The image of his father's weak, emaciated face filled every recess of his mind. He wondered whether, seeing him as he was now, Seròp would understand the meaning of his gesture, have continued being proud of his son. No, nobody would have justified him, not even his mother. Of this he was dead certain. The only person who would have was Novàrt, his little rosebud, perhaps because she was too young to realize what was happening.

«My dear little rose, I didn't want them to kill papa» he would have told her and she would have smiled, tossing back her jet-black curls.

«Off with you, nothing doing!» said Gara pulling his head out from under the blanket.

Gabriel turned around and stared at him.

«I just wanted to see how much you love your father.»

An awful knot in the boy's stomach loosened.

«Get out of my bunk», said his mate, pushing him away.

«Shut your trap!», grumbled an inmate.

«What about my dad?»

«Get down from this fucking bunk!»

Gabriel moved cautiously. He let his legs drop over the edge of the bunk and sought a foothold on the bed below. His temples were throbbing with anger and humiliation. He had just reached the ground when Gara took him by the wrist. In the gloom, the man's eyes shone like two beads of amethyst. For some reason he found it hard to explain, Gabriel believed these eyes contained a promise, a tacit vow. Despite this, he withdrew his hand as if it had gone too close to the fire.

Then, heartened again, he nimbly set off in the direction of his own bunk.

«Did you like it, at least?» muttered Maggot, chuckling. Despite being half dead, he understood what had been going on.

Gabriel did not answer but simply threw himself down on his bed where he remained awake until Sergej ordered them all to get up.

He rose and dressed, then gulped down his scalding hot tea which burnt his throat.

As they walked towards the site, he noticed that Gara was marching next to him as usual, as if nothing had happened the night before. He strode on, his shovel on his shoulder.

The temperature was forty degrees below freezing.

Don't stop moving, otherwise you're dead!

You need to hop about like a madman, slap your companions on the back to generate just a little heat.

Poor wretches! They force you, tools in hand, to build a world from scratch. You went out this morning and worked all day nonstop. It's almost dusk and you can't wait to return to the camp, to warm yourself up beside the stove. Your body is soaked, damp, your lips, eyelashes and chin all covered in hoar frost.

«Maloletok[2], now you know what face you'll have when you're old, if you ever get that far», quips the foreman, but you don't even hear him, because suddenly the wind begins to roar like an angry lion.

«The **buran**, *the snowstorm!» shout some of the men as they throw themselves down to the ground. You follow suit, your heart pounding in your breast, bearing overawed witness to the force of Nature. You just lie there, helpless. Millions of flakes spin and churn in the air, along with pieces of cardboard and a chisel which comes hurtling down to land dangerously close to you, missing you by a hairsbreadth. Someone helps you to your feet. You can't make out who it may be because you can't see a thing. The outline of the camp, the stars in the sky, even the beautiful northern lights, everything has vanished. You're shrouded in an algid fog, just like your miserable, lonely existence.*

A shower of ice, stones and snow hails down on you like yet another divine punishment.

Mikael leapt to his feet, his shadow cast by the light of the projector onto the big screen as if in a lantern show.

«Sit down!», protested someone from the audience.

The boy complied.

It was the usual Sunday afternoon at the cinema in Campo Santa Margherita. The *Cine Vecio* — the old cinema, as they called it in the Venetian dialect — was an old church, unconsecrated during the period of the Napoleonic reforms, when many religious buildings and monasteries were closed down. The building was dominated by a chopped off dome, which had remained the same for a century and a half. At its base stood two white marble statues: a sea monster and a forked-tongued dragon. Recently, the parish had decided to turn it into a cinema dedicated to screening films of lofty social and religion content only.

That Sunday, Wolf had insisted that none of the collegians should miss *Ladri di biciclette*, Bicycle Thieves, an Italian film he deemed a true masterpiece. The theatre was packed and the audience deeply engrossed. They all sympathized with Antonio, an unemployed worker in Rome, dealing with life's hardships immediately after the end of World War II. Many spectators were smoking nervously while some of the women were weeping. Mikael, who was particularly sensitive, felt the need to move. He rose again, this time with extreme caution, bent in two as he passed to the end of the row and slipped out. Just then, he heard a voice whisper:

«Mikael!».

Looking over to his left, he managed, to make out in the half-light, the shape of a girl sitting in the sector below the balcony.

«I've brought your book back.»

Straining his eyes, he saw Francesca's lovely face. He had not seen her again after their first encounter. He had often climbed onto the boundary wall in hopes of coming across his golden-eyed «fairy». He had even dared call out her name, without, however receiving any answer. And now, the fact that she was sitting right there overjoyed him and his heart began to race wildly.

«Come and join us for a while», invited Francesca pointing to an empty seat next to her.

Silently, Mikael sat down beside her.

«We've just arrived; this is Marina», Francesca told him, nodding at the friend sitting on the other side.

Gabriel smiled.

«*Papà, papà!*»

The hacking sobs of a little boy on the screen hushed the theatre. It was Bruno, Antonio's son, in utter despair seeing the people try to lynch his father for the bicycle he had stolen. Francesca's head sank into the hood of her duffle coat; her blond hair disappeared beneath its tartan lining, while her perfume filled the air. It was a fragrance Mikael breathed in blissfully, though unable to name it for the moment. Then, suddenly it struck him; it was orange blossom.

«*Thief, rogue, throw him into prison!*»

On the screen Bruno, his father's hat in his little hand, looked pleadingly out of his huge eyes at the crowd, begging to leave his father alone.

Mikael peeped at Francesca and realized she was crying, overcome by that moving scene. This made him sad, so he tried to think of words that might console her but, as he was about to say something, her hand, soft and warm, began to stroke his tenderly.

A whole world of wild orange trees had just bloomed.

We are walking back from the cinema and are at a few yards from the college when the stench of the canal catches me by the throat. There you are! Your feet are wet, your clothes sopping, you have been working for days in the water, digging on the banks of a frozen river. You have to build a bridge, and in a hurry, because if you don't get it done in time, you'll get nothing more to eat. But you are no longer afraid, not even of hunger. Like some kind of a robot, you clench your teeth and go on splitting the hard earth. You strike and strike again, until you feel absolutely nothing.

«*The director is looking for you*», *the foreman tells you.*

You've just returned to the camp and are changing out of your dungarees.

«*You know where, don't you? The billet with the flag outside*», *Sergej informs you. You dress again in a hurry and head for the* **baraki***, where you find your father standing just under the photo of Stalin, whose penetrating gaze seems to crush that poor little man.*

«*Have those blokes been annoying you again?*» *you ask him, putting your arm around your father's shoulder.*

«*No*», *he murmurs, shaking his head, but you insist on studying his face, puzzled by his tone of voice.*

«*You must report it immediately if they touch you again*», *you are telling him as the director shows up. You notice his moustache trimmed like that of the savior of the fatherland.*

«Sit down!», *he orders, without even bothering to look at the two of you.*

No useless forewords.

The director fishes out a letter from amongst the papers on his desk and reads it in a neutral and impassable tone, as if reading the contents of a work report. You lean forward, paying attention like you did at school. You want to understand the words in Russian, that legal terminology which you are not perfectly familiar with, as yet. You soon realize that it's no joke, because if you understand things properly, with this letter, your mother is repudiating you. Your mamma, the woman who gave you life, is disowning you, as well as your father. She condemns you both as dangerous, treacherous individuals, who undermine the integrity of the Union. She dissociates herself from you and declares not wanting to see you, ever again, for any reason, for the rest of her life. You remain open-mouthed, look at your papa who seems even smaller than you recalled. You feel the urge to take his hand, but the officer's next words nail you to the spot: «Here is the wedding ring which the lady returns to you», he states as he hands the little velvet box over to papa who takes out the ring and clasps it in his fist so tightly that his knuckles turn white. You are about to protest, ask for some kind of explanation, when the letter flutters on the desk close enough for you to recognize the signature of that villain of a mother of yours. It wounds you to the quick and you feel your guts gripped in a vise, like a lamb caught in the jaws of a wolf.

I feel all your pain, the unbearable cruelty of the moment and stop.

«My dear boys, you are going through a difficult and dangerous age», began father Elias.

He was an elderly, tall, lean man with a crown of white hair like a halo framing his face and bearing an extraordinary energy for a man of his years.

«As long as the Lord gives me strength…» he used to answer those who would marvel at his vigor. Father Elias claimed he could cover the distance between *Riva degli Schiavoni* — where the water busses from the island of San Lazzaro stopped — and the college in twenty minutes, a time improbable even for a far younger man.

«Nothing to it! You see, I cross the bridge of the *Academia*, turn right and there I am», he would say with a wave of his blue-veined hand.

A Persian by origin, he had now lived for over half a century in his monastic cell on the island. He was considered the Mekhitarist *par eccellence*, a pillar of the Armenian community, respected and revered as if he had been an angel fallen straight from Heaven. Voted to the closed order, he never left the monastery except when he came to the college where, on his own initiative, he taught that infamous subject known as «Sexual Education and Behavior».

«Numerous temptations torment your unripe existence.»

His voice boomed in the hall like that of a Shakespearean actor. His figure, standing out backlit by the windows, instilled fear in the pupils who listened in silence, paying the utmost attention.

«Keropé, my son, there's no need to feel ashamed…» he added as he went over to the student, who had blushed violently. He tousled the boy's hair with affection, perhaps because they both hailed from Persia, or maybe because he denoted in him that childlike innocence the others, in the throes of their hormonal storms, were losing.

«Satan is always lying in wait, let there be no doubt about that. He will visit you in the evening, at night, when least you expect it, to plague you. You will have disgraceful dreams and burn with sordid lust. But the Lord…» he added, his arms raised to the heavens, «will offer you a haven, if you invoke him.»

A ray of sunlight lit up the palm of his right hand.

«Bakunìn…» whispered Aznavour.

Mikael turned to look at his friend, who was pointing at the palm of his own hand, and then, with a look, indicated that of the monk.

«The wounds!» mouthed Aznavour.

Mikael winced: a deep gash, as if a sharp instrument had slashed the old man's palm just above the lifeline.

In the college, the figure of father Elias was shrouded in mystery. For quite some time it was rumored that he had received the *stigmata* and that these bled at times of great distress and tension, like a kind of gauge measuring the pressure of the torment the devil was inflicting on the brothers of the community.

«The sisters who do your laundry have informed me that they found some sheets stained with sperm. I know who it is. I was able to work it on the basis of the bed number marked on it. I won't reveal his name because I can only pity his sad conduct.»

The boys threw furtive glances at each other. Who could this sinner who lived among them possibly be?

«There are things you are unable to understand. Not yet, anyway. The great gift of love, the reciprocal complementary nature of man and woman. The union of the two sexes in matrimony, which mirrors the bountifulness and fecundity of the Creator. But in marriage, only in marriage, I repeat, to which appointment each one of you must arrive pure in body, pure of heart.»

Sobs and low groans echoed in the classroom. One of the boys, his bent head between his hands, had burst into heart-rending tears. He was so tall and corpulent that he could barely fit into his desk.

Father Elias reached him, quick as lightning. «Hampò, my son, you surrendered to the devil, but confess and humbly beg pardon for your sins from our Lord. I'm certain it won't happen again, that you won't lower your guard, that you will be vigilant and strong when temptation assaults you again.»

He then placed his hand on the boy's shoulder inviting him to rise.

«It wasn't my fault», he said between one sob and another, «I was asleep, I don't remember a thing. Next morning when I woke up my bed was all damp.»

Keropé, deeply disturbed by his friend's anguish, tried to justify him.

«It's true, I saw him in the bathroom trying to wash out the stain» he said.

«Two Coca-Colas, please.»

The waiter smiled down at the young couple seated at the back of the bar.

«Aren't you afraid they'll find out?» Francesca asked Mikael as she took off her duffle coat, revealing her slim body and small budding breasts.

Mikael shook his head. «My schoolmates are still at confession.»

«But why at the Chiesa degli Scalzi?»

He shrugged. He had never explained to himself why the fathers had chosen the Church of Saint Mary of Nazareth, that of the congregation of the barefoot Carmelites, as their collegians' place of atonement. He looked up through the bar window and noticed the Madonna and Child on the façade of the church.

«I don't know, but it's beautiful», he said at last.

It just happened that, every so often, some of the boys felt an urgent need to go to confession, probably because they were allowed to go there alone. It was the only occasion they were free to go anywhere unsupervised. They only had to abide by one rule: to be back by the time established by the rector.

«One, two.» said the waiter setting the two little bottles down on the table.

Francesca looked at the Coca-Cola bottle with a certain uncertainty.

«Have you never tasted it before?» Mikael asked her.

«Yes, but my mother says it's not good for you.»

«I like the way the letters of the name hug each other.»

«True.» said Francesca examining the little glass bottle.

«Which one?» Mikael offered, waving the two straws.

«How nice! The blue one.»

The bar was empty and a woman was sweeping some crumbs from underneath the counter.

«Do you ever miss your family?»

«I get homesick at times.»

«Are your parents old?»

«My mother is fifty-one, my father…»

«Yes…»

«He died two years ago»

Francesca took a long deep sip through her straw. Suddenly her eyes filled with tears.

«You need to drink it slowly, otherwise it'll make you cry», Mikael joked.

«Sorry.»

«What's the matter?» he asked gently.

«It's a bad moment for our family. Dad has another woman and that's not all.»

«Meaning?»

«They're expecting a baby. He'll be leaving home in a few weeks' time…»

Unable to finish, she burst out crying.

Mikael put his arms gently around her shoulders.

«Come now. Don't do that, please don't!» His fingers brushed her wet cheeks. «Francesca!»

Two sparkling golden eyes rose to meet his. They remained gazing at each other for several moments. She studied the boy wondering if she could trust him while he admired her beauty and hoped she might find him attractive too.

Driven by a sudden impulse, Mikael kissed her. It was a spontaneous gesture, a sincere way to tell her "I'm here, if you want me. I won't leave you. I'll stay by your side". Francesca remained motionless, overpowered by her emotions. He drew back, afraid he might not be able to control that sense of bewilderment, of having lost himself in an ocean of orange blossom.

«Had you ever kissed anyone before?» asked Francesca blushing, after a short pause.

«Yes», he lied.

Someone knocked on the window outside. They both swung around to see a nose pressed up against the fogged-over pane of glass.

Francesca laughed out loud. «But isn't that?…»

It took Mikael a second to recognize Aznavour. Behind him, Keropé and Hampò, smiling, were beckoning to him to come outside. It was time to go back to the college.

«Waiter, the bill, please», called Mikael, rooting around in the pockets of his trousers for coins.

«Let's make it every day. At two! On the boundary wall», Francesca suggested.

He nodded and brushed away the last tear that hovered precariously on her long eyelashes.

10

«What does Mephìs know about love? A celibate, old man who's always lived shut up behind the walls of a monastery...» whispered Aznavour.

«Who are you talking about?»

«Father Elia, Mephis, Mephistopheles»

Signor Peppe had just put out the dormitory lights and, as usual, had turned the key twice in the lock. Mikael could hear his friend breathing in the dark. There was barely a foot between their two beds.

«They say he speaks to the devil himself, that he's even more powerful than him!»

«What's that supposed to mean?»

«That he has the power to chase him away, exorcise him. But you know what? If God exists... what's the phrase?»

«If God exists, then men are slaves», said Mikael completing the philosopher's quote.

«There's my Bakunìn!»

From the garden came the sound of an ear-splitting screech. An owl had just flown away.

«You, for example, know far more about love than he does», continued Aznavour. «You've already touched a woman's body.»

Mikael did not say a word.

«Do you like Francesca?» his friend insisted.

«I believe I do», he shrugged.

«Ooh, she's perfect!»

«She's not, she's just perfect for me», said Mikael to put matters straight.

There was a long silence; nothing could be heard but the snores of their dorm-mates.

«Do you think we can know only the reality we live in, the one we can actually feel through our senses?» posited Mikael sitting up suddenly in his bed, changing the subject.

«Bakunìn, please don't, this is no time for philosophy...» the other suggested feebly.

«No, honestly, do you think there's another world beyond the one we can see?»

«Why ask me?»

«Please, answer me!»

«I don't really know. Maybe. Dreams, for example.»

«No, I don't mean while we're asleep.»

Aznavour looked perplexed.

«I mean, some kind of a mysterious reality. It appears out of the blue while you're walking, or studying, any time whatever. You can see it, feel it and suddenly you dive right into it.» Mikael halted for a moment, groping for the right words. «It's as if you're living someone else's life», he added sotto voce. «A life of torment, in a place you don't even know, in a situation you've never experienced before. As if you were in a play, where everything is gloomy, hard and desperate, written almost on purpose in order to make you appreciate the life you have which, despite everything, is far less distressing.»

He stopped suddenly, fearing he had gone too far. He pricked up his ears hoping for some kind of answer, a word of comfort. Alas, there was no response from the neighboring bed, just silence.

«Have I bowled you over?» he asked raising himself up on his elbows.

His friend's chest was rising and falling slowly; Aznavour was snoring.

Blood gushed from his mouth...

The boys were helping themselves from the breakfast serving table: hot chocolate, bread and jam. That very morning, the usual discipline which reigned even at mealtimes was rather relaxed because none of the fathers had turned up as yet at the refectory.

Aznavour put his tray down and sat down next to Hampò.

«*Pareluìs*[3]!»

Hampò responded, muttering indistinctly, his mouth full of food.

Mikael, sitting across, remained silent.

«What's wrong, aren't you eating anything?» Aznavour asked him.

«Just a little jam.»

«He says he's got nausea», Hampò intervened.

Mikael pushed his tray away. A slice of bread with a thin layer of jam lay among the crumbs. His cup was still full, the chocolate dried out around the rim.

«No wonder he feels crappy! All these white nights! What have you two got to talk about every night?» Hampò burst out in his marked Sirian accent with its tell-tale French-fried "r".

«Ghosts, isn't that right Bakunìn?»

Papa is lying face down on the floor, his body motionless among uppers and pieces of leather. A little further on, there's a wide-open tin box. It looks like a landmine which had just exploded, scattering tiny cobblers' nails all over the place.

You look on in utter shock like a spectator at some grotesque show.

«How did it happen?» asks the officer as the guards crowd the building.

Among the bystanders the one-eyed prisoner and his mate shake their heads in disapproval.

«It's got nothing to do with us, we were at lunch», an elderly man mumbles.

One of the guards leans over papa and turns him face up.

«I think he killed himself», he says.

«Let's put it down in writing and waste no further time», the officer orders.

Mikael wobbled and fell off his bench, banging his head on the tiles.

«What the hell are you doing? Is this some kind of a joke?» exclaimed Aznavour, utterly bewildered.

A soldier starts kicking papa, harder and harder. He now jumps on top of him making his body dance like a puppet; legs shuddering, head rocking, arms jerking…

«Hurry up, Bakunìn's not well; he's fainted!»

Lying on the floor, Mikael was thrashing about in convulsions. His companions crowded around in agitation, as Aznavour tried to hold his friend's head steady.

«Oh God, there's blood coming out of his mouth!» he exclaimed, seeing his friend's red-stained neck and chin.

«No, he's simply vomited. It's only cherry jam», responded Hampò, rubbing the purple mush between his fingers.

«Come on, lift him up. Wolf is coming», warned another boy.

Gabriel's eyes wandered over his father's dead body. A small, thin man, looking even tinier in his oversized dungarees. At every kick delivered by the soldier, a spout of blood came gushing from his mouth. Gabriel just stood there stark still looking at the outrage, as if riveted to the spot by some kind of morbid, masochistic need to take the whole scene in and brand it forever onto his memory.

Tired and annoyed, the officer knelt down and lifted up Seròp's head to examine it closely.

«He's gone», he said.

Then suddenly, he prized the dead man's jaws open and poked his fingers into his mouth pushing them far back into the throat, as if trying to reach for his stomach and turn it inside-out. When he took his hand back out, a dozen of nails bounced off the floor.

«This jerk has torn his guts to pieces!» he exclaimed, shaking his head.

A sharp dart of pain speared Gabriel's soul, he jolted like a fish that had been impaled on a harpoon.

«Shit!»

The officer rose and, noting Gabriel among the bystanders, started striding over to him as he dried his hands off with a rag.

«I'm sorry, Armenian», he said, so closely that he almost brushed the boy's face with his fur hat. Gabriel looked into his eyes, hoping to find a spark of pity in them.

«I'm sorry», the other repeated, «I mean about the nails…»

The walleye and his mate suffocated a snigger.

Two of the guards lifted the body up. Gabriel felt a strong urge to jump on them, prevent them from touching his father, but he held back. There was no point in giving in to useless outbursts of emotion. He had already been prepared for the worst when he had been summoned urgently back to the camp: he would never have been allowed to leave his work had it not been for something really serious.

«Where are you taking him?» he asked as they passed in front of him.

«Outside with all the others. We'll bury him in spring.»

«Wait!» Gabriel lifted up his father's arm which hung down touching the earth. Something shone on his little finger; he took it off and hid it quickly in his pocket.

It was his mother's wedding ring.

He followed the guards carrying the corpse until they disappeared behind a mound of snow, and then he returned to his billet. As soon as he opened the door, he found his companions having a furious row.

«Where the fuck is my bread?» snarled a man still wearing his work clothes, half-melted frost on his face. «I left a half slice under my pillow. Where is it?» he shouted.

A small group of men were gathered around Maggot. They were violently shaking and shoving him about.

«I don't know», he protested, defending himself.

«You were the only one left here. Who else could it have been?»

«We work our ass off and you nick our bread?»

The raging men lifted him up by the hands and feet and tossed him into the air.

«Stop it!» howled the airborne Maggot. His face was still full of the bruises from the last beating. He had not recovered from it as yet, therefore he had been exempted from work on the site. That was the reason why he was only given a half ration of bread; at times not even that. Maggot, however, had not resisted against the pangs of hunger and had simply taken his companion's food. According to one of the camp's unwritten rules, the sentence for whoever took another man's bread was death. You could steal a man's underpants, blades, comb, but you could not steal his bread. Never! That was considered downright immoral, cowardly and unacceptable. *Hlebushka*[4] was sacred and untouchable.

The men let go of Maggot who plummeted onto the hard floor to a crunching noise of splintering bones.

«No, I beg you, have pity», he whined, lying in a heap on the ground.

«Out with that bread!» Gara's voice said above all the others.

«I haven't got it anymore. I was hungry.»

Gara nodded and the others bent down to pick Maggot's broken body up again. Gabriel, totally disgusted, backed away. He could not bear to witness any more suffering. He hurried off in the direction of his own bunk and, kneeling down, rummaged among his things.

«Enough!» he yelled, standing up again.

The other froze and stared at him. Nobody had the right to interfere when scores were being settled, let alone a *maloletok* like him.

«What's missing?» he asked as he approached slowly.

Gara elbowed his way through the gang and stood right in front of Gabriel, believing he would intimidate him with his bulk.

«You think you can make amends?»

«I'll give you this if you'll leave him alone.»

Gabriel opened his hand. On the palm lay a chunk of bread.

«You're willing to give me your bread? Have I got that right?» asked the bloke in the dungarees, incredulous and unable to take his eyes off that morsel.

The boy nodded and the other pounced on it. He immediately smelled it and took a deep breath, as if wishing to fill his lungs with that mouthwatering aroma.

«You try that once again and I swear, I'll smash your face in!», Gabriel vowed, bending over Maggot.

The miserable fellow tried to get up but fell back onto the floor with a groan of sheer agony.

Gabriel met Gara's infuriated gaze, but did not take any notice of it. He had not been allowed to pay homage to his father's body. Not even a prayer, one last caress. Nevertheless, he had saved a man's life surrendering something very precious: his piece of bread. He prayed this gesture might convince the Lord to receive his father's soul, and embrace it in all his infinite mercy.

He opened the door and stepped outside, tottering. A gust of icy air whipped him in the face like a thousand needles pricking his skin. He walked over towards the clearing, unsure where to go, perfectly aware he was in the sights of the armed guards on the watch out tower, prepared to shoot. It was dark already and the lamp posts threw grey shadows on the frozen clump of snow. A dog in chains barked furiously, straining forward, making the links of his collar rattle.

Gabriel stopped, his knees gave way and he collapsed onto the muddy ground. He remained there at length, until the heat of his body began thawing the ice beneath it. His jacket became soaked and the chilly water reached his skin. He thought of his father, lying dead in a heap of other corpses, somewhere behind that mound of snow.

Just then, the fact that he was left alone in the world dawned on him painfully.

11

Patras, 1938

The autumn of 1938 got off to a very bad start. In any case, without promises of anything good.

There were visible rips in the world's precarious balance of political power, soon to come undone giving rise to World War II, the world's worst ever conflict, destined to cost six years of pain, suffering and carnage, for an estimated total of fifty-five million victims.

Europe's major powers were steadily forming two coalitions: one comprising the German-Nazi and Italian-Fascist Axis, the other the Franco-British Alliance. Further west, Spain lay in ruins due to a devastating civil war, after Generalissimo Francisco Franco, with help from Hitler and Mussolini, had defeated the nascent Republic and seized power as the country's Dictator. In the heart of Europe, Nazi-Germany's mighty armed forces were amassing troops along the French border, in blatant defiance of the terms of the 1920 Treaty of Versailles, while the regime had also sanctioned the Anschluss, by which Austria was annexed to Germany. Before long, Bohemia and Moravia were to be invaded and Czechoslovakia ultimately dissolved.

None of these events had much of an impact on Greece. The Country was too small, its role on the international checkerboard irrelevant, standing as it did way out there on a limb, at the tail end of the Balkan peninsula. Furthermore, it was an extremely poor country. Greece still bore the signs of Turkish dominion and struggled daily with countless grave problems: its virtually non-existent industry, its agriculture incapable of feeding the population, while the million Greek and Armenian refugees who had flowed into the country after the Greco-Turkish war, had dramatically worsened the situation.

The inhabitants of Patras, on their part, were facing a veritable climatic disaster: after an epic-making drought that had destroyed almost all the crops, autumn had scourged the area with storms and floods as destructive as tropical hurricanes, wiping out acres and acres of vineyard and even uprooting centuries-old olive groves.

«There'll be neither wine nor oil. We are damned!», the peasants commented as they crossed themselves. Hundreds of animals had starved to death. Their carcasses piled up in the fields, the lakes and the forests, even on the sides of the roads, where they rotted, slowly infesting the air with a stomach-turning stench. The western marshes now full of slime, swarmed with mosquitos and their larvae.

Soon after the animals, it was the turn of people to die of the so-called swamp-fever, alias malaria. They suffered from sky-high fever for days, agonizing headaches, while their urine turned a terrifying black color. Those who managed to recover were the few who could afford to buy a substance extracted from a therapeutic tree: the miraculous quinine.

The majority of the population, poor if not destitute, was obliged to pay with their lives.

They simply dropped dead, cluttering the roadsides just like the animals before them had done.

«Let's we go out?» Satèn invited the twins who looked at her in astonishment.

She wrapped them carefully in two blankets and placed them upright in the carrier-bag she had made especially for them on the sewing machine. It was a kind of saddlebag with two large pockets held together by a long strap she could sling over her shoulder. Originally it had been a sack containing flour that the American Red Cross delivered to the camp every so often; on one side, in faded lettering, was printed *Manitoba*, a word Satèn was unable to understand.

It was rare for her to leave the house. If she ever did, it was only to go into the yard to empty a basin, fetch fresh water from the pumps, or pick some fruit from a nearby tree: figs, pears, a handful of olives, but always anxious about having left her two little angels on their own at home. This was the first evening in months of fine weather, a clear, cloudless sky spangled with myriad stars. She felt like taking a breath of fresh clean air in the company of her two babies.

Seròp was away from home, trying to sell his slippers in the surrounding towns and villages. Sometimes he stayed away for days, trying to do business in some of the more prosperous hill towns of Aetolia, trading his *kundure,* or rather, bartering them for a loaf, homemade pasta, even a whole chicken when he was particularly lucky.

Hunger, after all, was far less urgent than the scourge of malaria. In the camp, the refugees were falling like flies. Every morning a cart, drawn by a scrawny little donkey would turn up at the camp to the sound of a tiny bell and wait a while to pick up the corpses. The weeping, mourning relatives would haul the bodies of their loved ones out from their shacks and pile them, one on top of the other, on the cart. As it moved off, they would bid them goodbye for the very last time.

Lussià-dudù had been one of the first to pass away. Seròp had found her one evening stretched out on the floor, the pupils of her eyes turned back in her head, her body still warm. He had waked her corpse all the night in the light of a candle and said the prayers he had learnt from her. The next morning, he had carried her over his shoulder and walked across the camp, solemn as a priest, to lay her down gently on one corner of the cart, begging the coachman not to cover her with anyone else's body.

«Take care of my mother», he had implored the man.

Then, as the wheel had begun to creak on the dirt track leading to the cemetery, Seròp had felt his legs sag and had collapsed in despair among the puddles of mud.

«Well then? When do you two intend speaking?» said Satèn to the children as she hoisted her load onto her back. «Can't you see how lonely I am?» she added.

The twins smiled and gurgled so sweetly at her that she,

heartened again, could only smile back. Then she drew the heavy curtain aside and took a peep outside. In the yard across the street, Fitìl's chair was empty and on the ground were a handful of sunflower seeds and hulls. She had stayed in for days now, sick, and rumor had it that she was on her last legs.

The rest of the camp was swathed in darkness.

Satèn knotted her headscarf and slid out silent as a shadow. A puff of warm, damp air brushed her cheeks and she felt that nature itself was promising her a better tomorrow and that, if only she hung on in there with all her might, just a little while longer, things would take a turn for the better. She walked on, her face bearing the signs of fatigue: she had worked very hard, bent over, embroidering slippers for hours on end and it showed. Only a few more remained to reach thirty, the quota established by Caputo. Then, Seròp would bring them down to him and show them off with great pride. «See how beautiful they are», he would have boasted before receiving the agreed sum of fifteen Drachmas.

At the mere thought of that money Satèn quivered. For days now, they had almost nothing left to eat, and she had even gone into the fields to pick edible herbs so they might put something on the table. It seemed too good to be true that soon she would be able to dispose of a similar sum. She would buy meat, butter, warm rolls; maybe a new toy for the children, a shirt for Seròp and, if there was anything left over, maybe some perfume for herself, roses and cinnamon, like Lucy's.

«So what would you like your mamma to buy for you?» she asked the twins, then waiting a moment as if expecting an answer.

For months now, Satèn had the habit of speaking to them as if they were grown-ups and could understand everything she said. She desperately needed to do this, because the children were her only company.

The boys gurgled incomprehensibly. She assumed they could not agree on the toy to buy and that each one wanted something different.

«If that's your attitude, I won't buy you anything», she cautioned them.

They looked up at her in wide-eyed, puzzled silence. Then, one of them began to smile only to be mirrored immediately by the other and, so, Satèn, recovering her good humor, hugged them both as closely as she could.

Shortly afterwards she reached the top of a barren, bare little hill, studded with greenish rocks which the eroding wind had sculpted into strange forms. One looked like an angry roaring lion. Satèn straddled it, settling the bag containing her children over its wide-open jaws.

«Your father is somewhere out there, doing his best for us», she told the babies as her gaze wandered in the vague direction of the Kryoneri mountains, «You two are the fruit of our love. You were a surprise, because we weren't expecting both of you in one go. But as soon as you left my belly — because that's where you were, in here, for nine months», and she passed her hand over her midriff, «we were overjoyed.»

Clasping them even closer, as if to assure herself they were safe right there beside her, she added:

«You are my sun and my moon. Could one of you exist without the other?»

Then she turned their bodies around so that they faced each other.

«Look at one another», she ordered them.

The two little brothers smiled at this amusing game their mother had just invented. They stretched their arms out and touched each other's hands, each fingertip-to-tip with its counterpart. It was funny to watch two identical little creatures act in specular unison. Their mother then took hold of their wrists and tore off the little colored wristlets, now very much frayed. Then she wound the two lengths of thread around each other, until they became one, and offered them up to the wind.

«There we are», she breathed as she watched the red and green offering vanish in the dark. «Now you're inseparable.»

She straightened up and heaved a deep sigh, her eyes raised to the star-studded sky.

«*Surp Astvàtz*», she invoked the Heavenly Father, listing her arms on high. «You watch over them.»

«A curse on whoever may wish them harm!» she shouted in rage, as if overcome by some strange premonition. «Forever!», she concluded, turning to the moon as it peeped out from behind a cloud. It was a full moon and, with its silver halo around her head, Satèn looked like a Madonna and Two Children.

The universe listened in silence, aware, perhaps, of the bad luck about to rain down on their heads.

Seròp advanced slowly, his sack on his back, along the main road to Neochori.

He was exhausted after three days walking in the rain and wind. To keep his strength up, he had eaten the *aghinari* — thorny, spiky, wild artichokes — some black currants and mulberries. He had drunk rainwater and a cup of goat's milk a compassionate shepherd had offered him one day. In the daytime he rested in the shade of some tree, at night he slept in the shelter of some ramshackle byre.

He had gone into all the villages he had come across, offering his lovely handsewn *kundure* to the people.

«Try them on at least», he would say, laying them out on a sheet of canvas in the main square.

Some passers-by would stop, wary and after a furtive glance at the merchandise, just make a face. One old lady went so far as to reach out and touch a pair. But nobody wanted to try them on, let alone buy.

«Where are you from? We want no foreigners here», one man had told him with a defiant air.

«You lot bring disease», another had added. Someone went so far as to threaten him by raising his fists and trampling on his wares.

«Away with you. Go back to where you belong!»

The people were frightened. Malaria had reached these villages too, spreading suffering and death.

Seròp had arrived in Neochori late one afternoon. His meanderings had led him far into the hinterland and to this village at the end of a remote valley.

As he gazed at the main street of the little town, he could not understand why there was not a soul in sight. The square was empty, the door of *kafeneio* padlocked. The houses, their shutters closed, were as silent as the tomb.

Suddenly, from behind a crumbling wall, he saw a small funeral procession approaching headed by a priest, his black cassock flapping in the wind, his long hair gathered up into a topknot, his hands holding a cross and a censer which he swayed gently. Right behind the celebrant, Seròp caught sight of two coffins, one, small and white, certainly that of a child. The air was alive with the laments, cries and groans of the mourners. A young man, supported by another - presumably his brother, given the resemblance - stumbled over the cobblestones. Distraught, his beard unkempt, he frequently stretched out his right hand to touch the caskets as if expressing the wish to join those inside. Beside him walked a little girl, his daughter by all appearances, who held his left hand and rested her head against his side.

«Where's mamma, where's my baby brother?» she asked between sobs.

Stunned by this excruciating scene, Seròp halted so abruptly that his sack fell from his shoulders, scattering slippers all over the ground. Flustered, he bent down to gather them up. When he rose again, the cortège had stopped right in front of him. The coffins were being lowered to the ground for the blessing and the priest turned around to face them.

«In the name of the Father and of the Son and of the Holy Ghost», recited the pastor swinging the censer, «dust thou art and unto dust thou shalt return.»

Then, at his nod, the lids were removed from the coffins.

In the larger one, Seròp saw a beautiful young woman, with long straight chestnut hair and a slender face, wearing an ample dress in black lace which highlighted the waxen color of her complexion. In the small casket lay a little boy, an angel, his hands joined gently on his chest, his nails yellowed by the cruel ravages of death.

«No!» shouted the young man, breaking away from his brother and throwing himself upon his wife's body, raising her head up from the pillow strewn with flowers, clasping her to himself and showering her with passionate kisses. He then fell on the other casket, embracing the corpse of his little son knowing it would be for the very last time.

«Why, oh, why?» he sobbed over and over again, the tears streaming down his cheeks. Seròp was unable to look away from the scene, at once macabre and heartrending. Sympathizing with the young father, Seròp was so distraught that he had the impression he could see Satèn's features in the dead woman's face.

Then, as the procession went on its way, he asked God why, in His infinite mercy, he did not bring those bodies back to life. Overcome by ineffable fear, he began to run at breakneck speed as far away as he could from that place, dragging his sack behind him, even losing some of the slippers as he went. He could not have cared less. All he wanted was to get straight back home, hold his Satèn in his arms, tell her how much he loved her, how lucky he had been to find a wife as precious as her; how content he was to have the twins whom he loved more than anything in the whole world.

He wanted, above all, to promise her that he would find a dignified way of supporting them all, that none of them would suffer from cold or hunger ever again.

Satèn was in the throes of a raging fever.

On returning home, she found she was shivering with the cold so, having put the twins to bed -her teeth chattering in her head- she had got straight into bed, wrapping the quilt around her body. For years now she had not felt that sense of bewilderment and numbness that had always ushered in one of her epileptic fits.

«Oh my God, what's happening to me?» she asked herself, frightened. Who would take care of the babies were she to fall ill, she wondered anxiously as her temperature rose. She wanted to remain vigilant, not to yield to the attack, but soon her strength forsook her, and after she had retched violently several times, she collapsed back onto the bed, exhausted.

«My love...» called Seròp, in utter terror.

He had just got back, drenched to the skin because a raging storm had burst out bringing a downpour of rain, blinding flashes of lighting and deafening thunder which made the Earth tremble.

«Satèn-*giàn*, what's the matter?» he shouted as he shook her by the shoulder. Then he felt her all over. He did not remember her being so thin and worn out. But now, poor woman, she was roasting, giving off heat you could feel at a distance.

«What can I do?» Seròp asked himself in anguish as he examined his wife's face, her yellowing skin, her closed purple eyelids, her lips chapped and stained with vomit. She was still breathing, but for how long?

He was petrified with fear. He could not even think, find a way of helping her. He felt he was being sucked down, faster and faster, into quicksand.

«Help!» he felt like yelling.

But there was nobody there to hear or give him a hand.

Just then, a flash of lightning illuminated the cradle.

One of the twins had woken up and was staring at him in silence. Seròp had the sensation that the child's eyes were full of the scorn he felt for his father's inertia, his inability to deal with the trials of life. He noticed the baby's position. It was always the same one; the one who insisted on facing outward, so, it seemed, to scrutinize him better, judge him with that know-all air of his, mocking him, sneering at him.

The evil one, the jinx.

The devil in person.

Years later he would wonder, damning himself, whether that notion had been suggested by despair or, worse still, a mere, low ploy he used to absolve himself for what he was about to do.

He pounced on the baby in the cradle. The child drew back, clinging to his brother and pressing his face close to his chest, one of his legs entwined around his twin's. Nonetheless, the father pulled him up violently and out of the cradle, paying no heed whatsoever to the tiny boy's screams, prizing him out of the arms of his twin who also wailed desperately, as if perfectly aware of what was happening.

When Seròp left the house, holding the child wrapped in blankets in his arms, the sky was rent by a flash of lightning so strong that it blinded him and made him stagger.

«*Meghà Asdvàtz*, May God forgive me!» he howled as the earth trembled beneath his feet struck by a deafening thunder bolt.

He reached the port in the pouring rain, ran across to the clearing where the lorries for Athens were parked, and looked around for Jivan, in whom he was about to place all his trust. He soon recognized the truck with the yellow cabin which stood out among all the others, parked in a line waiting for the storm to end. None of the drivers wanted to set out for the capital in that downpour. Seròp approached the vehicles, sticking close to the wall of a building, the child hidden in the ample folds of his raincoat.

«I see you have come slinking back», said the driver, maliciously, from under a lean-to near the truck.

Seròp pretended not to understand.

«Brother, you must help me», he implored.

Jivan took another pull on his cigarette, straightened the peak of his cap, gave Seròp a sideways glance but said nothing more.

«I have him; he's here, under this…» Seròp explained indicating his raincoat.

Jivan burst out laughing.

«The merchandise?»

«My wife is ill, she might even die, and I've no money for a doctor or medicine.»

The other shrugged. «What the hell do I care?»

«If I give him away, I may have some chance of saving her and the other baby, otherwise we'll all die.»

Jivan turned on his heels and was about to make off.

«I'm begging you…» said Seròp his trembling hand on the driver's shoulder.

«That was a bargain to jump at then, at the time. It's no longer valid», Jivan replied.

Seròp overtook him and blocked his way.

«Look! He's beautiful», he whispered, gently lifting up a corner of his coat. The child's face peered out. The baby batted his eyelids against the glare, annoyed too at the rain wetting his little face, then looked around mesmerized and bewildered like a cub who has just ventured outside of his den.

Jivan threw Seròp a glance and snorted.

«I don't know. I can't guarantee anything.»

«He's healthy and good-looking, where will they find another like him?»

«I see you've learnt how to make a sale.»

«If my wife dies…» said Seròp, and burst into tears.

«Stop it!», ordered the other looking at him in scorn. «Wait here and don't move. I'll make a phone call.»

He discarded his cigarette with the flick of a finger, pulled the collar of his jerkin up, tugged his cap down and started to run in the pouring rain. Seròp watched him as he disappeared among the people flocking into the custom house. He screwed up his eyes to read the time on the nearby clock. It was already half past eight in the morning though it was still quite dark. A wail from the baby made him start. The child was kicking wildly under the coat, writhing as if gasping for air. Seròp noticed two abandoned crates in a corner of the lean-to. He dragged them over, sat on one and used the other as a cradle for the baby.

Then he simply waited for Jivan to return, his eyes moving constantly between the custom house door and the clock tower. He was trembling like a leaf, his damp clothes drying into him. He had had nothing to eat or drink for a whole day.

As soon as Jivan reappeared he jumped to his feet, his heart in his mouth, lifted the child up, held him tight, breathing in his scent, the scent of home.

«You're lucky!» the driver called out to him.

Seròp straightened.

«Pay attention to what I have to say.» Jivan's tone was brusque and sharp. «No questions, no second thoughts», he warned, brushing him with the tip of his cigarette. «Agreed?»

Seròp nodded. The other hesitated an instant, trying to decide whether he could trust the other to stick to the arrangement.

«This is the address», he said at last. «Number 7 Villari Street, you press "Three Alpha" on the intercom. It's near Omonia Square, in the heart of Athens.»

As Seròp listened to him his eyes clouded over.

«Did you get that?»

«Yeah.»

«Repeat it to me.»

«Number 7 Villari Street, Three Alpha, Omonia Square», said Seròp.

«Buzz and go up to the third floor; Martiròs will be there waiting for you. Got it?»

«Yeah»

«Have you the money for the train?»

«No. I thought we'd go together in the lorry.»

Jivan laughed out loud.

«I wouldn't be caught dead in your company» he grunted and poked a finger at him.

Seròp lowered his head. His feet squished with mud.

«Here you are», said the other, tossing him a few coins.

«Only for the one-way trip, mind you. You'll have enough to pay for the return ticket.»

Seròp grabbed the money.

«Well, I must be off!» Jivan exclaimed looking at the sky that was clearing up at last.

He walked off in the direction of his truck, opened the door and hauled himself up into the cabin.

«I've been a friend to you, haven't I?» he shouted from a distance, leaning out the window and raising his cap slightly by way of a salute.

«Thanks» mumbled Seròp.

He stood there, motionless, the baby in one arm, his other hand clutching the money Jivan had given him.

12

This evening we come to you singing Hope
Along the pathway from the field,
oh haylofts, haylofts,
through your gloomy walls
let the new sun shine in
onto the verdant roofs
let the moon sift flour. [...]
This evening we come to you singing the Bread,
Down the pathway to the barn,
oh granaries, granaries...

«Why did you choose this poem?» Wolf interrupted him, overcome with emotion and sniffing just a little. Mikael had an innate bent for acting.

«Because I adore Daniel Varujan, and think *The Song of the Bread* is one of his best works.»

«A rather banal answer, Master Delalian.» commented Wolf, leaning up against the window ledge, fiddling with his reading glasses.

Mikael heaved a sigh. He watched the chalk-dust spiral gently in a ray of sunshine and thought of the photograph in his anthology: the poet dressed in a dark double-breasted suit. He could have held a conference on the reasons for his choice but decided to disclose only one.

«Because he was a student in this college and because I wanted to pay homage to him», he exclaimed. «I admit, I still shudder every time I pass the door of the room that was once his.»

He remembered how he had felt the first time he had entered that room, so small it resembled a cell. It was down at the very end of one of the dormitories, one of the six they reserved for senior pupils.

«This is where Daniel Varujan used to sleep», they had told him, and his heart had skipped a beat.

«I understand», murmured Wolf. «Were you familiar with *The Song of the Bread* before now?»

«Yes, though I'd never plucked up the courage to read it out loud.»

«Meaning?»

Mikael bit his lip.

«It is the last thing Daniel wrote before they murdered him. *The Song* remained unfinished, he was about to complete it but they stabbed him to death. He's a martyr of our people's genocide; this poem is his last will, a testament, in a way.»

Outside the college, the bells of the Carmelite church began to toll and this made the atmosphere inside the room even gloomier. The boys were all silent. Very few decades had passed since the Turkish massacre of the Armenians. Memories of their extermination were still very much alive and the wounds bled again at the least mention of those terrible events.

«Father!» said Hampò, seated at the back of the class, asking for permission to say something.

Wolf nodded and the boy stood up.

«At home, in Syria, in the Der-Zor desert», he began, faltering a little, «they say you can still find human remains, those of our fellow-countrymen deported there.» He reddened, intimidated by Wolf's penetrating gaze. Fearing his words might be inopportune, he hesitated a little before continuing.

«My father, when he was young, went on a trip to the town of Al Mansurah. Once he got off the coach, he took a walk in the nearby area where, digging a hand into the sand, he discovered a gold cross with a name and date inscribed on the back»

He slipped a finger beneath his pullover and drew out a chain and a small cross which he then showed the class. «This is it», he said turning it over awkwardly and reading, «Hampartsum, nineteen-hundred-and-fifteen».

Wolf straightened up and righted his shoulders out of sheer respect.

«Years later, when I was born and they baptised me, they decided to call me after that little boy who perished in the desert.»

Hampò turned to his classmates, his voice a little broken and added,

«That's why, since then, I've always borne not only his name, but also his cross».

Aznavour sprung to his feet. At first it was as if he wanted to say somethings. Instead he simply remained there, his head held high, his lips tight, like someone standing solemnly to attention. Keropé followed suit, then a few seconds after that, Levòn from Chile, Sempò from the Lebanon, Aram the Greek, Flick and Flock, the Hungarian cousins, and soon the entire class was on its feet.

All erect, motionless, lost in a sorrow they all shared.

«Mikael!»

The boy spun around.

«Where are you going?»

«I'm taking my watch to Father Nicoghòs.»

Wolf smiled. «Ah, you trust him, then?»

Padre Nicoghòs, nicknamed Tick-Tock, was a monk who hailed from Istanbul and had resided in the college for many years now. He was not a teacher nor did he work in administration. His only task was to mend timepieces of all kinds: wrist and pocket watches, grandfather and cuckoo clocks. He had a cubby-hole on the central, second-floor corridor, right next to the laboratories. There, Tick-Tock meticulously and with amazing enthusiasm fixed watches and clocks belonging to the students as well as to the whole of the Laguna's Armenian community.

«What's wrong with it?» Wolf inquired.

Mikael turned his wrist over and pointed at his father's old Omega.

In the middle of the face a cloud of condensation fogged up the glass.

«It must have got wet. I have to wind it all the time, otherwise it keeps stopping.»

They continued down the corridor as far as the watchmaker's

room. A bulb, swinging from the ceiling, lit up the tiny place, empty for the moment.

«Padre Nicoghòs!» Mikael called out, leaning over the workbench full of with cogs, springs and screws. A Lilliputian tweezers and screwdriver glinted in the light.

«Maybe he's hiding under the table», Wolf joked. «He's sure to be in the chapel. This is the time he usually prays.»

The boy nodded, a little annoyed.

«How are things, Mikael?» asked Wolf as they retraced their steps.

«Pardon?»

«Life in college. Do you like it?»

The boy was reluctant to answer.

«After Dick ran away, I noticed you were troubled», added the teacher, «you raved in your sleep.»

«It was a pretty distressing experience, father.»

Wolf threw him one of his inquisitor's looks. «And what about the episode in the dining-hall? You practically fainted!»

«I was suddenly overcome by a violent sense of nausea.»

The teacher slowed his pace.

«Mikael, you know we're here to help you. I mean, if ever something should happen, anything, you can feel free to come to me. As a friend, an older brother.»

They were going down the stairs to the floor below.

«I'd prefer to hear things directly from you rather than have others come and tell me about you», he added in a low voice. «Don't you agree?»

Mikael was saved by the arrival of Tick-Tock, bounding up the stairs at an amazing speed. His slim figure and eternally jovial, smiling countenance gave him the air of a boy who had simply grown old.

«I was looking for you!» Mikael exclaimed, indicating his watch.

The monk stopped and looked as if trying hard to recall something.

«An Omega, isn't it?» he asked, after a few seconds.

«Yes.»

«Calibre Noir movement?» he said glancing at the watch again.

Mikael, puzzled, did not know what to say.

«You're lucky to have a jewel like that. He is, isn't he, father Keshishian?»

Wolf smiled in amusement.

«Come along with me. We'll operate on it immediately and without anesthetic.»

And linking arms with Mikael, he led him back upstairs to his operating theatre.

«If we run, we should make it.»

Francesca looked down at her shoes, a pair of worn-out, misshapen suede slip-ons.

«I can't, Mikael.»

«You can, come on!»

And so, they ran, hand-in-hand, with childlike enthusiasm racing against the clock. They had just a little over thirty minutes all to themselves as Mikael had to be back at the college before three. But in the meantime…

«Wolf is not well so he's called off his lesson», he explained.

«Therefore, you and your cronies felt a sudden urge to go to confession, eh?»

They both burst out laughing. It was just one of those carefree, euphoric moments when nothing could trouble them except their unspoken mutual attraction.

«Where would you like to go?» Francesca asked him.

«I've no idea. You choose. You're the Venetian.»

«I'd like to take you to Rialto.»

«That's fine by me.»

«Come on, then, this way», said the girl dragging him through shortcuts that only the locals knew.

At a certain point, out of breath, they stopped in a small square in front of a palazzo with arched windows.

«This is the Naranzaria!» Francesca announced.

Then looking right they beheld a truly enchanting sight.

«Rialto», they whispered in unison.

The white marble bridge, like a majestic sailing ship made of stone, straddled the Grand Canal. The two adolescents lingered a while in the square, uncertain where to go next, surrounded by the buzz of the crowd wandering among the stalls. They could make out the gleam of the shop windows on the bridge. Rialto's goldsmiths were famous for their masterpieces.

«Have you ever been to the goldsmiths' shops?»

Mikael shook his head.

«Why not go to the fish market?» he suggested.

«All right, let's go!»

In the colonnade on the banks of the canal, stood a row of stalls with their colorful awnings. The paving stones were wet and smelled of brine. Several greedy seagulls circled above all that abundance lying there for the asking. Men in rubber waders glorified their wares at the top of their voices. Bass and bream, twitching anchovies and sardines, shellfish and sea food, all on display in wooden crates garnished with slices of lemon and bunches of yellow-green seaweed.

«Two Liras the kilo!» shouted one of the fishmongers as he watered the silver mackerel.

That strong pungent smell reminded Mikael of the small fish markets back in Athens and he thought of his father who had been mad about fish and convinced it was awfully good for your health. «All that comes from the sea does you good», he would say, «eat your fill of it, my son.» In the college they never served any, only stock fish, so that the mere thought of a fresh fish fry-up would make his mouth water.

He was suddenly distracted by a nearby commotion. One daredevil gull had swooped down on the stall in front of him and, having speared a handful of sardines, had flown away like some Levantine thief. A truly amusing scene.

«Franca!»

A sharp, nasal voice made Francesca freeze. Mikael turned around to see a slim lady with greying blond hair and the same gold-flecked eyes as his friend's.

«What are you doing here?» the woman exclaimed, putting her shopping bag down on the ground. «Weren't you supposed to be at home doing your homework?»

Francesca just stood there speechless, still as a pillar of salt.

«And who may I ask is this young gentleman?» she continued

«Good afternoon, ma'am. My name's Mikael», he said offering her his hand, which she didn't shake. She simply nodded and looked him over from head to foot: his unkempt hair, his sloppy turtle-necked pullover, his baggy canvas trousers. He would certainly have cut a better figure in his school uniform.

«Home!», she ordered, shoving her daughter in front of her.

«But mamma, I...»

Francesca was looking for something to say by way of excuse, when a resounding slap across the face made her jump and stifle a cry of pain. Mikael felt his soul being pierced to the quick. For one split second he toyed with the idea of telling this woman that it had been all his idea, make his feelings known, confess his love for that delicious creature who smelled of orange blossom and now held an important place in his heart. However, he did nothing, simply let her be led away, under the astonished eyes of the onlookers.

«*Da novéo tuto se beo*, young couples get away with murder», mocked one of the fishmongers.

This made the other vendors laugh and shook Mikael out of his lethargy.

«Francesca!» he shouted.

But the girl had vanished already.

13

Stalin's death has deprived the Soviet Union of its leader, the workers of the world of an indisputable, steady guide. Stalin enters history with an enormous amount of work and huge numbers of projects to his credit [...]. Certain that Stalin's work will be brought to completion, it is with profound emotion that we Socialists bow before the mortal remains of Lenin's successor and heir and convey our most heartfelt condolences to the Soviet government and peoples. No other head of state, upon his death, has left a void as great as that of comrade Stalin. Since yesterday there is something missing from the world's equilibrium.
—Pietro Nenni, 6th of March 1953

Wolf laid the *Avanti* — the Italian Socialist Party's daily newspaper — down on his desk and reflected on this important news item. He dwelt, in particular, on the closing remark of socialist leader, Nenni, which placed the accent on the precariousness of world politics, something that worried him too.

What would happen to Armenia now that this great statesman was dead? Father Keshishian had heard about Stalin when he first landed in Venice. As soon as he had arrived from Istanbul, he had been assigned a cell in the monastery on the island of San Lazzaro, where he had spent his novitiate. Father Athanàs, an elderly priest, had told him the story of a certain *Bepi del Giasso* — Joe of the Ice — a young Georgian who, as far back as 1907, had escaped the clutches of the Czarist police. Bepi, an exponent of the Bolshevist political current, had fled from Russia on a merchant ship carrying grain from Odessa to Ancona. The young revolutionary had wandered around a number of Italian cities before ending up in Venice where he had found refuge among the Armenians, because, as the elderly prelate maintained, he could speak Armenian and knew how to serve mass according to both the Orthodox and Latin rites. Furthermore, he knew how to ring the bells in keeping with the liturgical requirements of these two denominations.

«What do you think of that? Everyone has been through here!» father Athanàs had exclaimed. «Venice has always been the center of the universe.»

Wolf had looked at him in wonderment, unable to grasp what the older man was really getting at. He had heard of the painters, writers, politicians who had found a safe haven in the Armenian monastery, like Lord Byron, for example, but when the abbot spoke to him of the legendary Bepi, Wolf had not had the foggiest idea whom he meant.

«Soon, that verger became famous all over the world with a new name, Stalin, meaning man of steel, the most feared political condottiere of all times», the old man had continued, leaving Wolf in utter astonishment.

«But why did he leave the island?» the novice had asked an instant later. Father Athanas had simply laughed out loud.

«He was as mad as a hatter. He'd got it into that stubborn head of his to ring the bells only the Orthodox way. At the hegumen's first reprimand he had packed his bags and run away, back to Russia.»

For a long time afterwards, Wolf had been content to consider Stalin simply as the bell ringer of Venice's Armenian island. He had always imagined that between the statesman and his people there was some kind of special link, blessed by fate. What Stalin had done seemed to confirm this notion. Thanks to him, after decades of suffering, the downtrodden Armenian people, he believed, had found a strong, respectable country belonging to a union excelling in industry and science, with a solid economy, where hunger no longer existed and everyone was guaranteed food, work and an education. Like a true bell ringer summoning the faithful to church, Stalin had permitted the Armenians of the diaspora to find work in their native land, provided them with a safe haven and allowed them to leave those countries where they had been subjected to continuous humiliation and scorn at the hands of those who had no knowledge of history and considered them illiterate nomads, worse still, little more than a barbarian subspecies from the Caucasian highlands.

Wolf was convinced of this. Comrade Stalin had been the undiscussed architect and promoter of that homeland they had all so ardently desired for so long: the Socialist Soviet Republic of Armenia.

He took off his glasses and nibbling on one of the shafts, he took another look at the newspaper. On the left-hand side of the front page was a photograph of Stalin. He lifted up the paper to take a closer look at the picture: unfortunately, just above that thick slightly upturned moustache a smudge of ink had covered the face. So, the priest had to content himself with admiring the uniform which, although here it was in black and white, he could imagine turf-colored golden pips on the shoulders, red stripes on the lapel and the ever-present red star, shining on the left.

He pondered for a few more seconds and then, finally, decided to bring the newspaper to class.

On the morning of that 6th of March it was not Sergej who sounded the reveille, but the camp's loudspeakers.

Gabriel had arisen to the crackling sound of a military march, cadenced by orders to the prisoners to assemble in the central clearing for urgent communications. The inmates of the camp had rushed outside, some still wearing their pajamas under their jackets, and waited patiently. The comrade commandant of the camp had emerged from his billet—the one with the flag hoisted outside—, climbed up onto the platform, and solemnly announced that:

«At 21.50 last night, Radio Moscow transmitted an item of news that shocked the world. Stalin, Iosif Vissarionovič Džugašvili, President of the USSR's Cabinet of Ministers and Secretary of the Central Committee of the CPSU, is dead».

Gusts of wind distorted his words making the announcement practically incomprehensible. Some of the prisoners, still half asleep, thought it regarded some new kind of punishment about to be meted out to them.

«His life has been a concrete and unforgettable example of devotion to the cause of the working class and the Revolution. We are distraught at the loss of the great leader of the Soviet people and of all those who aspire to freedom elsewhere.»

«Did I hear that correctly? Stalin is dead?» murmured some of the prisoners, exchanging furtive glances.

The commandant's eyes panned slowly over the crowd which had remained impassable at the announcement. A strange silence, which he was unable to decipher, reigned. Was it due to the sheer laziness of that band of traitors or were they simply stunned and anguished upon hearing the terrible news?

«I repeat, Stalin is dead!» he had howled in indignation.

«Hurrah!» A cap had flown into the air, high enough to be seen even by those in the very last rows.

«It's now or never», another had cried, he too throwing his cap sky-high.

«Yes, we're going home», a group of prisoners had exclaimed. Suddenly the entire camp came to life. The prisoners, having grasped the fact that the tyrant was dead, began to express their feelings in ways that only a little earlier would have been unthinkable: comments of triumph, expressions of hatred, lewd gestures, curses, sighs of relief, murmurs of hope.

Those in charge of the camp, even the guards, seemed to be at a loss and confused.

«What will become of us?» asked an apprehensive sentry posted atop the watchtower.

«Keep calm», another ordered.

To everyone it appeared clear that the passing of Stalin meant the end of a system and the beginning of a process of inevitable change.

Behind him, Gabriel heard someone sobbing. Turning around, he saw Maggot laughing hilariously as he usually did, only this time his eyes were bright with tears.

«I never thought I'd live to see the day», he confessed to Gabriel looking him straight in the eye. «And this I owe you.»

The shiny, black Bosendorfer grand piano stood on a raised platform in the right wing of the Hall of Mirrors, considered the only place worthy to house such prestigious instrument. It had been gifted to the college by one of its benefactors, Manoukian, and was played only on very special, solemn occasions.

«What piece are you studying, Mikael?»

Father Ayvazian's voice echoed through the empty hall. He was sitting with Wolf, in the center row of the chairs that formed a small parterre.

«I thought of Rachmaninov, *Prelude, opus 23, number 5*», the boy answered.

«I hope he will be up to standard by the day of the ceremony», muttered father Soghomon, seated beside Mikael on the piano bench. He was a musician who had come over especially from San Lazzaro to help the boy with this committing task.

«We cannot afford to make a disgrace of ourselves. Kamil Shamoun, the Lebanese president, is a true connoisseur of classical music. It would be better to change the piece», replied the rector, as if issuing an order rather than a piece of advice.

«What does the pianist think?» asked Wolf. Mikael wagged his head from side to side not knowing what to say.

«What better proof than listen to him play?» retorted father Soghomon.

The boy cleared his throat and looked down at the keyboard, then he nervously righted the score. Suddenly the notes on the pentagram looked like a clutter of incomprehensible squiggles and, for a moment, he feared he would find it impossible to play even a children's nursery rhyme.

He began the piece thinking of the angular face of the Russian composer. He was well acquainted with the tormented life of Sergei Vasilyevich Rachmaninov, his anguish, his sorrow and he concentrated on the piece with the sole intention of trying to interpret the piece as the composer had conceived it, placing the accent on the sweet melancholia of life, its unfulfilled expectations, the disappointing utopias and shattered hopes, while also foregrounding humanity's unshakable desire for survival in the face of hardship, mustering up all its energies.

The notes invaded the grand hall, caressing the frescoes, the gilded stuccos, the antique mirrors. Mikael moved his head to the rhythm of the music, its impelling tempo, requiring a sure touch and noteworthy precision. At times like these he had the exhilarating sensation that he was all one with his instrument. Soon his brow was beaded with perspiration, but he continued to play with passionate eagerness, beyond this world, bent on surpassing the spatio-temporal confines of existence, losing himself in that ecstasy that only music can bring.

The piece ended in a short cascade of notes, the pianist's hands flying swiftly over the keys to the final light cadence, which brought this excellent performance to a an almost silent conclusion. Pianissimo.

Immediately afterwards, Mikael's fingers remained motionless on the keyboard, uncertain of their function in a world from which music had suddenly disappeared.

«Fantastic!» Wolf exulted unable to contain his enthusiasm.

«Not bad, was it?» asked father Soghomon, seeking the rector's approval.

«Well, I actually thought it was going to be worse», Ayvazian conceded, «although there was a note missing from the first bar», he added, rising.

«Wait», Wolf exclaimed, stopping him, «you haven't heard *Dlè Yamàn* yet. Mikael will sing it at the end of the ceremony.»

The rector smiled, something he rarely did.

«I have no doubt that he will sing it perfectly. Almighty God has made Master Delalian the gift of a truly beautiful voice.» And he walked away in the direction of the marble columns and his bare room.

«I think that went off well», Wolf said addressing the two seated at the piano.

«Yes», answered father Soghomon, loosening the white collar beneath his cassock.

«Mikael?»

The boy shook his head. «No, actually», he said. «That missing note was an unforgivable mistake.»

«You will excuse us, father Soghomon», said Wolf catching a hint of irony in Mikael's words, «but I urgently need to speak to Mikael privately in my study»

He rose and waited for the boy to come down from the platform and together they set off without a word until they entered the office.

«Sit down», said the teacher sharply as he closed the door behind them.

Mikael took a seat. On the desk, beside a small copy of the Bible, stood a half-empty cup of tea.

«Listen here, young man», began the priest before sitting down in the armchair «your behavior is unacceptable. This is a school, not your own private fan club. Only self-criticism will help you to excel in what you are good at. Talent is worthless unless accompanied by commitment and dedication.»

Wolf's words came out like a volley. He was red in the face with anger.

«How dare you, therefore, feel you are special?! The road is long and you are only at the start.»

«I was only expressing my opinion. As long as we live in a free country that should be my right, no?», retorted Mikael.

«Meaning?»

«I have decided to avoid useless hypocrisy. You can't always silence me the way you did the other day.»

Wolf's scowl expressed his intention to appraise the boy's every word with the severest criticism.

«What are you referring to?»

«When you brought the newspaper with Stalin's obituary into class the other day.»

«Well?»

«I didn't agree. Stalin was not the magnificent hero described in the article. He was a tyrant, a monster that only totalitarian systems can spawn. Why did you not allow me to express my point of view?»

Wolf was caught off guard and was wondering what to answer when the boy surprised him with an aphorism he had often quoted in class: «*Je désapprouve ce que vous dites mais je me battrai jusqu'à la mort pour que vous ayez le droit de le dire.*[5], Francois-Marie Arouet, alias Voltaire».

Mikael almost whispered this universal dictum which did not need to be shouted from the rooftops.

«I have here a list of the names and now I shall read them out», the camp's commandant announced addressing the prisoners lined up in equidistant rows.

«So: Suubat Kazaka, Igor Sheghevili, Victor Kristenko, Gabriel Gazarian…»

Gabriel started upon hearing the name by which nobody had addressed him for months now. In the billet, the prisoners did not use their real names. You guessed by the tone of voice who was being spoken to. If anything, you were called by a nickname. Gabriel's was simply Armenian.

From the day when Stalin's death had been announced the entire gulag — especially the guards — were on tenterhooks. There were fears of fresh episodes of bloodshed and revenge all over the country and it was rumored that the Kremlin was planning to make radical administrative changes to the camps. Many of the commandants, sentries and prison guards were literally terrified. Each man tried desperately to do his utmost to prove his commitment to improvement of this forced labor system and justify his own role. Suddenly, it had become an absolute priority to reawaken this sleeping elephant.

«Those who have been named shall line up here», ordered the commandant indicating a spot to his left. Nine prisoners advanced from the ranks to form a new line. Gabriel was surprised to find Maggot there too. The fact was that, until then, he had no idea what his real name was.

«I'm Gerasim Miusov», said Maggot, «nice to meet you, companion Gazarian», he added with an air of complicity as he stood right behind him. He was still limping, although he had spent a month in the infirmary.

«You nine are leaving tomorrow.», said the commandant, «We've received instructions to transfer you to another camp, where you will be better able to serve the fatherland.»

The prisoners, worried and confused, made a feeble effort to voice their disagreement.

«Silence!» warned the officer while two guards approached, their rifles at the ready.

«Tell us at least where you're sending us!» one of them shouted.

«Just think about working, *kontrik*, you still have many more years to serve!» thundered the commandant, sizing him up.

Maggot whispered in Gabriel's ear: «The uranium mines. In the north, in the bloody back of beyond».

«Attention!» growled the officer. «I haven't finished yet. I have more names to read.»

As he continued calling out these names the numbers of prisoners destined for other camps increased.

Many of the projects begun in Altaj had ground to a halt; the site where Gabriel had worked had been suspended, seeing that the Ministry for Justice had deemed it «of no use to the economic needs of the nation». Orders from above privileged projects favoring the development of technology and industry. The particular focus nowadays was on the extraction of gold and other minerals, in particular uranium used to fuel nuclear reactors. It was, therefore, mandatory to colonize areas rich in these materials, like the legendary territory of the *ciukci* tribe, the «bear worshippers», with no regard for the consequences. This meant that the northernmost gulags, devoted to the extraction and enrichment of uranium, were veritable extermination camps. Nobody ever survived there more than a year, because of the prohibitive environmental conditions, above all, as a result of deathly radiation.

Everyone who went there, died there, prisoners and guards alike.

«We'll bite the dust, Armenian» Maggot joked, and then broke out into his usual cackle, mocking destiny as always.

«So, you're leaving.»

Gabriel had come outside to smoke one last machorka in the camp where he had spent six months of his young life. It was a brilliantly clear night, the wind less cutting than usual, the sky all a-sparkle with millions of stars.

«Yeah», he replied, turning towards Gara, whose voice he had recognized as his billet-mate drew closer rolling a cigarette.

«Are you worried?»

«I've nothing to lose, one place is the same as another.»

Gara nodded. Since his father's death, Gabriel had clammed up, become aloof. He no longer exchanged even the odd word he used to before that. He remained on his own, as if he felt the need to grieve alone, something practically impossible, given the promiscuity of the camp.

«You're taking Maggot away from us...» he joked with a touch of contempt.

Gabriel pretended not to hear. He inhaled deeply and blew a

big puff of smoke into the air; a falling star drew a luminous arc in the sky.

«If you don't feel like a chat, if I'm breaking your balls, you only have to say so», snapped Gara, vexed.

«No, you don't trouble me», Gabriel replied. «being here has taught me a lot, in a certain sense...» he added.

«Really?»

«Yes. Not to judge by appearances, for example.»

A dog barked in the distance to be answered by another. Gabriel faced those ice-cold eyes that continued to pierce him.

«I believed you», he said, «I was convinced you'd protect my father. Seeing you were so big, strong and bold, I thought your word might mean something.»

He took two steps forward, his cap grazing Gara's chin. «Your size makes you even more ridiculous. I don't know whether your behavior is the result of the wretched life you've led or just your inborn nature. But, I'm telling you, I really pity you. Even Gerasim, whom you despise so much, has far more guts than you.»

Gara grimaced in anger, clenching his fists and preparing to strike him, but that did not make the least impression on the boy.

«There's no use. You don't frighten me anymore». With a smile full of disenchantment, he added «How can one be afraid of a man who is not a man at all?»

There they stood, facing each other, David and Goliath, against the backdrop of that Siberian sky studded with myriads of stars.

Athens, 19th of March 1953

My dear son,

How are you?

Today, I received a letter from father Keshishian. It is somewhat short but it worries me so much that I feel I need to write to you at once.

Your teacher informs me that your behavior is not at all fitting for a student of the Armenian college. «Although he is an intelligent and gifted boy, he is inclined to flaunt discipline, one of the mainstays of our educational system», are his textual words. He also informed me about your discussion on Stalin and the arrogant way in which you contradicted him. You are not in college to preach your political views — a boy with a little more worldly wisdom would not — but to study and learn.

What is happening to you, my dear child?

I needn't tell you how displeased and disappointed your father would be were he still alive. He had great plans for you, convinced you were so gifted, your character sound, your behavior respectful and tolerant. The choice of this college imposes a number of sacrifices on us — your being away, the enormous expense involved, our not being able to see and embrace each other as often as we'd like — but in exchange, I always thought you would uphold the family's honor and name.

In three weeks' time it will be the third anniversary of your father's death which this year will coincide with Easter. Like every other Sunday, I shall go to the cemetery, bring him flowers and have a little talk with him. It's the only place I know where I can still find that peace of mind I fail to find anywhere else. What can I say to him about you?

Every evening I pray God to bless you and give you the courage and wisdom to face the difficulties and challenges of this life.

I want you to know that I am simply counting the days until you come back to Athens.

You know how much I love you.

Hugs and kisses

from your adoring,

Mamma.

P.S. These flowers are from the tree in our garden you used to call the "bride" when you were little because it was all dressed in white. The petals I am sending you are the first of this year's blossoms.

Mikael turned the envelope upside down. They had delivered it to him slit open, the letter attached to it with a clip. A small shower of white petals fluttered out, landing on his face and on the pillow of the bed where he was lying. The fragrance of wild orange blossom filled his nostrils. He thought of the «bride» in the little garden at home, but also the trees bordering the streets in the district where they lived. On his way home from school, he used to pull off a few buds and rub them between his fingers to release the perfume.

Through the dormitory window he could hear the voices of his companions playing football down in the yard. Suddenly, everything seemed so distant and meaningless.

He closed his eyes and thought of his sole *raison d'etre*: Francesca, his own little «bride».

14

The ship pitched and tossed at the mercy of the waves. It creaked and strained as if every rivet which held it together were about to burst. It rose to the top of the crest, where it shuddered a moment, before diving back down into the trough.

Gabriel was huddled up on the tarred floor of the hold, in that dark, narrow space crowded with hundreds of other prisoners. The smell of unclean bodies mingled with the stink of rancid fish failed to disgust him. After months in the gulag his nose had grown accustomed to it.

They had sailed first from the port of Vladivostok, where they had arrived by freight train which, as it made its way eastward, had collected other men and women sentenced to hard labor in the gulags of the north. On the port's main dock, they had been mustered into groups to await the sailing. The women were the first to climb aboard.

«Fresh meat», observed a prisoner sentenced for common crimes who looked them over as they made their way up the gangway, a remark which made some of the other prisoners chortle.

The poor wretches were muffled up in such heavy, shapeless dresses that there was little way of telling what sex they might be, except for the headscarves they wore. They were lined up in a queue like so many ants, then they slowly clambered up the gangplank to the vessel with its two red funnels.

«*Vanya*», Gerasim had whispered reading the red Cyrillic lettering on the prow. «D'ye know what that means?» he had asked Gabriel, who simply shook his head.

«The grace of God», he pointed out, faking profound religiosity. «Remember, it's our stairway to heaven.»

The men had gone on board several hours later, in lashing rain, so dense that it blotted out the line between the sea and the sky on the horizon. As he climbed, Gabriel stopped a moment at a point where the step iron had been corroded by the saltwater. He had suddenly felt the urge to jump overboard and yield to the waves and, for one last time, taste the thrill of freedom, that inalienable human right of which he had been so unjustly deprived. Just then someone behind him had pushed him forward and, as there was no time to be lost, he was forced to climb aboard, to begin a journey he imagined would be without return.

A dim bulb hung from a girder at the end of the hold. It swayed to the surge of the waves making flitting shadows dance in the dark. A few bodies farther on, Gabriel caught a glimpse of Gerasim snoring on the floor. Strangely enough, the presence of this old mate from the camp reassured him, as if he were a bridge to the past, a life-raft they shared, as they were tossed about together on a sea of memories.

At a certain point there was a loud clang as a soldier opened one of the hatches leading up to the deck. A beam of white light flooded the hold.

«Water!» shouted the guard, slowly lowering a metal pail with mess tins hanging from its side.

Immediate turmoil broke out. Waking up, men and women alike hurled themselves against the iron railings which kept them caged in and separate.

«Open up, we're thirsty!» howled the men shaking the iron bars.

«Easy does it!», ordered the guard jangling his heavy bunch of keys. «Ladies first.» he shouted over lewd comments and rude noises.

The women, once free, pounced on the bucket, panting and squabbling over the mess tins. They snatched them from one another's hands, because without one it was impossible to drink.

«Cut it out! There's enough for everyone!»

The golden glow of a head of blond hair captured Gabriel's attention. He approached the grating and, straining his neck, caught sight of the profile of a slim girl patiently waiting on the edge of the group crowding around the pail. When the time came for her to drink, another woman shoved her aside and took her place.

«No!» shouted the guard. «It's her turn now.» He was a stocky type whose tightly buttoned jacket held his chest up. He took the girl by the hand and thrusting the others to one side, led her up to the bucket. Then he filled the tin and handed it to her. «There!», he said looking into her eyes.

Suddenly the voices hushed. This gallant gesture seemed so surreal that it silenced everyone.

She reached out with her slender fingers and took the tin, then drank a mouthful of water, wetting her shining crimson lips.

«Please allow me to take some to my mother. She's got a temperature and cannot even stand up», she whispered, keeping her eyes lowered.

Gabriel held his breath as he observed the scene. The young girl had turned around and the light, falling on her from above, made her look like a vision, a mirage in that emotional desert his soul had become.

«Yes, but first you must tell me your name», answered the guard.

She hesitated a moment as if uncertain of what to say. «Nina», she finally whispered before walking away carrying the tin. When she passed in front of him, Gabriel clutched the grating lest he faint and followed her with his eyes until the darkness of the hold swallowed her up. He just stood there paralyzed by the sight of that gentle apparition, drinking in the perfume left in the wake of her flowing blond hair. He did not even come back to his senses when the sentry opened the gate and his companions fought like cats over a drop of water.

«Here, have some.» said Gerasim offering him a drink from the cup he had stolen from camp number 11.

«Why do they keep us below deck?» asked a white-bearded prisoner.

«On deck they wouldn't be able to control us. Afraid we might make a run for it», responded another as he bit off the head of a smoked herring and swallowed it whole, without chewing it.

«Fiddlesticks», Gerasim contradicted him. «Run where? Throw ourselves into the sea?» And he burst out laughing.

«We are rounding the Japanese coast. They don't want those yellow faces to know what the cargo is.»

«Why? What reason would they have?» the bearded man objected.

Gerasim spat out a fishbone and cleaned his mouth in the sleeve of his jacket. «Because! Better not to arouse the suspicions of the Japanese, let them know what the Russians are up to. They're meant to believe this is a merchant ship or a fishing trawler. Look at what they give us to eat! Herrings and more herrings!»

Gabriel continued to listen, while chewing on the tail of a fish. After the first mouthful, so salty it made his eyes water, the taste grew less unpleasant. The more he held it in his mouth the sweeter it got, as if the saliva somehow managed to revive the taste of the sea by dissolving the white crystals that kept it buried.

The ship was no longer being tossed about by the waves.

All that could be heard was the growl and throb of the propellers like a hypnotic lullaby intoned by a Mermaid, locked away in the engine room down below.

Gabriel moved, avoiding and shifting the bodies of some of the other prisoners. After a few days' journey, the majority of them had fallen into a state of torpor. Only the strongest managed to remain awake for a few hours on end.

He made his way slowly to a less crowded part of the cage only to be assailed by the reek of urine and excrement. One corner of the bulkhead which divided the hold in two, acted as a latrine and Gabriel was one of the few who insisted on using it, not allowing himself to yield, as many had done, to the temptation of wetting and soiling themselves.

A light shuffling in the woman's sector made him even more alert. He tiptoed forward, paying attention not to tread on the rivulets of urine trickling across the floor. Holding on to the grating and stretching his neck, he peered into the other side. He caught a glimpse of a blond head, and smelled that scent which somehow managed to drown out the disgusting stench of the place, a perfume which vaguely resembled ripe apricots.

«Nina...» he whispered.

The girl straightened up, slowly, as if floating in a world where gravity held no sway. Gabriel caught sight of one of her cheekbones in the light of a distant bulb, and when she turned full face, he saw her inquiring eyes, the color of corn, peering at him.

«Nina…» he called again.

She approached until she came face to face with Gabriel. She was as tall as he was, so their eyes met on a level. For an instant, they studied each other's unknown faces on either side of the iron barrier.

«My name is Gabriel», he managed to say before she spoke.

Nina nodded.

«How is your mother?»

The girl lowered her eyes.

«Have you got any medicine?»

«No», she answered with a sigh.

Gabriel perceived her anguish and despair and his heart sank.

«I'll see if anyone here has any aspirin», he said, in an attempt to reassure her.

He then lowered one of his hands which brushed hers, the one still holding on to the rail. Nina did not pull back.

A creak in the aisle startled them. Looking around, they saw that the guard, standing a mere arm's length away, silent and motionless, was spying on them, his hand nervously rattling the keys that dangled from his belt. This made the two of them jump. Despite his bulk, the man had managed to move so silently and stealthily that neither of them had heard him approach.

«Lev the lion is watching you», he warned them smugly.

They withdrew their hands, but only after lightly touching fingers one last time. Then they allowed themselves to be swallowed up by the darkness of their separate prisons. The guard waited until they had vanished. Then he trod heavily away laughing at the two young people's lack of courage.

Gabriel returned to his place and squatted down once more among his companions. Reverently, he brought the tips of the fingers that had touched Nina's to his lips. He then closed his eyes and was soon fast asleep.

«It reminds me of your eyes.»

Francesca smiled puzzled.

«The golden light from the mosaics. Awe-inspiring, isn't it?»

They were in Saint Mark's Basilica, standing below the dome of the Pentecost. The golden walls sparkled in the sunlight that poured in through the windows in the drum above.

«Come here.» Mikael took the girl by the hand and led her a few paces farther under the dome, until they were standing right below a throne in mosaic, from which twelve rays spread out, one for every apostle.

«There's a dove on the throne», she observed.

«That's the Holy Ghost. They say that if you stand directly under it, your mind will be illuminated with immensity.»

Francesca shook her head

«What about the heart?» she teased.

«For that...» he answered, pretending to give it some thought, «well, that's what I'm here for.»

The girl's eyes shone like the Byzantine mosaics. She snuggled close to Mikael and would have thrown her arms around his neck had it not been for the awe this holy place induced.

«That's enough culture for one day, don't you think?» muttered Mikael as he pushed her gently out of the church into the square packed with tourists. Every time he came here, he felt so alive. He loved the cosmopolitan atmosphere and the vague sense of never-ending festiveness he could breathe here, with all the ladies in long organza dresses and the gentlemen in tight dark suits strolling around.

«What's happening?» Francesca asked as she pointed at a cluster of people near the Caffé Florian.

«Luchino Visconti's here», said a gentleman who was just passing by.

Francesca smiled and stopped. She was attracted by that little crowd but, at the same time, a little hesitant.

«Come on, let's go! Let's make him take notice of us, he might offer us a part in his next film», mocked Mikael pulling her by the arm.

She shook her head. «I'd rather go up onto the *paròn* instead.» And she pointed at the bell-tower behind her.

«That way we can enjoy the sunset.»

Mikael glanced at his Omega. «Yes, we should be able to make it.»

They ran off, paid the entrance fee and climbed the steps up to the top. On the balcony, panting and perspiring, they embraced leaning their backs up against the wall, listening to each other's hearts beating in unison.

«My grandfather saw it collapse», said Francesca. «In the summer of nineteen-o-two the whole tower fell down. It was terrible, he used to say.»

«But they built it up again, exactly the same as before.»

«That's right, but how can a foreigner know these things?»

«I don't know», he answered, «it's just a matter of making educated guesses. I often get things right.»

Francesca dwelt on this for a few moments, then, stood back, looked over the parapet and pointed upwards. «So, what's that at the very top?» she challenged him

«The statue of an angel.»

«Yes, ah, but which one?»

«The Archangel Michael.»

«Wrong!» she exclaimed with a faint smile of triumph. It was hard to catch Mikael out, but she had succeeded.

«The Archangel Gabriel.»

Mikael assumed an air of defeat.

«Don't take it too hard, come on!» Francesca consoled him, giving his nose a tender tweak.

The name Gabriel had a strange, upsetting effect on him. He had always been convinced that that golden angel that watched over Venice, a hundred meters above the city, bore his name. He had always thought so and had even boasted about it on several occasions, saying that it was his destiny to study in a city protected by the Archangel Michael. How had he got that wrong? He had read all about the basilica, the tower, even knew the names of the bells. How could he have made such a crass mistake?

He gazed up at the sky as if seeking an answer there. A cloud over Rialto bridge seemed to have been set on fire by the last rays of the sun. The Church of Saint Mary of Health, the Giudecca, the Island of St. George, the entire city was covered in golden dust.

«What shall I do now, poor dethroned angel that I am?» he asked out loud, his pride wounded.

Francesca noticed a veil of melancholy cloud his eyes.

«You could always watch over me» she suggested.

By way of an answer, Mikael drew her close to him and sealed her lips with a kiss which meant to be a promise.

«I love you», he murmured, just as the sun sank below the scarlet surface of the Laguna.

15

Patras, 1938

As Seròp set foot on the platform, the sound of the shrill whistle and the puffing engine of the approaching locomotive could be heard already.

The station was all a commotion as it awaited the train's arrival. The porters were hurrying to the beginning of the platform where the first-class carriages would stop. Railway men in their blue uniforms were running up and down blowing their whistles as a warning to people not to stand too close to the edge. Policemen mingled with the crowd and, every so often, stopped some poor wretch or other.

«Hey, you, where are you going with that baby?» one of them asked Seròp, the peak of his hat drawn down so that it practically touched the tip of his nose, giving him an air of severity if not of meanness.

Seròp started. At first, he had tried to keep the child hidden under his coat, but the baby had kicked and wailed because he wanted to see the world.

«He's got a temperature, he's been terribly hot for two days now», he stammered.

«So?»

«I'm taking him to Athens, to look for a doctor who might be able to cure him», he said, bursting into tears like a seasoned actor.

The platform quaked as the train came trundling in.

The gendarme was about to ask Seròp for his documents but, as there was no time left, he let things be. He had to be at his assigned post before the train halted because arriving passengers always needed to be checked.

«*Perastikà*, the very best of luck», he wished Seròp in the end.

The locomotive entered the station in a shroud of steam, like a giant serpent slithering back into its den. Then, it stopped with one big, final, choreographic snort. The carriages shuddered as they screeched to an ear-piercing standstill on the rails.

Seròp was still shaking.

For one absurd instant, he had actually hoped the train might not come at all, that it might bypass its Patras halt, that some miracle would prevent him from embarking on this ill-fated journey of his. Nonetheless, the train was there, right in front of him and its locomotive would soon propel its wheels all the way to Athens.

The loudspeaker crackled; the railway men slammed the doors as the passengers boarded the train.

«Athens?» the guard asked him.

Seròp came to his senses again and groped for an answer as he looked into the grey eyes of the man, the tip of whose whistle was a mere hairsbreadth from his lips.

«Are you travelling?» the railway man insisted.

Seròp pulled the ticket out of his pocket and showed it to him. Then he began to run because the carriage the man indicated was the very last one, way down at the end of the platform. Finally, he reached the carriage and made his way to his compartment, exhausted and breathless, not a shred of energy left. He then collapsed onto the seat next to the window, taking no notice of the glances of the other passengers. Just then, the train left the station to the sound of another whistle. Standing on the platform, the guard was waving to his baby who smiled back at him in amusement, his button of a nose pressed up against the window.

The smell of feta, sharp and sour, almost made Seròp retch. Even though he was famished, the overpowering aroma of cheese that filled the compartment was sickening.

«What's your name?» the little boy munching a roll overflowing with olives and feta asked the child in Seròp's arms, fixing him with his bulging sloe-black eyes. He was skinny and his bony shoulders could barely hold up his head, too big by far for his height.

«Come here, he's too small, he doesn't know how to speak yet», scolded his mother, a tiny, exhausted-looking woman in a red and yellow floral-patterned scarf. «He's not even a year old, is he?» she asked Seròp, looking at some point on his face but not into his eyes.

Seròp shook his head in a vague manner which failed to satisfy the woman's curiosity.

«Mine is seven, but he's not well, poor thing», she continued, indicating her son, who smiled, all pleased as if illness were some kind of gift that made him special.

«Is yours sick too?» the woman asked, swaying to the movement of the speeding train.

«No.»

«Ah. So, I didn't get things right back there in the station; I though you said he was running a very high temperature.»

«No», insisted Seròp both perplexed and amazed.

«May God protect him!» she exclaimed as she made the sign of the cross. «But tell me now, what sin can my poor child have committed to suffer like this! Dolichocephalism... it took me a whole year to learn even to pronounce it. When he has one of his attacks it's heart-breaking; he writhes, bangs his head from one wall to another, yells, whines.»

Her eyes filled with tears. «Unless he's cured, his head will burst», she said, wringing her hands.

The old lady, sitting next to Seròp, stiffened in horror.

«*Po', po' Panaghià mu*[6]», she murmured, crossing herself.

«'Take him to Professor Alivizatos', they told me, 'he's a true magician'. For years now we travel up and down every three months from Pyrgos to Athens. We've nothing left, not a Drachma to bless ourselves with, we've sold everything. I've no regrets, no! If only he'd get better.»

«Mamma, show them the chicken», shouted the boy, his mouth full, a little piece of feta stuck to one lip.

«Don't shout, there's a good boy!»

«The chicken!» he roared, insisting, his face now frighteningly red. It was clear that he had no intention of relenting until she contented him.

The mother shook her head, exasperated.

«He wants me to show you the present we're bringing the professor.»

Muttering, she bent down and began rummaging among some bundles under the seat and brought out a straw basket. Then she raised the lid slowly revealing a hen, its head lolling to one side, its red tongue sticking out between its half-open beak, its pink crest quivering a little, its silver and red feathers reflecting the compartment's weak light. On its throat, a long, deep cut.

Frightened, Seròp's child burst out crying and clung to his father's neck, seeking refuge.

The hen's open, blood-stained eyes stared at Seròp.

Number seven Villari Street was a neo-classical building.

Seròp had arrived in Athens at dusk after a seven-hour journey. He had got off at the Piraeus station and, having asked people for directions, had taken the «Beast», the new tram which crossed the city from north to south. This had brought him to the underground stop in Omonia Square, in the heart of the capital. On first seeing Athens, this vast alluring metropolis, his mind had been taken off the thoughts that plagued him, for a while any way. As to the child, he had grown accustomed to being in his father's arms. It was the first time that the two of them had ever spent so many hours together. The baby had hugged him, clinging tightly to his neck and, as they made their way through the crowd, had even planted a kiss on his father's cheek. This way, they had passed through the *leoforos*, the city's broad, elegant avenues; they had stopped and gazed into shop windows, they had admired the stylish clothes of passing gentlemen, the lines of shining cars. Seròp had even shown him, towering in the background on the top of the hill overlooking the city, the massive, majestic Parthenon. He could have been just any other man visiting the capital with his son, had it not been for his rags and that expression on his face that seemed to announce the crime he was about to commit.

He stopped in front of the hall door, looked up and counted the storeys. On the third floor a wide-open window was banging in the wind. He stood there staring at it. "If someone closes it within the next five minutes, that will mean that all will go well ", he told himself. He was already at minute four and nothing had happened as yet. So, he held his breath but felt he was going to suffocate. He was about to give in, when he saw a young woman lean out of the window. She had a very pale complexion and her blond hair flew about like silk threads in the breeze. Her arms reached out beyond the sill; her open palm seemed to contain something. A dove landed gently on her hand and began to peck at what he thought were some seeds.

"A gentle soul," mused Seròp.

The woman's eyes crossed his and she stood there a while observing him, the dove in her hand. Seròp believed she would say something to him, or at least that is what he hoped, but all she did was smile. And, as the dove flew away, she simply drew back inside closing the shutters behind her.

«Where are you going?» asked the concierge, one of his eyes half blind.

Seròp had entered the hallway dragging his feet and carrying a baby in his arms so, the concierge had taken him for a beggar.

«Three Alpha», said Seròp, as if it were a military password.

The other looked him over incredulously. What had a scruffy fellow like this to do with the import-export office? In all his years, he had only seen very well-dressed men, with white starched shirts and patent-leather shoes, go up there.

«Third floor», he decided to tell him at last, indicating the lift.

«Can I take the stairs?» He was not sure he knew how or even wanted to use that iron and wood contraption box swinging precariously from those cables.

The concierge shrugged.

«If that's what you want», he griped without even addressing him as sir. Then he lifted the receiver of the telephone and pushed a few buttons.

Seròp climbed the stairs very slowly, panting because he was weary and exhausted. The door with the Three Alpha plate on it was slightly ajar. He pushed it gently and entered a small waiting-room with a desk and two little sofas pushed up against the walls. A telephone was ringing somewhere down in the heart of the apartment and immediately afterwards Seròp heard the booming voice of a man speaking in a foreign language.

«Brother, how are you?» said Martiròs taking him by surprise.

Elegant as always, he had appeared suddenly from a side door. He was about to embrace Seròp, when he drew back, noticing the child in his arms.

«You look really tired», was all he managed to say.

Seròp nodded.

«Does he need something?» he asked indicating the baby. «He's bound to be hungry, both of you must be.»

Seròp did not seem to be listening to him, because he just stood there motionless in the middle of the room, looking lost and confused.

Another man, rather short and thin, appeared from the depths of the dark corridor. He was wrapped in a huge scarf which covered half of his face; his eyes were hidden behind enormous dark sunglasses. It was as if he did not want to be recognized. This stranger barely mumbled a greeting but appeared extremely interested in the little boy.

«Let me see him», he said in broken Greek.

Martiròs took the child out of Seròp's arms but with the perfectly natural gesture of a helpful uncle seeking to give the tired father some respite. Seròp handed him over to his friend, never imagining that he would never get his son back again. After all, Martiròs was his brother, he could trust him.

The two men immediately lay the child down the top of the desk and hastily undressed him. Then, they began examining the baby's helpless, naked, little body. They explored his mouth, his ears, poked him all over, flexed his arms and legs, brought a lamp up to his eyes. Seròp just stood by, inert, looking on while the two men treated his son as if he were some kind of merchandise on sale at the market.

At some point he noticed the baby's wrist waving about.

There was no red thread on it.

«Wait, I've made a mistake», he whispered.

«I've made a mistake!», he repeated this time shouting, his heart about to burst.

The other two turned around and stared at him.

«I thought everything had been made perfectly clear; Jivan explained that there could be no second thoughts», warned Martiròs.

Seròp saw a callousness in those eyes he had never noticed before. He gathered that the rumors about him must have been all true.

«I want my child back!» he said in a firm tone, straightening himself up to his full height.

Martiròs was about to react, but there was no need to. The bloke with the scarf simply took a wad of notes from his jacket, cleared his throat and began to count them out in a deliberated loud voice.

Thirty hundred-Drachma bills.

He put them down on the desk next to the child. Seròp looked at them transfixed, like a prey mesmerized by the serpent about to devour him.

Martiròs took them up, went over and thrust them into Seròp's pocket.

«You won't regret it, you'll see», he whispered in his ear and then, as the stranger disappeared down the corridor, a boy from the bar entered with a tray of coffee and warm cheese pies.

«Where is he taking him?» shouted Seròp.

«He'll be back in a jiffy», lied Martiròs. «Meanwhile, just sit down, make yourself at home and have something to eat», he added pushing him onto one of the little sofas.

Seròp gave in without opposing resistance. He bit into one of the pies with a trembling hand and, as he swallowed a mouthful, he looked down at the fixer's two-tone brogues.

There was still, he noticed, a smudge of dirt on the toes.

Satèn was walking cautiously downhill near the top of a cliff. In the sky the moon was rising slowly while the sun was sinking rapidly. Despite the uneven terrain upon which she was treading, she felt quite happy. She kept walking, admiring the sun on one side, the moon on the other, amazed that she could see both at the same time. Then she remembered that she had two identical heads on her shoulders, holding them both high with enormous pride, as if her physical deformity were some kind of divine gift, a prodigious attribute.

She could see double, hear double. She had two noses for smelling, two mouths for tasting. Two brains for thinking and loving.

Loving.

Just like a goddess of some primordial cult.

All of a sudden, the sun disappeared and the moon hid behind a boulder, and only the stars were left to light her way. Satèn stopped and looked around dumbfounded. She turned her two heads, watchfully, warily, in all directions. She did not trust a world without either sun or moon. Just as she was racking her brain wondering what to do, she felt an excruciating pain: an axe had fallen down on her neck cutting one of her heads clean off. Blood gushed out, soaking her clothes and drenching the ground as the head rolled away down the slope.

Satèn screamed and woke up with a start. She brought one hand to her neck and stretched the other out to touch the cradle desperately looking for what she knew she had lost forever.

Seròp's return journey was sheer agony.

The sale of his child had stunned him as if he had received a strong blow on the head: the bruise, which initially seemed to vanish, began to spread right into to his brain, with dire consequences.

Sitting in the train, he was unable to sit up straight. It was as if his backbone were missing. He simply lolled and flopped from right to left to the rhythmic motion of the carriage. Every time he toppled, the polite passenger sitting next to him pushed him back gently, but he kept falling back on top of the poor man. The other passengers in the compartment began to look at him in bewilderment, unable to understand what the cause of his torpor might be. At first, they thought he might be drunk, but he did not smell of alcohol; then they thought he might be asleep, but this was not true either, because Seròp continued to mumble a kind of litany. Now and then, he half opened his eyelids and stared with moist, misty eyes into empty nothingness, only to close them again. He had not even stirred when the inspector asked to check his ticket. The man had been obliged to shake him several times before he took it out and showed it to him in dazed, unsteady slow motion.

One lady had suggested that maybe he was suffering from malaria, a hypothesis which caused considerable commotion, and, although a railway man had come around several times spraying the compartment, some of the passengers decided to leave their seats and put up with the discomfort of standing in the corridor, given that the train was packed.

At the station in Patras they even had to help him off the train.

«Have you got a family? A home to go to?» asked the station master.

Seròp did not answer but simply stared at the other man with those sad, desperate eyes of his, like a dog expecting a beating.

They accompanied him over to a bench and left him sitting there. But then he swayed dangerously and seemed about to fall flat on his face.

«Let's call the police», said one of the men.

«No», whispered Seròp at last, having mustered up all the strength he had left. «It's only the journey, I'll soon get over it.»

When he caught sight of the *govush*, the Armenian camp, in the distance, he began sobbing, his body quaking and shivering violently, knees beginning to give way.

«Oh my God, please take my soul», he whispered, «I don't deserve to live.»

Instinctively, he dragged himself as far as the shack, his heart pounding frantically in his breast. A few steps further ahead he halted. What would he find inside? A mutilated, broken family. Everything looked different, alien, unreal, and he was terrified that he would soon smell a rotting corpse, believing his wife was probably dead.

He was about to pull the curtain aside, having plucked up the courage to enter, when Satèn preceded him. She stood there on the threshold, straight as a die, barring his way.

Seròp backed away, amazed at seeing her alive and out of bed. He looked her over, but could see no signs of the critical conditions in which he had left her two days earlier, except that her eyes were red and dry and that her motionless eyelids failed to blink. The joy he felt gave him energy, making him forget his heinous deed for a few moments. He drew close to his wife intending to embrace her and make sure she was no figment of his fevered brain. He wanted to cling to her, weep with her.

He wanted them to share their grief.

Satèn held him back with one hand.

«Where's my baby?»

Her eyes were ice-cold, her amber irises more brilliant than ever.

He lowered his eyes.

«Where is he?» she repeated without betraying the least sign of emotion.

He shook his head.

«If you come in, I want something to be perfectly clear.» said Satèn, biting her lip which had begun to tremble a little. «I am no longer your wife and you're no longer my husband», she warned him and spat on the ground in contempt.

And as Fitìl, or what remained of her after the ravages of her illness, was tearing her hair and chanting a lugubrious tune about a lamb being led to the slaughter, Seròp entered his hovel and put the wad of notes down on the table.

The thirty pieces of silver he had received in exchange for his son.

16

«Lev!» called the soldier opening the cargo hatch leading down from the deck above.

The guard raised his head and frowned.

«Here's what you were looking for.» said the other as he threw something down to him.

Lev tried to catch it in mid-air, but it escaped his grasp and went flying through the grating of the men's section. Then it fell onto the floor, bounced a couple of times, and spun like a top, ending up amid the bodies huddled up in a heap on the floor.

«Too fucking bad, chum!», sneered the soldier before battening down the hatch again.

The hold was plunged back into darkness.

«Shit!» swore Lev looking around, trying to find what his mate had managed to get him. Gabriel had already located it and, while the guard was busy rummaging on the ground, he picked it up furtively. It was a little brown glass bottle full of whitish tablets.

«Hey, have any of you seen a little bottle?» asked Lev shaking the railing to wake the prisoners up.

Nobody answered.

«I swear you'll regret it!», he growled as he strode away.

Gabriel opened his hand holding the tiny flagon and turned it to the faint light of the bulb.

«Aspirin», he read and smiled, convinced that for once fortune had been kind to him.

When he saw Nina again, he was struck by her pallor.

The women had come out from their cage again to drink the

water lowered down through the hatch. Gabriel had given her one of his eloquent nods and she had received his message.

A few hours later, she had appeared at the usual spot, taking advantage of that brief moment when Lev went off to wash. It was one of the two chances they had of meeting without running risks; the other occasion was when the guard snored like a pig after guzzling down an entire bottle of vodka.

By now their lives centered around those few stolen moments they were able to share: a precious gift that lit up these horrible days, something that helped them face the ugliness and squalor of their surroundings, give them the strength to carry on.

During these few fleeting meetings Gabriel had fallen deeply in love with Nina. He felt they were made for each other and was amazed to have found her here amid similar riffraff. His mood had improved, even Gerasim had noticed it, teasing him about his sudden spurt of optimism, his dreams of a rosy future.

«I want to marry her», he had confided in his companion who had burst out laughing, this time, however, out of sheer joy.

When Gabriel needed to meet Nina, Gerasim gave him a hand. He would keep an eye on the guard and, using a series of conventional signals, inform him of the man's movements. As soon as Lev would leave his post, Gabriel, as quick as lightning, would set off in the direction of the latrine and wait for his beloved. At times, she would arrive first and stand there on the other side of the grating, her long blond hair cascading down her back, the way he liked it.

«My love», he would whisper as soon as he saw her; sometimes he called her «my beloved» while she smiled revealing her small pearly teeth like those of a child and wrinkled up her nose to greet him in her special funny way.

As for her, she used to call him «*Angel moy*», just «my angel» nothing more, alluding to his celestial name.

Then they would beat their breasts with their fists twice, lightly, like the wings of a butterfly, a sign that, in their secret language meant: «I live only for you.»

«Everything all right?» he asked her, brushing his fingers against hers.

Nina nodded.

Gabriel took the bottle out of his pocket. It was wrapped in a piece of paper.

«I've brought you some aspirin.»

Her face lit up.

«Where did you get it?»

Gabriel shrugged but did not answer.

«And what's this?» asked Nina touching the paper around the bottle.

«Promise me you'll read it, but not now. And you must answer me in writing.»

«Thanks.»

The tone of her voice was so polite and well-educated that it always reminded Gabriel of her genteel origins. Nina was the daughter of a large landowner from the Ukraine. Her family was one of the few *kulaki* that had survived the Revolution; they had not opposed forced collectivization of the land and had spontaneously donated theirs to the Party. But in the fertile Cherkassy Valley where they lived, hatred and resentment had never died down completely. Years later, someone had accused the family of being opposers, crafty *kontrik*, members of that despicable, odious clique. Nina's brother and father had been killed right before her eyes while her mother, Tatiana, and herself had been deported.

«Has she eaten anything? Your mother, I mean?» asked Gabriel.

«The smell of fish makes her sick.» she answered staring into space. «I'm afraid she won't make it.» she added.

«No. You must convince her to take these. She should put a tablet under her tongue until it melts», he explained.

Nina nodded. «Angel moy, you're the only beautiful thing around here. Sometimes I think I'll go mad. I can't believe what's happening to me, to us! It's so absurd! All I'd need would be a cabin and your smile. Nothing else.»

Nina's tears ran down her cheeks and spilled onto Gabriel's hands. They were warm and innocent.

«Please don't...» he entreated her.

She stifled a sob.

«Look!» he exclaimed, holding out his open hand, on the palm of which Nina saw something sparkle.

«This is my mother's wedding ring. The only thing of hers I still possess. I want you to have it.»

He took her hand and slipped the ring onto her fourth finger. It all happened so quickly that it took her breath away.

«But, I can't...» she protested, overcome by emotion.

Gabriel silenced her. Her mouth, framed in a space between the bars, had remained half open. He drew near in hopes of touching her lips, only to discover to his amazement that miracles could still happen even in that squalid, sordid place they were caged in. And as they had kissed for the very first time in the stinking hold of a floating prison, Gabriel believed that, despite everything, life was worth living. He beat his chest with his fist and fled, afraid someone might see the tears in his eyes.

My love,

not a minute, not a second goes by when I don't think of you. I now live for those few moments when we are able to meet. At night I fall asleep thinking of you and pluck up the courage to face the inhumane conditions in which we find ourselves.

But soon, I'm sure of it, all this will end. I have faith in God. I am convinced he won't leave us here to die like this: we are too young; our lives have just begun.

Will you marry me, my dearest, loveliest Nina? Here, right now?

Let us make each other a promise, pledge our love. Let us openly declare our desire to live as husband and wife as soon as fate allows it. If not ... well, I cannot think of anyone else who deserves more than you to wear my mother's ring.

Answer me in writing. My heart would break if it received a refusal from your lovely lips.

I live only for you,
your angel.
P.S. Gerasim has offered to be our best man.

Nina put the letter down feeling a little dizzy.

She got up from the floor her heart aching, as if someone were trying to rip it out of her breast.

She had never known anyone who expressed their feelings so spontaneously and sincerely. Nobody, ever, not in all her tender fifteen years. And yet the beautiful words written by her Angel had troubled her deeply, ineffably. She was well aware what her hard-labor sentence really meant. She was upset because she knew she had met the love of her life at a time when she could see no promise of a future.

«Nina…» called her mother, coughing.

She hid the letter quickly in her pocket and rushed over to Tatiana who was lying on the floor among the other women.

«I'm here, mamma», she said softly, stroking her mother's brow which was beaded in perspiration.

«Thank God, I'm feeling a little better», Tatiana whispered.

Nina smiled and righted the bundle of rags beneath her mother's head.

«God be praised», she breathed softly looking into her mother's blue eyes.

«I see you are back on your feet, comrade», commented Lev sarcastically as he poured a ration of water into Tatiana's mug.

The woman, leaning on her daughter's arm, had patiently queued up with all the others, awaiting her turn.

«Thank God», she answered.

«What God, imbecile? You mean the aspirins», said a voice from behind, scoffing at the lady's faith. It belonged to a woman with a shaven head and a scar that disfigured one of her eyes.

"Aspirins!?" growled Lev.

«You bet! With a daughter like her you're sure to find what you need» she shouted, elbowing her way so aggressively that she threw them, literally, into the arms of the guard.

«Where did you get those aspirins?» exploded Lev, shaking Nina so violently by the shoulders that the ladle fell from his hand into the pail.

The girl started, alarmed.

«Where?» insisted her tormenter.

«Between her thighs, that's where she found them», intervened the shaven-headed woman, making the rest of the prisoners in the line roar with laughter. «Can't you see she's got a wedding ring and all?» she added lifting up the poor girl's hand and waving it about for all to see.

«No, please don't», Tatiana begged her, in a barely audible voice. «It was a gift from a charitable soul.»

«Shut up, you slut, the good old times are over and done with», said the other, abusively. «You can put on all the airs and graces you like, but you're scum just like the rest of us.» And, as her maimed eye twitched, she threw the contents of her mug all over the elderly lady.

«That's enough!» yelled Lev furiously, kicking everything in his vicinity, including the bucket which fell over, spilling all its precious contents on the floor. He was hurt, disappointed. He had gone to no ends of trouble to get hold of those aspirins because, for once in his life, he felt an impelling desire to do something really noble. He had wanted to be the one to make a gift of the aspirins to Nina, so she would realize that, despite everything, he was a sensitive, thoughtful man. Instead, that snotty-nosed Armenian — who else, if not? — had beaten him to it, acting the lovely at his expense.

«Away, back into the cage, the lot of you!» he barked at the women.

The poor wretches scurried away, muttering and complaining.

Gabriel ranted behind the bars, cursing himself for having got his truelove into trouble. He had behaved like the reckless, imprudent, stupid greenhorn that he was. And seeing her there, all alone and defenseless at the mercy of that thug, made his soul bleed.

«I did it», he wanted to yell, but Gerasim, guessing what he had in mind, covered his mouth with his hands.

«Don't you say even one word, enough of your foolishness for now», he said.

Tatiana, white as a sheet, staggered. Nina, seeing that her mother was about to faint, wanted to rush over and help her, but Lev held her back and dragged her into a corner.

«If you don't want your handsome Armenian to bleed to death, come to the grating this evening», he whispered into her ear. Then he let go of her and thrust her roughly away, over to her mother who had fallen to her knees.

«Out of my sight! Both of you!» he ordered, his jacket so tight across his chest that it looked as if it might burst any moment.

Nina helped her mother back onto her feet and they shuffled slowly back into the cage full of restless shadows.

«My child, let us reflect on the error of your ways.»

Mikael, in the company of his friends, was in the Carmelite church for the usual confession. He had wanted to go in first, hoping that — through the sacrament — he might free himself of the torments that had been plaguing him for some time now, especially at night, when he was haunted by abominable images and monstrous visions. He had even been obliged to get up and lean out the window to catch a breath of fresh air, his heart beating wildly, because he was overwhelmed by the dreadful sensation that he was going to die.

Mikael quaked nervously on the kneeler of the confession box. On the other side of the grille, don Antonio's profile waited in silence. The boy coughed, embarrassed, but was unable to utter a word.

«Well, my son?» The priest's fingers began to beat an impatient tattoo on the wooden partition. «Have you ever had impure thoughts?»

«Yes, father», Mikael answered at last.

«Tell me about them.»

«I wanted…» he stammered while looking through the lattice, catching only fragments of the priest's face.

«I'll help you. Have you ever touched yourself while thinking of a woman's body?»

«Yes.»

«Have you ever lusted after her?»

The boy swallowed. His throat burnt as if his stomach were on fire.

«*Ma ti se sbregà? Parla, muso da mona!* Are you cracked or what? Speak up, loon-face!» growled don Antonio, evidently vexed.

Mikael could hardly believe that this was the same good-natured priest who had heard his confession so often before. But maybe he was having one of his attacks. It must have been that, for, suddenly, he thought he could see, there, on the other side of the lattice, the devil himself and even catch a whiff of the sulphur believed to accompany the hellhound. In the throes of an uncontrollable attack of panic, he leaped to his feet and ran away as if Satan himself were hot on his heels.

«Hey, finished already?» asked Hampò, in amazement.

Mikael shook his head, mumbled something unintelligible, and dashed off, straight out of the church.

«Come back! Where are you going?» cried Aznavour following his friend outside, but he did not turn around, not even for a split second. He just kept on running like a bolting stallion.

He only stopped in front of the green door of *Calle de l'Avogaria* where Francesca lived, and bent in two as he strove to get his breath back. From the windows of the little two-storey house came the muffled sounds of voices and kitchen noises: indistinct words, the clinking of dishes, the hum of a radio. Mikael gazed up at the last half-open window of Francesca's room. Then he picked up a pebble and threw it up against the glass. Without any delay, she came to the window at once.

«Come up», she mouthed as she beckoned to him with one hand.

Mikael hurried up the stairs.

«Did anyone see you coming up?» she asked him as he reached the landing.

He shook his head.

They sat down together on Francesca's bed, in the room with pastel-colored walls. Her mother was not at home and would not be back until midnight.

«What's the matter? You're as white as sheet.»

«I've just seen the devil; I mean in person», he began, passing his hands over his face.

She frowned.

«In the Carmelite church, in the confession box, don Antonio is possessed.» he insisted, his voice all broken with terror.

Francesca said nothing and hid her worry beneath a warm, gentle smile. Then she held him close like a mother does with a child that has just had a nightmare.

Mikael relaxed in her arms.

«If only the world were as lovely as the one you belong to», he murmured caressing her soft shoulders.

When he raised his eyes, Francesca was still beaming. It was a smile he had never noticed before, one of subtle pride in her femininity, as if she had fully grown into a woman there and then, so quickly that neither of them had noticed.

«Will you ever grow tired of me?» he asked her.

«We'll see...» she teased and silenced him with a kiss, pushing him back onto the bed.

Mikael surrendered and lay there without moving, while she passed her fingers through his hair and nibbled at his lobes. He suddenly blocked her head with one hand while the other held her close, making their eyes meet and lock. He meant to ask for some sign of consent rather than of permission. Francesca blushed and stopped smiling. The modesty he read in her eyes inflamed him and he was overcome by an impelling desire to possess her, a yearning that took hold of his entire being and throbbed in his groin. Both of them, overwhelmed by passion, clumsily undressed in all haste before rolling down, wrapped around each other, onto the squeaking bed.

«I'm yours», she whispered, as she straddled him.

When he penetrated her she only gave one little stifled moan, somewhere between a sigh of pleasure and a cry of pain. The curtain fluttered and danced in the breeze full of the scent of orange blossoms.

Mikael closed his eyes.

Suddenly the room seemed to have been pervaded by a heavenly melody and for a few magical moments his existence assumed complete meaning.

«My love», he said, panting.

At the peak of his pleasure, he believed he had gained thorough understanding of the miracle of life.

A rose nipped in the bud before it could even bloom.
There shall be no more dew, no more spring.

Mikael had fallen asleep and was dreaming.

A group of men were encircling a girl and he thrust them aside like puppets in his haste to reach her and see who she was. As soon as he had dragged the last man away, an appalling sight met his eyes: Francesca lay there on the floor, lifeless, in a pool of blood, naked, her thighs wide open.

A fox was crouching down beside her like the one in Gauguin's *Loss of virginity*.

«No!» he cried, waking up startled in the pitch-dark room.

Confused, and not knowing where he was, he glanced at his watch: its phosphorescent second-hand was not moving and he could not even hear it tick.

Time had stopped.

Suddenly, a reading lamp was switched on and a naked body sat up in the bed beside him.

«I'm dead...» said Francesca, yawning.

Mikael shook in terror.

Just then, as the girl bent over him intending to hug him, he was downright uncouth, pushed her roughly away and jumped out of the bed.

«Keep away from me», he shouted.

During the days that followed, he tried to justify his despicable deed, blaming it on the shadows. Long morphing shadows, that distorted her features and changed the shape of everything.

Francesca fell out of the bed, hit her head off a chair and gave a little cry, more out of surprise than pain. Mikael started dressing himself like a shot and, flinging the door wide open, fled down the stairs into the empty alleyway.

Nina was raped by five men.

That night the ship had tossed and moaned loudly, almost as if it were trying to protest and tell the world about the atrocious crime about to be committed within her dark, secret entrails.

The girl had risen and staggered as she groped way stealthily as far as the railings. She had not been able to sleep because the guard's threat had frightened her so much that dreadful thoughts had kept her awake. However, in all her candor, she thought she could keep him at bay by going along with some of his whims.

Lev was there waiting for her, all smiles, and had even greeted her politely as he carefully opened the gate for her. Continuing to smile, he had taken her by the hand and led her down the corridor, passing right in front of the gate that sealed off the men's section. And it was exactly from here that four more men had emerged. Nina was frightened so Lev had clapped his hand over her mouth lest she call out and had not let go until another man, grabbing her by the hair, pulled her into a cubbyhole under the stairs and shut the door behind them.

Once inside, they had ripped her clothes off and, having gagged her with her own headscarf, they had raped her, first, taking turns, then all together. They had deflowered and sodomized her, treated her to every imaginable sexual abuse without paying the least heed to her laments, her cries of pain and humiliation.

«Let's pleasure her, the whore!» Lev ordered.

Nina moaned and implored them with her eyes, hoping to move them to pity, convinced that somewhere in a remote corner of their souls nestled that tiny spark of humanity that all men, however ferocious, possess.

She was wrong.

None of the brutes even spared her a glance. All they were interested in was her delicate, white body which now lay there, completely at their mercy.

They simply pounced on her like hungry jackals with a carcass to savage.

At a certain point, a blade glinted in the faint light of the bulb.

«What the fuck!?» asked one of the rapists, hooting.

«Too narrow», grunted the criminal holding the knife.

Lev would have stopped him had he not been so busy mauling the girl's breasts and licking her tiny nipples.

A deep gash was slit in the top of Nina's vagina.

The girl jolted and the blood spurted out.

«You mother fucker!» howled Lev.

Too late.

His face, the walls, the entire cubbyhole, everything was covered in that sticky, warm, sweetish liquid.

17

Kamil Shamoun, the Lebanese president, was tall and stout. His heavily brilliantined hair shone in the sun as he helped his wife out of the launch. Dressed in an elegant grey three piece he wore a sash bearing the colors of his country's flag: red and white with a green cedar at the center. Madame Shamoun, beautiful and several years younger than her husband, was swathed in a light-colored suit and had a patterned headscarf wrapped around her perfectly coiffed hair.

To honor the guests, the main door to the college had been thrown open and a red carpet rolled out as far as the landing pier. The wooden dolphins were decked out in colored ribbons while three flags, Italian on one side, Armenian on the other, the Lebanese at the center, flapped in the springtime breeze.

The entire college staff stood to attention at the door to welcome these illustrious guests. The rector first shook their hands then embraced them, affectionately, to underline their longstanding friendship. They exchanged a few words in Lebanese, a language father Ayvazian had learnt while studying at Saint Gregory's Armenian Seminary near Beirut.

The collegians, all decked out in their uniforms, waited silently in the atrium in orderly lines. As soon as Shamoun crossed the threshold, they bowed their heads slightly and saluted him.

«*Bonjour, monsieur le Président. On est honoré de vous accueillir dans notre collège.* Good morning Mr President. It is an honor for us to welcome you to our college», they chanted in chorus.

Then, they all moved to the Hall of Mirrors where a blue velvet curtain hid the platform set up especially for the occasion and, as the President entered, it opened to reveal the college choir. The Bosendorfer grand piano shone brighter than ever. Mikael, the pianist, stood beside the long stool and bowed to the audience. Although he had practiced the Rachmaninov prelude late into the night, he was still afraid of not playing it perfectly.

He was overcome by his usual anxiety; too many strange events had troubled him profoundly in recent times. Furthermore, he knew that, as soon as the solemn visit was over, the fathers would punish him severely for having come back late to the college the evening he had been with Francesca.

«Ah, Your Excellency Monsieur Delalian, we are honored with your presence», Wolf had quipped mockingly, surprising him as he was running up the stairs. «Do you know, by any chance, what time it is?»

«I'm sorry, but my watch broke again», he said, justifying himself and pointing at the Omega on his wrist. «I need to take it to Tick-Tock again,… sorry… hmm… father Nicoghòs I mean», he had corrected himself.

«The two of us will sort this matter out in due time. The day after tomorrow our illustrious guest will be here. If I were you, I'd practice all night», he had rebuked him, as strict as only he could be when he deemed it necessary.

Moreover, Mikael was angry with himself for his behavior towards Francesca. Their first time should have been unforgettable, wonderful and he reproached himself for having ruined everything. If only he had been able to explain his anguish to her: his certainties had collapsed, his faith crumbled, visions of violence, blood and death came to haunt him out of the blue.

He threw a furtive glance at the illustrious guests as they were taking their seats on the little nineteenth-century sofas. He took a deep breath and held it for a while, hoping that — as he had read in a magazine — that would rid him of the headache that had started to plague him again.

The conductor, father Soghomon, baton in hand, called the choir to attention. To the sound of the first few bars of the Lebanese national anthem, everyone rose and listened to the boys' pure, clear voices chanting:

«All for our fatherland, our flag and glory»

President Shamoun, standing pompously to attention, listened, his eyes moist with emotion. «The best gift you could have made us», he said, thanking them.

As soon as everyone was seated again, Mikael announced the prelude by Rachmaninov.

«Please, indulge us…», the rector whispered in Shamoun's ear, «but I wanted to honor you with your favorite piece.»

The president and his wife smiled cordially and focused on the young boy with the handsome profile preparing to play.

Mikael began the opening march with impressive impetus. The notes rang out throughout the hall, enthralling the audience. Mrs. Shamoun, enchanted, was nodding her head in approval to the rector when Signor Beppe suddenly appeared at the door of the salon. Wolf grew alarmed; the janitor would never have dared show his face there unless there was some terrible emergency. The poor man was gesticulating desperately when he was overridden by the intrusion of the Carabinieri, who burst into the room without further ado. Mikael raised his head and caught sight of a woman who made him trip over a note; along with the military police Francesca's mother had entered the hall.

«*Col Vostro permesso,* With your permission…» began the police officer.

Everyone turned to stare at the intruders.

The rector, stunned, rose to his feet. «What's happening? How can I help you?» he said without, however, managing to conceal his disapproval.

The officer was about to explain the situation when the woman rushed over to the platform, to the young piano player, breaking through the armed guards lined up to protect the president. Her hair was in a mess, her eyes red and swollen, as if she had wept at length. Mikael sprung up from the stool in utter amazement rather than as a mark of respect.

«Madam, you…», he spluttered.

The woman examined his face as if trying to ascertain that he was really the person she was looking for.

«Where's my daughter? I waited for her all night, but she didn't come home. Where is she?» she yelled, her face livid with rage and despair.»

Mikael did not utter a word.

«Talk, you wretch!»

«Madam, why not speak to me?» the rector suggested courteously.

«Indeed, you are all here to celebrate», she turned to him, getting down from the platform, «but my Franca, my only child has disappeared, duped by...» she spun around and screamed pointing at Mikael: «By one of your pupils!»

A murmur of incredulity and indignation filled the hall. The president and his wife looked furtively at each other, perplexed.

Francesca's mother collapsed. «I want my baby», she sobbed in despair.

The rector, moved to pity, put an arm around her shoulder in a fatherly way.

«Get your hands off me», she screamed in hysterics, «You Armenians should be ashamed of yourselves!»

On the evening of the eighth of May, the Vanya reduced the speed of her engines as a tug drew up alongside to lead her into the port.

The ship had arrived at Nagayevo bay, a few miles away from the city of Magadàn. In 1953, the capital of Kolyma was only a small town where prisoners were registered and divided into groups, before being sent to one of the many mines in the hinterland.

Gabriel disembarked, exhausted.

It had been a month long, taxing voyage which had sapped him completely of his energy. He wondered how he would be able to continue; he had no wish to go on after the horror and grief of Nina's death. That awful morning, just after dawn, he had been awoken by women screaming and shouting and then by great, general commotion. He had risen and gone over to the grating where several other prisoners were already gathering. Initially, he had caught sight only of her blond hair then, as the others began commenting, distraught by what had happened, he saw her lying there before his very eyes.

His own Nina, stretched out on the floor, completely naked, her back propped up against the gate, her head on her chest, her long blond hair grazing her breasts. Her arms were folded across her abdomen, her hands joined between her open legs. A stream of red liquid flowed from her thighs as far as the corridor, where, inexplicably, it stopped. Her clothes, all stained with blood, lay by her side. Tatiana Petralovna, embracing her beloved daughter, shook with the sobs of agonizing grief. The scene was like a Pietà conceived by a seriously warped artist.

Gabriel felt his heart stop, that he was about to die.

Lev stood there, a few paces away, jangling his keys and shaking his head.

«This is not going to end here», he growled.

A few hours later, they had come for the corpse. None of the officers had shown the least interest in the death of the prisoner. Never before, in the course of history, had human life been held so cheap.

Tatiana Petralovna and Gabriel had gone up on deck escorted by two guards. The woman had clung to him to prevent herself from falling; she stumbled, rocked by the ship moving to the rhythm of the waves. On a hazy, sunny day, Nina's body was thrown overboard, down into the sea, like a sack of rubbish, without any kind of funeral service. The foaming waves had soon swallowed up his love and pushed her under the keel.

«I live only for you»

He had struck his breast with two light beats, like the wings of a butterfly: his last goodbye as the golden tresses vanished forever into the deep torpid waters of the Sea of Okhotsk.

It was a scene that would remain vivid with him for the rest of his life.

At the sight of his darling Nina's massacred body, Gabriel had felt a strong urge to kill everyone without sparing even one life of those aboard: prisoners, guards, officers, the entire crew. After that, he would take his own life, too.

He wanted the *Vanja* to become the symbol of floating death.

Then, he had slowly come back to his senses, but — swearing revenge — he had decided to punish the murderers. So, patiently and with some caution, he had begun to investigate matters, even ask risky questions trying to unearth those responsible for that atrocious, inhumane act. However, the wall of silence the prisoners had built up around themselves was hard to break through. He had only managed to obtain some faint clues and nothing more. His initial fury had gradually given way to dismay and profound melancholy. For quite some time he had remained in a state of total inertia, without either eating or drinking and, had it not been for Gerasim's insistence and caring deeds, he would surely have died. His companion obliged him to take a few sips of water from his mug and, always, saved a mouthful of herring for him and make him eat it. In the throes of an unjustified sense of guilt, Gabriel had even avoided Tatiana, lowering his eyes every time they passed each other. Not only did her features remind him of Nina's, but he felt too distraught to speak to her, try to comfort her; even hold her hand and listen to her despair.

«I have something for you», the woman had whispered to him one evening, appearing in the place where he and Nina used to meet; he had not stopped going there, he needed to remember those moments of joy and tenderness, although it hurt him terribly.

Upon seeing Tatiana, Gabriel had started. He had tried to say something to her, but she had simply pushed a little sheet of paper between the bars.

«I found this among her things; I believe it's for you», she had whispered before backing away and vanishing amid the shadows in the hold.

Gabriel had stood there for ages, staring in silence at the paper which smelled of that vague scent of apricot. He was barely able to find the courage to read what it said…

My dear sweet Gabriel,
Your letter made me cry a lot and at length. I never thought I would meet true love on a ship like this, of all places, as it brings us all to prison. My mother and I have been convicted to thirty years' hard labor.

Despite this, your proposal overjoys me. It gives me hope. I want to believe in a better tomorrow. Imagine a family of my own, children fathered by you.

I wear your mother's wedding ring. I stroke it, fondly. Although your parents are strangers to me, I feel, oddly enough, that they are close.

You ask me if I want to marry you… Feel assured; I am yours already. And this is all that matters.

I promise to be faithful to you and to love you unconditionally, till death do us part.
Your wife,
Nina

«So, you were saying you took your clothes off?»

«Yes.»

«And?»

Mikael swallowed. The marshal did not take his eyes off him. He was about fifty, short and stout, his neck as thick as that of a calf.

«And then?» he insisted.

«We hugged.»

He exchanged glances with the brigadier, younger than himself, though equally stout.

«Hugged?» mocked the latter.

«Listen, boy», said the marshal suddenly springing to his feet, «we don't intend staying here all night playing with words?» He went over to Mikael and, leaning up against the desk, asked point blank: «Did you or did you not make love?»

The boy looked around him. The room was little more than a cubbyhole. On the wall facing him was a mirror he imagined was a window through which Francesca's mother and the fathers could listen to the adventures of two young people, until then believed to be exemplary and well behaved.

«So?»

«No, we did not», lied Mikael.

The policeman sighed. «So you embraced, naked, on the bed but did not… consummate, that is, make love.»

«No.»

«Why not?»

«Because…»

«Well?»

Mikael could not understand why the policemen were so obsessed by something so absolutely private. Not only, but he could not see any connection between that and the disappearance of Francesca.

«Because I had a terrible cramp in my stomach.»

The marshal threw his arms akimbo in utter amazement.

«Can you explain yourself better?» insisted the younger policeman.

«I'd probably eaten something that was bad for me... so, I had to run to the bathroom.»

«Where?»

«I rushed back to the college.»

The two men shook their heads in disbelief.

«You young people, I can't make head nor tail of you», sighed the older man, utterly disappointed. «But don't think I'm letting you go, we have to check matters», he threatened.

Mikael had to spend that night in the lockup, despite the fathers having tried to use all their influence to have him released.

«I hope this will teach you a lesson», chided Wolf who had insisted on accompanying him there.

Mikael kept his eyes lowered.

«Tell me, have you anything to do with the girl's disappearance? You can talk to me, and it would be better to do so now», the teacher added.

The boy shook his head and remained silent.

He loved Francesca above all else. The news of her disappearance had troubled him greatly, adding to the sadness that marked that period of his life. In the beginning, he had feared for her safety. But when he overcame his initial shock, he had reflected on matters seeking an explanation. He had left her there, lying on the floor, her eyes full of bewilderment, as he had taken to his heels without the least explanation. Maybe her flight was an attempt at drawing attention to herself. Recently, she had confided in him saying she felt neglected. She often felt lonely because her mother had to work till late while her father had abandoned them to create another family. Last but not least, he had repaid her with that unpardonable behavior of his, rejecting her after she had made him the gift of her virginity.

«If this affair is not sorted out by tomorrow, we shall have to inform your mother», threatened Wolf.

«She won't believe you, my mother knows me better than you do!» he objected, on the point of collapsing.

Wolf allowed himself to be moved. He took his little Bible from his pocket and offered it to him, but Mikael did not move a finger.

«I hope you will find the strength you need in here», he added, putting the book down gently on his boy's bunk.

He waited a few more seconds and then walked over to the door, nodding to the guard.

«Father!» called Mikael before he had gone.

Wolf turned around.

«What do you think, father? Do you think I'm innocent?»

The priest hesitated, not knowing what to say.

«It doesn't matter, I didn't mean to embarrass you», the boy said, disappointed, saluting him with a wave of the hand.

That night he dreamt of the sea.

It was not the Aegean with its sparkling waters, but rather a cold, colorless ocean. He was on a ship and was examining it fore and aft, from hold to bridge, without finding any sign of life. The engine room had been deserted, despite the fact that the ship was chugging full steam ahead, and all the cabins were empty, the doors flung open.

«Is there anybody here?» he shouted in the wind. «Can anybody hear me?»

Out of nowhere, a sailor appeared on the forecastle. He was lowering the anchor, his back turned to him.

«Hey!» he called to attract the other's attention as the sound of the engines ceased unexpectedly.

The sailor did not turn around but continued to tinker with the ropes in an effort to complete his task. He then squatted down on the deck, his back resting against a lifeboat.

«Why did you do that?» asked Mikael going over to him, but the other remained silent with his head bowed. «Why? We haven't arrived yet», he continued to protest and, in order to look at the other's face, he pulled his head up.

«You...» he then stuttered, dumbfounded: the face looking back at him was identical to his own.

«Surprised?»

«You look just like me.»

The other smiled. «Like two peas in a pod», he pointed out.

«What are you doing here?»

«Waiting for you.»

«Why?»

«To say farewell, we'll never meet again.», and a shadow of sadness clouded his eyes. «I wanted to meet you», he concluded and put out his hand to take Mikael's.

«It's you, really and truly?»

The sailor smiled, reached for Mikael's hand and clasped it tightly.

«I'm your brother», he declared.

Mikael burst out laughing. «Impossible, I'm an only child!»

He woke up startled, someone was shaking him.

«Get up! They're coming to fetch you», a Carabiniere was saying.

Francesca had returned home.

«So, they're taking you away…» sighed Gerasim, coughing as he spoke.

Gabriel had been given permission to visit him in the military hospital to which he had been admitted.

«Yes, the ship sails in a few hours.»

His friend smiled. Despite the treatment, he had not improved.

When they landed in Magadan, Gabriel had disembarked looking like a ghost, all skin and bone, his heart in shatters. Gerasim on the other hand, who appeared to be in better condition, had begun to vomit a few moments after the prisoners had been lined up on the dock.

«It must be the sailor's disease», he told Gabriel who had rushed over to help him.

«Not to worry, they'll find a way of curing you», Gabriel tried to comfort him, even though he felt that the dark stains of clotted blood were an ominous sign.

According to protocol, all newly transferred prisoners had to undergo a medical examination at the military hospital, a three-storey building reserved especially for prisoners. The real purpose was to separate the healthy from the sick, if not the dying. Those deemed fit continued their journey to the minefields, the others were admitted to hospices to await their end.

«Have you found out where they're sending you?» asked Gerasim in a whisper of a voice.

«I've heard talk of Pevek.»

«Pevek? Even polar bears would refuse to go there!»

A prisoner groaned in the next bed. The huge swelling on his neck was choking him.

«Yesterday, the fellow over there died», whispered Gerasim, pointing at the empty bed opposite.

Gabriel looked out the window: Magadan stretched out before his eyes in blinding shafts of sunlight. He allowed his gaze to wander over the port, the two docks like the claws of a gigantic shellfish embracing three ships, one of which was ready to sail. Further up, he saw a gaggle of huts, factories with smoking chimneys, the surrounding hills sprinkled with snow. In the distance, a winding road leading northward.

«Will you miss all this?» joked Gerasim.

He turned around. He was used to seeing people fade away, but Gerasim's head looked like a skull to him. He remembered the first time he had seen him at the camp: a thin worn-out man with no teeth and rotten gums. But now his skin had taken on that yellow hue, typical of those whose days are numbered.

«I'll miss you», he said.

Gerasim chuckled, intending to playthings down, but a fit of coughing almost choked him.

«D'ye know the last time someone said that to me?» he said, making a great effort to speak.

Gabriel shook his head.

«I was five, it was my mother, the day I was leaving for summer camp.»

The soldier in charge nodded to inform them that visiting time was over.

«I have to go.»

«Okay.»

Gerasim mustered up his usual smile and stretched out his hand, his fingers curved like claws.

«You've been a wonderful travel mate», whispered Gabriel and, as a handshake seemed far too little, he bent down and hugged his friend to express the sincere affection he felt for him.

18

Standing next to the lifeboat, the sentry watched the port vanish slowly in the mist. The smoke from his *machorka,* clamped tightly between his lips, was borne away on the wind.

The *Linka* had just sailed out of Magadan. It was an old whaler that had been adapted for the transport of passengers. Its tonnage was less than that of the *Vanja,* and it travelled the route to the mines of northern Siberia, a territory impossible to reach overland, because of its few, often impracticable roads. On board the prisoners were no longer kept in the hold though each one was obliged to perform hard, menial tasks.

Gabriel took notice of the man as he was scrubbing the floor of the upper deck. There was something about his stance, maybe the way he held his shoulders back, that seemed familiar to him. He slid the bucket along a little to get a better view of him.

On hearing the noise, the man spun around. It was Lev, the lion.

«Surprise!» he burst out, cackling and raising his hat just a little to salute him ironically.

Gabriel looked him attentively, examining his face. In daylight, he was far younger than he had imagined before. His Caucasian features — oval face, high cheekbones, broad forehead — reminded him of those of his own people.

«Aren't you going to greet me back?» said Lev, taunting him.

Gabriel continued washing the floor and barely nodded to him.

«Look at me; that's an order!» barked Lev.

Gabriel stopped scrubbing, lifted his eyes and planted the handle of the floor brush firmly on the deck. Lev had drawn closer to him. Straight, cock sure, one hand on his waist, while with the other he gestured to him to obey. In the pale morning light, a red gold wedding ring flashed on his little finger.

«S-S-1935», he spelt out with a sneer, shoving it under his eye. «You shouldn't have got so cut up over that girl, you know! After all she was only a little fucking slut» he said, underlining this cutting remark with a lewd gesture as he passed the tip of his tongue slowly along his upper lip.

Gabriel felt the anger boil up inside of him. Seeing his mother's wedding ring—the love token he had given his adored Nina—on that hand made his stomach lurch. He would have liked to hurl himself against Lev, knock him to the ground and strangle him right then and there. So, at last, he had found the person who had murdered his darling and the desire to avenge her death overwhelmed him. «No foolhardy actions, though», he told himself recalling his friend Gerasim's words of advice. There was no question of a fair fight, he needed to be cunning, catch that louse off guard. He just lowered his eyes and, although his heart pounded wildly in his breast, he resumed his work under Lev's contemptuous gaze.

It was the 25th of May 1953, the feast of Pentecost. The college staff had decided to celebrate by taking the boys on a trip to the island of San Lazzaro. Pentecost was a feast the Mekhitarist fathers celebrated with the greatest solemnity because it recalled the gift of the Holy Ghost to the faithful.

«Bakunìn, why this long face? Swear you aren't thinking about her!» exclaimed Aznavour sitting on the waterbus next to Mikael.

He shook his head

«Fiddlesticks», said his friend, laughing.

«I'm just a little tired», he answered, lying.

Had he been more honest he would have admitted he was thinking about Francesca, as he did every single day. When the girl had returned home, Mikael had been released from custody with no further action. The brigadier had told him that she had simply stayed with a friend of hers, Marina, a student who lived alone and that she had remained there a day and two nights. Then, because she had felt sorry for what she had done and was fed up hiding, she had decided to return to the fold.

«No charge, you can go», the officer had informed him.

Mikael had taken Wolf's Bible and with the priest, who was waiting for him outside the barracks, had returned to the college.

The fathers had been surprisingly indulgent with him. Maybe they had taken pity on his terrible plight or maybe they thought it might be better not to make too much of a fuss over such a delicate matter. His mother had not even been informed and when Mikael had made some mention of it in one of his letters home, the priests had confiscated it and then read it out to everyone.

«First you create havoc, then you go around prattling to all and sundry about it», the rector had declared while his companions just tittered with amusement.

Despite this lenience, Mikael had received three kinds of penance: fasting, prayer and alms. He had been banned from the refectory for a whole week and given only bread and water, he had spent hours in the college chapel reciting the Hail Mary and had been obliged to give his food away to beggars. Luckily enough, Aznavour had smuggled some leftovers from the dining hall into the dorms, and he had devoured them under the blankets.

«I saw you yesterday, still waiting there beside the boundary wall», his friend insisted as the waterbus left the pier.

Mikael shrugged, unable to contradict him. He had turned up on that very spot every day, waiting in vain for his Francesca to show up…

«Hey!» Keropé and Hampò said as they came staggering over in their direction.

«Move over», said the Persian lad sitting on the wooden bench.

«No place here for ladies», joked Aznavour.

Keropé sat down just the same shoving his friend aside to make room.

Looking at his friends' behavior, Mikael thought they were still such children. Even with regard to what had happened to him, his companions' attitude had been immature, and this had hurt him. Some simulated embarrassing indifference, others took it all as a joke, sniggering and grinning allusively. Although for quite some time now, all of them fantasized about their «first time», discussing it at night and during their free time, none of them had dared discuss the matter with him, question him about the experience, ask him for «particulars». Nobody, except Aznavour, had made any attempt to understand what it had been like and how he was feeling now. Somehow, his long-time companions seemed to spurn him. Or, was it just him who had grown aloof after that incident?

«I'm starving...» complained Hampò.

«I hope they give us something good to eat», said Keropé.

«The monks? Rye bread, goat's cheese and a few black olives. If you're lucky, maybe some *vartanoush*», laughed Aznavour.

«What's that?»

«The jam made from the roses in their garden.

«Yummy! I can't wait to get tucked in. I hope Mass won't last too long.»

«Half a day at least», said Hampò, butting in.

«Yep! They have to read nine Gospels», Aznavour joked.

Then they all burst out laughing.

Mikael envied their carefree mood, their desire to fool about, their light-heartedness.

«Next stop!» Wolf called out.

Mikael sprang to his feet, feeling slightly more optimistic. Soon the school year would come to a close and all the students would be going home for the summer holidays. Maybe, away from the college, he might find some way of putting things into proper perspective.

«Time will cure me,» he thought as the launch docked at the island of San Lazzaro of the Armenians.

In 1717, San Lazzaro, once a leper colony, had been entrusted by the Venetian Republic to the care of Manug di Pietro, an Armenian monk known as Mechitàr, founder of the order which bears his name. Mechitàr and his followers had escaped persecution by the Turks and fled to Italy. The Republic of Venice, the Most Serene —which had always greatly appreciated the culture and history of the Armenian people with which it had traded in the lands of Byzantium—granted the island to the Mekhitarists so they might set up the new seat of the order there.

The monks had set down to work, restored the church and the remains of the monastery, in ruins at the time, with the help of wealthy Armenian benefactors. Even the island itself was enlarged and on this reclaimed land a marvelous garden full of rare plants and exquisite flowers had been planted.

They had refurbished and redecorated the old Gothic church dedicated to San Lazzaro, the patron saint of lepers. The apse was hidden by a curtain in keeping with the Armenian rite, and the altar was brought forward to make room for the choir and rebuilt using precious marble following instructions laid down by Mechitàr himself. Three tall stain-glass windows from Innsbruck, the central one portraying the patron saint, had been installed behind the altar, throwing beautiful colored patterns on the floor when the sun shone through them.

That Pentecost Monday the church was full of worshippers who had come to attend the solemn Eucharistic service. An intense, almost sickening odor of incense hung in the air. The Mass was officiated by father Samuel, a thin young man with a crewcut, whose hieratic, severe mien reminded one of a Byzantine monarchs. Swathed in a red damask mantle he solemnly intoned:

«Oh God of the old and new covenants / who revealed yourself in the fire on the sacred mount/ and in the Pentecost of your spirit/ make one pyre of our pride».

Mikael paid great attention, forcing himself to grasp the true significance of the invocation and, although the liturgy had always fascinated him, that day it disturbed him.

The celebrant took a step forward. He wore embroidered slippers with gold thread and two red gems woven into the uppers.

«I have come to cast fire on the earth.», father Samuel thundered, his flowing mantle enveloping him, giving the impression that he was surrounded by flames.

Mikael was hypnotized by his voice.

«Fire», repeated the priest looking him straight in the eye, «And what will I, but that it be kindled?»

On hearing these verses from the Gospel of Saint Luke, Mikael felt the heat of the flames. The word fire was obsessing him. As his gaze swept over the congregation, his eyes met those of father Elias, notorious teacher of sexology and exorcist, who was staring at him with a stern, inquisitive air.

Red petals rained down from the altar on the heads of the faithful, like so many tongues of fire, symbolizing the Holy Ghost who would illuminate men's minds.

«Veni Creator Spiritus, come oh Holy Spirit, Creator blest, enlighten our minds», sang the choir.

Mikael felt his head swim, his eyes cloud over; moments later he passed out.

When he came to again, lying in a bed in one of the cells where the fathers had brought him, he did his utmost to make some sense of what had happened. He tried to find a reason why during the mass he had risen from his place, and leaving his companions behind him, had burst into the nave. Why he had stood facing father Samuel and, overcome by terror, had howled: «*Vivi missi sunt hi duo in stagnum ignis ardentis sulphurae[7]*».

Above all, he wondered from where those words from the Apocalypse had surfaced and which he had quoted in perfect Latin, where the fire of hell had appeared so terrifying to make him fall to the floor as if struck by lightning.

«Your enemy, the devil prowls around like a roaring lion looking for someone to devour», asserted father Elias, quoting the famous words of the Apostle Peter.

«Admitting you are right», said Wolf in an effort to indulge him, «how did you arrive at this conclusion?» In the past he had often held discussions with this old monk and was well aware that it was useless to challenge him on matters he believed belonged to his domain of competence.

After Mikael had fainted, the two priests sat there together reflecting on how best to help the boy, who was evidently affected by some serious disorder. Father Elias looked out the window of his cell. In the garden, in the cloister, several students were talking and playing.

«Do you see those boys down there?» he asked Wolf. «Those are normal. They shout, play, laugh. Now, I know Mikael well enough by now to claim that he's always behaved- and things have worsened- in a very peculiar fashion. You told me yourself that his roommates have often heard him wake at night, that he suffers from frequent stomach cramps and nausea and that during your lessons he has shown a certain aversion to religion and everything sacred.»

«Well, actually, he was only asking questions; normal at his age.»

«That's not true and you know it», father Elias retorted, «the boy shows signs typical of those possessed by the Evil One. I saw him today, during mass. Just before he fainted, he looked right at me in sheer bewilderment. He was looking for help, this is what I read in his eyes.»

Wolf decided not to reply. He needed to protect Mikael at all costs, but prudently and with arguments capable of undermining the old monk's ideas.

«He is the most brilliant boy I have ever met,» he began, «acute, profound and, compared to his companions, incredibly mature and wise. Not to speak of his musical talents. His playing sends shivers down your spine and when he sings...» At a loss for words to describe the boy's extraordinary voice, he simply pointed to the heavens. «Are these not gifts from God? An unequivocal, divine blessing?»

Wolf was standing facing father Elias and looking inquiringly into his eyes.

A brief sarcastic smile appeared on the old man's chapped lips.

«Ah, so you don't know what Satan is capable of.», he responded shaking his head. «The devil showers his servants with wonderful gifts. He makes them shine of their own light, raises them up to the heavens before casting them down into the infernal pit. Beauty, eternal youth, talent, intelligence. Everything. He can grant whatever he chooses to any luckless wretch willing to sell his soul. Today, Mikael quoted verses in Latin, doesn't that surprise you?»

«Well, he does speak five languages perfectly», said Wolf in an effort to justify the boy.

«The ancient ones too?» answered the monk, scoring a point. «He's possessed», he pontificated.

Wolf shuddered upon hearing this sentence.

«No, you're wrong. It is not the case with Mikael», he objected. «He is only somewhat stressed, overtaxed. That story with the girl, I'm sure you've been told, disturbed him greatly. That night in the barracks, the cross questioning, his anguish over her disappearance. We shouldn't underestimate the facts.»

«Exactly; let's not underestimate the facts», said father Elias with considerable emphasis. «I'm telling you that I'll hold you personally responsible for what he does from now on. Don't try to hide his doings and strange fits from me, you know I'll find out anyway.»

Then he opened a drawer in his writing desk and took out a wooden cross with a Christ in ivory and kissed it reverently.

«Our Patriarch gave it to me as a present many, many years ago in the holy monastery of Saint James in Jerusalem. The wood», he whispered touching it lightly with trembling fingers «is part of the True Cross.»

«God be praised!» exclaimed Wolf, drawn not so much by the cross as by the stigmata in the palms of the monk's hands. He had already heard the story of the cross which father Elias told him every time he was given the chance. His devotion to the relic had always amazed Wolf. It was the only material object the monk had ever possessed in the whole of his long life.

«All right», he said eventually «I'll keep you informed if I notice any strange behavior on his part. But now, please let me go and see how he is.»

Father Elias held out the hand with the crucifix. Wolf bowed and brushed it with his lips and made the sign of the cross.

«He never lies», the old man reminded him «and he will help us understand whether Mephistopheles had taken possession of this pupil of ours. If I am right, we'll free his troubled soul», he concluded with an impetus worthy of a fearless warrior.

The *Linka*, with its human cargo, ploughed the calm waters of the Sea of Bering on its way to Pevek.

They had set sail from Magadan three days before. Three days during which Gabriel had brushed floors, cleaned out cabins, scrubbed the deck and performed all the tasks assigned to him, his head held low to avoid meeting Lev's gaze. Nevertheless, his hatred for that man had not subsided. On the contrary, it had increased second after second, so much so, that it prevented him from getting any sleep.

He was downright obsessed by Lev, he could feel his presence everywhere.

The sun was vanishing behind the verdant Petropavlovsk peninsula. It was the time of year when it set late and the scenery was shrouded in a lingering twilight. The prisoners had finished their day's work and they were putting away their buckets, brushes and cloths. Soon they would go down into the hold. They were veritable living corpses by now; their shoulders stooped, their legs weak, their breathing labored. They just could not wait to throw themselves down on their miserable bunks. In the morning they would count the dead; someone always died in his sleep, but Gabriel would not be among these.

Not yet. The desire to kill would keep him alive until justice had been done.

He could hear the sound of his enemy's voice, which the roar of the engines did not manage to drown out. It was loud, clear and rude. Unable to bear it any further, he lifted up his head. Lo and behold, Lev stood there with two fellow soldiers smoking his usual *machorka*, leaning up against one of the lifeboats.

«This is the last trip», he was saying, «then I'll be on leave for two months.»

«How's that?» asked the private with curled-up whiskers.

«Well, it's just that I know some people.»

«You asshole!» joked the other.

«Actually, there is a reason», Lev explained, «I'm marrying my *kukla*, my little doll, could I miss my own wedding?»

«You lucky bastard!», cried private Whiskers.

«All the very best!» exclaimed the third man.

They clapped each other on the back, laughing, while Gabriel's teeth chattered uncontrollably.

An explosion made the ship rock.

A deafening blast knocked Gabriel, as well as Lev and his friends off balance. In a split second, the crew, the guards, the prisoners were all thrown into a state of sheer panic.

«Fire! The ship's on fire!» shouted a man struggling up from the engine room. His eyes were watering, his face a mask of soot, his hair disheveled. Then he started choking, spluttering, spewing black mucous.

The smoke siren went off, bellowing like the pitiful lament of a beached whale.

A second explosion, stronger than the first, ripped through the entire vessel and flames began to devour the deck. Metal began to melt, girders to collapse, parts of the ship to cave in. Men were amok all over the place trying to escape the fire. Some had become human torches already, others were injured, while those as yet unscathed were looking for an escape route; anyone would do. Some of them, in utter despair and believing they might save their lives, threw themselves headlong into the freezing waters of the Bering Sea.

Amid the flames and turmoil, Gabriel caught a glimpse of Lev. The sentry was in utter terror, fidgeting with some ropes, trying to lower a lifeboat.

This was the chance he had been waiting for, for so long.

«It's now or never!» he thought, as he jumped on him in one leap.

Taken completely off guard, Lev looked straight at him. He did not even try to defend himself, instead he seemed to be imploring him with his eyes, to launch the damned lifeboat together and save their lives.

He could not have been more mistaken.

Overpowered by an uncontrollable rage, Gabriel caught him by the neck and dug his teeth in his flesh, so deeply he could taste his blood. Then he pulled back to take stock of things: Lev was wheezing as he stared at him in horror, knowing that he was done for. Gabriel caught hold of his head and drew it tightly to himself in an incomprehensible gesture of despair. He stood motionless for a while before he took to banging it as hard as he could against the deck, over and over again until it was smashed in.

«There, it's all over now» he told himself, thinking that Nina had been vindicated, at last.

A few seconds later he came back to his senses as if emerging from a trance. He let go of his enemy's crushed skull and began to tremble with sheer repugnance.

"How did I do something so awful?" he broke down, bursting into floods of tears.

His rage had spiked into uncontrollable, blind, murderous fury that had brought him to commit an abominable crime. He recalled the past, the sweetness of his not so distant childhood and realized that his innocence had been irretrievably lost.

The awareness of what he had become pierced his soul like a dagger.

He looked at the lifeless face of his enemy, the man's wide-open eyes, his throat and chest covered in blood and suddenly he felt the curse of God upon him, like the one the Almighty had inflicted on Cain after he had murderer his brother.

«A fugitive and a vagabond shalt thou be on earth!» he murmured to himself.

He fell on his knees alongside Lev, sobbing, as the flames began to lick his feet. Overcome by despair, he had decided to let himself die, allow himself to be consumed by these tongues of fire.

He just stayed there, on the blistering hot deck, like a sacrificial victim on a pyre.

On the motorbus taking them back to Venice, Mikael felt he was beginning to burn, a sensation that grew more and more intense. It was if he were sitting on a bundle of red-hot wood. He was so frightened that the only urge he felt was that of escaping. He rose from the bench in silence and sprung lightly up onto the bulwark of the launch, where he teetered precariously examining the Laguna in the twilight.

For a fleeting instant, he had the impression he was in the place he used to see in a recurring childhood dream, where, on the shores of a bay, he used to play with an imaginary friend of his.

A sudden dive. Nobody could stop him.

Contact with the water barely alleviated the burning sensation on his skin. The fire that seared his heart needed a different cure.

«Mikael, no!» shouted Wolf, aware all too late of the boy's foolish deed.

19

«How are you feeling?»

Mikael acknowledged the priest's presence with a nod.

«Better?»

«Yes», he answered in a very weak voice.

Wolf sat beside him on the edge of the little bed and settled the blankets around his charge.

«Would you like some tea?»

«Not now, thank you.»

«You vomited so much; you need liquids.»

He lifted up the old cast iron teapot and filled a cup.

«Try to sit up.»

The boy complied but with some effort.

Wolf raised the pillow behind his head and brought the cup on the table a little closer to him.

«It's not too hot, you may drink it», he said.

Mikael began to sip, his hands trembling slightly.

«Why are you staring at me?» he asked his teacher.

«I'm worried.»

The shadow of a smile crept over the boy's lips.

«I'm not dead yet, you know…» His eyes were red, his hair combed back, except for that rebellious lock which fell across his forehead. «Is Emil still here?»

«They've all gone back to the college. We're alone, you and I.»

It was almost midnight. Wolf had waited patiently in the cell for the boy to reawaken and, telling his beads, had said the rosary.

«Why did you do it, Mikael?» he asked him point blank.

The boy turned his eyes away.

«Don't you want to tell me?» insisted Wolf, disappointed.

«I would if you listened to me, if...» he broke off and looked up at his teacher, «if you swore you'd try to understand me.»

Wolf drew nearer, pulling his chair closer to the bed.

«Tell me about yourself. I promise I'll always stand by you.»

«But you don't understand? I don't need allies; I'm not at war. Above all, I don't feel the need to justify myself. What I need is someone who will listen without judging me.» He had spurted out this spiel, prompted by a kind of rage he found hard to control. «If I find myself in this state, I fear it's because we've all got things wrong. Me, you, the whole college. If you'd been more available, I'd certainly have told you about my Calvary.»

«Calvary?»

«Indescribable suffering.»

«Due to what?»

Mikael shrugged.

«How long has it been going on?»

The boy did not answer.

«How long, Mikael?»

«Ages and ages, since I was a child, but it's grown worse here in college», he added with a shadow of resentment.

«Have you spoken to anyone about it. Emil maybe?»

«I tried once, one evening, chatting in the dorm.»

«And he?»

«He was snoring before I could finish telling him about what was happening to me.»

«Nobody else?»

«Francesca, but I only mentioned the vision.»

«The vision?»

Mikael nodded.

«What form do these attacks take?» whispered Wolf.

For the first time, Mikael caught the note of sincerity and affectionate interest in the priest's voice.

«It's quite simple, really. It's just that at times I have the feeling I'm living somebody else's life.»

«And whose life would that be?»

Mikael sighed.

«Well. A boy who looks a lot like me. Once I dreamt he told me he was my brother, weird thing, I have no siblings.»

«But why does it make you suffer so?» insisted Wolf.

«Because his life is sheer torment. A gap is thrown wide open, all of a sudden, like a secret passageway taking me into his world. I am forced to witness the cruel events of his life, feel his pain.»

He examined Wolf's eyes. He wouldn't have continued had he caught the slightest hint of disbelief there. But the teacher was shaking his head gently and seemed to be reflecting seriously on his words.

«What made you leap into the water?» he asked in an almost inaudible voice.

«He was burning. And I with him.»

Wolf was visibly disturbed.

«The ship he was sailing in, was on fire, but he didn't want to save himself. He wanted to burn to a cinder.»

«I don't understand…»

Mikael burst into tears.

«He had just killed a man!» he shouted. «He had killed a human being, and he wanted to kill himself!»

«You mean, you threw yourself into the sea out of despair?»

Mikael raised his tear-filled eyes. «No. I wanted him to follow my example, give him the strength to resist. I wanted him to save himself. I couldn't bear to see him die.»

He broke off and the cell fell silent.

«Had he died, I would have died with him», he affirmed with such vehement sincerity that Wolf shivered.

Mikael fell back soon into a deep sleep.

Wolf stayed in his cell watching over him like a guardian angel, aware of the shock the boy had experienced. As he walked up and down the cell, he couldn't help mulling over the dramatic moments of that evening.

After Mikael had plunged into the water, havoc had broken loose aboard the launch. Although he had had the presence of mind to order the helmsman to stop the boat, Wolf himself had got into panic.

«He's fallen into the sea. Mikael's fallen into the sea!», he kept on saying, as if it were a mantra of some kind.

It was Aznavour's prompt reaction that had avoided the

tragedy. An expert swimmer, he had removed his shoes in a jiffy and dived into the water to save his friend.

«Bakunìn!» he kept calling, his head above the waves while Wolf, his eyes glued to him, had prayed with all the fervor his soul could muster.

As darkness fell on the Laguna, Aznavour's mission became more urgent. He could no longer see a thing amid the sloe-black waters. A strong beam of light was then pointed from the launch onto the sea, while he desperately fought to find his beloved friend.

It was Mikael's white trousers he noticed first suspended a few meters below the water's surface and his hair floating like the dark tentacles of a squid. Without wasting an instant, Aznavour had caught hold of him by the waist and pulled him up above water.

«Hold on to the lifebelts!» yelled a member of the crew as he threw the orange-colored rings to him.

Mikael's inert body was hoisted onto the launch. Like a fish that has just been caught, he lay face downwards on the deck, as the teachers and the students gathered round.

«Stand back, stand back!» one of the sailors shouted.

«Make room», echoed Wolf.

They had turned him over on one side, and, hitting him on the back, had made him throw up all the water he had drunk. Mikael had coughed several times before he began to breathe normally again.

«May the Lord be praised!» Wolf had exclaimed without succeeding to hold back his tears. «Emil, may God bless you», he had whispered to Aznavour who, wrapped in a blanket was drying himself.

A knock on the door shook father Keshishian out of his reverie. He checked his watch: it was four in the morning.

«Who is it?» he whispered behind the door.

«Me, Elias», croaked a voice.

Wolf turned the key in the lock and let him in.

«It's a good thing you shut yourselves in», said the elderly monk. «It's better to be prudent.»

«Isn't it a bit early?» objected Wolf. «He's worn out, he needs to sleep.» «No», sentenced Elias, «the sun rises in an hour's time, there's no time to lose.»

Wolf was about to protest, but Elias's ice-cold eyes riveted him to the spot.

«Has he said anything?» asked the old man.

«No, he only asked for Emil, he probably wants to thank him.»

After having rescued Mikael, the launch had returned to the island bringing him back to the monastery. Aznavour had had just enough time to take a warm shower and get into some dry clothes. Then, although he had asked, with a certain insistence, to remain with his friend, the monks had denied their permission and he had had to return to Venice with all the others.

«Let me stay with him», Aznavour had pleaded, this time entreating the rector, as soon as they had reached the pier again.

«Only father Keshishian is staying. There's no need for us here. He'll be back at school again tomorrow, anyway», he had added, playing things down as he looked at the other boys who listened all worried.

The two boys had been unable to meet or talk to each other, even though Mikael would have preferred his friend's comforting company to that of his teacher.

«I've already let father Samuel know. He'll be waiting for us in church. Wake him up as soon as I've left», Elias ordered Wolf.

The boy muttered in his sleep and tossed in the bed.

Father Keshishian hurried over to Mikael and felt his forehead.

«I'm afraid he has a temperature», he said and went to pick up the thermometer from the bedside table.

«Leave it», said the old monk, blocking his hand. «There's no better remedy than the one we are about to administer. Exorcism. This is not a disease of the body but of the soul», he asserted in irrevocable tones.

«Most Glorious Prince of the Heavenly Hosts, saint Michael Archangel», began father Elias, standing up straight in the middle of the church. In his left hand he held an old prayer book, in his right the cross, the celebrated relic from the Holy Land.

In the apse, father Samuel, draped in his ceremonial mantle, swung the thurible diffusing incense at every one of the exorcist's utterances.

Mikael, accompanied by Wolf, was seated in the ciborium on a straw-bottom chair turned towards the altar. They had dressed him in a white tunic, one of those worn by postulants, and tied at the waist by a cord. Around him, facing the four cardinal points, stood four tall candles.

At seventeen minutes past five in the morning, the first ray of the rising sun struck the boy's forehead like a luminous shaft and rippled down to his breast.

It was the perfect sign for the exorcism to begin.

Wolf, visibly moved, stood behind Mikael as the boy's paladin. He had tried to stop all this and rebuked himself for not having opposed the ceremony with sufficient determination.

That night, after Elias had left the cell, Wolf had waited a while then had gone in search of father Samuel.

«I need to speak to you», he had told him, stopping him as he was coming out of his cell. «But what's that?» he had asked as he pointed inquiringly at a small leather case the other priest had in his hand.

«A tape recorder. Elias wants to record everything.»

Wolf had stiffened. «This is pure folly, a colossal mistake», he burst out.

«I don't understand.» Father Samuel had retorted, turning the light off and pulling the door shut with one hand.

«Mikael is not possessed.»

«A difference of opinion», said the other cutting short and hastening away.

«He's simply confused.»

«Didn't you see him yesterday at mass? He began raving, quoting from the Apocalypse, staring at me in scorn!»

«What if he were ill? Have you never heard of diseases of the spirit? Sigmund Freud, Carl Gustav Jung. Do these names mean nothing to you? Religion is not the alpha and omega of everything. The psyche, my dear brother, the psyche has extraordinary powers. Superior even to…»

«To?…» Father Samuel had halted suddenly, staring at him inquisitively, without hiding his vexation.

«I'm worried», continued Wolf.

«About what?»

«The trauma this may cause. After all, he's only a boy.»

«Frankly, I don't agree with you. Don't you know he's already a man. We all know about his amorous adventures. Anyway, dear father, prayer can only do him good.»

They had both stood there studying each other for a few seconds.

«Let's not lose any more precious time. The rite must begin as soon as the first ray of sunlight strikes the altar. You know that, don't you?»

Wolf, disheartened, unable to utter another word, had gone back to the room to fetch Mikael.

«We have to go», he whispered shortly afterwards, waking him with a gentle shake of the shoulder.

Mikael had opened his eyes wide. «Where?» he had asked lifting his head from the pillow.

«To church.»

«At this hour?»

Father Keshishian had remained silent, with a guilty look on his face.

«Why?» the boy had insisted.

Wolf would have given anything to avoid this thorny, embarrassing situation.

«Morning prayer», he had murmured.

Mikael had shaken his head.

«It's for your good, you'll feel much better afterwards», Wolf had added sitting on the edge of bed.

«Father, I pray every day, I always have. What's so different about this morning?»

Wolf had taken one of the boy's hands and held it with affection, something he had never dared do with any other student. He could see Mikael was deeply disturbed and shaken.

«My dear child, it's a special mass, dedicated to you, to your illness. Father Elias, and many others too, believe that your predicament is caused by the Devil, by Satan in person.»

Mikael had drawn his hand back.

«This is absurd. I have just confided in you. Told you things nobody else knows, not even my mother, my friends, my girlfriend.»

«It's only a prayer meeting», Wolf had objected feebly.

«No, that's not what I mean. I'm unhappy at the superficial way you face my plight. You swore you'd try to understand. I was wrong. Seeing how highly I think of you, I thought you'd help me get to the heart of the problem, the root of my suffering although...» he broke off suddenly.

«Although?»

«I fear there's no real cure», he had concluded, getting up, an embittered look on his face.

Father Elias's voice boomed amid the pink marble columns. The monk stood facing Mikael waving the cross while father Samuel, from the altar, intoned a Gregorian chant with his hoarse voice, waving a sun-shaped flabellum adorned with chimes in the air and continuing to diffuse incense. The rays of the sun played on the golden walls forming a gigantic halo that surrounded the entire place. The atmosphere was particularly suggestive and Mikael allowed himself to be carried away into that mysterious world of double existence which dwelt within him. For a moment, only one instant, he believed that prayer was the only solution, the only remedy possible.

Jump! Jump now!
I have forgiven you already.
Wash the stains of blood in the sea, no-one shall know.
Swim, on, don't cry, don't despair.
I'm praying for you.

Father Elia's brow glistened with sweat as he pressed the cross down against Mikael's breast with all his might. The boy jolted and writhed, while from behind, Wolf put his arms around him, as if seeking to protect him from the dark forces of evil.

«I command you God the Father; I command you God the Son; I command you God the Holy Ghost», father Elias recited, visibly exhausted.

For a fraction of time, Mikael and Gabriel were one, coexisting into a single being, as if someone had abolished the barrier — physical or mental — the space can create.

I with you.

Gabriel made a great effort to remain afloat.

Although he had made up his mind to let himself die after killing Lev, some mysterious force had urged him to jump into the sea. And now he was trying desperately to reach one of the lifeboats which the crew had managed to launch. But the water was freezing and he grew more and more exhausted. He turned over on his back, allowing the waves to carry him along — resigned to his fate — trying to turn his last thoughts to pleasant things. He imagined his father heating milk, his mother cutting bread, himself and Novàrt, his little rosebud, sitting down to breakfast.

«You want my slice, little one, don't you?», he whispered.

He breathed in the air of the setting sun and a vague aroma of ripe apricots played with his nostrils: the smell of his darling Nina. He made one last effort, bringing his fist to his breast. Two light beats like the wings of a butterfly.

«I live only for you», he was tempted to say, but he almost burst out laughing, realizing he had no life left to live.

He decided to lie still. Floating, he stared at the sky, at its wonderful colors, ranging from blue, to violet to red. He asked himself whether there had been anything missing from his short existence.

«Nothing»

Out of the blue, a piece of Gregorian chant rang out in his head, along with a series of broken images: a smoking thurible, a flabellum shaped like the sun, a crucifix of worn-out wood. In the middle, surrounded by a halo of light and incense, he thought he saw a boy who, absorbed in prayer, offered him salvation and hope.

He smiled.

Then, quickly, harmoniously, with the grace and ease of a young man on the flying trapeze, he emerged for a moment from his body and joined that of the other boy, identical in every way.

He then looked up at the sky again.

Motionless, perfect, waiting for life to slip away from his young body.

Cognition

20

Toronto, 1991

«Ladies and gentlemen, the captain informs us that in a few minutes we shall land at Toronto Pearson airport», crackled the voice on the loudspeakers.

Mikael shifted nervously in his seat. He rummaged in his pocket for his pill box and took out two whitish tablets which he gulped down with the help of water from a paper cup. He then fastened his seatbelt as tightly as he could and looked out the window. A handful of small clouds floated in the blue sky, like soft fluffy lambs in a celestial meadow. Down below he could make out bean-shaped Lake Ontario stretching out as far as Toronto. The plane continued its descent and the aircraft's poor pressurization blocked his ears.

Aznavour was right, he should have flown with one of the European airlines, instead of having to settle down for a cheap flight.

Then, he thought the Mekhitarists would never have paid more for his ticket nor, clearly, would he have accepted a dearer one either. That trip was a mission on behalf of the Moorat-Raphael college: in one week he was expected to convince the Canadian community to offer funds for the school which was now on the verge of bankruptcy.

Mikael was about to crumble under the burden of a similar responsibility.

He swallowed several times to free his ears as his eyes continued to wander over the city below, its skyline defined by hundreds of skyscrapers. In the distance, the famous CN, the Canadian

National Tower, stood out needle-like reaching for the heavens. It was the building that Aznavour had celebrated most frequently in his letters, with a certain pride, as if he himself had had a hand in building it. He had even promised that had he come over he would take him to dine in its revolving restaurant at the very top.

«It's like dining in paradise!» he had exclaimed one evening on the phone.

He closed his eyes and conjured up the face of Emil Megoyan, now bald and plump, judging by the photos he had sent. Since he had moved to Canada, Emil had put on some weight and Mikael wondered if he would recognize him in the crowd at the airport. After all, they had not seen each other for almost forty years, although they had always written and telephoned each other.

When, at last, the plane landed, Mikael felt his heart race overcome by deep emotion at the sole idea of embracing his old friend again.

"Who knows if he will still call me Bakunìn", he wondered and smiled.

«What's the purpose of your visit to this country?» asked the emigration official.

She had markedly Asian features but spoke perfect English, except for the phoneme «R» which sounded more like an «L».

«Tourism», Mikael answered.

The lady nodded and continued to flick through his passport, filling the air with her strong jasmine perfume, a little too much for Mikael at such an early hour in the morning.

«Why were you in the wrong queue?»

«Sheer distraction, as I said before. I'm so sorry.»

«Distraction», she repeated, shaking her head.

Shortly before that, Mikael, lost in his thoughts, had gone with his luggage to stand in a shorter queue and, having arrived at the desk, had handed his passport in to the official. But the man, annoyed, had invited him to look at the notice above the window.

«Canadian and US citizens only», he had read.

All red and stammering an excuse, he was about to join another queue when the man signaled to him to stop. Then, he had lifted up a receiver and spoken in a low voice to someone. The lady with the oriental features had appeared and invited him to follow her into an office, where Mikael soon understood that he was suspected of trying the enter the country illegally.

«So, I see you live in Rome.» she was now asking.

«Yes.»

«But you were born in Athens.»

«Yes.»

«How come you live in Italy?»

«I went to boarding-school in Venice and…»

«And it was there that you learnt English so well?» the woman prompted.

«Precisely.»

She nodded and began scratching the corner of his passport with one of her nails before taking it over to the window and examining in the light for a few seconds.

«What's your job, Mr Delalian?»

«I have an antique shop.»

«Hmm…», ventured the woman, her expression less rigid. «And what exactly do you sell?»

Mikael sighed. «Ancient objects, Byzantine relics, icons and manuscripts and so on. As you may have gathered from my surname, I am of Armenian origin. So, I'm on the outlook for objects associated with my people; I travel frequently to Anatolia, Syria, Cyprus, Egypt, that is, to all those countries where the Byzantine and Armenian cultures have left their mark. I also have a personal collection in my shop which is, obviously, not for sale.»

That was his job, in brief, but he also took an immense interest in theology and philosophy, wrote for dedicated journals, and had even published some excellent essays.

The lady listened to him, enchanted, her hands steepled, her elbows on her desk. Mikael's voice had always fascinated listeners, especially when he spoke about what he believed in and loved most.

«All right», the official said at last as she stamped his passport. «You have a tourist visa of one month, Mr Delalian», she concluded rising and handing him back his document.

«Thank you.»

She accompanied him to the door and indicated the way out with a gesture.

«I beg your pardon, again», Mikael whispered, shaking her hand.

«Well, *'allivedelci Loma!'*» she exclaimed in Italian. «That's what you say, no?» she asked with a smile.

«Precisely», he answered smiling back and, picking up his case, headed towards the arrivals hall.

«Bakunìn!», shouted a voice from a distance.

Mikael turned around but failed to recognize anyone in the crowded arrivals hall.

«Mikael», called the voice again, this time closer.

A tall, stout man was making his way through the crowd asking permission, smiling broadly and waving his arms frantically. It was Aznavour, beside himself with joy and contentment.

«Aznavour, old man», Mikael said, deeply moved when he saw him, and hastened over to embrace him, holding him tightly. The happiness on seeing each other after decades was authentic and sincere.

«Oh, how I've missed you!» exclaimed his friend, pummeling him on the back.

Mikael stepped back to look at him. Emil had aged really well, unlike what the photos seemed to say. He had very few wrinkles, his skin was pliant and healthy-looking, while his bright eyes had maintained their youthful expression. For a moment, he thought he was looking at the face of the boy he once knew.

«Had you a good trip?» Aznavour was saying, jerking his jeans up and adjusting his big, blue sweatshirt with the Toronto Maple Leafs logo, his favorite ice-hockey team.

«Yes, fine», Mikael lied.

Aznavour lifted up his friend's suitcase and headed for the exit.

«A short walk to the parking lot, do you mind?»

«Not in the least. I really need to stretch my legs after ten hours nailed to that seat», grumbled Mikael stopping before the lifts. «How far is your place?»

«I see you haven't changed a bit», his friend commented examining him attentively, observing his grey suit, his white shirt, his cream dustcoat folded over his arm. «Still the same, even the way you dress. Where did you leave your college badge?»

They both burst out laughing and did not stop even when they got into the lift.

Seated in his friend's brand-new Cadillac, Mikael relaxed and took an interest in the countryside outside the car window. He was struck immediately by how spacious and neat everything seemed to be. On both sides of the road, green fields stretched out as far as the eye could see, studded with farms, villas and shopping centers. The traffic was smooth and nobody seemed to drive dangerously; they all proceeded in an orderly manner in the various lanes. The signposts were legible and clean. The 401 motorway they had just taken was indicated with large green panels, a white crown embossed above the number.

«Why the crown?» asked Mikael, out of curiosity.

«For the Queen. We're a Commonwealth country, remember?»

«So? You mustn't forget it while you're driving?»

The two of them burst out laughing again. Aznavour's presence had always had this effect on Mikael. It calmed his anguish, mitigated his fears, put him in good humor.

«Have you got your speech ready for Sunday?» his friend asked him all of a sudden.

«I jotted down a few ideas on the plane.»

«Whatever you say, you'll charm us all and arrive straight at our hearts. The Culture Centre is all abuzz about it. It's a great honor for the community to have you here at last. A world-famous intellectual, a philosopher of your caliber.»

«Cut it out, Emil.» said Mikael somewhat uneasy. «It's no joke. It's a matter of money and you know how hard it is to get people to fork out.»

«Yes, but it's for a noble cause. They need to understand that if the donations stop, if they continue being tight-fisted, the college will have to close.»

The idea of a future without the college was so unbearable to them both that they had sworn to do all in their power to prevent its closure.

«Are things really that bad?» asked Emil.

«Terrible. Worse. No more enrolments, at least not of boys from wealthy families who can afford the fees. Now and then, just the odd boy from Beirut, Damascus or Baghdad. So you see how things stand. They barely scrape through on donations and subsidies, but they can't resist much longer»

Aznavour nodded. «You told me you'd been back recently.»

Mikael sighed. «Yes, for Carnival, but it would have been better not to go. It left such a bitter taste in my mouth. Peeling walls, the garden all neglected, dirt and rubbish all over the place. I literally fled!»

A long silence fell, during which both relived the emotion of the time spent at Moorat-Raphael.

«Do you remember, you had carved the date of your arrival on the headboard of your bed?» asked Mikael after a while. «Just think, it's still there!»

The sound of a loud ringtone filled the car and Aznavour picked up the phone. «Hello», he said lingering on the «o», in his hand a portable phone as large as a brick, with an aerial several centimeters long. He listened in silence for a few seconds. «Negative», he protested, then «Josh can say what he likes but I want a smoke machine and a twenty-thousand-watt projector. We have to bring that stage alive! We're talking about a show, that's what they pay us for, Dominique!» Then he smiled, resuming his sweet voice once more. «Yes, my love, he's here beside me in the car and I'm bringing him straight home to you», he said, as he swerved to take the Don Valley Parkway exit.

Emil lived in a beautiful villa in a residential complex immersed in a green park full of tall leafy trees — turning russet just then — elegant, automatically-sprinkled, perfectly manicured lawns, and steep driveways leading up to the houses, all set on a height to make them seem even bigger and more imposing than they actually were. Big dogs with long pedigrees frolicked contentedly alongside children on bikes or skates.

«Welcome to Canada,» thought Mikael as his friend's Cadillac drove royally down the ramp to the garage.

They entered the house through an open plan basement as large as the villa itself.

«We'll leave your case here, your room is just behind that little sitting room», said Aznavour shortly afterwards.

Mikael caught a glimpse of some gym equipment, sofas, a television set. At the center a billiard table with colored balls in a wooden frame.

«If the weather holds up, we'll have a barbeque in the garden on Sunday», Aznavour promised. «Now let's go up, Dominique is waiting for us.»

They took the stairs and arrived up in the main hall which led into a spacious living room full of designer furniture. A divan with big comfortable cushions stood against the far wall surrounded by some armchairs including two bergère chairs. On the wall above the divan, hanging on a taut steel wire were several framed silver and gold disks, each one with a plate bearing the name of a singer or group that had won the award in question. Nearby, on an Empire-style carved playing table was enthroned an enormous vase of white orchids facing a ceiling-to-floor window, through which it was possible to admire a lovely maple grove. Finally, at the center of the room stood a white grand piano which even the most distracted guest could never fail to notice.

Smiling to himself, Mikael mentally compared his home in Rome with this veritable barracks square.

His was a simple, two-roomed apartment in an area of the Eternal City known as Trionfale, which he had chosen for its sheer convenience. On fine days he could reach his shop near Borgo Angelico after a short walk. He had always lived in rented flats, and had not bought the apartment until many years after his arrival in Rome, and only when he had saved up enough to avoid getting a mortgage or asking for a loan. His friends, all said his house was a «jewel, a true treasure», especially because of the terrace from which one could enjoy a magnificent view of Saint Peter's dome. Moreover, at break of day, the first ray of sunlight struck his bed, filling him up with a long-lasting, positive energy.

«This is Dominique, my wife», said Emil with a touch of pride.

A tall, slender, youthful woman with a dazzling smile approached, her swaying hips sheathed in tight jeans, her long chestnut hair swinging behind her.

«Hi, Mikael», she greeted him, taking care to put the accent on the last vowel of his name. «For me you're one of the family, Emil is always talking about you», she said with the ease of the typical bourgeoise.

«Dominique, at last!»

Mikael embraced her affectionately. Even if this was their first meeting, he knew everything about her. She was a rare diamond, Aznavour's most precious possession. His friend had provided him with every detail of their love story from the first day they had met.

«This morning while I was boring myself to tears at the Lobarts Library, this marvelous creature appeared before me. It must have been minus twenty outside but my heart was on fire», he had written in the first letter where he described the woman who was to become his life companion.

Dominique was a true Canadian, the daughter of a cultured, wealthy Quebecoise family. Aznavour had met her in 1959, shortly after having «got off the boat», as the saying went over there when speaking about less fortunate emigrants. Both had been enrolled in the Law Faculty at the University of Toronto. They had gone out together for a while, then, for some stupid reason, had broken up only to meet again by chance a few years later, on a tram.

«Hi Dom, tu vas bien?» he had greeted her in French, the language that always made her feel at home.

Dominique had scrutinized that big lad with the black curly hair and that good-natured smile and suddenly realized how much she had missed him. It was a snowy February evening and when they got off the tram, Dom had invited him up for a cup of tea in the Victorian house where she lived. As soon as they came through the door they had made love passionately, above all, tenderly, like those destined to stay together for the rest of their lives.

A week later, Emil had moved in and never left. He had put his toothbrush in the bathroom, his size eleven and a half slippers under the bed and lived with Dom in the house she shared with five other girls, regardless of the looks and comments of the neighbors. Dominique had found work in a legal practice specialized in copyright while he had begun to produce programs for a private local TV station. On Saturday evenings they drank Budweisers until dawn, smoked joints, leaving empty bottles all over the house while Mick Jagger sang *Time's on my side, yes it is!* with that heartrending, hoarse voice of his. Their relationship had grown stronger and stronger, day by day, despite the disapproval of Dominique's parents, who would have preferred her to marry WASP and wealthy, besides.

Despite their ferocious opposition, Dominique and Emil had got married one Sunday in May, accompanied by a group of intimate friends, at Toronto's Government Eye, the town's futuristic, recently inaugurated city hall.

«Come here», said Dom inviting the men over to sit near her on the couch. «Let's have some coffee and biscuits.» she said handing a steaming cup to Mikael, as he sat down on one of the armchairs. «I hope you don't suffer too much from jet lag», she added.

«Is this how you imagined my best friend?» asked Emil springing back onto his feet after he had sat down beside her. Mikael blushed slightly as Dominique looked at him with her lovely hazel eyes

«He's actually younger and more handsome», she pointed out looking at Mikael as he put two lumps of sugar into his coffee. «Do you know, I've just finished reading your *Revelations*», she continued in more serious tones. «I liked it even if there is one point which perplexed me, but we'll talk about that some other time.»

«Thanks», said he.

«Lucky to have the author in the house, eh? So, he can explain it to you personally», mocked Emil, taking a cigar from a box.

Mikael looked at him askance.

«Now he's going to scold me. Wait and see», Aznavour confided to his wife, «I didn't dare smoke even once during the drive from the airport.».

«So, that's what it was! I could smell tobacco but thought it was the leather on the seats.»

They all laughed, not as much at the remark but because they were happy to be there all together.

«You've said nothing about Canada yet. Do you like it?» asked Dom.

«What I've seen so far, yes!»

«This, dear Bakunìn, is a true multicultural society», Emil declared.

«At work, we have people from seven different countries», continued Dom, «each of them carries a little of their native culture. This can only be an advantage».

«And, I have never felt discriminated against, expect by her parents», Emil broke in, chuckling.

She elbowed her husband and then in tones that admitted no objections said: «My love, why don't you call Josh? There is something he's not too happy about».

Emil grumbled and rose.

«Excuse me, old man, we're organizing a concert for a new group called Nirvana. Heard of them? They're going big time and my partner is all excited… I'm warning you, don't tell her anything she's not meant to hear», he joked, indicating his wife before disappearing behind a partition.

She smiled. «There's no point in telling you he's over the moon having you here. He's been so excited for a month now, ever since he heard you were coming.»

«Well, I was thrilled and a little nervous myself.»

«Yes, I'm sure», Dom broke in wishing to explain herself better, «You see, he's become so reluctant to speak about France and Italy, not to mention Marseilles or Venice», she said emphasizing the name of the latter. «It's as if he were stubbornly trying to forget some old deep-set trauma. When he is asked to go there on business, something that happens frequently, believe me, he always finds a way of sending somebody else. Had you not come, I fear you two might never have met again.»

Mikael nodded. He would have liked to tell her how well he understood his friend's state of mind but held his tongue.

«Today he wants to celebrate at home, 'this year it'll just be a small family affair, with Mikael staying with us', he said to me some time ago.»

Mikael appeared perplexed.

«You've forgotten, haven't you? Today's the 14th of September. Emil is turning fifty-three»

Later on, when Mikael appeared again, he was dressed impeccably.

The house was shaking with rock music and by an angry raucous voice booming from the end of the corridor.

Exhausted, he had slept five hours in the guest room — in realty an apartment with a private bathroom —, only to be woken up by that infernal racket. Looking at his watch, he saw it was six pm already. He had got up with a splitting headache and taken three tablets hoping it would pass. Then he had taken a hot shower and donned an elegant steel-grey suit and a clean white shirt.

«Is there anybody there?» he asked from the top of the stairs. He waited a while and listened a few seconds. When nobody answered, he walked in the direction of the deafening noise. He passed in front of several doors, some closed, some thrown wide open, before arriving at the one he was looking for.

«Hi there!» he said from the threshold.

A colored youngster lay sprawled on the bed fondling a puppy he held in his arms. On seeing the intruder, he sprang up and hastened to switch the stereo off. A sudden silence fell over the house.

«Good evening, you must be Mikael», he said holding out his hand.

«And you're surely Mathias. How do you do?»

The boy smiled. He was wearing black jeans and a sweatshirt bearing obviously intentional splashes of red dye.

«I hope I haven't disturbed you, but I'm crazy about this band. I pump it up full volume when my parents are out. I thought you'd all gone somewhere.»

«No problem.»

«So you heard me singing too?»

«That was you?»

«Oh my God, I'm so ashamed!» cried Mathias grimacing.

«You were rather good, you know.»

«Yeah, but to reach their level…» he murmured.

Mikael looked at Aznavour's son and, however absurd it was, he thought he looked like his father although he knew right well that the boy had been adopted. His face was round, his skin the color of chocolate spread, his flat nose was slightly upturned, his full, prominent lips were vermillion, his curly hair done Afro style. Mathias had arrived after Emil and Dom had done everything they could to have a child of their own. In the end, they had given in and flown to Martinique from where they had returned with a beautiful infant. Mikael still had photos of the boy as a baby: two huge black eyes piercing the Polaroid. «This is Mathias», was written below with a green marker.

The pup whimpered, obviously wanting to be petted again. The boy ran over and picked him up.

«And this little one here is Romeo, our present for papa.»

«Lovely! A greyhound?»

«No, a whippet, they're smaller.»

«He's like a little gazelle», said Mikael stroking his shiny, wet snout.

«Mamma and I were wondering whether it was a good idea to get him another dog or not; he was so cut up when Spike died.»

Mikael realized how fond Mathias was of his father and this moved him.

«If my son gave me a dog as a present, I'd be very happy indeed!» he exclaimed, intending to please and reassure the boy.

«Have you got a son? How old is he?» asked the boy, enthusiastically.

This question made Mikael hesitate a little:

«Tommaso… is… thirty-six, no, thirty-seven».

«Wow, I'm only fourteen».

He was about to tell him that he had become a father at more or less his age, but refrained.

The roar of an engine in the garage made the floor quake.

«They're here», said Mathias, all excited, «I'd better go and hide him.» And hurriedly placed the pup in the bathroom.

Romeo, feeling he had been abandoned, whimpered again behind the closed door.

«*Happy birthday to you…*» Dominique sang brining in the cake.

«And is that supposed to be me?» asked Emil indicating a long white candle in the middle of the *gateau.*

«It's your soul, pure and candid», Dom quipped, placing it before him as Mathias chuckled, amused. Then, they all sang *Happy birthday* and waited for Emil to blow out the candle. He waited for the song to end and looked at them all with one fond glance.

«What a lucky man I am», he whispered, before quenching the flame with one energetic puff.

«Many happy returns!» they all shouted and took turns to hug and kiss him.

«You look young enough for an old man», said Mathias, pulling his leg.

«Happy birthday my love», murmured Dom.

Just then the phone rang.

«Hello», answered Dom, «Certainly, here he is». She handed the cordless receiver over to Mikael. «It's for you, your son» she mouthed.

He rose and walked away from the table, speaking in a low voice in the half-light of the salon.

«Is everything okay?» asked Emil when he returned.

«Yes, he just wanted to know I'd arrived safely.»

«How kind», Dom remarked.

«What time is it in Italy now?» asked Mathias.

«Five am», volunteered Emil, «he's an early bird, I see…»

«He was telling me he has to fly somewhere, but we got cut off…»

«Call him back, what are you waiting for!» objected his friend.

The phone rang again, and Mikael pressed the button reflexively on the receiver he was still holding.

«Hi, it's Rose», said a deep, soft female voice, with a marked foreign accent.

Mikael was taken by surprise and remained silent.

«Sorry for calling so late, but I just wanted to wish you many happy returns, dear Emil», the woman continued.

«This is Mikael speaking, a friend of…» he finally mumbled.

«Mikael Delalian?» she exclaimed.

Aznavour, his curiosity aroused, signaled to his friend to tell him who was on the phone.

«Rose?» mouthed Mikael.

Dom appeared both incredulous and astonished.

«But what a pleasure, really», said Rose in Armenian, «I knew you were coming, I cannot wait to meet you on Sunday», she concluded with true enthusiasm.

«Thank you, it will be a great pleasure for me, too. See you soon then. Here's Emil», answered Mikael handing the cordless over to his friend.

Emil did not stay on the phone for long, though he spoke in cordial, almost formal tones to the lady, as if dealing with a client or a person of some importance.

«There's someone who can make a great contribution to our

cause», he told Mikael as soon as he had hung up. «Rose Bedikian. She and her husband have a clothing firm, *the Rose*, a veritable goldmine...»

«Come on, papa let's open this champagne, you still have to unwrap your presents», Mathias urged, fidgeting impatiently on his chair. «I really must let him out of the bathroom.» he then murmured to himself.

On their own in the living room, Aznavour and Bakunìn chatted quietly after the party.

Mikael was seated in one of the armchairs while Emil was reclining on the divan, Romeo by his side, napping peacefully.

«Are you sure you're not sleepy?»

«I got some sleep before; but what about you?» answered Mikael.

«Tomorrow is Saturday, I can take it easy. I just have to look in at the Opera House, to check the stage.»

«It's been a wonderful evening.»

«Yes, I haven't felt so well in years.»

«Meaning?»

«Surrounded and spoiled by those I'm fondest of.»

Aznavour gazed at his friend.

«Do you know what I've learnt in these fifty-three years? That what really counts is the happiness of those I love. For me that's fundamental.»

A noise from the road woke Romeo who, rising on his long legs, pointed his nose inquiringly.

«What's the matter mooch?» he murmured stroking the dog's short grey hair. The dog turned once around itself on somewhat shaky legs and lay down again on the couch. The two had already bonded in a peculiar way, maybe because their first encounter had been a little unusual.

Mathias, at the opportune moment, had run to the bathroom to get the pup. But the long wait had exasperated the animal who had shot out like a missile into the lounge, and under Emil's gaze of amazement, had raced around stunned and frightened before catapulting himself literally into his new master's arms. «*Tsakùg*, puppy, where have you come from?» he had exclaimed hugging him tightly.

«Are you happy, Bakunìn?» he burst out all of a sudden.

Mikael bristled. He had no idea what his friend was getting at. In different circumstances he would have been able to hold a conference on the topic of happiness, quoting philosophers and thinkers, demonstrated everything and the opposite of everything, but such a point-blank personal question had caught him off guard.

«I... I think, I am, yes», he murmured, floundering.

Aznavour nodded.

«It was nice of him to call you.»

«Tommaso?»

«Yes. Do you see him often?»

«We met up a few months ago, he was in Rome for work.»

Mikael took a photo from the wallet in his breast pocket and showed it to him. «This is quite recent», he said handing it over to his friend.

Emil examined it turning it to the light. Father and son, they looked about the same age.

«A good-looking boy», he said.

«Man», Mikael corrected him.

«Yes», he said, «he's got something of you in him, but I find he resembles Francesca more.»

«You're the one who's good at faces.»

«Is he still in the same job?»

«Yes. Interpreter, at a very high level.»

«You were telling me he speaks seven languages perfectly.»

«Yeah, Russian in particular, very much in demand these days.»

«He's surpassed you. You speak only five.»

«He has surpassed me indeed.»

The two friends remained in silence for some time. Romeo, twitched and whined softly now and then dreaming about who knows what.

«Tomorrow, let's go downtown.»

«Okay.»

«Just in case there's still something we need. It will be hard to find anything on Sunday.»

«Naturally.»

«Coming back to Rose», continued Emil, «she is the queen of the community, or rather, she has become its monarch.»

«Age?»

«About forty, but it doesn't show.»

«Is she from Yerevan?»

«Yes, no mistaking that accent. She arrived here about ten years ago with her mother, an old woman, tried by life, who passed away the following year.»

Mikael stared into the darkness; his eyelids heavy with sleep.

«Then she married Hagop Bedikian, he too from Yerevan. He'd been here in Toronto and had set up a clothing company. But then she came along, a very tenacious and determined lady, and together they made it big time. She's the one who really decides everything. Designs the clothes, checks the sizes, chooses the colors. Last summer they dedicated a whole article to her in the People's Magazine's Sunday supplement. *A Canadian dream come true* was the title, with several photos of her in their Forest Hills mansion. So there you are!»

«Good for her. Are you friends?»

«No, acquaintances, I dare say.»

«So why did she call you at home and so late in the day?»

«Well, in spring, when they moved to that castle of theirs, at Forest Hills, she asked me to get in touch with a famous tenor for the housewarming party. I gave her a hand, that's all. She probably found out late that it was my birthday and wanted to wish me all the best just the same. She's a stickler for formality», he added.

Mikael tried to stifle a yawn. «Let's go to bed, Aznavour, I'm beginning to feel the brunt of the journey.»

«It's only age, Bakunìn», his friend joked, managing to make him chuckle.

21

«Thank you, thank you!», exclaimed Mikael putting an end to the applause with a gesture of his hand. «What flattering words Emil has used to introduce me to you!», he said, addressing his friend who was descending from the platform to return to his seat in the front row. «I guess he just wants to butter me up lest I publicly tell tales about our life at the college»

The audience burst out laughing.

«Well, thank you all once more.»

That Sunday afternoon, Toronto's Armenian Cultural Centre was packed. Even the corridors were full of people who, unable to find a place inside the hall, were content to stand outside. The most important members of the Canadian Armenian community were there, along with many others who had travelled up especially from the States, as well as several members of the North American Apostolic Church. The deputy Lord Mayor was seated beside the Archimandrite, father Ghevonz, who had flown from New York for the occasion.

Mikael's strong, clear voice rose above the applause.

«Thinking things over, however, my dear friends I don't know whether you'd be more bored by accounts of our boyhood adventures or the speech I am about to deliver now.»

More laughter and applause.

«I arrived the day before yesterday in this beautiful country of yours. I'm somewhat dull at the moment due to jet lag which I'm finding it hard to shake off. If someone were to ask me what time it is right now, I'd say two in the morning. Therefore, I beg you all to bear with me if I look like someone who has just fallen out of bed.»

«Bravo!» said someone in the audience and there was further laughter.

«Not too long ago, in Paris», continued Mikael, now assuming a much more serious tone, «I met a boy no taller than this», he said indicating his hip, «'Hello', I said to him in Armenian, 'what's your name?' For me it seemed normal to address him in our language seeing we were in the community's cultural center. Guess what he replied: *'Je m'appelle Armén, mais je ne parle pas l'arménien'*. I'm called Armén, but I don't speak Armenian...»

Mikael remained in silence for a moment to let his message seep in.

Nobody breathed a word.

«That's right, ladies and gentlemen, that's what the child said, 'My name is Armen, but I don't speak Armenian'. So then, I asked him why. 'Because there's no longer an Armenian school in Paris', he answered. That boy does not speak his own tongue, although his name — ironically — is associated with it, because there is no longer a school for Armenians in the French capital...», he stopped and: «There is no longer a school for Armenians».

A thundering applause burst out.

«I», cried out Mikael beating his breast with one hand, «graduated from the Mekhitarist college in Venice and, frankly, I don't know what kind of person would stand here before you this evening had I not attended that legendary institution. I am the result of the teaching I received there and carry with me the literature, poetry and music of my people, an incomparable spiritual wealth which I owe the Mekhitarist fathers, to the effort they made to instill in me what every young person should be encouraged to feel: pride in belonging to one's own people. A value, my dear friends, that we are slowly losing», he added, shaking his head.

Some groans and comments were heard, but Mikael continued, with decision: «Our children are experiencing a new massacre, a bloodless one, I admit. No gore, no wounds, no visible enemy, not even the Turks to blame. Yet the outcome is the same: the disappearance, the extermination of the Armenian people. Today, unfortunately, the sword of Damocles hangs over our heads, our identity, over our very survival. It is a sharp sword and held up only by a single, slender strand of horsehair». And he looked above his head as if he were looking for that sword.

«Whether that fateful strand breaks or not, depends on us, on our conscience, our determination.»

Aznavour was amazed by his friend's words and moved to tears like a child. There was something about Mikael, he had known so for ages, which made him really special when he spoke to people. An innate quality, the gift of enflaming and moving the souls of those who listened.

«We cannot allow this to happen. We need to act, react. At once!» his friend was now thundering, as the hall resounded of the applause that exploded. «The Moorat-Raphael college is about to close. My, our school, the school of our fathers, of our children, is dying», he continued fixing the audience with his piercing gaze. «Let's give it a helping hand! William Saroyan, the famous writer we all know, was thunderstruck when he first set foot in the college. 'This is a true temple of Armenian culture', he said, grasping, as he knew how, the genius loci, the very spirit of the place. Let us support this temple lest it fall.»

«Let us help it for the sake of the writers, philosophers and scientists whom the Moorat-Raphael College has provided with the best possible tools to permit them to excel in their various fields. Let us help the college, in memory of those apostles who have spread a very simple but fundamental message worldwide: despite everything, we Armenian still exist.»

The audience hung from Mikael's lips; over five hundred respectful, moved people held their breaths.

«And now, dear *hayrenaghìz*, I wish to conclude with a few lines from one of our most illustrious poets, he too an alumnus of our Venetian college: Daniel Varujan. These lines of his have been my constant companions since childhood and have instilled my soul with love and hope. I dedicate them to you all with immense affection.»

Abandoning the lectern, he took a step closer to the audience. He fastened the top button of his jacket and standing tall recited:

Sow, sow, even if far from the borders
like the stars, like the waves
Sow, what matter if the sparrows devour your seeds?
God will replace them with pearls.

An emotionally charged standing ovation greeted Mikael's final words.

It had been a triumph.

«Bakunìn!»

An athletic man, no longer in his prime, was calling Mikael from among the crowd at the buffet. His tousled hair had blond streaks bleached by the sun and over his golf outfit he wore a green trench coat that was far too tight and short for him.

Mikael clutched at the glass he had in his hand, trying to make out who this fellow might be. A crowd of people flocked around him; they all wanted to meet him personally, congratulate him on his speech, exchange views concerning the future of the Armenian diaspora.

«I've brought something for you», he now heard someone whisper in his ear. It was the stranger who had reached him having made his way through the swarm of guests.

Mikael jumped, taken by surprise, then, perplexed and bemused, began to examine the man who had addressed him.

The first thing he recognized was his boastful, challenging attitude which time had not succeeded in taming.

«Dick?»

«Your trench coat...» he muttered as he struggled to take it off. «For fuck's sake, it's always been too tight and short for me», he added as he wriggled out of it.

Mikael noticed a slight tremor in his hand as well as that air of vulnerability Dick had always managed to mask with his swaggering attitude. Ignoring the coat, he simply embraced his friend. «Yes, that's true. Oh, how I've missed you», he said holding him close.

Aznavour, only a few paces away, was moved to tears and when Mikael caught sight of him, he tried to hide among the crowd.

A merry, rejoicing crowd, unaware of the small miracle which had just taken place.

«You knew about this, but said nothing!»

«He called me only a few hours ago from Detroit airport telling me he was coming», said Emil justifying himself.

The three friends were now standing in a corner chatting, excited at meeting again after so many years.

«Thank you ever so much for coming», said Mikael to Dick.

«Well, sooner or later I just had to give you back that trench coat.»

«I hope it's brought you luck», added Mikael.

«Yes, I have a great job and two wonderful kids, a boy and a girl.»

«You have before you none other than the President of the Detroit Golf Club who is also a much-feared businessman.»

«Someone who went by the name of ' thief'...» said Mikael, in jest.

The three friends roared with laughter.

«I heard you have a son.»

«Yes, Tommaso.»

«Age?»

«Thirty-seven, yes, thirty-seven», answered Mikael.

«What a stroke of good luck, I'll have to wait ages before my two grow up», Dick commented.

«But he was always precocious», quipped Aznavour.

«D'ye know, you said something that impressed me deeply. It went something like, 'I am the product of the education I received from that school'. I agree absolutely. Even I, the deserter, believe I was given the Mekhitarist benchmark.»

«Very true, and he's also quit stealing», said Aznavour, who was irritated as usual when the college was mentioned.

«*Touché!*» exclaimed Mikael.

«Do you know why I stole your raincoat that evening?» Dick continued, relentless.

«I haven't the foggiest idea. I always thought it was because you'd found nothing better to keep off the rain», answered Mikael with a shrug.

His friend smiled. «Negative, the reason was another. I knew it was going to be hard for me to make it, that I had very few chances of succeeding, so I took it as a good luck charm. I always considered you a person with a pure heart, an angel fallen from heaven. I needed to feel you were close to me somehow.»

Mikael glanced a moment at the coat.

«You know what? I think it belongs to you by now», he said, draping it over Dick's shoulders.

«You're right», agreed Aznavour, «I think it suits him better, too.»

The three of them burst out laughing once more.

«Emil», called a hoarse, decided female voice Mikael recognized instantly.

«Rose!» Aznavour exclaimed running over to embrace her warmly yet formally. «How are you? Come, let me introduce you to my friend Mikael.»

«I'm so sorry», she excused herself, offering Mikael her hand, «I arrived just as they were dimming the lights so I couldn't greet you before this.»

The first thing Mikael noticed was the color of her eyes: thyme-flavored honey struck by sunlight which was, strangely enough, the scent she seemed to be wearing. Her complexion was milk white framed by her shoulder-length, lustrous, black hair, her lips full and red, illuminated by a soupcon of lip gloss. She was tall and slim, her hips narrow in contrast with her generous bosom shown to its very best by a plunging neckline.

«How are you, Rose?» Mikael asked her, unable to take his eyes off her.

«Better now, but before, in there», she said nodding towards the hall, «I was distraught. Every word you said sent a dagger through the heart; I felt like crying.»

«Yes, you're right», said Dick, butting in. «Oh, I'm sorry. My name is Dikran Samuelian, from Detroit», he added introducing himself.

«Rose Bedikian.»

«I know, I read an article about you recently.»

She smiled. «So, I asked myself», she continued, «what it means to be Armenian if we don't fight to keep our culture, our common memory alive. Your cause, my dear Mikael, is also mine, ours, and I want to help you.» Aznavour threw a furtive glance at his friend who remained in silence.

«I have decided to hold a big party at our place to raise funds. I've already spoken to my husband Hagop about it. He sends his apologies, he couldn't make it this evening, you see, one of our children, Toròs, is in bed with a high temperature.»

«How many children have you?» Mikael asked her.

«Two, you'll meet them at the party. Emil, will you help me organize it? I'm convinced everyone has to make some contribution, whether they be Armenians or not. The college is an institution of great international relevance, as any guidebook may testify»

«I couldn't agree more!» exclaimed Aznavour.

«I just adored your quotation from Saroyan, dear Mikael: the temple of Armenian culture. He is great, a true maestro. That *Daring young man on the flying trapeze* was a true cult for me and my family; it accompanied me all through the years of my not too happy childhood.» Here voice broke, but she tried to cover this up with a cough. «Sorry I was nibbling a *boerek* and a crumb must have caught in my throat», she said, smiling again.

Dick took a glass of wine from a passing tray and offered it to her.

«No alcohol», she said, declining the drink with a wave of her hand: on her ring finger shone a dazzling emerald.

Mikael, looked at her clothes. She was wearing a moss-green dress. The cut was very simple and the skirt reached just below her knee. On her feet was a pair of swede ballerinas of the same color.

«I was thinking, next Friday would be best for our party. I'm told you're leaving on Sunday», continued Rose, turning to Mikael.

«Thank you, that sounds perfect to me.»

«Friday would be a bit of a problem for me, you see, I have a concert with a rock group», said Aznavour.

«Have it on Saturday, then», suggested Dick sipping the wine he had been left holding.

Rose shook her head. «I'm afraid Friday is the only evening possible. There are some people I wish to invite, most of them go away to the lakes on weekends.»

The friends all looked at each other perplexed.

«So, all we've left is Friday, then», said Mikael who could not conceal a certain touch of irony.

«Ok», Aznavour conceded, «Friday's fine with me too. After all, Rose, you don't really need me to be there, our enchanter's presence will be more than enough», he said putting his arm around his friend's shoulder.

Rose smiled, satisfied, showing the gap between her two front teeth: a tiny flaw which made her all the more fascinating and particular.

It was ten pm and the Centre was almost empty.

Mikael had stayed behind at length speaking to his fellow countrymen and women. Old and young alike were anxious to meet him if only to exchange a few words. Everyone had some story to share with him. Some had come from Persia after the fall of the Shah, others from the Lebanon torn by continuous war, others again from Turkey which was not to be trusted or from Syria where matters were not looking good at all. The majority of the refugees, however, came from Armenia itself.

The Soviet Union had been showing signs of disintegration for years now and the *Perestroika* and *Glasnost* reforms had led to the final dissolution of the USSR. Some of the smaller nations of the Union were advancing claims of independence and Armenia was fighting for its autonomy, which seemed imminent. However, the country's political instability and economic uncertainty had caused huge migratory flows towards North America where Canada was a destination many preferred.

«Sixteen thousand two hundred dollars», Aznavour announced as he sat down next to Mikael.

«That's barely thirteen thousand real dollars, US dollars I mean», Dick pointed out, sipping a second glass of wine.

«No, we've already changed them into US money», explained Dom who looked quite tired after registering all the donations.

«You'll find them on the college's account when you get back; I'll fax you the details», added Aznavour.

«Thank you for everything; you've all been so generous.» Mikael sprang to his feet and gave them a low bow.

«What can they do with this little nest-egg? I don't think it's enough to save them», mused Dick.

«No, but it's something to begin with. It's important as a signal to the whole of the diaspora, it can trigger trust, rekindle that flame of interest in the college which is fading fast.»

«I agree with Mikael, trust and interest are the hardest things to recover», commented Dom.

«Papa!» Mathias called as he arrived all hot and bothered in the company of a friend.

«Yes?»

«Garò and I must, absolutely need to go to the Nirvana concert on Friday.»

«Impossible.»

«Come on, papa, do us this favor!»

«*Baròn* Megoyan, please, oh, please, they are my idols», insisted his friend, a lanky lad with hair down to his shoulders, jeans slashed in several places, one big frayed cut halfway down his leg revealing a knobby knee.

«You're too young. You wouldn't be allowed in.»

«No, not in the audience, backstage with you.»

«Nope», Aznavour insisted.

«I'm begging you, papa. Please! Please!!»

«Listen, Mathias, you've got the whole week to try and convince your father», suggested Dom. «My love, we'll go home now, I'll take Romeo out for his run», she said rummaging in her bag for the car keys and she left with the two boys.

«Signor Delalian? Great speech!», cried out Garò reappearing on the threshold, as he signaled his compliments with a raised thumb. «But you forgot to say that the first school is the family. I learnt Armenian at home.»

Mikael was about to reply but the boy had already disappeared.

«There are no flies on them, eh?» mocked Dick.

Mikael shook his head.

«Today's young people...» was Aznavour's banal complaint.

«Adolescence is a terrible period, I see it even in my own kids», added Dick.

«Just imagine, Mathias wants to be a rock star.»

«You can be his road manager, like the father of the Jackson Five, no?», Dick joked.

«Emil looked really well in Afro curls, don't you remember?» chuckled Mikael.

«My kids don't even know what they want, they think only of having a good time», Dick complained.

«Yeah», sighed Emil.

«They'd need Wolf...» said Mikael with a smile.

«Bakunìn has been lucky, he found a son in the box, fully grown and everything», Dick remarked.

«Well, to tell you the truth», retorted Mikael, «it wasn't all that easy. I'd have much preferred to watch him grow.»

«Oh, oh, we're entering a mine field…» warned Aznavour.

«No, not any longer», Mikael reassured them, tidying his long grey hair. «I've admitted that I've really lost out, but I've got over it»

The other two lowered their eyes to hide their discomfiture; Mikael's declaration had been so sincere that it embarrassed them.

«I'd like to share this experience with you. After all you are my best friends.»

«No, I don't want to know», Aznavour protested.

«Stop acting the dickhead. If he wants to tell us, let him. There's only the three of us. Look around you. There isn't another soul left in the place.»

«All right», sighed Emil. «But only if you'll allow me smoke a cigar», he grumbled as he searched the pockets of his jacket.

«Well…», Mikael began making a swift mental count of the time, «seven and a half years ago, on the second of February 1984 precisely, someone rang the doorbell at the shop. It was nearly two pm and it was strange for anyone to come at that hour, during the lunch break. But, as you say, business is business, so, I went to open, curious but vexed at the same time. I peeped out through the shop window and saw a young man waiting patiently on the steps outside. I was about to ignore him, when he rang again.

«Who can this nuisance be? I asked myself.

«*'What can I do for you?,* I asked opening the door just a little.

«The young man said nothing for a while, and I had the impression that, he too, was observing me through the slit in the jamb of the door.

«*'The shop is closed,* I told him rather annoyed.

«*'I beg your pardon, are you Mr Delalian? Mr Mikael Delalian?'* he asked me at last, as I was about to shut the door in his face.

«*'Yes.'*

«*'Sorry to disturb you, I'm not here for… for the shop,…I've actually come to see you.'*

«I looked him over carefully: he couldn't have been more than thirty, regular features, long boned, dressed in nonchalant elegance. *'I haven't got much time. If it's a matter of a few minutes, do come in',* I finally gave in opening the door completely, thinking he might be a journalist from one of these local rags given that my first book had been quite successful.

«We sat down in my study, a corner of the shop where I had placed a writing desk I found in the Keghàrt monastery, in Armenia.

«*'Listen, Mr....?'*

«*'My name is Tommaso'*, he volunteered, without adding anything else. His eyes wandered over the furniture and the antiques until they came to rest on a blackened icon hanging on the wall. He seemed to be trying to pluck up the courage to continue.

«*'Is this about my book?'* I asked him point-blank.

«*'No, sir, although I have read it and enjoyed it very much... but, then again, my opinion is biased.'*

«*'Meaning?'* asked I

«*'Look, it took me several years to reach this decision: that is, whether... I should come to see you or not'*, he stuttered.

«*'Per favore, Tommaso, come to the point, I'm expecting customers,'* I snapped, which made him feel uneasy.

«*'Today is my birthday,'* he whispered, fidgeting on the chair. *'I was born exactly thirty years ago, in 1954.'*

«I listened somewhat perplexed and confused.

«*'I decided to make myself a special present this year, thirty is an important birthday, no?... something I really wanted for so long and never found the guts to do.'*

«I was struck by his voice: deep, mellow, sincere, at times veined with a touch of earnest melancholy. Then I noticed his eyes, those amber flecks, and my heart lunged. No conscious awareness, not the slightest suspicion, only the resemblance, a facial expression I had buried in my memory for so many years.

«*'My mother used to say that it was you who introduced her to Coca-Cola, as well as to the classical authors and to the great composers. That you taught her, above all, we should all be ourselves, regardless of the rules and prohibitions of polite society, to have the courage of our convictions even if nobody else takes them into consideration... she also used to tell me...'*

«Tommaso halted for a moment and, as I continued to stare at him, I realized where he was coming from. I felt paralyzed, overpowered by affection and emotion.

«*'She used to tell me*, and his voice was almost a whisper by now, *'that you were her angel, her own Archangel Michael, that once your heart beat only for her, that she was eternally grateful to you because you had made her the most precious gift a man could ever make a woman: your love along with a child.'*

«He stood up facing me. I was so bowled over that I had to hold on to the desk to pull myself up onto my feet. I went over, close to him, almost touching his shoulder, feeling a strong urge to embrace him. Above all, to ask his forgiveness.

«*'What exactly are you trying to tell me?'* I mumbled on the verge of collapsing.

«Fortunately he smiled; a smile of relief.

«*'Well, if Francesca, my mother, tells me the truth, you must be my father.'*

«Upon these words, I finally gave in. I yielded to my instinct; I took my son into my arms and held him tight. I must tell you this, my friends, just then the shop was filled with an aroma I had long forgotten.

«I swear, it was orange blossom, the scent of my beloved Francesca.»

22

«What kind of a person is this Delalian you like so much?»

Hagop Bedikian was sitting in the *Rose & Co* board room. That morning he had taken more trouble than usual with his attire. He was waiting for some American clients with whom he expected to do business and really wanted to impress them.

«He's truly fascinating», answered Rose as she busied herself with some press cuttings she wanted to show them.

«Does he look like the photos on the dustcovers of his books?»

His wife lifted her eyes and smiled at him with a coy hint of malice. «More», she said provokingly. «Sexy too, with that long grey hair of his», she added batting her lovely honey-colored eyes at him.

Hagop fixed the knot in his tie and Rose studied him attentively. With his grisaille suit, white shirt, silver cufflinks and brogues he could have passed for an English lord. He was perfect, just too perfect, she thought. True elegance must always have something casual about it.

She got to her feet and walked around the big crystal table to join him.

«How beautiful you are...» he whispered with sincere admiration and fondness. Rose stopped and brushed his swivel chair with one of her knees. He put his cup of coffee down, reached out and, wrapping his arms around her thighs began to pass his fingers slowly, gently over the skin between them. An almost imperceptible gesture which made her thrill with pleasure.

«Do you think they'll sign if they find us here making love on the table?» he jested. «We might go back to the office and lock the door; they won't be here for half an hour at least.»

«Only half an hour?» she teased, raising her eyebrows. She broke away from him and sat down softly beside him. «On Friday evening… I want everything to be perfect, elegant», she said caressing the hand he had placed on the table.

«Yes, maàm», he reassured her. «Liù-hò has called all of the Golden Agenda people, one by one. Some of them have already signed up».

«Maybe I'd better look after it personally, with Liù, of course.» Though she had no doubts whatsoever about the efficiency of her Cantonese secretary, Rose wanted to organize Friday's party herself. It was too important.

«Why all this hype for a dingy college on the other side of the ocean?»

Rose got up again and walked over to the board room's ceiling-to-floor window. Despite suffering from vertigo, she insisted on looking down from the office's twenty-third floor. Her shrink told her she needed to do so to remember how far she had come up the social ladder.

Utter nonsense!

In reality, she had always sought and faced up to challenges, tackled her demons, fears and weaknesses.

«This place is surely worth every dollar it costs!» she exclaimed contemplating the breath-taking view.

«You haven't answered my question.»

She turned around, her pony-tail bobbing, and Hagop saw that familiar look in her eye that told him she had no intention of yielding.

«Because Delalian convinced me. Will that do you for an answer?»

He smiled; it was his way of inviting her to put her cards on the table. Ten years of marriage had taught them that between a couple sincerity was indispensable.

«All right, then», she whispered, as she decided to tell him all. «Do you remember Mc Lean?»

«Edward Mc Lean? The journalist?»

The telephone in the room began to ring.

«I'll take it», she offered, lifting the receiver. «Thank you, Liù, you can put him on to me… Hello?»

She listened a while then silently mouthed «Hong Kong» to her husband, who glanced at his watch and grimaced.

These Chinese never took a break.

«Listen here to me, Chan. I'm willing to examine the goods; when did you say they are due to arrive? Okay. This is what I intend to do. I'll unpack every single one of them, item by item. If, as you say, the color has acquired an imperceptible hint of purple, maybe we can talk about it. Otherwise, I'll send them all straight back to you; I came all the way over there to check the feasibility of that dye with you. I am not open to surprises. Is that clear?»

Hagop could hear the voice pleading at the other end of the line. Rose winked at her husband craftily.

«Half price then. If I can have them at half price I am willing to take them all, as from now», she promised. «Okay, for everything else you can speak to Liù, Thanks. Talk to you soon», and she hung up.

«And if they're not up to standard? If they're really awful?» Hagop asked.

She grinned. «If he's willing to take half price, he'll go even a quarter. If all come to all, we won't label them; we can sell them at the flea markets. We'll see.», she replied convinced, her face flushed.

Her husband shook his head. «You can deal with it, I'm sure you'll manage. Back to Mc Lean then, what's that you're saying?»

She looked at him, puzzled for a moment. «Mc Lean? Ah, yes. Well, in the latest interview for the People's he asked me a question off the record. *'It's a rather sensitive issue, madam'*, he said. *'Is it true you had an unhappy childhood, that your family was dismembered? Your father deported to Siberia?'*» Rose stopped as if she had run out of breath and could not continue.

«So? Is that why you want to help Delalian?»

«Yes, but not only that. Today it's not enough to be just rich, not to mention being *nouveau riche*. I believe that money should be used to help people become, I don't know, artists, philosophers, writers, great patrons of the arts. Nowadays, people believe that what really matters is being, not having.»

Hagop listened to her with an air of astonishment.

«What I really mean is that being rich, only rich and nothing more, is not elegant», she summarized «It's actually… it's downright vulgar.»

«Don't tell me!» Hagop burst out laughing.

Rose turned her back on him and he immediately stopped. «That day», she said in a solemn tone, «I wish I had been able to say to Mc Lean: That's perfectly true my dear Edward. But I am going to fight in the front line lest anything like that ever happen again, lest any family in my native land be dismembered, destroyed ever again. That is exactly why I have set up the Rose Foundation, to help the needy in my own Armenia, a Country fighting for its independence from Russia. Can't you see what a noble cause that is? Now go and write about it.»

«You're raving, my love.»

She sprung around and faced him, using her index finger to admonish him. «People don't care how big your bank account is. To truly admire you they have to know what you do with your money, how you invest it, to what purpose. Then, the Mc Leans of this world can write all the long, tear-jerking articles they like and ennoble every move we make. We shall have earned our halo of sainthood. And if anyone doubts the legitimacy of our profits, seeing that we exploit the third world and all that balderdash, we shall have risen above attack.»

«And what's the college got to do with all this?»

«It's only a start. I want to associate my name with something noble… prestigious. Don't forget that the college has been one of the most important Armenian schools ever, attended by illustrious men, famous worldwide.»

Hagop pondered on what his wife was saying. «In short, we might say, it's not gold alone I seek, I want glory too», he commented with an air of complicity.

Rose had taken him by surprise once again, as she had from the very first day he had met her. He had first seen that girl, no longer in the first bloom of life, at the Cultural center frequented by the numerous Armenians, most of them refugees who had arrived from the Soviet Union following the laws passed under President Reagan. Back in the eighties, of the tens of thousands of Armenians who had arrived in the United States many migrated to neighboring Canada.

Tall and slim, her bearing proud, she looked like the kind of woman who would not even deign to look at a man unless he were a prince or a tycoon. «Who is she?» asked many members of the community in a whisper as she passed, but nobody was ever able to provide a satisfactory answer. All they knew was that her name was Rose, a strange name for an Armenian, and that she had come from Yerevan with her ageing, ailing mother.

The first time they had spoken was at the Centre, in the little kitchen where the automatic drinks and snacks vending machines stood. Hagop had opened the door and found her standing there, rummaging in her purse for coins to put into the slot. She had not even looked up to see who had come in.

«Hi», Hagop had said.

«Hi», she had replied, counting her money.

«We've bumped into each other now and then», he had continued.

She had simply nodded.

«My name is Hagop», he had dared to say, introducing himself, «and I know yours is Rose.»

At that, she had lifted her gaze slowly.

Hagop had swallowed hard. It was like looking at a field of ripe corn.

«Have you got fifty cents?» she had asked him, unperturbed.

«Yes, I should have some change», he answered thinking he was about to faint. He found the only coin he owned and hoped it would be enough to buy drinks and snacks for both of them.

«What'll you have? It's on me.»

«A *Perrier*, thanks», said she, ordering the most expensive item in the machine.

As they drank, they began chatting, leaning up against the dispenser.

«You're from Yerevan too?»

«Yes, is it that evident?» he asked blushing.

«A little. What do you do?»

«I have a small fashion company.»

«Fashion?»

«Clothes.»

Rose's expression changed. «Really? I attended the school of tailoring. I design clothes.»

«A stylist?»

«Yeah.»

«And where do you work?»

The girl shrugged. «For the moment I work as a secretary for an import-export company; they needed someone who could speak Russian.»

«Do you live nearby?»

«Scarborough», she replied indicating one of the city's northernmost suburbs, the haunt of refugees who could only afford very low rents. «In a two-roomed apartment, my mother and I.»

Hagop scrutinized Rose's clothes. «How should a stylist dress?» he asked himself. To his surprise he noticed she was very simply attired: a long, loose jersey skirt, a sleeveless cotton blouse, flat shoes. She certainly dressed outside of the box, unlike the other Armenian girls who preferred the showy, pompous style. It was as if Rose were trying to convey the message: «Please take no notice of me or, at least, try not to».

«What about you?»

«What about me?»

«Where do you live?»

«Oh, downtown, in Yonge Street. I live alone.»

«Good», she said putting down the bottle of the French mineral water. She stood right in front of him and smiled; a vulnerable smile which showed up the small gap between her top two front teeth.

«Maybe we might…» gulped Hagop in a low voice, so confused because of the attraction he felt for that most unusual girl.

«What?»

He took a card from the back pocket of his jeans.

«These are my phone numbers», he said handing it to her, «the bottom one is my company.»

«Smart Clothes?»

«Yes.»

«A funny name», she commented, a little disappointed.

«Don't you like it?»

«Not too classy.»

«I didn't really give it much thought. Let's talk about it, if you like.»

«Okay, when are you free?»

«Monday afternoons»

«Fine», Rose answered slipping the card into the pocket of her blouse

The following Monday she had called him.

«Do you feel like a drink in Yorkville?» she proposed and when Hagop had turned up at the appointment, all in a flap, she was there with a cardboard folder under her arm.

For years afterwards, when Rose had been his wife for some time, Hagop often wondered whether that meeting had been prompted by an authentic desire to see him again or simply as an excuse to show him her portfolio, full of sketches and drawings, all perfect in style and form, enough for an entire collection.

Bemelman's, in downtown Toronto, was the favorite haunt of people in show-business, but also of politicians and businessmen. In perfect New York style, it was always dimly lit, had a huge counter with brass finishings, black lacquered tables and chairs, antiqued mirrors on the walls and a swarm of attractive waiters and waitresses, all perfectly decked out in black trousers and white shirts.

«You're costing me a fortune, Bakunìn!» Aznavour jested, putting an arm around his friend's shoulder.

As soon as they entered, an Asian waitress came over to them. «Have you booked?»

«Yes. Megoyan, for three.»

«Oh, sure!» she exclaimed after having checked her reservations book. «You're expecting Big Luciano.» «Shhhh», joked Aznavour his finger on his lips. «Nobody is to supposed to know.»

The girl laughed outright. «Please follow me», she said picking up three menus.

They sat down in a secluded corner, darker than the rest of the place. From the loudspeakers Marilyn Monroe's simpering voice sang *I wanna be loved by you*.

«I must thank you; I really must», whispered Mikael.

«*Dudu, bidù*», Aznavour mimicked in prefect synchro with Marilyn.

«I'm not joking, come on.»

«It's Dom's doing, it's she who called him and, above all, succeeded in persuading him to come here alone, without his manager.»

«Dom is perfect.»

«No, not perfect, just perfect for me.»

«This line...»

«Yes, I stole it from you; I can now, can't I? So many years have gone by. Almost forty!»

«So I was wrong.»

«But you never even gave Francesca the chance to prove it!»

Mikael bent his head. «I was going through a period of enormous confusion; besides I was only fifteen...» he murmured.

«You could have patched up the relationship later on; you'd had a child together after all. Why did you never try?»

«When I found out about Tommaso it was too late; we'd become strangers.»

«People change, so do feelings.» Aznavour rested leant against the back of the chair and took his cap off. «Well, if you must know it all, when you began dating Francesca I was quite put out; I was very jealous of you, of our friendship, I didn't want to share you with anyone. I too was fifteen, remember, and had still a lot to learn.»

«You think Luciano will be on time?» asked Mikael trying to change the subject.

«Then, when I realized that Francesca was good for you, calmed your darker, more troubled and tormented side, I accepted her», continued Emil unrelenting, «and when you told me you'd made love to her I actually cried. My friend had become a man, I told myself, we're no longer equal.», as Aznavour fidgeted with his cap his hands trembled slightly. «For me you were the most beautiful couple in the world and I was such an idiot to think I'd see you grow old together», he added looking him in the eye.

Nobody else but you, chirped Marilyn, in her falsetto, totally out of tune with what they were saying.

Mikael cleared his throat and twined his fingers. «Well», he sighed. «You don't know; I never told you, but I did call her.» He paused for an instant, trying to put his words into some kind of order. «Do you remember Marina? Her friend? Well, I met her by chance a few years later, in Saint Mark's Square. We chatted for a while and she told me about the baby. Francesca had moved to Milan with her mother and the child. I asked Marina for her number and so, I called her».

«Wait a moment, when was that?»

«Easter 1970.»

«Damn it all, he was six then!»

«Tommaso? Yes.»

«What did you say to each other?»

«Not much… I called her.»

«No», his friend broke in, «I want to know the exact words.»

"Ok, ok!" burst out Mikael. He took a deep breath and then pretended to dial a number in mid-air.

«*'Hello?'*»

«*'Hello'*, she answered.

«*'Hello, Mikael here.'*

«*'I know,* she answered, catching me off guard straightaway.

«*'Marina gave me your number.'*

«*'I know,* she said, cold as ice.

«*'Listen, Francesca, I didn't know where to find you. I called at your house several times but the shutters were closed and…'*

«*'Our neighbors knew where we'd gone '*, she interrupted. *'We left our address with them.'* When she wasn't speaking I could hear the child's joyful chatter in the background.

«*'How is he?'*

«*'Fine'.*

«*'May I speak to him?'*

«*'What could you have to say to him? If it were all that important you wouldn't have waited six years!'*

«*'Don't be so mean.'*

«*'I'm not, just disappointed.'*

«*'We can meet if you like, try to set matters right.'*

«*'Mikael, honestly! We two have drifted so far apart that all we can say to each other is maybe Happy Easter.'*… and she hung up.»

«And you never called her again?» asked Emil, with a touch of wonder veined with indignation.

Mikael remained silent.

«You never did, did you?»

«No», he answered, shaking his head.

«There!» snapped Emil and, picking up a menu, pretended to study it in silence.

«I see a car drawing up» whispered Mikael.

Aznavour leaned closer to the window and screwed up his eyes in an attempt to focus better.

«It's him», he said. «Listen to me. You must enchant him as only you know how to. Big Luciano was rather perplexed about the authenticity of the cause, but you need to convince him. It would have been easier to get him to sing in an institutional context, not in a private home, but Rose couldn't be persuaded otherwise. I think you know what she's like by now. She's got such a subtle way of delivering messages: take it or leave it! Dom and I found ourselves with our backs up against the wall.»

Mikael was about to say «I'm sorry» when Aznavour jumped up suddenly, all excited.

«Luciano, how lovely to see you again!»

The big tenor threw his arms wide open to embrace his friend.

«This is Mikael», said Emil, introducing him at once.

They sat down and chatted about this and that, opera in particular, and its foremost stars.

«You Armenians are tremendous, amazing!» Luciano exclaimed. You're so good at music! Let alone all the languages you speak. Mikael, you speak Italian better than me!»

«All thanks to the college. By the way, I wanted to say a few words about the school», Mikael began.

«No need, I know all about it already. His wife delivered a lecture to me on the subject already», said the tenor looking at Emil and laughing. «Let's talk instead about what we need to do. Dom was telling me you sing and play beautifully.»

«Too kind of her altogether»

«I recently listened to a piece by an Armenian composer, Komitas, a monk, if I'm not mistaken. A truly splendid melody. I believe Peter Gabriel is going to use it as the soundtrack for a film.»

«*Dlé Yamàn*, all played on the *dudùk*?»

«Exactly. How does it go?»

Mikael intoned the first few lines softly, timidly «*Dlé Yamàn, arèv tibàv massis sarìn.*»

«It's absolutely superb», exclaimed the tenor, enthusiastic. «We might do it together, one verse each.»

Mikael glanced rapidly over at Aznavour, who was beside himself with joy.

«What a great idea, Luciano; absolutely genial, isn't it, Mikael?»

«Indeed!»

«Are you ready to order?» asked the waiter in a mellifluous voice.

«What's on the menu here?» enquired Luciano.

«They serve the best *soupe à l'oignon* in the world here», Aznavour suggested.

«That's true, you can have it simple or *au gratin*», commented the waiter, the tip of his biro poised on his lips.

«But I'm on a diet...» the tenor exclaimed.

The waiter pretended to be upset. «What a pity. So what will you have instead?»

«Too bad... I'll have the soup, and make it au gratin!», and he guffawed the way people in his native Emilia do, so contagious that everyone else was obliged to follow suit.

«Do you want me to remove the photos from the shelves now, madam?» asked Lina, the young Moldavian maid, duster in hand.

Rose pondered a moment. «No, leave them there, just try to put the other rooms in order for now.»

The basement, which was really the ground floor of the Bedikian's sumptuous residence, was an immense open space leading up to three guest apartments, a glass-roofed swimming pool and a health spa with a *hammam* and sauna.

Rose had come down to check how the house had been cleaned, as she always did when she got home early from work, not due to any lack of trust in her domestic staff, but because she was unable to remain idle. The basement was the area of the house where she felt least at ease, because it was some kind of an Ark containing the memorabilia of her past.

She often thought Hagop was right, that she should not keep the things that reminded her of that unhappy period of her life in plain view. However, she had insisted, had been adamant about not wanting to hide those things away in boxes; a little to spite her husband, a little because they were like scars of the wounds in her soul with which she had learnt, little by little, to cope with.

When Lina left, Rose went over to the shelves and examined the silver-framed photographs which, even if arranged in impeccable order, she arranged again, passing her fingers gently over each one of them. Except for the more recent ones, they were all old snapshots of her brother, her mother, and herself as a child.

Of her father no trace.

«Nothing can cancel the little girl you once were, no matter how many years have gone by» she mused looking at the pictures.

She reached out and picked up the first photo in line. There, her mother, with her careworn face, slightly vacant expression and gold-crowned teeth smiled out at her, her profound melancholy well concealed.

«Mamma, I'm safe now», she whispered, stroking a blackish mark in the picture, a scar on her mother's left nostril.

Her heart began to beat wildly, the blood throb violently in her temples. She would have liked to dash the photo to the floor, trample it to smithereens. Instead, with admirable self-control she put it back in its place. Insisting on hurting herself, she passed on to another photo. It was the only precious image she had of her only, adored brother. In this picture he, an adolescent, was hugging her, a small child, kissing her fondly on the cheek. In the background, the colossal statue of the Mother Country. Below, someone had written *Yerevan, 20th March, 1952.*

The snap was full of affection, tenderness. Above all, happiness, a feeling that time would never be able to tarnish, corrode, spoil.

Weighed down by emotion, her legs began to sag and she had to drop into the nearest armchair. Yet, not knowing how to calm her pain, she opened the drawer of the sideboard and threw the photo into it. The heavy frame fell with a thud, the glass cracked, and a line ran across their smiling faces, marring that impression of eternal bliss.

Rose started and picked up the picture again with the air of a mischievous child. She ran the tip of her finger over the line, tenderly, hoping it might mend by magic.

«Mamma!» called the sweet voice of a child from somewhere inside the house. It was that of Toròs, her favorite son.

She recomposed herself, immediately, breathed deeply and stood up.

«Coming», she answered, standing the photograph back in its place.

«You know how much I love you?»

«Again?» huffed Mathias.

«You must never forget it. Ever!»

«Papa, give it a break. I'm studying!» The boy looked up from his desk. His father was leaning up against the lintel of the door.

«You must never doubt it», continued Emil, without paying the least attention to his son's vexed expression, as he did when he had something important to announce. «Do you hear me? Never!», he repeated. «Even if you are not the fruit of my loins, you… you're the fruit of my soul», he concluded, his eyes moist with emotion.

Mathias just sat there staring at him, trying to understand the deeper meaning of his father's words. «Why are you telling me now?»

«There is no right time and it's never too soon. I'm telling you, that's all.»

The boy thought for a moment, puffing away the tousled curls falling over his brow. «Prove it to me, then!» he exclaimed at last, all hyped up. «Let me come to the concert on Friday».

Emil sighed. «I knew it would come back and bite me», he griped. «Well, we'll see, but I'm not promising anything, mind», he added as he turned around to leave.

«Papa!» called Mathias, bounding after him and throwing his arms around his neck, something he had not done since he was a little child.

Emil hugged him as tight as he could.

He was crying. Ridiculous, silly middle-aged man that he was, prone to tears, weeping like a baby. Luckily Romeo, barking, jumping, getting under his feet, making a general nuisance of himself, created such a rumpus that he managed to cover the man's sobs.

Nobody was supposed to come between his master and him.

He alone was his pet.

23

Sitting in front of the mirror at her dressing table, Rose examined her face from all possible angles.

That Friday she had not gone down to the office because she wanted to devote herself to preparing the party, above all, to getting herself ready.

She had to be in splendid form.

She had woken early, as she always did, and had breakfasted with her children and husband. Then, as the caterers had begun invading the kitchen with crates, boxes, trolleys and all the necessary utensils, she had driven the boys to school, feeling — as she often did — proud and fulfilled as she cruised calmly around the gentle bends of the road leading down from the hills.

This was Forest Hills, her neighborhood, a district for the privileged, for those who had made it.

«I'll send Lenny to pick you up», she had told the children referring to the chauffeur, as they banged the doors of the car and scampered over to the majestic building which housed their school.

As soon as she arrived back, the domestic staff had stormed her with questions:

«Madam, would you rather have salmon mousse or quiche?»

«How many tables in the gazebo?»

«What sauce would you like with the lobster claws?»

«Shall we set up tables along the edge of the swimming pool? Shall we heat the water?»

«Which *flûtes* for the champagne, ma'am?»

«Would you like us to put Brazil nuts into the bread we're baking?»

Rose answered them all, in every last detail, even indicating the exact distance between one place and another, telling them how to dispose the seating arrangements, where each of her illustrious guests was to be placed.

«Never seat two politicians next to one another, worse still, two beautiful women», was her famous joke regarding seating plans.

At a certain point, the chef had asked her to come down to the kitchen to deal with an important matter. Rose was just entering the kitchen when a distracted waiter had knocked over a bottle of Chablis, which had crashed to the ground spraying wine and scattering shards of glass all over the floor. Rose had started and begun to scream, insulting the waiter, unable to keep her fury under control, reacting excessively to what was really a minor incident. Eventually, she had managed to calm down and ask them to forgive her outburst. «Let's forget the matter. No harm done. Back to work, everyone», she had said in the calmest tones she could muster. Then she had escaped to her room, picked up the phone and called a number she knew by heart.

«Arthur?» she asked. «I need to see you. Now!»

She had rushed to her car, got in and driven down to the city center, her hands trembling on the steering wheel as she slammed on the accelerator, leaving her sedan in a *no parking* space, right in front of the obelisk-shaped skyscraper. She had whooshed into the lobby, got straight into one of the lifts, ridden up to the fifty-fourth floor where she had got out and rung at a door.

«Rose, here already?» Arthur said, amazed, as he let her in.

«Tell me what's happened...» her analyst asked, sitting down behind his desk, signaling to her to lie down on the couch.

«They broke a bottle of wine» she began, «and I...» she stopped suddenly as if unable to explain how she felt.

«You panicked»

«Yes.»

«It was not the noise...»

She shook her head.

«Oh Arthur, it was awful, I felt as if nothing had ever changed. Must admit, I was quite uptight about the party but, you know me, I can manage with these things. I'm used to it, I do it every day; it's my job.»

Arthur nodded.

«I felt like the old Rose...» she murmured staring at the ceiling.

«Who, Novàrt?»

«Yes...her», she replied, as a shroud of suffering fell down over her face; the pain due to the chronic ailment for which she had found no definitive cure. «I went through that evening all over again. The same hovel in Yerevan, alone, with my mother... the shards of the bottle scattered all over the floor.»

She coughed, as if to free her throat of the knot that was almost choking, and tried to rise from the couch.

Arthur stopped her.

«Stay», he gestured with a gentle wave of his hand. «Breathe», he urged her. «In and out...» he bid her calmly, rhythmically, to help her relax, gain control over that malaise whose roots lay deep in her past and continued to torment her.

Rose obeyed.

As she grew more composed, she began to speak with greater ease and less uncertainty. «Now that Satèn is dead, I find it easier to find excuses for both herself and my father. Somehow I feel the need to justify them.»

«Tell me about that evening» Arthur had asked as if truly curious, as if listening to it for the very first time, though he knew it by heart.

Rose had passed the back of her hand over her lips and started to tell her heart-rending story all over again.

«I was sixteen at the time, I remember I drank a lot, I would guzzle entire bottles of stuff without knowing or even caring what I was drinking. All I wanted was to dull my senses...»

She paused for a moment and looked him straight in the eye. «I was an alcoholic, Arthur.»

He had steepled his fingers and rested his nose on his joined hands, impressed by the nonchalance, the apparent ease with which she told the tragic story of her former self.

Rose was mesmerized, almost hypnotized.

Every relationship between a therapist and a patient may be compared to a love affair, with attraction and repulsion always lying in wait. Over the years, Arthur had managed to create a positive transference, a rapport based on the affection and trust he and his patient shared. Rose — he was convinced of this and often wondered if she was aware of it —, had projected onto him the feelings she had once had for her brother, her idol, the person she had loved most in the whole world, and who had been brutally torn from her when she was still a little girl.

«Tell me about that bottle» he had asked her in his gentle, low voice.

Rose let out a deep sigh.

«Living in Yerevan in the sixties was really hard for my mother, left all alone, with a daughter to bring up, especially after she had been branded as the wife of an enemy of the people. I saw her decline day by day, though she knew how to dissimulate, pretend that nothing had really changed. Oh God, she suffered so much! She worked constantly, without pause, at home, cutting and sewing, cutting and sewing... We spoke to each other very little, almost never, said only what was absolutely necessary. We quarreled often, we even came to blows at times. We never went anywhere, had no friends. You know the way lepers were treated once? There was something profoundly wrong with our lives. As if someone had secretly poisoned the water we drank, slowly contaminating our very existence...»

She swallowed repeatedly, moving her head uneasily on the leather pillow.

«...At fifteen I began going out on my own and there was no way she could stop me. Physically I was a fully-grown woman burning with repressed rage. I had never forgiven mamma for resigning herself so easily to her fate, for never having looked for her husband, worst still, for not even having tried to find her son, my only, adored brother.»

She winched with pain, but clenched her teeth and continued:

«I used to slam the door and leave, and the few times she tried to stop me, I simply shoved her out of my way. Stay away from me!»

Rose was screaming, writhing on the couch, her face becoming terribly red.

«Tell me about that bottle» Arthur insisted.

She shook her head, gasping.

«The bottle, Rose», he urged.

«…Once I arrived home at break of day, I had been out all night. I was staggering all over the place and about to collapse on the floor, I was blind drunk. Satèn was waiting for me. I saw her as soon as I came in the door, spying on me from her armchair. She was scrutinizing me — my clothes, my makeup — above all, she was staring at the bottle of wine I was holding in my hand. She rose, outraged: *'That will be the end of you, it will kill you,'* she said. I paid no heed to her and headed to my room when I heard her sobbing. *'I can't take this any longer, if I lose you as well, I'll kill myself, you're the only child I have left, the only one left'*, she cried…

…then she said something…»

Arthur noticed how labored her breathing had become and signaled her to take it easy, but Rose did not even deign him with a glance.

«*'God gave me three children and he's taking them all away from me,'* she shouted. *'One at a time'*.»

«Three? You said three?»

She nodded.

«I turned on her. *'I may be an idiot but I can count'* I said to her, *'you only ever had two children. You've got your sums wrong, ma'am! Are you out of your mind, or something?'* But my mother insisted, raising three fingers and showing them to me as she burst into tears again. *'You're raving?'* I howled, and the more I shouted the more she sobbed. *'Who's the third, who is it?…'* I goaded her. *'Tell me who it is?…'*.I threatened her with the bottle until…»

Arthur had given her a compassionate, benevolent look which made her feel loved, sustained. She needed help to bear this terrible agony.

«*'The one your father cancelled from our lives… my baby.'*» Rose let out an excruciating scream as if someone had stabbed her through the heart and lay back on the couch, thrashing about.

«Easy Rose, easy does it», Arthur had entreated her.

She was gasping, her hands flailing at her neck as if she were trying vainly to free herself of a lump in the throat that was suffocating her.

Arthur had jumped up and sat down beside her.

«There, it's all over now», he murmured soothingly, holding her tightly in his arms.

«I hurtled the bottle at her...», stammered Rose between one sob and another, «with all my might, with utter scorn, I wanted to silence her forever... and... I cut her on the nose...

...My God, her blood and the wine... all mingled together...!»

Arthur began to stroke her back gently. He did not behave like this with all his patients, but Rose was special. There was something about her life story that touched him deeply. He allowed her to cry, to relieve her pain and free herself of the suffering her heart was destined to bear forever.

«Thank you», she murmured after some time had elapsed. «I am feeling better now.»

She had backed gently away from Arthur, her shrink, the man who for many years now had known how to appease the anguish, the torment which threatened to crush her in its coils.

«Madam I have brought you your dress», whispered Lina, as she appeared on the threshold carrying a large box and jogging her out of her reverie as she viewed herself in the mirror.

She had taken refuge in the *boudoir* of her private suite after she had returned from the session with Arthur. She used to shut herself in there whenever she wished to be alone and recover her energies, on the pretext of doing her makeup, her nails or applying a face mask.

«Well, open it, please», she asked the maid.

The woman undid the wrapping with great care and pulled out a vaporous tulle gown from the tissue paper.

Rose's face beamed with enthusiasm.

«Do you like it, Lina?»

The maid blushed. She looked carefully at the simple dress with its tight bodice and ample skirt. She took note of the color: a tea-stained white, with a pale pink underskirt. Then her eyes lingered on the raw-edged neckline.

«I'm sure you'll look very well in it», she lied.

Rose chuckled out loud, realizing that Lina did not like the gown at all. In reality, this model was not supposed to be pleasing, but striking, provoking. This time, this is what she had decided.

«Have they brought the flowers yet?» she asked going over to the window and looking down on the garden below where a team of workmen were feverishly working, building a stage.

«Yes, they're putting them into the vases.»

«No, not those; I meant the rosebuds for this dress!» she said.

The girl shrugged.

«Go and find out… and as soon as the dressmaker arrives send the flowers up. They are to be sewn on the dress, one by one, only I have to tell her where.»

Lina curtsied slightly and tripped away as lightly as she had come.

In the late afternoon the house rang with the joyous shouts of the children.

Rose heard them arrive at the pool, where she had decided to swim a length or two in an effort to keep her anxiety at bay. Later, she would check the preparations once more, in her usual pernickety fashion.

«Attention, don't run on the wet floor», she scolded the boys as she emerged from the water and donned her bathrobe.

The children halted in front of her. Although they were vivacious, they obeyed the strict rules their mother imposed on them. Rose looked at them and smiled. They were standing to attention, side by side, like two little soldiers.

«Well, how did school go today?» she asked, stifling a chuckle.

Levòn, tall and stout, the elder of the two, shrugged.

«Fine, I got top marks in French», he burst out.

Rose was assuming an air of amazement and admiration when Toròs, her second born, anticipated her with great decision, as was his wont.

«I got top marks in everything, though».

She looked at him adoringly, feeling a strong urge to hug him tightly and shower him with kisses. That Toròs was the apple of her eye, her favorite, was an open secret, therefore she had disciplined herself not to show the visceral love she bore him, especially not in front of her other son.

«Is that so?» she commented without saying any more, as she pushed back a wayward lock of his hair from his eyes.

Toròs had just turned seven. He was slim, and although still small, he promised to be long-limbed and muscular. His face was his mother's in miniature: the same amber eyes, the same long, narrow nose and full lips.

«What shall we call him?» Hagop had asked her a few days before he was born. «We called his brother after my father, he should be called after yours.»

«No!» she had exclaimed, impulsively. «Let's call him after my paternal grandfather. An easier, more cosmopolitan name: Toròs, Theodore, don't you think?»

Later on, as the years passed and she watched him grow, she often wondered why she had not christened him Seròp. She was only four when the secret police had taken her father away. If she had some vague recollection of him, it was of an extremely thin man with bent shoulders and an expression of defeat on his countenance. She could not recall anything else about him however hard she tried: a gesture, a caress, a hug, a tender word... nothing. All cancelled, as if someone had pressed the delete button on the tape where her father was recorded.

Rose had removed everything.

On the few, rare occasions when Satèn mentioned Seròp, it was never with malice, but with sad, grave resignation, which made Rose rebel. «I don't want to hear one more word», she used to say, and would stop her ears, because the mere mention of his name made her tremble, at times even retch. Inside herself, especially after the incident of the broken bottle, she had reached her verdict, she had condemned him, relegating him to the ranks of the weak, the cowardly and the useless, deciding that he was not even worthy of the name father.

However, as the years went by and she had pondered matters over again, she had softened her appraisal, her firm conviction that her father had been a good-for-nothing. Little by little, she had discovered than not even she was as strong as she had previously imagined. She had grown milder, wiser, and so, without admitting having pardoned Seròp, she tried to ascribe his cowardly behavior to the terrible compromises life, at times, imposes on people.

She had even begun to regret having called her second-born after her grandfather. She felt guilty, because by doing what she had done, she had failed to follow the tradition of her people. She had broken a chain, shifted a link, upset an order of things that had been established many centuries before.

But of this all she made no mention to anyone except Arthur.

«Off you go and get ready», she told her children. «Tell Bessy to dress you elegantly.»

Toròs smiled revealing his gapped front teeth.

«Can I wear my bowtie?» he asked.

Rose nodded as her eyes filled with tears.

«Chop-chop!» she ordered them, clapping her hands.

She watched them as they skipped down the corridor, Toròs gesticulating to explain to Levòn the proper way to tie a *papillon*. She observed his profile and wondered whether her father's name would have suited him; the name of such an unhappy, unlucky man.

«Never!» she exclaimed with all the love she felt for her son.

She pulled her bathrobe tightly over her shoulders as her stomach twitched with fear.

«Hello, Rose, How are you?»

«Who's that?»

«Sorry.... Emil speaking.»

«Hi! I'm in the garden on my mobile and I can't hear you very well. How are you?»

«Great and you? How are things faring?»

«Splendidly. Your men are fantastic, the stage is truly magnificent.»

«I am happy to hear that.»

«I mean it, seriously, we'll be sorry to have to dismantle it afterwards.»

Both of them laughed.

«Here's hoping the weather holds up», added Rose.

«No worries! I've consulted a very trustworthy met office.»

«Ah, yes?»

«They say it may rain, but not before dawn.»

«Good, though there's no knowing when the people may decide to go home», she said jokingly.

«Too true.»

«When is Mikael arriving?»

«At seven. Our driver will pick him up, and wait to take him back here afterwards.»

«Is he coming with Luciano?»

«No, Luciano is coming on his own.»

«He will come, won't he?»

«He will, he will.»

«Will he sing only Dlé Yamàn?»

«Yes.»

«And if they ask him for something else?»

«That could be difficult, he has another appointment at half past nine; he has to rush away.»

«Hmm. Okay. I understand.»

«I'm sorry.»

«Do you know what I was thinking, Emil? Maybe we need a third violinist.»

«A third one?»

«Yes, in the orchestra; do you think you could find one?»

«It's a bit late, but I'll try. There is this Japanese violinist…»

«I hope he's familiar with the repertoire…»

«… and that he's available», he added.

«Thanks… and Mikael…what kind of a speech has he prepared?»

«He never prepares anything. He always speaks off the cuff.»

«As long as he doesn't go on for too long.»

«That's not his way.»

«The guests already know what it's about; he needs to be pleasant and convince them to cough up.»

«That's not his style either but, when he wants to, he can charm the birds off the trees.»

«Yes, he is rather particular, special, isn't he?»

«He is indeed. He's my best friend! Anything else, Rose? Sorry, but I must be off.»

«Of course.»

«This evening I have Nirvana in concert.»

«Well, then, best of luck!»

«All the best with your party, too.»

«Emil!»

«Yes?»

«I am so grateful, for everything.»

«Don't mention it. Talk to you soon.»

«Bye.»

Hagop arrived a couple of hours before the party.

«Surprise!» he exclaimed, taking Rose by the arm as she came back in from the garden.

«Here already?» she asked smiling at him. Hagop looked as if he had just come from a beauty parlor all perfumed, groomed and impeccable in his double-breasted suit.

«Shall we go up?» he suggested.

«Yes, I've just finished checking everything», she said, «and I've had a swim in the pool.»

«Well, fancy that! I thought you were dressed already...» he whispered as he gave her a light, languid kiss on the lips, fondling her soft white robe without paying the least heed to the looks they were receiving from the domestic staff that came and went.

He took his wife by the hand and led her upstairs and into their room.

«How did it go?» Rose asked as she filled the bathtub.

«There's a price war on», sighed Hagop, «someone had made the Americans an offer they couldn't refuse. What saves us is our reputation, our guarantee of quality.»

«Where did they have the clothes made?» she asked as she let the bathrobe slip off her shoulders.

«Guess...» He was unable to take his eyes off two particularly pronounced dimples, on his wife's lower back. «China is turning the world market topsy-turvy. In ten years' time nothing will be produced in the West anymore!» he burst out.

Rose was not listening, she had already climbed into the tub and lowered herself in the foam.

«Is there any room in there for me?»

One foot after the other he stepped into the bath sending foam all over the place.

«No!» she cried putting her hands up to ward him off.

He was a little put out by his wife's remark and stood there in the tub, his strong thighs all splattered with suds, his huge hardened penis standing to attention.

«I did my best to get home early, just for you», he pouted, his big brown eyes full of desire, of yearning for her. He took a small step forward and stared at her with mounting passion, letting his penis dangle in front of her mouth. Rose caught hold of it and squeezed it with an eloquent smile.

«Yeeessss...» he groaned, with his big hands on her head, pressing her face against his groin.

«You've come home all randy?», she whispered giving him a lascivious look.

He was about to answer but Rose put the tip of his penis into her mouth, licking it gently, feeling how wonderfully velvety and smooth it was, stroking his testicles too, just the way he liked it.

Hagop closed his eyes and shuddered with sheer pleasure.

Later on, with the taste of her husband still in her mouth, she asked herself whether sex was enough to make a woman feel she belonged to a man. A query which kept tormenting her even as the dressmaker made sure the gown fitted her perfectly. And even though she knew it was not the right moment for certain questions, yet she could not stop quizzing herself whether there was anything else, besides their sexual attraction and their unquenchable desire for money, that held herself and Hagop together.

Unfortunately she could find nothing else, no matter how hard she mused.

Nothing.

At least not until the first guests began arriving at the door.

24

The Bedikian residence was a neo-Gothic Victorian mansion surrounded by a ten-thousand-square-meter park.

It had been built in 1870 when lord Cavendish, an aristocratic high-ranking British official related to the royal family, had been obliged to move to the Canadian colony. His visceral love for his native country and for all he had known in childhood, had led him to build a replica — exactly the same down to the very last detail — of his English home outside Toronto. For this reason he had shipped stones, doors, furniture, even ornaments across the Atlantic to Canada and hired a team of architects, builders and bricklayers to work seven whole years to build Toronto's most beautiful and imposing residence.

And now the Bedikians were its new owners.

«Not bad at all, this place», the young chauffeur who was taking Mikael to the soirée commented ironically. They had already driven through the gateway and were motoring up the maple-lined driveway to the mansion. The young man glanced fleetingly in his rear mirror at the gentleman seated comfortably in the back seat. He reminded him of an older Sean Connery, playing the part of a professor or a writer with a complicated and mysterious personality.

He was dressed impeccably, he had already noticed this when he had picked him up at the Megoians'. A dark grey suit, a white shirt and a lovely blue silk tie with white lilies on it. During the drive he had tried to engage the passenger in some small talk, but as the man did not seem inclined to cooperate, he had let the matter drop.

«What's your name?» Mikael then asked him out of the blue, surprising the chauffeur.

The young man cleared his throat in an effort to hide his embarrassment.

«Dave, Mr Delalian.»

«Dear Dave, you'll be waiting out here, won't you?»

«Of course! Mr Megoian told me to do so, sir.»

«Good; so, we can escape whenever we feel like it», quipped Mikael, and for the first time he even managed a ripple of a smile.

At last, through the branches of the trees, they managed to catch sight of the sumptuous façade of an enormous three-storey dwelling, all the windows lit up. Numerous luxurious cars, including a limousine, were already parked in the gravel-covered yard, where gigantic cypresses in huge Tuscan terracotta pots flanked the walkway up to the splendid entrance. Liveried footmen hastened to receive the guests, take their names and usher them into the magnificent atrium with its enormous crystal chandelier.

«Wow!» exclaimed Dave without making any attempt to conceal his astonishment.

A man knocked on the car window near the driver.

«Name, please?»

«Mr Mikael Delalian» said Dave.

The other expressed contentment.

«Mr Delalian, it's an honor», he said with a slight bow as he addressed the guest seated in the back of the car. «We've been waiting for you.»

He circled the car whispering something into his walkie-talkie, he opened the car door and stood to attention as the illustrious guest alighted.

«Don't send his too far away», Mikael joked. «He's my guardian angel», he whispered in the man's ear indicating Dave.

«He can park over there.», he replied showing the driver a space close by.

«Thank you, that's so very kind of you. I hope you've brought a good book with you, Dave» he then said looking at the young man in the car.

He hurried up to the entrance where a footman was already waiting to lead him inside.

As soon as he entered the hall, Mikael saw the lady of the house descending the stairs in a flood of light and flowers. Photographers, journalists and cameramen who were already crowding around the foot of the stairway, immediately surrounded Rose, storming her with questions, photographing and filming.

«Mrs. Bedikian, over here, please!»

«Your dress is awesome!»

«Smile, please!»

Mikael stood looking at her attire. Rose was wearing a white tulle dress with a tight-fitting bodice and a full-length skirt with ample flounces around the bottom. The model was rather conventional, nothing that had never been seen before, had it not been for the tens of rosebuds sewn onto it: white at the bottom, pink around the middle and red from the waist up. A single crimson rose was pinned to the top of her perfectly coiffed hair.

«Boys, not now, please; later on», said Rose, inviting the press and the television people to make way with elegant gestures of her hands.

«Mikael!» she exclaimed as soon as she saw him.

She picked up her skirt with both hands and gliding through the crowd ran over to him. Dressed like that, emitting that little squeal of delight as she ran over to greet him, she reminded him of a heroine from a Tolstoian novel. Rose embraced Mikael and kissed him on the cheek with great affection, as tens of flashing cameras clicked to immortalize the event.

This Rose was quite unlike the introverted, sober lady he had met at the Cultural center.

«Come with me», she said stepping to one side, taking him by the hand and leading him out into the garden.

As soon as the lady of the house appeared in the portico, a buzz of wonderment and surprise rose from among the guests. She descended the steps gracefully and began to circulate among them shaking hands with these members of the city's jet set who had accepted her invitation.

«You're more beautiful than ever», said the mayor's wife, a short plump lady sheathed in a dress with a plunging neckline.

«Who is hiding beneath this enchanting masquerade?»

asked her best friend, the wife of one of the city's most powerful entrepreneurs.

Rose smiled at everyone. Although her gown, her hairdo and all the preparation for the party had tired and stressed her considerably, she appeared perfectly at ease, natural and spontaneous. Leading Mikael by the hand, she greeted everyone with amazing poise.

«This is Mikael Delalian, the Moorat-Raphael college in person», she said as she introduced her guest of honor with a few choice words.

Mikael shook his head modestly, smiling and doing his best to maintain his aplomb.

From the stage set up at the center of the garden came the sound of violins as the orchestra struck up a waltz.

«Dear Mikael, shall we have this first dance together», she asked him.

«But I...»

«Please», she insisted.

Mikael took her by the slender waist while she placed her left hand lightly on his shoulder. They both began to twirl gracefully to the notes of the waltz.

«Mikael, where did you learn to dance like that? You're perfectly charming», Rose commented.

«In the college, my dear friend, in the college.»

She smiled again, and as other couples joined them, she began to observe the guests with immense satisfaction for they all seemed content and to be enjoying themselves.

Rose thought this was going to be one of the happiest evenings of her life.

«Hagop», she called to her husband, «stop boring our guests.»

He turned around. He was standing in the midst of a group of people, including the Russian ambassador and his lovely wife, chatting amiably in their language.

«My love, they've been asking me what this evening's secret may be, why there are so many rosebuds on your dress», he answered drawing her close to him. «Someone must have leaked something.»

Rose feigned a scowl.

«My dear friends, you'll find out in your own good time. The real secret is certainly not my dress», she added as she looked at Lindsey, a well-known folk singer who was also her keenest rival in mundane circles.

The other woman's face was the epitome of envy.

«Myriad rosebuds, as many as the ways of our Rose», was all she managed to utter.

Mikael, not so far away, surrounded by a crowd heaping questions on him, involuntarily overheard this spiteful repartee. He had taken note of the rapport between Rose and her husband whom he had just met. They seemed to collaborate perfectly. In the course of the evening, he had noticed how complementary their remarks and gestures were. He provided the words and she delivered the remarks; he could have sworn they had rehearsed.

A guard came up to Rose and spoke quietly in her ear. She became alert, sought Mikael out with her eyes and signaled to him with a barely perceptible nod of the head. Then they both set off in the direction of the stage and disappeared behind it. Just then, the violins began playing the lead-in to a well-known aria, the lights dimmed and the silhouette of a stout, imposing man entered. A thunderous applause erupted among the guests as his impetuous voice broke the silence intoning the three heroic words:

«Vincerò! Vincerò! Vincerò!…»

The audience went crazy.

«Thank you, thank you», said the tenor as the lights came up again and Rose and Mikael mounted the platform.

«Dear friends, venerable guests», exclaimed Rose over the microphone, her voice trembling a little with emotion, as she took a few steps to the left of the singer «This is the most wonderful evening of my life. I am truly honored to host Luciano», she said turning towards her guest, «this world-famous tenor whom we all admire. It also gives me immense pleasure to welcome Mikael Delalian, whom you've had the occasion of meeting this evening. A very warm welcome also to all of you, who have come here this evening to support a cause in which Luciano, Mikael and I sincerely believe. Luciano?»

Below the stage, the turmoil among the photographers and cameramen was hectic. The tenor smiled warmly. «Yes, Venice is a wonderful, beautiful, unique city, full of historic treasures that are sadly vanishing, like the Armenian college and, for the salvation of which, we are gathered here this evening. But I wish to hand you over to Mikael who has a few words to say to you all», he concluded in his rich warm voice.

«Thank you, Luciano, I intend to be brief so as not to ruin this wonderful soirée. First of all, I wish to thank you all, not only on behalf of the college's past pupils but, hopefully, on behalf of its future pupils too. I thank you all on behalf of the Mekhitarist fathers who have been the beacons of Armenian consciousness for so many years. Thank you! Thank you all so very, very much!»

«And now», Rose taking over the microphone once more, «a small taste of our people's wonderful musical tradition which I dedicate to you all with the deepest affection and gratitude.»

The lights dimmed again and the sweet sound of the *dudùk* filled the air. Soon the string section and harp wove their harmonic way into the strains of this ineffably heavenly melody.

Dlé Yamàn, arev tibàv Massis lerìn[8] sang Luciano's powerful voice piercing people's hearts.

As Mikael's mellow voice joined in at the beginning of the second verse, arousing comments and comparisons in audible whispers, a light started to flicker somewhere. The electrician who rushed in to fix it would later swear that he caught sight of Mrs. Bedikian break down and sob backstage.

It was well after ten when Rose began collecting the donations.

Luciano had left and the guests had eaten and drunk their fill, although half of what had been prepared still remained on the long tables decked out with bows and candles. The waiters wended their way among the guests with trays full of *flûtes* of vintage champagne and the tone of the evening grew less solemn. The waltzes had given way to tunes better suited to a nightclub; there were shouts and hoots of laughter, and now and then a loud guffaw.

«Rose!» called a stout man in a dark blue silk suit. Rose signaled to him that she would join him as soon as she had finished talking to her secretary who had followed her around like a shadow, notebook in hand, writing down names and registering donations. Although several hours had passed, Rose was still glowing, her hairdo still perfect, the crimson rose still in its place, her face radiant, beaming with satisfaction due to the success of the venture. Only her dress seemed a little worse for the wear; many of the rosebuds were missing, some swung head-down by their threads and, here and there, the material had been ripped.

«Here I am, Albert», said Rose as she approached the man who was evidently in his cups. He was seated at a table with three other people — his own wife, Mc Lean, the well-known journalist, and Mc Lean's wife.

«Ah, so we are honored with your company at last!»

«The honor is all mine», she responded. He was the country's most important corn broker.

«Sit down and have a drink with us.»

«I am drinking already», she lied, indicating the *flûte* in her hand and smiling at all the people seated around the table.

The man growled: «Well then, first to health and then to the college... to the Moorat... what's it called exactly?»

«Moorat-Raphael, Albert.»

«That's it, Moorat-Raphael», said he hiccoughing.

They toasted and Rose pretended to drink bringing her glass to her lips. Albert, on the contrary, gulped his down in one mouthful and shook his head already befogged with alcohol.

«Tell me when you're ready for the interview», Edward Mc Lean reminded her, «so you can tell me how much you managed to rake in...» he joked.

«Not yet», Albert butted in rudely. «I haven't made my donation yet.»

With a finger he gestured to Rose to bend down a little so he might whisper his offer into her ear. Rose obeyed pushing back an unruly lock of hair that had tumbled down onto one of her cheeks.

«Albert!» she exclaimed and laughed in amazement when she heard the sum: «This deserves a red rosebud, the reddest of them all!» she exclaimed trying to tear the loveliest one from the top of her bodice.

There were still many red flowers left. These were for those who made the largest donations; the pink ones were for less substantial offers and the white ones, nearly all missing from her dress now, for smaller sums.

«I want that one», said the man indicating the big red rose on top of her head.

Rose, who was busy seeking the reddest bud on her bodice, did not understand what he was saying. So, she simply said:

«Take it, it's all yours».

The man poked his big pudgy hand into her hair. Rose started and backed away touching her head. «What are you doing?», fulminating him with a look.

«That rose is mine», Albert insisted.

«It's not for sale», Rose contended, trying her best to remain calm.

He burst out laughing mockingly. «Did you hear that, Edward?» he said turning to the journalist. «There are flowers in this world that you can't buy.»

«Stop, that will do, my love», said his wife in an effort to calm matters.

Albert silenced her putting his hand over her mouth.

«How much to you want for that one?» He stumbled to his feet, his breath stinking of alcohol. «Fifty? Sixty?»

Rose remained impassable.

«All right, then, a hundred thousand for the college», and he began to shout at the top of his voice: «Ladies and gentlemen, listen to me, all of you, I offer one hundred thousand dollars for that decrepit, stinking Venetian school». He was ranting, his eyes bloodshot, as he addressed the guests who stared at him in shocked silence. Then he went over to Rose and spoke softly into her ear: «Now, can I take the fucking flower you have on your head?»

Rose clenched her teeth; she was about to explode but she kept her cool, hiding her rage beneath a benevolent smile.

«Of course you may, Albert.»

She bent her head down and allowed him to remove the flower from her hair. Freed from their clasp, her tresses tumbled down her back. As she straightened up again pushing back some rebel strands, her eyes met Mikael's severe gaze. Even at that distance it was evident that he was quivering with anger and disgust.

He stalked away decidedly in the direction of the house, mounted the steps up to the portico two at a time and disappeared into the atrium.

Mikael marched down a long corridor and ended up in a small sitting-room barely lit by a standard lamp. He felt he was choking, a lump in his throat was making it hard for him to breathe, so he rummaged in his breast pocket and took two tablets from his pillbox and swallowed them without water.

«It'll pass», he murmured.

In the silence of the room he thought he could hear someone sighing softly. He strained his eyes and saw the outline of a tiny body lying on a small couch. Approaching cautiously, he realized it was a child wearing a pair of Winnie-the-Pooh pajamas; he was facing the wall with his bare feet poking out beneath the armrest.

«Hi», Mikael whispered.

The little boy started.

«Everything okay?»

He sat down beside the child whom he recognized immediately: it was Toròs, Rose's younger son. He had met him and his older brother earlier in the evening, only then he had been dressed to kill, bow tie and all.

«Is there something the matter?» he insisted.

Toròs shook his head.

«I'm a bit sad myself», Mikael confessed unexpectedly.

The child turned around and looked up, scrutinizing him for a while as if to decide whether that man with the long grey hair could be trusted. He shifted position and curled up on the divan like a puppy.

«And why are you sad?» he finally asked brushing the tears away from his cheek.

«I wish the world were different.»

«Me too», grumbled Toròs.

«Meaning?»

«There are wicked people.»

«Do you know some already?»

The child nodded with a scowl.

«Who are they?»

Toròs shrugged. «That big fat drunk man who put his hands on mamma.»

«Did you see him do it?»

«Yes, from my room. I was in bed and heard the shouting.»

Mikael smiled sadly, reached out and stroked his tousled head. He was sorry the child had witnessed a similar scene. Children had the right to grow up in a safe world without nastiness, without baseness, where nobody could traumatize their fragile sensitive little souls.

Sheer utopia.

«That man was shouting only because he wanted the other guests to hear him», he lied, regretting this untruth as soon as it had passed his lips.

Toròs sat up all composed, mirroring Mikael's pose, his feet dangling.

«I saw mamma was so cross and I understand her, you know.»

«Maybe she was only very tired», ventured Mikael, «she had so much to do all day, organizing the party and everything.»

«Yeah», murmured the boy, dubiously.

«I think that you need to go to bed now and tomorrow morning you'll see it'll all be over. Ok?»

Toròs nodded.

«What are you going to do? Are you sleeping over?»

«No, I'm away soon.»

«Okay.» The child jumped down off the divan and smiled at last.

«Bye, Mikael.»

«Bye.»

His tiny bare feet trod slowly, reluctantly over the ancient parquet floor.

«*Torosìk*», Mikael called.

«Yes», he answered turning around.

«I need a toilet, where can I go?»

«There's one in the hallway… wait!» he exclaimed changing his mind. «There's another one nearer, under the stairs.»

Mikael raised his thumb and as soon as the boy had vanished, went off in the direction he had suggested. As he descended the stairs, one by one, leading to the basement he was overcome by a strange feeling, as if he were about to break a spell, or solve an enigma he had not been able to decipher until then.

Down below, he came across a big bookcase illuminated by bronze sconces.

On the shelves were tens of volumes, both old and new and a variety of bric-a-brac of all kinds, souvenirs from travels including a precious amber *comboloi*, the Greek rosary beads that the idle patrons of cafés tell to pass the time.

Then, on a deeper shelf he noticed a row of photographs.

One of the lamps threw a strong cone of light onto one of the frames making its silver frieze gleam. Maybe due to this or because of the crack in the glass, or, more simply still, because destiny had decreed it, Mikael reached out and took it up to study it more closely.

The picture showed a happy little girl in the arms of an older boy, who was kissing her on the cheek and hugging her close as if seeking to protect her from everything and everyone. The little girl was undoubtedly Rose. This was clear from the shape of her eyes, her nose, the unmistakable gap between her two front teeth. As for that boy who held little Rose with such adoration, who could he ever be? Mikael blinked convinced that his eyesight was playing tricks on him. He brushed his eyes with the back of his hand and looked again, closely, no longer able to understand what was happening…

That boy in the photo was identical to himself, when he was that age: features, physique, facial expression. He could still remember the snapshots in his family album and had no doubt whatsoever about the incredible resemblance.

Utterly shocked, he put the picture back in its place and looked for others, his hands shaking, his breathing shallow, his eyesight foggy. Finally, he found another portrait; it was a close up of the face he was looking for. He brought it over to the light and examined it in detail.

He then slumped into one of the armchairs, gasping, breathless…

«Mikael, there you are!»

Rose appeared on the threshold and stared at him in amazement, still holding the champagne glass in her hand. He looked up almost shaking and when their gazes met he realized how close he was to that woman, much closer than he could ever have imagined.

«One hundred and forty thousand dollars!» she announced in triumph.

«Excuse me, Rose», he said, «but… I'm… I'm not feeling too well.»

He stood up without uttering another word, and fled like a thief in the night, in the direction of the car park.

«Good evening, Mr Delalian, shall I take you back to the Megoians'?» asked Dave as soon as he saw him arrive all hot and bothered.

Mikael sunk into the back seat with a deep sigh.

«Can we call Aznavour somewhere?»

«I beg your pardon, sir?»

«I mean, call Emil on his mobile?»

«I'm so very sorry, sir, but he always turns his phone off when he's working.»

«Where is he now?»

«At the Opera House, the show is in full swing», answered Dave after a glance at his watch.

«How much does it take from here?»

«Hmm… twenty minutes, half an hour, maybe.»

«Take me there, please, as fast as you can», he entreated him with such urgency that the driver was worried. «Are you feeling all right, sir? Is there anything I can do for you?»

Mikael shook his head. «The sooner we get there the better», he answered and said no more until they drew up in front of the theatre.

«Here we are», Dave said, stopping by the pavement.

Mikael saw a simple red brick building, with a sign above the door; it might have been just any old English pub.

«Will they let me in?»

«Of course!» laughed Dave. «All you need to do is buy a ticket», he said indicating the box office.

As soon as he entered the theatre he was struck by the red backdrop, an almost throbbing hue, by the strident strains of the electric guitar scratching the air. The walls were quaking and the delirious crowd — the place was packed beyond capacity — was swaying to the beat dictated by those strings.

On stage, a young man with the face of an angel was singing *Endless, Nameless*, a song full of ire, indignation, sincere torment, swishing his long blond hair, as his thin body, naked except for his underpants, shook like a pneumatic drill. He reminded him vaguely of Jesus, when the Son of Man was stripped of his garments and hefted onto the cross.

«Kurt, Kurt!» urged the crowd in delirium.

Mikael, stunned, tried to connect with that strange atmosphere, and discovered that, all told, he did not dislike it. There was something soothing, sublime about that voice, that rhythm, even the scenery, as if inviting the audience to place its anxiety on the shoulders of that angel, who, like some latter-day Messiah, was willing to take on the suffering of the whole world.

«Do you like the Nirvana too?» shouted a boy into his ear as he sized him up from head to toe, somewhat amazed to find himself standing next to a guy in a dark suit, though his grey hair was acceptably long.

Mikael was about to answer when through the haze of smoke he caught sight of Aznavour. He was standing to one side between Mathias and Garò, swaying to the rhythm like everyone else. Mikael, stranded amid that horde of people, began to wave frantically at him like a shipwrecked sailor trying to attract the attention of those aboard a lifeboat.

«My friend, my dear friend», he said literally throwing himself into Emil's arms, as the image of the brother he had never met but had always imagined flashed upon his inward eye.

Aznavour smiled, amazed at this sudden outburst of affection.

«What on earth has happened? The sky fell down, or something?» he shouted trying to make himself heard above the wailing electric guitar.

Confession

25

Toronto, December 1991

Arthur opened the door at the third ring.

«Hi, Rose.»

Two amber eyes met his from beneath a Russian-style fur hat.

«Hi.»

«How are you?» asked the analyst with sincere concern and he pulled her gently over the threshold.

«You're absolutely lovely dressed like that,» he said referring to her fur hat and the Astrakhan coat which showed her figure up to best advantage.

She embraced him and did not let go of him for a while, as if trying to sap up his energy.

«I feel strange, at times I feel as if I'm caught up in a kind of theatre of the absurd»

«'All the world's a stage'», said Arthur with a smile.

«I'd much rather chat in the living room, if you don't mind» suggested Rose, glancing an instant at the half-open door of the study.

«Whatever you like»

«May I have a cup of tea?» she asked as he removed her hat. «Some biscuits, too. Those round ones» she called to Arthur who was already busying himself in the kitchen. She went over to the huge glass wall and looked down from the fifty-fourth floor.

«Are you going to stay standing there all day?» Arthur jested as he came back in carrying a tray.

Rose smiled and dropped into a comfortable armchair beneath a painting by Botero: an obese Mona Lisa.

«How's he coping?» inquired Arthur, putting the teapot down on the nearby coffee table.

«Who? Hagop?»

«No, Mikael.»

«First he ran away as I told you», she began. «I could not understand why until I called his best friend, Emil Megoyan.»

«His classmate from the college in Venice?»

«Yes, that's the one. For Mikael he's like the brother he's never had, at least until now.»

She spoke about the issue with such amazing composure that Arthur himself was rather impressed.

«Well, finding out all of a sudden about your natural sister, let alone your twin brother, must be pretty traumatic.»

«Yes», murmured Rose breathing in the gentle fragrance of ginger coming from the piping hot cup. «Mamma told me they were so alike that not even our father could tell the difference between them.»

The analyst steepled his fingers beneath his chin, something he usually did when trying to grasp a salient point.

«But that's not all!» exclaimed Rose. «I've been told that, as a boy, Mikael was haunted by a series of paranormal 'visions'.»

Arthur listened to her with the utmost attention.

«Apparently, he was mentally able to contact this imaginary friend of his, someone who looked exactly like him, and — in some way —'go through' his extremely painful, sad experiences...»

«Did he tell you this?»

Rose shook her head. «No, Emil did...» She lowered her eyes and sipped her tea. «He avoids speaking about these things. He seems to have removed everything. It must have been very hard to bear.»

«Hard?»

«Very. Due to these tremendous 'visions', Mikael often suffered from epileptic fits, or something like that.»

«How about you, Rose?» inquired the analyst point-blank, touching a very sensitive point.

She recoiled and sank into the armchair like a snail retreating into its shell. She evoked the telephone call she received from Emil the day after the party, his voice all embarrassed as he attempted to excuse his friend's behavior.

«What a let-down, after all I've done for him!» she had complained to Aznavour. She had asked herself numerous times why he had run away like that without even saying goodbye and thanking her.

«I'm really sorry Rose but, please, allow me to explain», Emil had entreated her in a grave voice so unlike his usual self.

«Besides, he's the one who should be calling me, not you.»

«Listen to me», he had broken in, «I'm sure you'll understand as soon as I tell you everything.»

«Fine, but only because I have so much respect for you.»

«Rose, something far beyond the imaginable, has happened. Mikael is shattered. He's shut himself up in his room since we got back home last night and won't come out. I am so worried about him, about his health.»

Rose did not speak, imagining that Emil was trying to spin some mendacious yarn to justify his friend's conduct. «Next thing we know he's caught brain fever, that he's going out of his mind», she had remarked with a hint of sarcasm.

«Well, that's closer than you realize. Oh, God I don't know how to put this... he says he saw a photo, an old one of you and a boy he believes must be your brother. He says that boy is identical to him... that he is his double... must be his twin.»

Rose had staggered and slumped into the chair in front of the mirror, with her ample dressing gown flapping about her.

«You see... Mikael was adopted, his mother told him so on her deathbed.» said Emil as he listened to her strenuous breathing on the other end of the line. «Rose, are you there?» he called, initially to no avail.

«I'm here», she said at last in a faint whisper, trying to control her wavering voice.

«Do you think he's raving?»

«No! No!» she exclaimed. «Satèn did give birth to twins, I'm sure of that», she asserted, coming back to her senses.

Neither had said a word after that affirmation. Both were reflecting on the new scenario that had just burst upon them all.

«Tell him, I beg of you, that I am waiting for him.» Rose's voice had taken on a pleading note. «I entreat you», she added staring at the tulle dress hanging in the wardrobe.

The withered red roses left over from the night before stood out like clotted blood against the backdrop of the white bodice.

She had received him in the little sitting room where he had come across Toròs that fateful evening. As soon as he entered, she had risen and offered him a slightly trembling hand saying simply «Hi, Mikael.» He was no longer the impeccably groomed gentleman of the day before: the collar of his shirt was soiled, his crumpled trousers had lost their knife-sharp crease, his face was wan and grey. He had shaken her hand listlessly and sat down in the armchair next to hers. The daylight showed up some of his white locks which had taken on a yellowish sheen and had fallen onto his forehead, down as far as the top of his narrow, aquiline nose. Tiny relentless wrinkles attacked the corners of his mouth.

«How are things?» she asked, visibly pale as if all the blood had drained from her face

«Fine. Forgive me. How are you?» Mikael had answered as if emerging from a trance.

They scrutinized each other a brief moment, each seeking in the other some sign, some mark that had escaped their notice until then, like a birthmark for example, capable of proving their blood relationship.

«Have you a photo of yourself as a boy?» she had asked him with amazing self-control.

«Yes.»

Mikael had searched in his pocket and taken out his college student card he had held onto as a kind of amulet. Rose had taken it over to the light and examined it carefully. A split second later, he had seen her shoulders heave, slightly at first, then violently as she sobbed uncontrollably.

«But this is Gabriel, my brother», she murmured, «my angel.»

She held the photo to her breast, like a long-lost treasure she was just given back and from which she had no intention of being separated ever again. Mikael, moved to tenderness, had risen from the armchair and gone over to sit beside her, while she did her best to recompose herself, drying her eyes and trying to settle her tousled hair.

«You're identical», she had whispered trying to hold back

further tears. «Now I'll never be able to look at you again without thinking of him.» She had lifted her head to look at him and Mikael has smiled at her fleetingly, embarrassed and equally shaken. «I don't know where to begin, what to tell you... it would take a lifetime...»

«My flight leaves tomorrow.» he joked.

This statement made her smile and gave her courage.

«Well, to begin with, I'd like you to know what Gabriel meant to me.» She broke off drowned in her feelings. No matter how hard she tried, she failed to find the right words to describe what she had and still felt for her brother.

«I can imagine», Mikael said.

Rose sprung to her feet and opened a drawer in the desk beside the divan. From it she took out something swathed in a piece of light-colored velvet. She unwrapped it carefully as if it were a precious relic; then she took out a book without a cover, with a slender spine and worn-out, much-thumbed pages.

«This is the cause of everything», she said returning to the divan. «I know it's crazy, to think of something of the kind now, but papa and Gabriel were arrested and deported to Siberia because of a stupid story, which is really not stupid at all.» She clasped the book to her breast and recited a passage by heart: «...*He fell face down upon the bed, saying, I ought first at least to give the coin to some child. A child could buy any number of things with a penny*».

«Saroyan!» exclaimed Mikael.

«Gabriel used to read it to me in bed», she continued shaking her head, «...we used to sleep together, get up together... when I was afraid at night he would hold me tight in his arms; he used to give me his bread when I was hungry... scold me tenderly, caress me fondly.» She looked straight at Mikael as if declaring some universal truth «'You are my Novàrt, my little rosebud,' he used to say, and when they came to take him away that evening, I...» She began to tremble and as she tried to steady her hands to cover up her reaction, the book escaped her grasp and fell onto the soft cushions. «I remember his face, his eyes looking out of the back window of the police car that was taking him far away from me... I was so, oh so, young and thought... I was convinced he'd soon be back. How could I have guessed I'd never see him again... ever?»

Rose's face caved in and she had begun to cry again. Mikael felt a strong urge to embrace her, console her, but he was utterly confused himself, lost, bewildered. That woman sitting in front of him was his sister, yet she remained a stranger telling him the story of how she had lost their father and their brother. It was enough to drive one demented.

«I think Gabriel is still alive», Rose suddenly declared. «Every day I read about ex-prisoners from the gulags, survivors, found again years after their families had believed them lost or dead. Many have changed their identity, taken refuge in some out-of-the-way village in Siberia. I know some people at the Russian embassy. They can get me all the documents I need... Please help me trace him! I can't do that all on my own.» she had pleaded with Mikael looking straight into his eyes. «I'm begging you to come and look for him with me. After all we are all siblings», she had said in a barely audible whisper.

Mikael wished she would hold her tongue, not be so precipitous. Rose was burdening him with the crushing weight of a terrible story; she felt she had the right to do so, but he was not ready yet to share this unbearable load with her. There were so many things to verify, to accept. Or was it that he was not prepared to, did not want to believe it, out of fear of the sudden turn his life was taking?

Out of sheer cowardice?

«Mamma adored you», she added, catching him completely off guard. «She once told me she felt she would die the day papa took you away. For months, years, she used to check beneath her clothes to see if her heart was really bleeding because of the pain.»

Mikael had remained silent, but something in these last words of hers had hit the mark. He lifted his eyes to heaven in vain hopes of holding back the tears that were burning his eyes.

«So you think he is Gabriel's twin?» asked Arthur, bringing her back to the present.

«When he showed me his photo, I just burst out crying, I couldn't believe my eyes. It wasn't only the physical resemblance but what the picture conveyed. The same warmth, the same tenderness. And yet...»

«And yet?»

«I don't know. How can I be sure?»

«What does your heart tell you?»

«I don't want to clutch at a straw, dream a dream that may turn out to be impossible. You know how I've suffered and how much I still do.»

«Did he ask you for information about his twin?» Arthur inquired.

«He seemed more interested in what concerned himself», answered Rose nibbling on a biscuit.

«Well, that's only normal. Try to put yourself in his shoes.»

«If he is my brother, as I hope he is», Rose continued, «I would like him to understand how much we all suffered. I told him about our repatriation to Armenia, the red terror, the arrest of Gabriel and our father. I told him everything. It was already dark when he left, profoundly troubled, distraught.»

She placed the cup and the half-nibbled biscuit down to the table and looked out the window.

«In actual fact, Mikael and I have nothing in common, there is nothing that binds us», she concluded. «Maybe pain, dear Arthur…» she added finally, «pain is the only thing that might ever draw us together.»

26

Rome, December 1991

«She's convinced he's still alive».

«I am too», Tommaso said, interrupting him suddenly, in a way so unlike his usual placid, patient self.

Father and son were strolling along the shaded gravel walk up on the Pincio in the direction of the terrace where they could enjoy the stunningly unique spectacle of a Roman sunset.

Mikael did not answer. He looked at Tommaso perplexed and somewhat annoyed. He believed his son had jumped to hasty conclusions, as if he knew facts of which even he was uncertain.

«So you don't like what I'm saying?» asked Tommaso. «I, too, am convinced your brother is alive», he repeated looking at him with his dark riveting eyes.

Mikael, his face the picture of gloom, remained silent.

«I do understand you, believe me. I know it's not easy to be presented all of a sudden with a birth family and being told stories you'd never known about, never even imagined, and which actually regard you very intimately. What you've told me has shaken me too. When you called me in Milan, saying you needed to speak to me urgently, I never imagined anything like this… a bombshell of these dimensions.»

Tommaso had joined his father in Rome a week after the telephone call, taking advantage of the fact that he was to act as interpreter to a Russian guest being televised live in the capital.

A few days earlier, Russia, the Ukraine and Belarus had signed the Belavezha Accords which dissolved the Soviet Union and stipulated the birth of the Community of Independent States. It was an event of worldwide import, which had, naturally, catalyzed the attention of the media. Tommaso, who had a perfect command of Russian, had been up to his ears in work. After the talk show, he had taken a taxi from the studios of the Italian National Broadcasting Company, RAI, and hurried to his father's home where — over lunch — Mikael had explained, in detail, everything that had happened to him during his week in Canada. Then, they had gone for a walk and continued to discuss the incredible affair.

They now stood in spellbound silence looking out over the balustrade of the Pincio terrace admiring the awe-inspiring sunset.

«She rang me up again yesterday», Mikael said, out of the blue. «Telling me she's found a way of getting us visas.»

Tommaso looked at him puzzled.

«Your aunt Rose», explained Mikael with the hint of a chuckle, as if there were something comical about calling her that, «she insists on trying to find our long-lost brother in Siberia, and wants me to accompany her at all costs, you see, she's afraid of undertaking the adventure alone.»

«And you?»

«I don't know… What I do know, however, is that I have always been so lonely that even the suspicion of having a brother, who may be still alive, makes me happy.»

As the darkness began to envelop the city sprinkling it with lights that sparkled like clusters of stars, Tommaso thought of Gabriel, his father's twin, deported as a mere boy to a gulag in Siberia, a hostage of time, kicking out wildly to break free.

«You must go, papà», he said at last, surprising even himself.

He had just called Mikael by the «magic» word he had never dared utter before.

Milan, 18th December 1991
Dear papà,
Thank you so much for your hospitality. Travelling to Rome now feels like coming back home, and it's all thanks to you.
I wanted to write to you to make it clear what I really think about the

*story you've told me. I just couldn't do it face-to-face; at times my courage
fails me, and I am somewhat ill at ease when in your company. I hope, with
time, we could establish a relationship where we shall both feel perfectly
free to tell each other what we are really thinking and feeling.*

*What happened in Toronto is a sign of destiny. Needless to say, the
tragic events you have discovered, your own and those of your family, are
truly devastating but they concern the past; the wound is healing, and you
are recovering already.*

*I was struck by something you said the other day: «I have always been
so lonely that even the suspicion of having a brother, who may be still
alive, makes me happy». I couldn't get these words out of my mind during
the flight back to Milan, maybe because I caught a hint of something so
familiar in them, a feeling so akin to my own.*

*Arm yourself with strength, with courage, and go on that journey to
Siberia. I understand your trepidation, your fear; the quest for your twin
may end well, or it could end badly. Despite this, I feel you need to face up
to this trial, accept the challenge, pick up the gauntlet! Only that way will
you be able to go on living without misgivings or regrets.*

I'll be with you all the way.

I love you, Tommaso

Mikael lay the letter down on the table. It was the first one his son
had ever written to him. He glanced at the clock on the wall of his
shop, at its swinging pendulum. If he were not mistaken, in Toronto
it was exactly seven in the morning. He lifted up the receiver and
dialed the ten digits he had scribbled down in his address book
under the name Rose.

«Good morning!», he said to the hoarse voice that answered,
«have you got your bags all packed yet?»

27

Petropavlovsk, north-east Siberia, June 1992

That morning Evgenij Koslov had risen early.

Standing on the balcony, wearing only his vest and underpants, he waited for the sun to appear behind the hills. Dawn splashed the sky with streaks of vivid color and, although it was already early summer, the morning breeze was chilly, sharp. He drank a mouthful of piping hot tea from the cup he was holding and immediately afterwards took a long, deep pull of the cigarette he held in his other hand. He puffed the smoke out into the haze and coughed, hacking the very depths of his lungs.

He allowed his gaze to wander and pick out the bay, which at that hour was painted in tints of mercury. The lamps on the docks shone yellow like the eyes of a pack of wolves. The cranes swung above the piers with slow, halting movements like those of the walking dead. From farther off the hum of the factories, tireless producers of wealth, caressed his ears like a lullaby.

Every morning, he allowed himself these few moments of respite to enjoy the panorama which unfolded before his eyes but, above all, to enjoy watching the fishing boats as they docked. This was the main reason why he had moved to this old *izba* on the slopes of the Petropavlovsk hills. It had been love at first sight — a veritable *coup de foudre* — as soon as he had set foot out here on this little balcony.

A vessel sounded three long hoots which echoed right across the bay like the cry of a whale. Evgenij glanced at his watch and went back into that house made of beams and tree trunks. That morning, unfortunately, he could not stay long enough to watch the sun rise, nor enjoy the glow of the first ray of light which struck, depending on the season, a precise point in his room. He regretted missing the breaking of this new day, an experience which always overjoyed him and rekindled fresh hope in his soul.

There was no time for all that today. He had to get ready and rush off to the airport to catch the first flight to Magadan which left at eight am. He hoped that the plane would take off on schedule: he had an appointment immediately after lunch.

For some years now, those people there had stopped calling him and he had fooled himself into believing that that kind of thing was all over. But, only a few days before, the telephone had rung again and the acid voice of a secretary had put him on to commissar Litvenko.

«Hey there, fishmonger, still rotting away in Avacha bay?» the officer had begun, trying to be funny. He was the kind of person who could suddenly switch from being affably cordial to being disdainfully harsh.

«You never got back to me so I've had to console myself with the salmons», Evgenij quipped in similar tones.

«We want you here on Tuesday afternoon, at two pm, sharp. Speak to the secretary about the details», the commissar had said before hanging up.

It was like being in an old film about the Cold War. Instead, this was real, this was his life. For the KGB, a dodgy past like his, open to blackmail, gave them every right to order him to carry out actions they could never have asked an ordinary citizen to do.

The past had the power of dictating the future.

Seated on the bed, pulling on the grey socks that lay on the grey quilt, completely naked except for his underpants, he examined his body. For quite some time now what he saw disgusted him: his dull wrinkled skin, his swollen, flaccid, sagging belly. With a touch of scorn and a hint of compassion, he began to massage his abdomen with brusque circular movements as if, by miracle, he could melt away the fat that had built up there over the years. He then dressed quickly putting on a pair of brown trousers and a pale yellowish shirt. On his way out he would have to get into the black leather jacket hanging on the clothes rack. He needed to be spruced up on these occasions.

In Magadan he was supposed to meet people of a certain importance.

Before leaving the house, he went to have one last pee. Although he was only a little over fifty he suffered from a bladder complaint; an uncontrollable, impelling urge to urinate, all day, wherever he happened to be. At the outpatients' they had suggested that he have some tests done, but had not called him yet. Meanwhile, he was supposed to stop smoking and give up drinking that smooth velvety liquor he enjoyed so much: vodka.

As he was leaving the bathroom, he examined his reflection in the mirror. There were days when he refused to deign the face he saw there with even a fleeting glance. He had come to the point where he had grown a beard to hide that stranger's face a little. But that morning the tension provoked by the journey and the unease the new mission aroused in him, made him yield. So, he plucked up the courage to look at that face. What had not changed was, certainly, the long scar running from below his left eye right down to the corner of his mouth. Evgenij focused on his disfigured eye: the lid scored with tiny cuts, the ball crisscrossed by a web of broken capillaries, the iris coated in white. He passed his finger over the rough skin, all creased like a badly fried pancake, as if trying to smooth out the distant memory of an event lurking in the back of his memory. The rest of his face was that of a badly-worn, middle-aged man, full of wrinkles, wisps of grey hair, yellowing teeth, a short beard which failed to hide his horribly marred cheek.

«Evgenij Koslov, you're an ugly toad», he told the mirror with a sarcastic smirk.

Back in the living room he checked his papers once, twice and then went to the door. Before leaving the house, he donned his black leather jacket, shoved his inseparable flask of vodka into his hip pocket and began mooching around for the keys of his van. Just as he was closing the door he hurried back inside and, all hot and bothered, rushed to the bathroom, picked up what he needed and shoved it into his pocket.

The eye patch he used to cover his maimed eye.

Once in the yard, he was struck as usual by the imposing bulk of the Koriaksky volcano. With its glittering white peak towering over the plane it looked like a huge meteorite fallen from the heavens. It was the only part of the panorama he could not see from his balcony, although it was visible from almost every angle of the city over which it hovered like a sentinel. Evgenij stopped a moment and saluted it with respect. He imagined that in its core waited a clock ticking away the time until the next eruption, when the earth would quake and the lava spew forth from its mouth like an incandescent river burrowing its way through the snow.

He opened the door of his pea-green Moscvich and settled himself laboriously into the rickety, broken-down driving seat. He stroked the steering-wheel fondly and switched on the engine. Evgenij was fond of his van; although it was over ten years old it had a four-wheel drive, a one-hundred-and-fifty horsepower engine and, at the back, a goods compartment. The few times he ever decided to push the accelerator flat out, his Moscvich took off like a racing car making most of all the other vehicles look like Micky-Mouse jobs. Back then, he had managed to get hold of it showing those who counted that he could not afford to drive around in a wreck. Evgenij delivered fish; he loaded the crates directly from the boats and distributed them to various retailers and customers in the city. That was not the whole story, though; the hardest part was getting to certain villages in the back-of-beyond down the peninsula, which could be reached only by impervious, dangerous mule tracks. Therefore, a trustworthy vehicle was vital if he were to carry out deliveries regularly.

He took the state highway and accelerated. At a hundred an hour, the sun making his windscreen shine, Evgenij lowered his window to clear the vehicle of its stink of brine and fish and not because that smell troubled him; he was used to it; it was familiar to him. He just wanted to enjoy the wind tossing his hair, caressing his face, making him feel he was stealing the fresh fragrance from the waters of the Arctic.

For him, this was one of the few sensations that resembled freedom.

A few kilometers before the airport he caught sight of a police car. He smiled. For years now, the police insisted on parking in exactly the same spot, behind the same tree, with a view to surprising their prey. This country was a place where everyone cashed in on unlawful trafficking of rubles and where the police, scum of all scum, fomented illegality and abuse. They would stop unknowing drivers threatening to suspend their driving licenses along with all their documents, even to confiscate their vehicles if they did not comply with their demands. The unfortunate victims had no choice but to cough up loads of money if they wanted the police to close an eye or two, and let them off.

Evgenij hoped things would change. He had listened to news on the radio, seen it on TV, about the radical changes being carried out, the transformations the country was undergoing, about the elephantine situation was about to dissolve. Boris Eltsin, the new President of the Russian Federation — there was no further mention of the Soviet Union — had banned the Communist Party and confiscated its assets. The old regime had its days numbered.

Maybe even the commissar would stop calling him, once and for all.

Perestrojka and *Glasnost* had saved Russia, he told himself as he passed slowly in front of the policemen. He looked closely at them and recognized them: the usual two, Pushka and his deputy Rubi. He waved to them and gave them one of his disarming smiles.

«Hello there, Evgenij», they responded, loud and in chorus

In other countries they would have stopped him, most likely. Pushka knew downright well that Evgenij should not be allowed to drive because he could see practically nothing with his left eye and that he had obtained his license thanks to the usual exchange of favors. God knows how many lobster claws that had cost him! In actual fact, the vision in his left eye had improved over the years. Evgenij could now distinguish shapes against a well-lit white background. He often fooled himself into believing that soon some doctor or other would invent a surgical technique capable of restoring his sight completely. Meanwhile, he was quite content the way he was, and often he preferred to leave off the eye patch which irritated his skin, and did not give a tinker's curse about the disgust his scarred face aroused in others.

After so many years it did not bother him any longer.

He entered the huge Elizovo airport area, surrounded by a barbed wire fence, left his van in the parking lot, and strode swiftly into the hall and looked around for the toilets. He emptied his bladder again and washed his hands with the reddish clove-scented soap. Then he took the eyepatch out of his pocket, placed it over his eye, passed the elastic around his ear and made sure it hugged his head securely.

He was ready.

«I have a pre-paid ticket to Magadan», he said later with a big broad smile to the attractive girl at the check-in counter.

The flight lasted a little under two hours.

At Sokol airport Evgenij decided to catch the minibus for Magadan. It could carry up to eight passengers, and although inside it stank of smoke and sweat and cost more than the regular bus service, it was faster, above all, more comfortable.

«Lenin Square», he said to the driver as he sat down beside him. He looked at his watch and settled down calmly: there was almost an hour left before the appointment.

The plane had left on time and even arrived ten minutes ahead of schedule. He had had sandwich for lunch at the airport cafeteria which helped swallow it down with a mouthful of vodka from his flask. He had then looked for one of the blue SibirTelecom booths and phoned the operator.

«How can I help you?» had asked a male voice which seemed to come from another planet.

«Seven-four-oh-oh, Yarkaiya Avacha nursing home.»

«Kamchatka?»

«Yes.»

He heard some strange crackling noises before the operator connected him.

«Yarkaiya Avacha », a woman had answered in a soft mellow voice.

«Evgenij Koslov speaking.»

«I can't hear you.»

«Evgenij Koslov, I'm calling for Anjushka Pechinova», he shouted making passers-by turn and stare.

«How can I help?»

«How is she today?»

The woman took her time to answer.

«Exactly as she was forty years ago», she said sharply, and he was shocked that such a gentle voice could be capable of expressing so much cynicism.

«Where shall I drop you off, comrade?»

The driver's voice shook him out of his reverie.

«At the central Commissariat.»

The other looked at him with diffidence and then drew up near the pavement.

«Seven thousand rubles», he muttered.

Evgenij alighted from the minibus in the drizzling rain. He jerked up his trousers, buttoned his jacket, fixed his eyepatch and mounted the steps to the building with the grey plaster façade.

It looked half deserted. There was no longer that frantic coming and going of people hurrying in and out that he recalled. Above it, the red flag with its hammer and sickle no longer flew and all the old insignia were gone. There was only a plate bearing three letters KGB, Kah-Geh-Beh, the Russian initials for the State Security Commission. Years previously, when he had frequented these offices assiduously, Evgenij would have tired his arm out saluting right and left as he encountered multi-decorated big brass, feeling he belonged to that magnificent, mighty mechanism called the USSR. In actual fact, the impression that the whole country was crumbling appeared more evident in the bigger cities than in smaller, remote towns like Petropavlovsk.

«Who do you need to see, comrade? » asked a skinny, sickly fellow behind the window at the information desk.

«The general commissar for internal affairs.»

«Documents?»

The chap examined the photo on Evgenij's ID and compared it with the person standing in front of him.

«You need to renew this», he said taking the document and handing him a plastic badge in exchange.

«I've already applied for a new one. »

«Third floor», grumbled the man clenching the butt-end of a cigarette between his teeth.

Waiting in the office for the persons who had convoked him, with his adrenalin soaring, Evgenij allowed his mind to wander and return to an episode which today, many decades later, still moved him to tenderness.

He was almost twenty at the time and already worked transporting fish. The seas of the Kamchatka were famous for their abundant catches; trawlers and boats returned every day laden to the gunwale with fish of all kinds: crabs, lobsters and the inevitable salmon, some of them over five feet long.

That morning he had loaded his vehicle with salmon heads, cut off at the gills, in great demand in hospitals and nursing homes because they cost so little and made a delicious soup. The recipe was simple and straightforward: a pot full of fresh cold water, onions, carrots, loads of potatoes and, of course, the heads of the salmon. It was allowed to stew until it became one big pulp to be filtered and served to patients and to debilitated elderly folk: a veritable panacea, light and nourishing.

Among the addresses to which to make a delivery was the squalid Avacha rehabilitation center. He had brought his van to a halt in front of the building and carried a pair of crates into the kitchen through the tradesmen's entrance.

It was only six in the morning and there was nobody in sight.

«I need a signature. Where's the administration?» he had asked a kitchen help.

«You have to go up there», said the boy who was lifting an enormous pot into the sink.

Evgenij had gone up the stairs smelling of a disinfectant which stung his nostrils. On the first floor he had pushed a heavy metal door and found himself in a long corridor. Not knowing which way to go, he had looked around to see if there was anyone he might ask for directions. An orderly was washing the floor but as he approached him, the man simply walked away pulling his heavy, noisy trolley after him. He was about to follow the man but, changing his mind, had decided to take the opposite direction. Dressed in his rough canvas trousers and waxed cape he walked down the corridor passing in front of half-open doors from which came groans, stifled laments, coughs: noises typical of a nursing home beginning to wake up. He was about to turn a corner when his was struck by the sight of a girl. She was sitting in a wheelchair on the threshold of one of the rooms. In the half-light that framed her, Evgenij was struck by her snow-white skin and the long blond plait which reached way down her back to her waist. She was very thin, her slender shoulders wrapped in a grey fringed shawl. She was staring into empty space and clutching a rag doll which, ironically, looked rather like herself with its lanky body and long straw plait. Evgenij had thrown an inquisitive glance at her and she had suddenly seemed to reawaken from her daydream. She looked at him with two big green eyes shrouded in melancholy.

«Excuse me, can you tell me where I can find the office?» Evgenij had asked her, feeling an inexplicable longing to hear her voice. The girl had whimpered some strange sounds and when he had drawn closer to her, a radiant smile had broken out on her red lips; a shy smile which had pierced his heart to the quick. Somewhat worried, he had taken a step backwards, lest the girl might have noticed his excitement, his throbbing eagerness. She, on the contrary, had motioned to him with gentle, suave, seductive gestures inviting him to draw closer. It was as if she were inviting him to kneel down and lend an ear to her close to the wheelchair so she might share a whispered secret with him.

Evgenij had got down on one knee, like a prince in a fairy tale about to ask his beloved for her hand. She looked him over with her two enormous eyes which now seemed to have begun smiling too. And just as Evgenij felt himself beginning to die slowly, the girl had dropped her doll and brushed his eye patch with her fingers.

«What on earth happened to you?» she seemed to be asking him.

«Anjushka, what are you doing?»

The oneiric bubble suddenly burst as a nurse came hurrying forward ordering the intruder to leave at once.

«Comrade Koslov, I find you in great shape!»

Vassilij Litvenko was entering the room: an imposing figure in a turf-colored uniform sporting several decorations. Aleksei Kalkin, short and thin, fussed in his wake like a duckling waddling after its mother.

Evgenij sprang to his feet and remained motionless until Vassilij approached and held out his hand. Aleksei, on the contrary, simply nodded.

«Have they offered you some tea?» the commissar asked him.

«No, thanks, no beverages.»

The two officers sat down at the desk facing Evgenij, laid down their red files and looked him over with great attention.

«We haven't met for three years», began Vassilij.

«Three years and a month or so», Evgenij pointed out, «I was beginning to miss Magadan.»

«You don't appreciate Magadan until you leave Magadan», replied the commissar with a certain gravity. «But now down to business.»

Evgenij felt his heart beat faster as it usually did when they briefed him on some mission.

Aleksei opened one of the files, flicked through the contents and took out a telex message. «Two suspects are about to arrive in Petropavlovsk», he said looking at him over his half-moon reading glasses. «Mikael Delalian, bachelor, fifty-four, place of birth not given, resident in Italy, Rome, antique dealer, and Novàrt Rose Bedikian Gazarian, married, two children, forty two, born in Yerevan, Armenia, presently resident in Toronto, Canada, entrepreneur. Date of entry the seventeenth of June, Moscow airport, flight KLM five-six-six from Amsterdam.»

«They have already arrived in Barnaul», continued Vassilij. «Our colleagues called us a while ago. It seems they wish to consult the registers of camp number eleven, Altaj. They are trying to trace a prisoner called Gabriel Gazarian, the woman's missing brother.»

With a nod he invited Aleksei to continue.

«A work visa has been issued regularly by the Russian Embassy, Ottawa, Canada», he read. «Official reason for the trip: Mrs. Bedikian wishes to study the traditional costumes of the Chukotka tribe for the Rose & Co clothing company, of which she is the owner.»

«What? The clothes worn by the Chukotka people?» exclaimed Evgenij with a sonorous guffaw. «Is this a joke, or something!?»

The other two were amused too, but stopped smiling as they realized, themselves, that the reason provided for the visit was rather ridiculous.

«That's the crappiest excuse of the century», added Evgenij, bringing one of his fists down on the desk with a thud.

«How should we go about this?» inquired the Commissar.

Evgenij sprung to his feet, trying to suppress what seemed to be a fit of laughter.

«Excuse me one moment, comrade, but I need to leave the room for a moment" he said pointing at the door. «I need the bathroom, I'm afraid this joke has worsened my... hmmm... little bladder problem.»

He winked his only eye pleading for their comprehension and fled the room as if he were about to pee in his pants.

Evgenij wondered how to spend the remainder of the day in Magadan; it was only six in the afternoon and his return flight was scheduled for midnight.

He knew the city well, as it had once been Siberia's largest prison-camp hub; he had spent many long months here in his youth. He had lied to the officers during the interview — and now he regretted it — when he claimed he missed the place. Bollocks! He had simply said it to gratify his superiors, due to that stupid uncontrollable sense of servility that triggered within him at times. He actually hated that city. Every street, every corner, every house in Magadan reeked with pain and angst.

Its very soil was drenched in blood and tears.

He sat down on a bench in one of the parks, under a tree, and remained there in meditation. There was nobody anywhere. Evgenij was alone as he had been for decades, though time had taught him how to bear the situation. Now, however, something was about to subvert that fragile equilibrium he had taken enormous pains to reach: his new mission. He did not want to, no, he could not drink this bitter chalice. He just could not face it.

Had he been at home he would have jumped into his van and driven off to the Yarkaija Avacha where his beloved Anjushka had lived all these years. He would have tackled the treacherous roads with their sharp bends and sheer drops just to hold her in his arms. She, with her marvelous smile, would have probably dropped her dolly to touch his hand again and feel his warmth. And they would have told each other so many things just by looking in silence into each other's eyes. Words often create confusion; sometimes it takes only a few moments of silence to generate happiness.

He sprang to his feet and walked down the slope towards the sea. It seemed like the right direction to him. Down there, the boundless stretch of waves and color held the promise of that infinite gift called oblivion. Like a match set to hay, a tiny spark of hope ignited his heart. He crossed the city taking the Street of Bones, walking purposely in the middle of it, trampling that asphalt made of pitch and bones: the remains of the convicts who had built it. He wished he could hear them yelling, he wanted to know if, in that other world, there were anyone who suffered more than he did in this one.

He would be more than glad to swap places with them.

The women were lined up against the wall; they looked like mannequins exhibiting the various models.

Evgenij looked them over carefully like a director trying to pick the starring actress for his film. He had no clear idea of the role as yet, a lot depended on the interpreter's qualities. Some were blondes, some brunettes, some thin, others well padded. If he needed another, tall or short, they would certainly have been able to satisfy his demands.

All you needed to do was pay.

With sly, allusive glances the girls took tiny mincing steps, swung their tightly-sheathed hips and puffed clouds of cigarette smoke into the faces of their potential customers. They were charged with attracting those men, slaves to passion and morbid lust. An elderly woman with back-combed hair sat at a desk. She was the *maitresse*. She handed over the keys hanging from the little closet nearby, took note of the girls' names as they went up to the rooms and collected the clients' fees in advance. Rigorously in advance.

In that brothel Evgenij began to feel he was alive again. He was sitting alongside the other men in the waiting room, like patients with a dental appointment. He could feel the heat of the groping bodies upstairs in the rooms, catch the smell of the fluids they released. The sound of them lurching and moaning gave him new, vital lymph. The next vacant room would be his. He would take the girl of his choice by the hand and take her upstairs in the dark.

There was no need to look one another in the face.

«Do you come here often?» asked the fellow sitting beside him who spoke with a strange accent. It was perfectly normal to come across foreigners here. The city was a veritable babel.

Evgenij shrugged. «Whenever I can.»

«They told me they know how to fuck well.» And he made a lewd gesture with one raised finger, grinning maliciously.

Evgenij shrugged once more.

«There's a little one this tall», murmured the chap bending forward. «They described her to me, but I don't see her.»

«Who, the Armenian?» butted in the man sitting on the opposite side of the room. He was gross and fat, and his stomach jumped when he spoke. «Forget her, she got the clap! Did the job bareback.»

«What a dumb-fuck thing to do!» remarked the foreigner.

«When I was young I wanted to try it, too, but now…» continued big-paunch waving a hand, «it's impossible, far too risky.»

«Room eleven», announced the *maitresse*.

Evgenij got up, went over to the row of girls and, without giving it much thought, took the first one in line. She was a minute run-down brunette, whose empty tits drooped down to her belly.

«You know who to choose», *madame* whispered in his ear as she passed him the key, «that'll be forty-five thousand.»

Evgenij paid and went upstairs dragging the woman he had just bought up behind him.

«I need the bathroom for a moment», he said not having noticed that the bowl was in a corner of the room.

She began to undress as he pissed. When he turned around, he saw she was already lying on the bed, naked except for a pair of black lace panties. She was rubbing her thighs together and massaging her groin slowly, sensually. She wanted to make herself desirable, fuckable and get the business over with as quickly as possible.

Time was money.

«Do you do just any job?»

«Yes.»

«With or without?»

«With… but…»

«But what?»

«If you pay more»

«How much more?»

«Fifty thousand.»

Evgenij thrust his hand into his pocket and pulled out a wad of notes He unrolled three twenty-ruble notes and lay them down on her belly. The woman jumped of joy, grabbed them, made a ball of them and stuck them under the pillow.

«Don't tell madame, though, or she'll sack me », she entreated him.

«Get down on your hands and knees», he ordered without even responding.

The woman turned over and on all fours, obeying to the man entitled to order her about. Evgenij got down between her legs, looked at her close up and sniffed her all over. On either side of the gusset of her panties the lips of her vulva protruded, while the rest was trapped behind its tight elastic. He pushed this aside with one finger and freed her sex, which looked like a small pink apricot. The woman feigned pleasure and groaned.

«Hush! I don't like it», he snapped.

He began to rub her genitalia, while she heaved her hips to accompany his movements.

«Don't move», Evgenij ordered again.

He widened her wet orifice, poked his finger inside and began to masturbate her, while she remained silent and motionless, just as her master had commanded. Evgenij's hand slid slowly upward, kneading her perineum before passing to her anus, where he lingered, rubbing it ardently. He spat onto his fingers and plunged them into her rectum several times, first his little finger than all the others.

He unbuckled his belt, lowered his trousers and with one hard, unflinching push, sodomized her. The woman stifled a scream as he clung to her dangling tits which bobbed to the rhythm of his thrusts...

He placed his head on her bony, curved back and closed his eyes. It was not his intention to satisfy some perverse impulse of his. He simply wanted to suppress his feelings, those which insisted on encroaching on his heart, trying to tear it apart.

He just wanted to annihilate love.

28

Barnaul, Altaj, western Siberia, June 1992

«Please, be seated; don't stay there on your feet», said the man in uniform.

«What's he saying?» asked Mikael.

«He's inviting us to sit down», whispered Rose pulling back one of the chairs facing the desk.

«It's always difficult for me, for us, to have to inform relatives about what happened to convicts who passed through here», began colonel Misha Nikitin speaking slowly so Rose would have the time to translate from Russian for Mikael. «As you can understand, we are speaking about a certain period in our history; many of the data have been lost and several roll books destroyed. Although the practice was to record everything down to the last detail, unfortunately, not all the documents have come down to us.»

His solemn voice boomed in the office with its unassuming furniture, its walls bare except for the one behind him which sported a map of the country and a framed photograph of the new president Boris Eltsin. In the picture the statesman, with his spiky hair standing on end like a hedgehog, seemed to have been unwilling to gratify the photographer with a smile.

«Fortunately, if you'll allow me to say so, in this case we have managed to come across some information about the members of your family; comrade...» Nikitin, a handsome distinguished-looking man of about forty, bent his head to scrutinize the document he was holding in his hand «comrade... Seròp Gazarian and his son Gabriel.»

Mikael noticed a slight tremor in Rose's hands joined elegantly in her lap.

«Well?» he asked in an effort to distract her, although he had got the gist of the man's words; but she sat there as if paralyzed, almost unable to breathe.

«We have some information about your relatives», the colonel said all of a sudden, showing off his English with its guttural accent.

«Don't worry», said Rose coming back to reality, «you can tell me everything in Russian and I'll translate for him.»

The officer smiled at her cordially. «As you wish», he replied. «So...according to the registers, Seròp and his son arrived at camp number eleven in Altaj on the twenty-first of November 1952. We have a photocopy of the list containing their names,» he added waving a grey-black page smeared in ink. «Now... a few months later, in around February, no precise date is given... though we are certain of the fact, Seròp Gazarian died.»

Rose gasped.

«Certain, you say?»

«Yes.»

«What happened to Mr Gazarian?» inquired Mikael, anxiously.

«Our father is dead», murmured Rose.

«The cause of death?» she asked the officer in Russian.

«Well, here it says...» It was evident that Nikitin was extremely embarrassed by the lady's piercing eyes.

«What does it say?»

«He took his own life.»

«I want to hear it too», Mikael insisted. «What happened to Mr. Gazarian?» he asked in rather peremptory tones.

«Suicide», replied the colonel lowering his eyes and letting the paper slide from his hands.

Rose turned and looked out of the window. They were in the public records office inside the commissariat of the city of Barnaul, on the seventh floor of one of its ultramodern downtown buildings, the place from where they had begun their quest for Gabriel. If there was the slightest hope of finding someone alive that, for obvious reasons, would be Gabriel, not Seròp. Yet, being told that her father had committed suicide cut her to the very quick. Before undertaking this mission, she would never have imagined feeling so deeply about him. She had always despised Seròp, avoided speaking about him in public, never missed him or felt the need to find out what had happened to him. Yet now, everything had changed.

«As to the young Gabriel Gazarian», continued the officer in his soft mellow voice, «we know that soon afterwards he was sent to the Magadan sorting camp, then embarked on the *Linka*, destined for the Pevek mines… but…» and here he heaved a deep sigh, as if something had gone fatally wrong with the story of a hero, some latter-day Ulysses dogged by fate. He gave his interlocutors a look meant to express compassion.

«It seems the *Linka* never arrived at the port of Pevek», he concluded.

«What?» exclaimed Rose.

«Can you tell me what he's saying?» asked Mikael jumping to his feet.

«It seems it sank for reasons unknown to us.»

«The ship sank», repeated Rose in such a low voice that Mikael could barely hear it. «So?» she asked then, but the question was addressed more to herself than to the colonel.

Nikitin shrugged, embarrassed. He would have liked to say something to comfort her, but words failed him.

«Can you tell us where it happened at least? Where exactly did the ship go down?» insisted Rose.

The official sifted through a sheaf of papers. Then he found one and scanned it rapidly.

«It seems the *Linka* was lost off the coast near Avacha bay.» He looked up wondering if they had any idea where the place was. «Do you know where it is?» he asked, like a geography teacher quizzing his pupils. Upon receiving no answer, he stood up and went over to the map. «This peninsula shaped like the claw of a lobster is Kamchatka and Avacha bay is here!» he exclaimed pointing to a tiny spot on the map with the tip of his pen.

«But that's hundreds of miles away from here», exclaimed Mikael.

«How does one get there?» inquired Rose.

«Why, what can we possibly do there?» Mikael asked.

«I believe that we can be given some more detailed and precise information about the shipwreck, no?» insisted Rose.

«Madam, it happened forty years ago.» said Nikitin throwing his arms akimbo.

«It's worth trying, don't you think so?»

«Well, Petropavlovsk is a fishing village; someone is bound to have seen something at the time… and if there were any survivors you might find out more about them there, I'll grant you that!»

He took two steps forward stroking his chin as he thought out loud. «The shipwreck occurred at the end of spring» he said. «Maybe a strong man with a lifeboat or a dingy might have reached the coast; the water was no longer frozen at that time of year… naturally I don't want you to get your hopes up… in vain» he concluded shaking his head.

«How does one get there?» insisted Rose once more, recovering her usual self-control.

«We're not going anywhere unless you explain everything to me first», Mikael exclaimed.

«Just bear with me a moment, will you? I entreat you» she replied, like a mother scolding her child.

«Well, you'll need to return to Moscow and catch a plane from there.» affirmed Nikitin.

«Isn't there a direct flight from here? It must be closer!»

The colonel shook his head.

«Can't we hire a private plane?»

The officer laughed out loud, although politely, as was his wont.

«I entreat you, you must help me; whatever the cost!» pleaded Rose.

In the half-light of the ultra-modern hotel room where they were staying, brother and sister were getting to know each other a little better. The mere blood relationship did not suffice to create understanding, warmth and affection between them; these are things that stem only from shared experiences, joys and suffering, in short, life itself. Both of them needed time to really «find each other», «encounter each other».

«There is one detail in all of this that I find really hard to explain», Mikael said point blank, as if something really important had dawned on him all of a sudden.

«And that is?» asked Rose.

«You said that the relationship between Satèn and Seròp had broken down beyond repair after the sale of the child, that is me.»

«Exactly; mamma always told me so.»

«Well then, how come they decided to go to Armenia together, not to mention...» indicating her, «have another child? I just can't understand it at all.»

Rose heaved a deep sigh.

«For a really long time, papa and mamma continued to live under the same roof but as strangers; rather than strangers, business partners really, because papa had reached an agreement with an Italian, if I'm not mistaken, to supply him with slippers that mamma embroidered.»

«So getting rid of me brought them luck, did it?» commented Mikael bitterly.

«But soon afterwards, the Second World War broke out», proceeded Rose, disregarding her brother's cynical remark. «Patras was one of the first cities to be invaded by the Italians. Everything ground to a standstill, business, schools, especially after the Nazis arrived and patrolled the streets with their machineguns at the ready.»

«Yes, I saw that kind of thing in some war film or other.»

«Yes... Papa took to the hills with the partisans; he had always been a member of the communist party. Had they found him they would surely have executed him.»

Mikael, who had been sitting cross-legged on the divan, now lay back and looked at his sister distractedly.

«Seròp used to come back home in secret under cover of darkness and leave again before dawn; he came only to see his son who was growing up, nothing more, because Satèn was adamant about denying her husband his so-called marital rights... Are you listening to me?»

«Yes.»

«At the end of the war, repatriation began, favored by the AGBU, the Armenian General Benevolent Union.»

«The association for the preservation of Armenian identity in the world!» Mikael burst out angrily. «Of all the infamous and ignoble deals in history... Stalin needed low-cost workers and reached an agreement in cahoots with the church and AGBU, in reality a clique of millionaires, fake communists, members of the American diaspora.»

«Whatever! There was an enormous publicity drive, public appeals in all the newspapers, a funding campaign to pay for the journey back to the homeland. Seròp thought it would be a wonderful way to begin life all over, put the broken pieces of his marriage back together again. In June 1947 he joined the massive caravan. From Greece alone over one thousand Armenians returned home.»

«I know, I remember it clearly as if it were yesterday, that poster portraying the family — the baby in his mother's arms — she looking adoringly in the direction of the rising sun of Armenia. My parents were almost falling for it too: mamma Veronìk would have loved to go, but papa stood his ground.»

«Why?»

«Because he knew the communist regime only too well. My parents were Armenians from Bucharest in Rumania, and papa had studied medicine in the nearby Ukraine. Even if the idea of returning home attracted him — he was a fervent patriot — he imagined that in a soviet Armenia there would have been little hope.»

«When did they leave Bucharest for Athens? Before or after...»

«The adoption?» Mikael, using his elbows as leverage, got onto his feet and went over to the big window. «In the autumn of 1938», he answered finally his eyes fixed on the Barnaul hills. «When they arrived at the Greek frontier they registered a son; someone had succeeded in sneaking the baby over to the other side. Papa must have paid someone handsomely, you see, he did not want the community in Athens to know about the adoption, he feared his boy might be traumatized by gossip, afterwards»

«And you... when... how did you find out?» asked Rose, immediately regretting her words and fearing that the question was too indiscreet.

Mikael spun around and scrutinized the woman as if deciding whether she, the sister destiny had foisted on him, deserved his confidence or not.

«Veronìk and I were really close», he whispered, slumping into the armchair nearest him. «I was her pride and joy, also because papa was always so caught up in his work. Papa, the famous doctor

Harutiùn Delalian was the community's only physician at the time. He used to leave the house before dawn and often returned home after dusk. When he died, mamma suffered a terrible shock, but she suffered even more when I left to the college in Venice. She was alone and lonely, all she did was wander through that sad house full of memories… Her life lost all meaning.» Mikael drew back his long grey hair and choked overcome by emotion. «She passed away just one year before I graduated. Luckily it was summer and I was there with her.»

«Mikael, don't, if you think…»

He raised a hand to silence her.

«I knew she was dying; the surgeon who operated her had given her only a few days to live. I did all I could to hide my despair. I told her that everything would surely improve, that I knew this fantastic doctor in Venice; that I would bring her to see him soon and that he would cure her completely. I sat by her bed and read to her; the novels, the poems she loved best. Well, one hot, clammy afternoon — have you any idea what it's like in Athens in August? — she suddenly lowered the book I was holding and whispered,

'Mikael I need to talk to you.

«*'Later, mamma*, just listen to this poem…

«*'No, no, now'*, she insisted in an inaudible though adamant voice, her eyes imploring me.

«*'You're so stubborn'*, I mocked, stroking her forehead which was burning with fever.

«Then she took my hand and held it tight as if looking for the strength to continue.

«*'You are not my son'*, she blurted out.

«*'What are you saying?'* I gasped.

«*'Mikael, you are not our natural son'*, she repeated looking me straight in the eye.

«*'You're raving'*, I protested, withdrawing my hand.

«But she kept shaking her head tossing her tousled grey hair.

«*'You were adopted. Papa and I couldn't have children. You were the necessary half of our happiness, without you we'd never have been complete.*

«I was utterly bowled over and my gaze wandered all over the room, alighting on the most banal of details: the lampshade, the medicine cabinet, a spider on the ceiling

«*'Mikael, look at me'*, mamma begged me, with the same authoritative tone she used when I was little. *'It's the truth'*, she whispered more softly, *'you are not our natural child, but I ask myself if we could have loved a natural child more than we loved you. Papa and I just adored you, like a treasure beyond compare, a gift with which the Lord had decided to bless us when we thought we'd grow old all alone.'*

«I was weeping, my head bent low, to hide my face from her.

«*'Take it as you please, but I have no regrets... whatsoever,* mamma asserted, *'I'm going to meet my Maker, soon, and I thought you were mature enough to understand.'*

«I knew that if she saw me in tears that would cause her pain, but I was distraught.

«*'The only thing that really matters is love, remember that, my dear delight,* she murmured and began sobbing her heart out. *'The only thing that matters is love '*, she reaped clasping my hand. *'I have loved you above all else in the world'*, she murmured kissing the palms of my hands with her chapped lips.»

Mikael, curled up in the armchair, was weeping copiously and sobbing his heart out.

Rose could not bear to see her brother in that state. She went over to him almost fearful of how he might take it. She threw her arms around his neck, hesitantly, in a gesture of sincere affection. He did not react, but — surprisingly enough — allowed her to fondle him like a baby in distress.

«Pain is the only thing that could draw us together» thought Rose, as she held him tight in this, their first fraternal embrace.

Early the following day Nikitin called Rose.

«Good morning Mrs. Bedikian, I hope I'm not disturbing you», he began politely.

«Good morning», she replied uncertain, imagining a piece of bad news.

«Madam, I've just received some further information about the shipwreck involving your brother.»

Silence.

«Madam?... Can you hear me?»

«I'm listening.»

«I'm sorry but I have to give you some very bad news, I'm

afraid. We now know the cause of the shipwreck. The *Linka* caught fire out at sea, off the coast of Avacha bay.»

«Fire?»

«Yes, it caught fire, though I can't tell you why or how. However, there were witnesses, fishermen who were out on the sea at the time»

«What exactly are you trying to tell me?» asked Rose in gelid tones. «To pack my bags and go back home?» Her teeth began to chatter so uncontrollably that she had to step back from the receiver lest he hear them.

The colonel hesitated for a moment. «No, not at all!» he exclaimed. «I have found a small military plane willing to fly you to Petropavlovsk at a fair price. The only thing I wish to tell you in all honesty, as you yourself will appreciate, is that the chances of finding survivors are extremely slim; I really have to tell you this, even if it sounds discouraging».

«I'm so grateful for your interest in the matter», she murmured though she felt nauseous. She had to change the subject at once lest she retch. «Tell me about the plane.»

«In actual fact you'll have to take a normal commercial flight back to Magadan and, from there, a military plane will take you on to Petropavlovsk. It's impossible from here; it's over four thousand kilometers», he concluded.

«Do you know at what time the flight leaves for Magadan?»

«Are you sure you don't wish to think it over, madam?»

«Just tell me, please.»

«There's one at 15.20, and it takes six hours.»

«So we'll arrive at 21.30.»

The colonel chuckled good-naturedly.

«Mrs. Bedikian, the Soviet Union is a very vast country; we have five time zones. You'll land in Magadan at about two a.m.»

«I'll talk to my brother about it, and let you know. Thank you!»

Rose hung up her heart beating in her throat.

«So he called you in the middle of the night to tell you this?»

«Yes.»

Rose spooned some scrambled egg onto her plate. She had decided to have breakfast with Mikael in the hotel lounge and discuss the next step to take.

«So, you're determined to travel to Petropavlovsk?»

«Positive!»

«To do what precisely? Would you be so kind as to enlighten me? To ask those stinking old fishermen — admitting there are any of them still alive today — if, by any chance, over forty years ago, they saw a boy in the bay as a ship full of convicts sank in flames, off the coast?»

«Stop it!»

«You know what? I don't know why you insist so much now. Why didn't you do something about it years ago?»

Rose remained silent. She continued to take her irritation out on the eggs, tormenting them with her fork.

«Well? Do I not even deserve an answer?»

«I was on my own before this.»

«Meaning, I'm to provide you now with all the energy you need, is that it?»

«You're downright cruel!» she blurted out, her eyes filling with tears.

«You're going to cry?»

«I'm much stronger than you think; if you want to go back to Rome, help yourself, I'm going out there anyway!», she asserted transfixing him with a look both stubborn and reckless. "Well then, Mr Delalian? What do you intend doing? Returning home, locking yourself up safely in your den, burying your head in the sand and waiting for the storm to blow over?»

Mikael stared at the buffet, heaped with of all kinds of food and drink. He was about to stand up, he wanted to flee from the embarrassing situation that had come to a head.

«He's you brother too, for God's sake. Your twin!» Rose blurted out.

He knocked over his chair.

«I have no siblings; I grew up alone. It was our father who decided to tear me away from our family. Remember?! It's better that things remain as they were, there's no sense in stirring up the past, it hurts both of us too much», he replied, his voice cracking. «I'd never have undertaken this distressing, senseless quest had my son not urged me to.»

«Tommaso simply threw light on something lurking in your

subconscious. Everyone wants to know where they come from, would wish to embrace the brother from which adverse destiny separated him. But, obviously, you're different»

Mikael remained dubious, lost in his thoughts, sipping his coffee, his head bent over the damask table cloth.

«Look here, Mikael, I can't step down now, I won't.»

«Why?»

«Because I've always felt guilty about his arrest and imprisonment. I cannot bear it any longer, I have to do something.»

Mikael failed to understand.

«Do you remember that book by Saroyan?»

«The one you keep wrapped in that piece of velvet?»

«Yes, I told you it was the reason for their arrest. But I never told you that we had kept it in the house, Gabriel and I, because I made him promise not to destroy it. At that time the secret police were fine combing the area. Papa had asked us to burn the book, but we disobeyed him; it was our little secret.»

«And you risked your lives for a book?»

«For us, that story not only exalted human dignity but also the price it cost not to renounce it. Gabriel was a dreamer, a born actor, in a way; he knew my weaknesses, my latent desires, my passions. When he read it to me he used to change the text to impress me, please me. There was that sentence at that end with a penny...»

«*A child could buy any number of things with a penny.*»

«Yes, that... well, until I had learned English, I thought he meant a little girl— although *child* can mean either in English—because that's what Gabriel had told me. An when I asked him why Saroyan preferred girls, do you know what he said?»

Mikael shook his head.

«Because girls are always better than boys... I used to take this seriously, as a personal compliment, imagining that the author had thought of me, that he had actually — forgive my naiveté — dedicated the book to his own little Novàrt. Can't you see?, I couldn't destroy such a sweet, intimate thing, could I? I was really little, stubborn and I had no idea, could not judge the gravity of certain actions. Besides, I was backed by Gabriel, who would have done just anything to make me happy.»

Although Rose spoke softly, it was clear how important the

recollection of these memories were to her. Mikael listened, fascinated in a way, impressed, and caught up in the artlessness of a little girl he had never known.

«We tore off the binding», continued Rose, «and stuffed it into a crack in the kitchen cabinet while I hid the book in the rag bag mamma allowed us to play with. They found the cover, that was enough for them.»

Mikael sought his sister's hand and caressed it lightly.

«Call the colonel... I want to box the ears of that rogue, that con man, that text-forger of a brother of ours!», he said getting up and going over to the buffet to pour himself another cup of coffee.

Rose was smiling.

The little Novàrt of bygone days was back.

She packed her bags in great haste, then called Toronto, getting Hagòp up out of bed at that unearthly hour.

«My love, is everything all right?» asked her husband in a hoarse voice.

«Yes, I don't know... they say he may have died in a fire on board the ship taking him to another camp.»

«What? So, what now?»

«Nothing, I'm going to look for him. I want to find out if, by any chance, he survived.»

Hagop was in no way surprised at her tenacity.

«Is there nothing I can do to help?»

«Tell Liù I need an urgent bank transfer to Siberia. I'll call her in fifteen minutes.»

«Okay, but you, how are you?»

«Fine»

«And matters with Mikael?...»

«Better, thanks. Listen I have to rush.»

«The boys were asking for you.»

«Kiss them for me. I miss them», she replied with a touch of sadness.

«What about me?» asked Hagop, but his wife had already hung up.

Rose had to stay quite some time on the phone with Liù to iron out the bank transfer issue. The whole sum of ten million rubles was paid, in one shot, into the foreign account Nikitin had given her. Had it been a matter of mere business she would have asked for discount, but to haggle over the price of the plane that might take her nearer to Gabriel was out of the question, it would have been downright sacrilege. Mikael had offered to contribute too, but Rose had declined. She had been the one to decide to hire the private plane and she alone was going to pay for it.

Before going to the airport, they had to go to the public register office to pick up a special permit along with the detailed flight plan. Colonel Nikitin had made provisions for everything they needed.

«At Magadan you will find the pilot, Major Anton Pavlovich waiting for you; he'll be holding a placard with your names on it. He's one of our very best pilots. He has ten thousand flying hours to his credit.»

«Isn't the plane somewhat small?» asked Rose, evidently alarmed.

«No, no worries», he answered stifling a chuckle, «it's a taxi-plane, we use them for short hops.»

«More or less two hours?»

«Let's say three.»

Thanks, colonel; I'm feeling better already. Have you received confirmation of the bank transfer?»

«Yes, that was really quick, thank you.»

«Don't mention it; we often have to deal with urgent payments.»

The officer beamed her a courteous smile.

«I also wish to inform you about the representative who will meet you at Petropavlovsk, I have written his name down along with details of your itinerary. His name is Evgenij Koslov; he's lived over there for ages and knows the territory inside out. He'll be an amazing guide.»

«Are there hotels?»

«A vast range, will a five-star do?… I'm only joking. Evgenij has been briefed about everything already; he'll bring you to where you'll be staying. He's an odd fish, but once you get over your first impression you'll see he's a real brick.»

«How can I ever thank you, colonel…» Rose realized she could not recall his name.

«Misha Nikitin.»

Mikael stood there in silence listening to Rose and the officer; his poor Russian did not suffice to satisfy his curiosity, so he tried to guess what they were saying.

«Excuse me asking, madam», Nikitin turned to Rose politely. «I presume the person you are looking for is your only sibling; you are so earnest about the whole enterprise...»

«No, that's not it at all; this gentleman here is his twin», she replied indicating Mikael.

«What are you saying about me?» her brother asked without receiving an answer.

«Oh, God, that never dawned on me. Your surnames are different.» The colonel looked perplexed.

«Well, that's quite another story. If we'd enough time I'd tell you.»

Nikitin smiled. «Bon voyage.», and he held out his hand to say goodbye.

«Thank you so much for everything, colonel.»

«Madam...»

«*Sbasibo*», said Mikael as he shook the man's hand. «Would you mind telling what you two were saying about me?» he grumbled as she was already walking away without paying him any heed. «I swear I'm going to learn Russian», he threatened as he punched the air.

They took off from Barnaul half an hour behind schedule.

Once the plane rose above the clouds that bore down on the city, the fuselage was flooded in blinding sunlight.

Rose had to put on her Hollywood-star-style sunglasses.

«This is the best part of a flight», she told her brother.

«Which?»

«The light you find when all seems dark.»

As they flew eastward the sun gradually sank behind the tail of the aircraft. By the time the flight assistants came with their trolleys to serve dinner it was completely dark.

«Sausage or chicken?» the attractive blond girl in the red uniform asked Rose.

«Chicken, please.»

«And the gentleman?»

«The same», she answered deciding on her brother's behalf.

«No caviar», jested Mikael.

«How do you open this?» said Rose trying to unseal the carton containing her meal. «I can't see a thing», she grumbled.

«What if you took your sunglasses off?»

«Ha, ha! Wise guy!»

A little later the lights were switched off in the cabin and Rose, exhausted, soon fell fast asleep, her head resting on Mikael's arm. He brother remained still as the scent of thyme from her perfume titillated his nostrils; he closed his eyes and thought of the most moving fairy tale he could recall: Hansel and Gretel, the two little siblings lost in the woods. He could still remember the illustrations in the book someone had given him as a present: Gretel with a broom in her hand freeing Hansel from the cage where the bad old witch held him prisoner.

As he slowly dozed off, the fairy tale became all confused; he was not sure who it had been that had shoved the witch into the oven.

Hours later. when the plane landed, he was the first to wake.

«Welcome to Magadan», he whispered to Rose, smiling.

She opened her eyes slowly and looked around, unsure of where she was.

«It wasn't all that far, now, was it?» she said, as she stretched and yawned.

29

Petropavlovsk, Avacha bay, North-East Siberia, 19th June 1992

That day, the beginning of summer was making itself felt even in Petropavlovsk. Evgenij had come home from work, undressed, filled the tub with cool water, and remained there soaking nearly all afternoon, a flask of vodka on the edge of the bath.

He had a lot of time on his hands: the guests he was to pick up would not be landing until the middle of the night.

Immersed in the water, he lit a cigarette, took a long pull the way he liked to and filled his lungs until he felt them protesting; then he puffed it back out accompanied by his usual hacking cough. The radio was playing an old folk song; a cascade of light, happy notes poured forth from a balalaika. Evgenij imagined the girls gamboling in a meadow full of flowers.

«What a fool I am», he scolded himself, chuckling. Caught up in the rhythm, he began to beat time on the side of the tub. «Da, dada dudu», he crooned.

His gaze fell on the ring he wore on his little finger that made a dull sound as he tapped the bath. He tried to take it off but could not; it was stuck on the finger where he had been wearing it for years. He massaged it with a little soap and pulled hard to slide it off. The ring went flying and plummeted into the bottom of the bath. Evgenij felt around for it beneath the floating foam and when he found it, he stared at it as if for the very first time. It was a simple wedding ring in old red gold. On the inside an engraving said S-S 1935.

«They were married fifty-seven years ago... so much time has passed since then!» he murmured somewhat amazed.

He twisted the ring around his finger as if trying to wind back time. Scenes of a ship on fire suddenly crowded his mind: the smoke, the choking coughs, the screams of the men burning alive. Then, two grappling men oozing with hatred, the taste of blood as one bit into the flesh of the other...

Willing to chase this nightmarish vision away, he lay the ring down on the edge of the tub beside his little flask of vodka. He took another mouthful of his favorite drink, this time bigger and longer, and flinched at his own loud belch. A wasp cut across his field of vision; it was bigger than average, its brown and yellow striped body kept buzzing around the window, bumping into the panes, flying stubbornly around the glass and crashing into it over and over again. Evgenij watched it mesmerized, struck by the insect's untiring desire for freedom. It was obvious it had no intention of giving up until it had found a way out.

«Silly little beast, can't you see it's closed?» he asked it out loud.

He rose from the tub dripping all over the floor, went over to the window and threw it wide open. The wasp buzzed for a while in his face as if trying to thank him.

«Off with you, now!» he urged.

They insect flew out the window and vanished on the light summer breeze.

«Shall we be flying over the sea?» Rose asked Major Anton Pavlovich.

«Positive», he responded. «Don't tell me you're afraid?» he teased guessing her apprehension.

«You must be joking!» said Mikael.

They had been flying for twenty minutes now, and although it was nearly three in the morning, Anton Pavlovich was as fresh as a daisy; tall and muscular, he might have been cast in the role of a war hero in a film. He had met the siblings in Magadan with broad, warm smiles, and after the usual small talk and a cup of coffee, he had led them out to the little green aircraft which looked like a mosquito compared to the regular airline planes. Rose had done her best to hide her embarrassment behind a rather silly grin as she sat down next to the pilot. As for Mikael, he had slumped down onto the seat behind them, having loaded their bags in the luggage compartment. Pavlovich had revved up the engine and the propeller had begun to turn very slowly, then faster and faster, while the little aircraft had skipped and jumped down the runway before finally lifting off to Mikael's big surprise.

"We're airborne!" he had cried out with a mixture of joy and terror.

«We're lucky», Pavlovich said, «the weather's so good.»

«At least that», Mikael muttered in Armenian. The propeller made such a racket that the major would not have understood him even had he spoken in Russian.

«How long will it take?» shouted Rose.

«Roughly three hours», replied the pilot. «Have you even been to Petropavlovsk before?»

«No», said Rose, shaking her head while she kept staring out the window not much bigger than a car windscreen.

«It's an enthralling place», the major added. «For the local tribes it's the place where dreams come true.»

«All dreams?»

The other nodded. «Even the most improbable ones», he said with some emphasis.

«What's he saying?» Mikael asked Rose, leaning towards her.

«That it's a wonderful place.»

Rose was still talking when the plane entered a patch of turbulence and shuddered all over. It was as if some invisible wave were trying to overturn it. The two siblings clung to their seats convinced their hour had come.

«No need to worry», soothed Pavlovich, «nothing serious; all perfectly normal.»

Rose and Mikael looked at each other in astonishment

«This is just the first of a series of similar quakes», the pilot warned them, «but rest assured it's nothing, just pretend you're on...»

«...a roller coaster!» exclaimed Mikael, who understood what he was saying, for once.

«From now on, this man will be your guardian angel», Pavlovich said.

A stocky bloke, with a black eyepatch and a cigarette clenched between his teeth, was smiling at them.

It was six the morning and they had just come through passport control in a sleepy, deserted airport.

Rose held out a hesitant hand, as she took a peek at their guide.

«My name is Evgenij Koslov. It's a real pleasure.»

«Rose Bedikian.» She drew back her hand and, discreetly, dried it on her jacket; Koslov's was unusually clammy. «His name is Mikael», she then said introducing her brother who shook hands too.

«Evgenij, look after them well, mark me!», advised Pavlovich. «Madam, sir, I wish you a very pleasant stay.», and he took his leave with a brisk military salute.

«Thank you very much, again, Major.»

«Thank you indeed», remarked Mikael, «especially for the breath-taking flight», he jested, though Anton Pavlovich could hear him no longer as he was already striding off in the direction of his aircraft.

«Give me your bags!» exclaimed Evgenij. «The car is just over here», he added, picking up their bags and rucksacks, «I bet you're tired.»

«I'm pooped! How do you say that in Russian?» said Mikael.

«You just don't», retorted Rose.

As they walked through the sliding doors, a new pale dawn was creeping across the hills to the east where day would soon break.

«Here we are», said Evgenij, indicating a pea-green van parked a few meters away, but Rose was not listening to him. She was looking at the diaphanous moon hanging in the sky, breathing in the bracing mountain air as if seeking to imbibe the energy of the place all in one go.

«What are you waiting for; aren't you getting in?» called Mikael, who was already sitting in the vehicle.

«Do we all have to sit in there?»

«If you like you can ride in the goods compartment.»

«Very funny.»

«Tomorrow we'll have a rented car, it wasn't possible to hire one at such short notice», said Evgenij, excusing himself.

Rose wriggled in next to her brother and closed the door with a sonorous thud.

«We'll have to squeeze in a bit; but we haven't far to go and… sorry for the mess.»

«Not to mention the stink!» chuckled Mikael.

«Cut it out», snapped Rose, silencing him.

«I feel it's only correct to inform you that I know a little Armenian. You are Armenians aren't you,?»

«Ah… yes… and where did you learn the language?» Rose mumbled.

«I be in work camp», Evgenij began in broken Armenian.

«As guard. Guard, how is it you say?»

«Sentinel?» suggested Rose.

«Yes, many Armenians in *baraki*.»

«There were many Armenians?» inquired Mikael.

«Yes, yes.»

«Where? In which camps?» Rose insisted.

«Oh, far away, Vladivostok, Magadan.»

A little man emerged from the guardroom at the airport gateway and was about to ask to check the van and its contents. Evgenij flashed a badge at him from a distance and the man simply nodded and waved them through. «But where do you hail from?» asked Mikael, a little later.

«Georgia… but we, I think same age», suggested Evgenij with a cordial smile. «How many years have you?»

«Fifty-five next autumn.»

«Me too», said he.

«Peers, then.»

«Yes, I from Batumi, many Armenians in Georgia.»

«Speak in Russian if you like, you don't need to force yourself to speak Armenian, my brother understands…» suggested Rose.

«Ah, he brother? I thought husband.»

«No, no, he's my brother.»

Evgenij glanced at the two guests.

«Now that you say so, there is a certain resemblance,» he said in Russian.

«Now what's he saying?» asked Mikael.

«That we look alike.»

«Because he's never seen me fresh as a daisy in the morning, my face all relaxed.» And he tucked up the skin on his face.

Rose burst out laughing. «But where does this comic streak of yours spring from? I'd never have imagined it existed.»

«It's tiredness, dear sister, simple tiredness… And fear», he added with a brusque change in tone.

«Afraid?» asked Evgenij amazed, while Rose tried to understand what her brother really meant by that last remark of his.

«If you're cold, tell me», Evgenij said a little later winding down the window, a wisp of his hair dancing in the breeze flopped all over his forehead.

The road cut through e green landscape crossed by a rushing crystal-clear blue river. Vast groves of trees painted the surrounding hillsides emerald green. Rose thought she could hear thrushes warbling amid the branches rustling in the wind.

«That's Koriaksky», Evgenij announced, indicating the snow-capped mountain to his left, «the most beautiful volcano in the world.»

Rose and Mikael leaned forward to get a better look through the windscreen.

«There are twenty volcanoes in Petropavlovsk.»

«Oh, how interesting!» exclaimed Mikael taking a photo of it with his Kodak Instamatic.

«Don't worry, they're all asleep», the driver reassured him with a slight nudge in the ribs, «many in sea, in Avacha bay, old times many tsunami», he added miming a huge wave in the air with one of his hands, mixing Russian and Armenian, which he presumed would be the best way to communicate with his guests.

«Awful», said the siblings in chorus.

Evgenij shrugged and turned on the car radio. An accordion, drums and a tenor voice crackled from the speakers.

«You like Russian music?»

The siblings nodded.

«I knew it!» he said satisfied. «Tomorrow musical evening at hotel.»

«Perfect», said Mikael.

«That's kind of you», Rose butted in, «but we're not here for tourism.»

«Yes, of course», agreed Evgenij.

«When have we got the meeting at the commissariat?»

«This afternoon at two, so you can rest a little.»

«Good, we'd like to take a look at the registers, the archives of the period. The colonel told you about it, didn't he?»

«Yes.»

«Do you think there'll be some account of the shipwreck, the fire aboard the *Linka*… the ship?»

«Asking does no harm», Evgenij remarked with a grimace full of doubt.

«Yeah», grumbled Mikael.

«But don't you know anyone who may have witnessed the disaster?»

«Madam, it was forty years ago.»

«There must be some older people living in this uncontaminated countryside», observed Mikael indicating the enchanting landscape around him.

Evgenij found this highly amusing. «I can take you to an old folks' home, if you like» he said as he thumped the steering wheel with a fist and guffawed sonorously.

Rose and Mikael glanced at each other perplexed.

«Sounds like a good idea, do you know one?»

«You bet… Yarkiaya Avacha», he answered his eyes bright with tears of laughter.

«What's the town's population?»

«One hundred and eighty thousand, I think», responded Evgenij. «Mostly fishermen and fishmongers like myself. In summer when the tourists come, I act as a guide… to supplement my earnings»,

They had just entered Petropavlovsk and were driving along the road down to the bay amid alternating industrial sheds and Soviet-style high-rise blocks. Now and then the odd wooden house, the traditional *izba* stood out among them. Rose had dozed off, her head resting against the window, her long chestnut hair blowing in the breeze. Mikael observed the traffic of the town which was just waking up.

«Lovely view, no?» shouted Evgenij, one of his arms indicating the sea, his voice waking Rose.

«What's the matter?» she asked, still a little hazy.

«Look, I live up there, in that little house.» he said, but neither of the siblings was paying any attention. They were looking in the opposite direction at an imposing white church with gaudy sky-blue domes.

«Every year, I come here to celebrate Easter», Evgenij added.

«Is it still far to the hotel?» Rose inquired in rather snappish tones.

The driver glanced at her. «There it is, madam», he said with all the politeness he could muster.

They went past a traffic light and then pulled up alongside a building in an undefinable style. It was a cube in cement with some rather frayed flags flying over the entrance. The doorman, in a red jacket, rushed over to meet the guests who alighted all stiff and awkward, stretching their limbs, as Evgenij carried their bags into the foyer.

«Welcome», said the receptionist greeting them. His head was clean shaven, his cheeks ruby red. «May I have your passports?» He filled in some forms paying particular attention to their visas. «Rooms 18 and 19», he said eventually, handing them two large heavy keys and keeping their documents.

«All right then», said Evgenij offering them his hand. «Shall me meet down here in an hour and a half, let's say?»

«Fine», nodded the two siblings, turning around completely, ignoring his proffered hand.

«If you need a snack, the restaurant here isn't half bad.» he muttered.

Mikael faced their guide again as Rose pressed the lift button. «Thank you.» he said softly.

Evgenij waited for them to enter the lift and then dashed outside, greeting the receptionist summarily as he passed him by. He did not head for his van, he furtively slid behind the hotel and hid among the birches in the garden. He leaned up against the trunk of a tree and vomited convulsively, his heart pounding like a hammer in his breast.

"God help me!" he whispered.

«What are you looking at?»

«Nothing, there's a garden down there», replied Mikael leaning up against the window frame to look at the view.

«I'm too tired to sleep. Do you feel like eating something?»

«Give me five minutes».

A few minutes later they entered the lounge. The tables with red cloths and gold serviettes were arranged around a little stage, decked out in garlands of red and gold balloons mirroring the cockades on the white walls. The whole place reeked of stewed cabbage.

«Ready for the Russian evening?» asked Mikael.

«Only if we dance the *kozachok*», jested Rose.

A pleasantly plump woman came over to them, smiling. «What can I bring you?»

«Breakfast and some tea, please.»

«We have smoked salmon, herring with onion, borsch with cabbage and beetroot.»

«No, thank you so much, just some tea, bread and jam.»

«But those are already included with the tea, madam», said the woman leaving a strong trail of lacquer in her wake as she moved away.

«What do you think of our guardian angel?» asked Mikael.

«I couldn't say, an odd bod.»

«He drinks. He stank of vodka.»

The waitress returned with a copper samovar, an ugly reproduction of one from the Czarist period.

«So it wasn't the fish then», Rose blurted out.

«I wonder what happened to his eye?»

Rose snorted. «He was a sentry at a gulag, I don't know if I explain myself.»

«Do you think we can trust him... he might be dangerous, no?» asked her brother as he poured out the tea.

«No, around here they all had something to do with the work camps, one way or another.»

«We're in good hands, then.»

The waitress returned with bread and butter and some small dishes of jam. «We make these ourselves!» she exclaimed with a touch of pride. «This here is rose jam.»

When she left, they spread some of it on a slice of bread.

«Not bad», commented Rose tasting it.

«This reminds me of my years at the college and the *vartanoush* the monks on the island of San Lazzaro used to make», Mikael remarked.

«What else do you remember about that period?»

He did not answer but stared at the samovar as if trying to figure out why it looked so ugly.

«Ok then, shall we go upstairs?» suggested Rose a few minutes later as she got to her feet.

«The pain», Mikael murmured out of the blue.

«I beg your pardon?» said Rose, sitting back down.

«The sheer torment» he added, «torment of youth thrown away.»

«Are you talking about your son's affair?»

«No, he was a blessing; I mean the fact that I grew up so much more quickly than all my classmates… I had to deal with too many, all at once.»

Rose felt all the unhappiness which time had failed to attenuate.

«I suffered so much, at times I thought I'd go mad; *le chagrin de vivre…*»

A golden balloon broke loose from one of the garlands and floated on the air. They both followed its course until it landed in a corner of the stage.

«Have you ever managed to work out the reason for all that pain, that profound suffering?»

«As a child I had an excessively vivid imagination. I even believed I lived the life of another.»

Rose shifted on her chair, visibly moved.

«Whose?»

He turned towards the window; a shaft of sunlight chiseled his face mercilessly. «A boy like myself, identical to me. I could feel all his anguish, his pain. All I wanted to do was console him, give him hope whatever the Inferno he was trapped in.»

Rose listened with bated breath.

«Once, I even felt my skin burning. I thought I was on a ship in flames — in reality I was on a motor launch in Venice — so I jumped into the Laguna in attempt to save myself… ourselves…»

Mikael bowed his head, haunted by ghosts from his past, as Rose began to repeat a name, like some kind of a mantra:

«Gabriel, Gabriel», she whispered.

You and me, as children. Playing together. Surrounded by enchanting scenery, in a spot I wouldn't be able to place yet so familiar to me, shying stones on the shore of a bay. The pebbles skim weightlessly, bouncing over the waves. Each of us pitches his own, as far away as he can. We stand side by side, our feet ankle-deep in the soft wet sand. We study our throws, serious as can be, but nobody wins. This is evident right from the start. Even if the haze prevents us from seeing clearly, we are dead sure that out there, on the deep, our flying stones, thanks to some strange optical illusion converge and join, becoming one. We look at each other, spellbound, as if watching a magician at work, then we throw two more, follow them, until they reach the point where they come together again, a veritable miracle. We smile, pleased with ourselves and throw several more, with childish doggedness, challenging the bay's spell, which never fails, anyway. I turn around to look at you, to capture your image so like my own, then, all of a sudden, I'm afraid because you're walking away from me. You're wading into the waves, fully dressed, your hand clutching one last stone. You want to get the better of it, break the spell that ties our pebbles together and, heedless of the icy water, you advance bravely.

I'd like to call you, only I don't know your name and then, suddenly, you disappear, as if swallowed into empty nothingness. I don't want to lose you, dear friend, so I dive in too, in your wake, looking for you everywhere. Finally, I find you, but only because, at a certain point, I look around: and there you are standing stock-still on the shore, right there where I had been a moment before, guilt all over your face for having made me run such a risk. And yet, I feel more surprised than angry, though I'm mad at myself for having been so naive, for falling for your hoax and following you. But then I realize that I'm holding the stone you had in your fist before and I find myself in the water instead of you, as if I were you and you were me. I swear I don't understand what we're playing at anymore, the sense of what's happening, so I just remain still for a while, thinking, suspended, like a particle of vapor in the fog all around us. In the end — and this is the absurd thing — somehow, I know what you know, but above all, I feel what you feel. It's not that I'm guessing and I'm certain of this now, it's because we are made of the same stuff, are a single being, split in two.

I see, that you, on the shore, are upset and worried, because you can see I'm not able to stay afloat. Don't do that, please don't! It wasn't you who made up the rules of this game.

Shhh, look!

The bay is turning into a river. A strong rushing stream. Easy does it, I give in to the current. Let it carry me away, wherever it wants. I don't feel a grudge anymore, only a little sadness, maybe, a strong longing for the happy moments we spent together.

You and me.

«Mikael, wake up!» called Rose knocking on his door. «Evgenij is waiting for us.»

He let go of his pillow soaked with tears, and glanced at his watch: it was almost two pm.

«Coming!» he exclaimed jumping out of bed.

The commissariat was close to the old port, a blue building facing the fish market. Evgenij had been quick and taken them there in a jiffy avoiding the afternoon traffic.

«You can take a walk, I'll go and park», he proposed as they alighted.

Rose and Mikael crossed the road and began looking at the fishing boats bobbing gently by the pier, their cables tied securely to their moorings. The fishermen had returned home after their night's work and one or two of them sat on the pier teasing out their nets. Farther on, were stalls offering freshly fried fish of all kinds.

«So unlike those on the shores of the Mediterranean,» Mikael mused.

Enormous salmon were laid out in long lines on marble slabs, the fishmongers sprinkling them with water from the dock; gigantic lobster claws, like huge rough, thorny orange talons, spoke eloquently of the size of the shellfish from which they had been taken.

«Imagine coming face to face with a monster like that on the reef?»

«Fat chance, I wouldn't even put the tip of a toe into this water», responded Rose.

«Smile!» Mikael took out his camera and immortalized the moment in a snap of her standing next to one of the giant claws.

From the other side of the road, Evgenij was hailing them, his arms flailing like a windmill.

Khalil Akhundov, the commissar for the Kamchatka region was waiting to receive them.

FIRE OFF AVACHA

At 20.39 yesterday a fire broke out in the engine room of the Linka belonging to the Dostroi fleet. The ship disintegrated completely following three strong explosions and sank almost immediately. The Linka, of medium tonnage, left the port of Magadan on Tuesday the 19th of May and was expected in Pevek on the 12th of June, where it was due to disembark provisions of all kinds. On board were twenty-one members of the crew and several prisoners in transit. There were no survivors.

Kamtcatskaya Pravda, Tuesday 26th May 1953

THE LINKA SINKS

Investigations are being carried out to ascertain the cause of the fire which on May 25th last broke out on board the Linka, causing it to sink in the bay of Avacha. The vessel, belonging to the Dostroi fleet, blew up while sailing to Pevek, probably due to a human error in the engine room. No member of the crew or any of the convicts on board survived the disaster. Pravda, Wednesday the 27th May 1953.

«Here», said Akhundov, «these are the articles published at the time of the tragedy.»

He searched among various newspaper and magazine cuttings and handed them over to his two guests.

«There are these too, only a few lines in each. Unfortunately, at the time, they published very little concerning the organization of the gulags.»

Mikael sat up straight. «Is there no possibility that someone may have survived? A convict, maybe, who managed to evade and come ashore in a lifeboat or a dingy?» he asked, gesturing to his sister to translate his question into Russian.

Akhundov shook his head. «If you'd been a convict at the time, would you have made your identity known? You would have been sent straight back to the camp!»

Rose and Mikael shook their heads, while Evgenij, seated behind them, followed the conversation with the utmost attention.

«But the locals never noticed a stranger in town, a face they'd never seen before the accident?» inquired Rose her cheeks red with excitement.

The commissar smiled at her understandingly.

«Madam, apart from the fact that we are speaking about something that took place almost forty years ago, this is one of Siberia's busiest ports. There's always been a coming-and-going of people, fisherfolk, sailors on shore-leave and so on. It would have been impossible to have them all stopped and checked, admitting someone would have noticed them.»

«So, the fishermen saw nothing?» burst Mikael out.

Rose was about to translate for Akhundov when he stopped her; he had grasped the meaning of Mikael's words. He sprang to his feet, went over to the shelf and pulled out a huge cardboard binder. He put it down on the desk and began to browse through the contents causing a whiff of musty old paper to fill the air.

«This is an old dossier from our archives. It contains the testimonies of the fishermen who were out at sea the night of the tragedy. You are free to see for yourselves.», and he pushed the binder in her direction. «Would you kindly read what they say out loud to us, madam?»

Rose stiffened — the man's tone irritated her — but Mikael's affectionate glance managed to calm her down.

«It was awful», she began to read:

«*I thought it was the end of the world, or that they'd launched another atomic bomb. Everything was covered in smoke and flames, while deafening explosions followed one after the other. We could hear desperate screams and saw men like human torches hurl themselves into the sea. Then the ship broke up into several pieces like a toy and sank before we could really understand what was happening.*»

Rose stopped and swallowed several times trying to free her throat of the lump lodged there.

«Go on. The next testimony», Akhundov urged her, «It's important... so you can understand.»

Rose impaled him with a chilling gaze, although she went on smiling.

«Of course.»

«*Our vessel*», she began again, «*was the one closest to the unfortunate Linka. We had actually saluted it shortly before and some of the sailors on deck had waved their caps at us. As soon as we heard the first blast, we threw ourselves face down on our own deck; we were so close that splinters and shards from the ship landed on our trawler. At the second detonation, the sea filled with petrol that spread all over the water forming a huge slick. The Linka was like a torch by now, and we could hear desperate cries 'Help us, for God's sake'. At the third explosion, the ship split in two, the prow sinking almost immediately, the stern, still afloat, lay on one side. Shortly after that, it too disappeared beneath the waves, while it continued, inexplicably, to burn even beneath the water. We did not know what to do, we were shocked. Finally, we sailed over to the scene of the disaster. We shouted as we tried to cut through that smoke screen looking for survivors. Nobody answered and we saw no living person. We sailed through a pool of petrol and blood from which only charred bodies were emerging.*»

Rose could not continue; she was struggling to deal with the pain that this eye-witness account was causing her; she had practically listened to her brother's necrology, heard about his cruel, inhumane death.

She covered her face with her hands and broke down. Mikael did not need her to translate; he had watched the train of emotions cross her face and heard her breath-halting sobs.

«Don't cry, there may be some chance he's still alive.» he whispered and he turned around to ask Evgenij to fetch a glass of water.

To his surprise their guide's chair was vacant...

30

«He must be here somewhere!»

In the hotel foyer, Rose and Mikael were looking for Evgenij. He had sent up to let them know he was waiting for them below.

«Good morning, I hope you haven't been waiting long, I just needed the toilet», exclaimed Evgenij as he appeared from around a corner. He did not greet them with his usual broad smile and Mikael immediately noticed his gloomy expression.

«Is everything okay?» he asked, more out of politeness than of sincere concern.

«Well, no. I'm just angry, I shouldn't have trusted certain people», he replied, as they were leaving the hotel and walking over to the usual pea-green van.

«Shouldn't they have sent us a rented car?» asked Rose.

«I beg you to put up with what we've got… you see, the agency let me down.»

Rose and Mikael exchanged glances.

«I can find you a car right away, if you like!» Rose burst out scornfully.

Evgenij bowed his head like a child being told off.

«Madam, this is the peak tourist season, and there are not many cars available.»

«You should have booked in advance», she retorted, vexed.

«I swear, I did!»

«Hey, there's no use talking about it», intervened Mikael. «What do we intend doing?»

«However, I tidied it up to make amends, cleaned it out completely», he kept on, justifying himself as he fondly stroked the door of his van.

The three of them piled inside the rickety old vehicle, once again.

«Where are we going this morning?» asked Mikael breaking the icy silence.

«I thought I'd take you north, towards Yarkaia Avacha.»

«What's that?» asked Rose.

«The nursing home I told you about, madam, remember?...»

«Ah, yes. And please call me Rose.»

Evgenij nodded, the first smile of the day playing on his lips. «There's an old man I know there, he was out fishing the night that...» He broke off unable to finish the sentence out of tactfulness.

They took the same road they had taken from the airport, only this time driving in the opposite direction. «*Dobre utra*, good morning!» Evgenij waved at Pushka and his deputy, lurking in their usual spot, under the same old tree, ready to carry out their usual con.

«Do you know them?» asked Mikael.

«Here everyone knows everyone else», Evgenij answered.

The fresh air filtering in through the window announced a real summer's day, something quite rare on this Siberian peninsula. The van was scudding along at quite some speed; the grey blob of the city down below grew tinier and tinier as they drove on.

At a certain point there was a fork in the road, and Evgenij turned right.

«Now we're in for a real climb», he said.

After a series of sharp hairpin bends, they took a road clinging to the top of a sheer drop; the deep azure hue of the sea below sparkled far below. A hem of early morning mist moved earthwards, halting on the sand, garnishing the coastline like a lace border. Down along the slopes of the cliff were clumps of trees, their trunks and branches all entangled and growing horizontally, the result of having been lashed for years by unrelenting winds and storms.

«How lovely!» murmured Rose. The wonder of the landscape had managed to calm her bad humor.

«Just look at that trunk, looks like a child lifting up its arms!» exclaimed Evgenij.

«True.» said Mikael leaning forward to take a better look.

«By the way, have you got children?» inquired Evgenij.

«I have a grown-up son», answered Mikael.

«I have two boys; they're still only children», said Rose. «What about you?»

Evgenij shook his head. «What's your son's name, Mikael?»

«Tommaso.»

«Is he a good lad?»

«Excellent.»

«Ah, what does he do?»

«He's an interpreter.»

«Interpreter?»

«*Perevodchik*», Rose explained.

«What language?»

«He speaks seven. But he's specialized in translations from Russian into Italian and vice versa.»

«Russian?! Why Russian?». He laughed unexpectedly, a twinkle of joy and mischief playing in his eyes.

«He's always been enamored of Russia, her history, her literature. Now he's finding it rather useful.»

«Can you leave his address with me? I need some phrases for Italian tourists; I say in Russian, he translate in Italian, okay?»

«You need to have some phrases in Russian translated into Italian, is that it? To use with your tourists, right?»

«Yes, but I pay, nothing free», he clarified at once.

«All right, I'll give you his name and address later on.»

«You lucky father, first you do many sacrifices, but now have great son.»

Mikael was struck by Evgenij's rather ingenuous comment. «Yes», he said softly.

Looking at the bulk of Kronotsky through the windscreen, the volcano dedicated to Kronos, the mythical Titan who devoured his own children, he let his mind wander back in time, focusing on an episode he thought he had quite forgotten…

«I'm going back to the college, I need to pack», said Aznavour running off and leaving him there all alone on Rialto bridge.

It was only a few days before Christmas and most of the students were preparing to go home for the holidays. This was his last year in college and the fathers allowed the seniors greater freedom, as they were quite grown up now. Aznavour was leaving for Marseilles, but he was staying in Venice.

There was no longer anyone waiting for him in Athens.

Mikael wandered about aimlessly, burdened by the immense weight of sadness which had weighed him down for many months now, since the death of his mother Veronìk. He dug his hands deep into his pockets to warm and protect them from the *Bora*, the freezing strong wind that made the fairy lights, hanging up all over the place, dance wildly. Despite the bitter cold, people were strolling around smiling happily. From the shops on the bridge came the sounds of joyful carillons, while the air was full of the aroma of freshly baked cakes and biscuits.

Mikael was about to descend the last steps of the bridge when his gaze fell on a little boy, all bundled up in his warm green coat. The child was pulling at his mother's skirt, insistently, in an effort to attract her attention, while in the other hand he was holding the string of a red balloon with the words *Buon Natale* written on it, and which jerked as if it were about to be carried off by the violent wind.

When the boy's mother turned around Mikael recognized her, at once: it was Francesca.

He froze and impulsively hid himself amid the crowd and spied on her from a distance. Francesca was walking in the company of a lady, probably a relative. He presumed she had come back to Venice to spend Christmas. She was more beautiful than ever, her body having blossomed into the soft curves one could easily intuit beneath her lovely coat. Her face was radiant, and as she bent down to attend to her child, he thought it looked warmer and sweeter than he had ever known it to be. He wondered whether this was the result of motherhood, that divine gift that made every woman glow.

He turned to look at the boy again. As if by magic, their eyes locked in the midst of the crowd and for a few instances they studied each other.

«*Amore mio, dobbiamo sbrigarci... We need to hurry...*», he imagined Francesca saying as she dragged the child off in the opposite direction.

All of a sudden, the idea that that little boy might be his dawned on him.

His heart started aching, utterly overcome by emotion. He felt he was dying and could barely breathe. Nevertheless, he stood there like a statue, unable to move or react in any way.

When he came back to his senses there was no further trace of what had seemed to be a premonitory vision. He imagined himself as a young Scrooge in a latter-day version of "The Christmas Carol" and thought that this vision was meant to be pursued, grasped… instead…

Happiness had passed at a hairsbreadth from him, but he had just remained inert, indifferent.

«No!» he shouted.

Rose started. Even Evgenij swerved dangerously as he rounded one of the bends.

«No!» he cried out again, this time sobbing.

«What's the matter with you?» asked Rose, bewildered and worried.

«You're right, I am an ostrich.»

«Can you please stop a moment?» Rose asked Evgenij.

The guide pulled over to the verge.

«An ostrich, my head buried in the sand, a coward… a damned coward.» Mikael was as white as a sheet.

«Come, let's get out of the van for a moment», she urged, pulling him by the arm.

They alighted into the fresh air and Rose led Mikael, dragging his feet, sapped of energy, over to a rock where she made him sit down.

«How are you feeling?»

He shook his head. «When Koslov spoke… about the sacrifices a father makes for his son… I completely lost my cool.»

«He was just talking for the sake of talking, you know how these things are…» she whispered with a nod in the direction of Evgenij, who was lighting a cigarette.

«I never did anything for Tommaso, I don't deserve him.»

«Come now, Mikael, you know that's not true.»

«I've wasted an entire lifetime; thrown it away…» he added bitterly. «I've studied loads of stuff, written books, taught brilliant theories but, I've… I've never learnt to live.»

«What are you saying? You're raving»

Her brother kept shaking his head. «You're right! I *am* a coward, I'd have abandoned you too, I wouldn't be here had it not been for Tommaso; it was he who insisted.»

«You were just afraid, I was too; fear is only normal.»

Mikael, distraught, burst into tears again, his nerves in shatters. The dam built up within his soul had just collapsed, crumbled, and the pain that was released overpowered him, tearing him to pieces.

«Hey!»

Evgenij had approached them almost on tiptoe and he was gesturing silently to them to follow him. It was obvious that there was something awfully urgent he wished to show them.

«What is it, Evgenij?» asked Rose.

«Come with me as quietly as you can», he whispered, his finger on his lips.

Rose and Mikael looked at him puzzled.

«It seems like we have no choice» she mumbled, helping Mikael rise.

All three crossed the road and came to the edge of a big meadow studded with myriad white dots, white as snow.

«What is it?» asked Rose sotto voce.

Evgenij smiled slyly.

«Wait and see»

He stepped gingerly into the field and clapped his hands once, twice, three times. Loudly.

Hundreds, thousands of buds rose into the air. It was a swarm of white butterflies all taking flight together, fluttering upwards like a snowfall in an upside-down world.

«Fantastic!»

Mikael was smiling at last and Rose was clapping her hands, both fascinated by this wonderful show staged by nature herself, especially for them.

«White butterflies are the souls of the good», Evgenij said lifting his arms to heaven, as the siblings continued to gaze, dumbfounded and enthralled.

«They're here to remind us of the goodness in the Universe.»

«How far is the nursing home?» asked Rose once they set out again.

«That's Melikovo», answered Evgenij indicating a village, «so… it's another half hour.»

The road had now become as straight as a die and crossed a lush valley. The sun was barely warm at this altitude. Even though it was summer according to the calendar, it was not in actual fact.

«Do you come here often?» Rose asked him.

«Yes, my sister was admitted here many years ago.»

«You have a sister?»

«Anjushka, but she's very ill, poor thing.»

«Other siblings?»

«One, but we lost him when he was only a baby.»

He turned and looked the other way, trying to hide his sadness.

«And there are… I beg your pardon, were, three of you?»

Mikael and Rose nodded.

«You must have been very young when they took your other brother away, weren't you?», asked Evgenij, «yet I hear your speak of him as if he were some kind of an angel.»

«You're entering a mine field», Mikael warned him.

«What's wrong? I am wanting to know just…» he continued in his Armenian-Russian grammelot.

«Gabriel had the name of an angel and I reassure you, he was one», responded Rose. «Have I told you about the pact we had?»

«No» Mikael looked at her in amazement.

She pulled back her hair in a bunch, draped it over one shoulder and cleared her throat:

«Ours was a world full of distress; Terror stifled Yerevan like a cloud of toxic gas; you could breathe it everywhere. It came to the point that we started at every little noise, even a book falling off a shelf. One night I woke up crying and Gabriel sought my hand under the blankets.

«*'My little rosebud, Novàrt-giàn, what's the matter?'* he asked me in a voice hoarse with sleep.

«I tried to lift up my head because I felt I wasn't able to breathe. Gabriel sat up crossed-legged on the bed, and in the dark he looked at me trying to make out what was wrong with me.

«*'But you're crying'* he whispered caressing my face.

«*'I've had a bad dream, aghbarìk.'*

«*'Really, really bad?'*

«'Yes.'

«'Come on, tell me all about it', he asked tucking in the blankets.

«'They'd taken me away… to an island, a castle in the middle of the lake.'

«'Like that of Sevan?'

«'Yes.'

«'It must have been beautiful?'

«'It was cold and…'

«'And?'

«'They wouldn't let me go home.'

«'And this is why you're crying?'

«'Yes.'

«'Silly little goose… don't you know I'll never leave you?' And he held me tight: 'You're my precious little flower, look at me…' he whispered, lifting up my chin. 'Could I ever leave my precious little rosebud unguarded?'

«'Really? Swear it.'

«'I swear', he promised with that solemn air of his that always made me laugh.

«'Now, isn't that better? Shouldn't we go back to sleep now, eh?'

«'And if I dream about that castle again?'

«'No need to worry,… had you continued to dream you'd have seen that I was coming to free you.'

«'How do you know?'

«'Because! I'm the one who writes your dreams.'

«I giggled as he laid me down gently on the bed.

«'Nite, nite', he whispered kissing me on the forehead. I remained there for a long time thinking over the fact that it was my brother who wrote my dreams. Though it was funny, it also made me feel safe.

«'Dear brother', I whispered when he had already fallen back to sleep, 'I would come to look for you, too, no matter where or how far away you were.'»…

Evgenij slammed on the brakes as the van rang with these last words.

«Please excuse me», he said, «only two minutes.» He threw the door of the van open, jumped out of the vehicle and ran towards a bush, on the edge of the road.

«What's wrong with him?»

Mikael turned around and caught a glimpse of his head behind the bushes. «I think he's having a pee.»

«He could have waited until we had reached the nursing home»

«Maybe he's got a problem with his prostate.»

Rose snorted with impatience.

«He's coming back now», Mikael said.

«Do you think he's washed his hands?»

«Washed and dried», he chuckled as Evgenij started the engine again and they skidded off.

The name *Yarkaia*, meaning bright in Russian, did not suit the nursing home at all.

It was a rundown old building clinging to the bleak slopes of a hillock; if the sunlight did not reach it in June, it would certainly not reach it the rest of the year.

They parked the van right in front of the entrance though the large parking lot was half empty. A cool wind smelling of moss enveloped them as they emerged from the van. Rose drew her jacket more tightly around her shoulders, her eyes fixed on the smoke rising from the chimneys: the sick and elderly needed greater warmth than others.

As they entered the hall, everyone turned their heads trying to figure out who they might be. The inmates of the home were not used to visitors; months, years even, went by without anyone coming to see them. They were sitting in a large lounge overlooking the valley. Some occupied the armchairs and sofas, while others, in wheelchairs, had their backs to the panorama, staring vacantly into space; maybe the view in the mind's eye was more captivating.

«Evgenij, you must be here for Anjushka!» exclaimed a middle-aged woman behind the reception desk. Her head was full of rollers, her lipstick a bright orange.

«No, Ekaterina… I've brought some friends…»

The woman rose and joined them, holding out her hand to greet the guests.

«They need to talk to Batjushka, they are relatives and have come a long way», Evgenij explained.

«He's just had his *kasha*, but… go up, go upstairs. Even if he's resting he'll be glad to see you.»

The threesome mounted the stairs to the third floor. From the rooms came the soporiferous buzz of television sets.

«Batjushka should be in ward eleven», said Evgenij, reading the numbers on the half-open doors.

When they reached the room, he knocked and, without waiting for an answer, entered, followed by the other two. An amazingly thin old man lay in the bed in the half-light, snoring, his eyelids fluttering as he dozed. The odor of disinfectant barely concealed the unpleasant smell of an ageing, old body. On his night table were a syringe, some phials of brownish liquid alongside a latex glove, that had been used and was now turned sloppily inside out.

«Batjushka, it's me, Evgenij, do you remember me?»

The old man opened his eyes and looked up while a smile played on his lips. «Such a long time...» he answered in a ghost of a voice.

«But... Batjushka, we saw each other only last week.»

The man tried to sit up.

«Wait, let me help you.» offered Evgenij who bent down and plumped up the pillows behind the man's back. «These are two friends, they have come all the way from Canada and Italy.»

A shaft of gladness shot through the old man's eyes.

«*Pajalovat*», he said, welcoming them.

«They lost a brother in the *Linka* fire...», and Evgenij indicated the visitors standing there in silence.

Batjushka shook his head.

Rose took a step forward and approached the bed. «Please, Batjushka, speak to us about that evening, you're the only hope we've left.»

«We've looked for other witnesses, but they're all dead», prompted Evgenij.

«I was young... strong», the old man began almost choking, overcome by a bout of coughing.

Mikael sat on the edge of the bed and brought his face right up to the old man's. «I... I'm his twin... look at me, we were identical», he said, naively.

«Even a few words will do...» entreated Rose standing behind her brother.

Batjushka smiled baring his toothless gums.

«You can whisper in my ear and I'll tell them what you say», proposed Evgenij, «that way you won't tire yourself or cough too much.»

He drew up a chair for himself and bent his head down to the old man's lips. Batjushka sighed and assumed a serious, pained expression. Then he began to mutter sentences that only Evgenij could understand and translate, interrupted frequently by breathlessness and coughing.

«I'd gone out in my little boat, as was my wont whenever the weather permitted it. The sun was about to set when three tremendous blasts boomed throughout the bay. I looked up and saw a fire. It was the *Linka*, as I found out later; it sank in a few minutes and I could hear the desperate screams of those on board. I was terrified, petrified, as I stared clutching my fishing rod. I trembled at the idea that at a stone's throw from me, dozens of people were drowning, dying, burning to cinders. I switched on the engine and sailed out in the direction of the tragedy, but I soon realized that I could go no farther. A dense cloud of smoke had enveloped the entire area and I could barely make out the silhouettes of some trawlers trying to cut through that black curtain in search of survivors. The stillness was surreal and broken only by the voices of the fishermen calling: 'Is there anybody there?... Is there anybody there?' I couldn't tell you how much time passed, an hour, maybe more, but I just sat there motionless in my little boat waiting for who knows what... the waves started to wash some debris slowly in my direction... bobbing tin plates, shreds of clothing, a shoe... when a mutilated arm thudded against the keel, I was utterly horrified. I switched the engine back on and headed for land, like a madman, without a backward glance. I could hardly breathe, I was so shocked. When I came close to the three reefs, the ones that guard the mouth of the bay, I slowed down and looked back at the site of the disaster for the last time...» Batjushka stopped, his breathing having grown shallow and labored.

«Here, have some water» Evgenij offered picking up a small plastic cup. The old man refused with a wave of his hand and continued his story.

«A body was floating near my boat. It was face up and swaying backwards and forwards on the swash of the waves against the reefs. It appeared to me like a mirage, some bizarre trick of the imagination… and yet, it was real. I dragged him on board… I saw he was very young, little more than a boy.»

«How old could he have been?» asked Rose instantly, anxiously, her voice cracking.

«Fifteen, sixteen, no more.»

Mikael sought his sister's hand and gripped it tightly.

«Once I had heaved him on board, I turned him over on one side and hit him on the back to empty his lungs. They were full of water. The more I struck him the more he retched, he vomited, and so… so he finally began to breathe again.»

The siblings looked at each other open-mouthed.

«Are you sure he was breathing?» insisted Evgenij, taking him by the shoulder. «Our friends must not entertain any false hopes.»

The old man nodded. «*Konechno*, sure», he said.

«Did he speak? Did he say anything? His name, maybe?» Mikael's breathing was as short as the old man's.

«Niet, nothing, he was dying.»

«What did he look like?» Mikael asked. «Hang on!» he suddenly remembered his student ID which he took out from his pocket and was about to show it to Batjushka.

«Let me have a look» Evgenij took it, examined it for a moment, and passed it over to the old man.

«I don't know», murmured Batjushka, «He was in a really bad state, half of his face burnt… a mass of skin and blood… I took him to the hospital.»

Rose knelt down beside the bed. «Batjushka, dear, kind Batjushka, do you remember where?» she asked, her eyes filling with tears.

«There was only one in the whole city at the time, now it's called the Novaya Kamchatka», Evgenij informed her.

«Let's call them!» decided Rose springing to her feet.

«Yes… there must be a telephone here we can use» exclaimed Mikael, he too excited.

«I'll call from here», offered Evgenij lifting the receiver hanging on the wall.

«Allo?» Ekaterina answered.

«Sorry, Katyusha, but it's urgent… we need to speak to someone at the Novaya Kamchatka, can you put us through, please?»

«I'll see what I can do, Zhenia, just give me a second.»

When the phone began to ring again, Rose thought she would die of anxiety. As for Mikael, he let himself collapse onto the side of the bed, his heart pounding in his throat.

«Good morning, I need to speak to someone in the archives, please», said Evgenij.

«I'm sorry, comrade, it's closed now. It reopens tomorrow morning.»

«Tell them it's urgent», mouthed Rose, «really, really urgent.»

«It's terribly urgent, may I speak to the person in charge?.»

«No, comrade, there's nobody here at this hour. Call tomorrow morning, the office opens at eight sharp.»

«But...»

In the silence that followed all they could hear was the hum of the interrupted connection; Evgenij was left standing with the receiver in his hand.

«Damn it!» snapped Rose, snatching the phone and dialing again.

«Allo?»

«Please», she began in perfect Russian, «we called a few moments ago to speak with someone in charge of the archives. It's absolutely necessary that we consult your 1953 records, today. It's vital!»

«Madam, if the question concerns something that happened in 1953 it cannot be all that important today. Call back tomorrow», said the voice and hung up.

The three of them just stood there speechless looking at each other. Meanwhile Batjushka was showing signs of fatigue and drowsiness.

«Now what shall we do?» asked Mikael rising from the bed.

Rose shrugged. «I'm afraid we'll have to wait until tomorrow.» She looked tenderly at the old man who seemed bewildered and confused by all this turmoil. «Batjushka, let me give you a kiss», she murmured brushing his bony cheek with her lips. «Thank you so much for everything, you've been wonderful, really wonderful.»

Mikael took the man's hand and stroked it.

«You've given us hope and we are eternally grateful to you», he whispered.

Batjushka smiled. «*Sbasibo, sbasibo*», he said thanking them in turn with slight nods of the head.

«He was astounding», commented Mikael, as the three of them filed out of the door, «such felicity of expression, all those vivid details! It's not that you added something of your own to the story, eh, Evgenij?»

«No, no worries, in his day Batjushka was an excellent teacher», retorted Evgenij shaking his head. «Excuse me, but would you mind if I went up to see my sister for a few moments?» he ventured with some trepidation.

«Not at all! Go!» answered Rose, though she was so anxious all she really felt like doing was rushing back down to town, straight to the hospital and wait there all night until the archives opened next morning.

«Shall we wait downstairs?» Mikael asked.

«Why not come with me? That way you'll meet her.»

They went down the corridor to the very last room.

«Here we are!» exclaimed Evgenij pushing the door open. «Anjushka?…»

The shadow of a woman in a wheelchair was visible in the middle of the room.

«What are you doing here in the dark?» he scolded her tenderly.

He went over to the window and drew the heavy curtains aside; a pale blue light flooded the room and fell on the woman. She looked about fifty, her chest and shoulders slender, her stomach and buttocks rather plump. Here short hair was blond streaked with grey. Her features were regular, her cheekbones pronounced, her big sad green eyes looked out from under dark eyebrows.

«These are some friends who have come from faraway», Evgenij explained referring to the two visitors standing embarrassed on the threshold.

Anjushka muttered something and shook her head indicating a colored object on her unmade bed; it was a rag doll.

«So, you want your *kukla*?» Evgenij picked the doll up from the bed and handed it to her. «She's mad about her dolly. It's as old as the hills, but she doesn't want another one. Only this one … isn't that so?» he asked Anjushka, kneeling down in front of her wheelchair and fixing her hair gently. «Look what I've brought you!» he exclaimed, taking a bar of chocolate out of his pocket.

Anjushka took it and began to study the colored wrapper inquisitively. Then she picked up her doll and pretended to feed it to her, trying to push it into her mouth like a good little mamma.

«She used to have a long blond plait that came down to her waist only they cut it off a few months ago... isn't that so, dearest Anjushka?» said Evgenij stroking her cheek.

Rose looked on, bewildered. There was something about the way Evgenij moved his hands, those huge hands with their unkempt nails, that touched her profoundly. It was crazy, but those tender gestures reminded her of Gabriel.

Anjushka threw an unexpected tantrum. She began to thrash about, move her hands randomly to the point of snatching the eye patch off her brother's head. Evghenij's maimed eye and terrible scar were now perfectly visible in the harsh light. Rose and Mikael winced at the sight and turned aside, highly embarrassed.

«That wasn't very kind of you», scolded Evgenij. He picked up the patch and put it carefully over his eye again.

Anjushka cackled, staring at the two strangers standing stock still in the doorway.

«Zhenia, when will you brings us some more salmon heads?» called Ekaterina after them as they prepared to leave the building.

«Soon, Katiushka», he promised as he held the door open for Rose. «But aren't you two hungry?» he asked.

«We could do with a bite», answered Rose.

«There's a place on the way that makes a wonderful soup.»

«As long as there's no cabbage in it», commented Mikael.

Outside, a strong wind bore distant sounds on its wings. Rose thought she could make out the desperate wailing of a child and stopped to look around, but Mikael took her by the arm.

«Everything all right?»

«I'll feel better when I've had something to eat», she murmured, shrugging and throwing the door of the van wide open. This time she sat between the two men.

They took a different road from the one they had driven along earlier. Evgenij told them that he was making a slight deviation but that the road was far better.

«Has this van got heating?» asked Rose, shivering. There were draughts everywhere.

«Sure!» exclaimed Evgenij fiddling with some knobs on the dashboard. «Five minutes; the engine is still cold.»

«Has your sister been ill long?» asked Mikael.

«Since our brother died; shortly after that», he responded, his eyes fixed on the tarmac.

«Would you mind not smoking?» Rose grumped. Evgenij had lit a cigarette outside the hospice and had continued to smoke it inside the van.

«I'm so sorry. Force of habit, really», he said stubbing it out in the ashtray.

«Was it a stroke?» asked Mikael turning down the window to change the air.

«Yes, she couldn't cope with his death. Anjushka had cared for him like a mother and when he died she just let go; a year later she suffered a stroke. Some people simply cannot bear pain, others seem to be fortified by it. I too was distraught, but only initially. Then I came to terms with it.»

«What did you little brother die of?» asked Rose in a barely audible voice.

«Misha?» Evgenij shifted nervously in his seat. «Burnt alive in a house fire, a stove went up in flames. We tried hard to save him… I almost lost my life.» he said pointing to his patch. «I jumped right in the flames to save him, but nothing doing.»

The two siblings glanced over at him astonished and full of admiration, impressed by his noble, brave gesture.

Little by little they were getting to know him and beginning to appreciate this guide of theirs.

«Here we are!» he announced at a certain point as they rounded a bend. He coughed, hacking his lungs to pieces as usual.

They sat in a booth with pink walls.

They ordered the soup after having informed the waitress that they did not like cabbage. They ate it up with great relish and washed it down with a glass of good Chinese beer.

They spoke about life, of how chance — destiny? — can often change the course of our existence from one moment to the next, about the joys and sufferings that are inextricably tangled in the skein of people's lives. They took leverage from Batjushka's story, the chance of finding of a survivor coughed up as it were by the sea, and reached the conclusion that one should never lose hope.

«I'm afraid», whispered Rose after all these lovely words, as she put her soup spoon down in her bowl.

«Tomorrow morning we'll go to that office and if...» Mikael tried to cover up his angst by saying something optimistic, but he couldn't even finish his sentence

«We can continue our journey back now, if you like», suggested Evgenij after a long pause.

«Where are the toilets?» asked Rose as she stood up.

«Downstairs.»

«I'll accompany you», offered Mikael getting to his feet.

As soon as the siblings moved away, Evgenij lit another cigarette. He drew the smoke into the very depths of his lungs, held it there so long that he started to cough. He then took his flask of vodka from his pocket and gulped down a huge mouthful to calm the fit.

They left the eating place under a flame-red sky which covered the whole landscape in purple dust. Rose looked at her hands, and couldn't believe the color her skin had taken on in that light; Mikael rummaged in the bottom of his rucksack for his camera.

«Let's take a photo...» he said.

On the way home nobody spoke.

Each of them looked straight ahead, lost in their own thoughts. They were crossing a bare, sandy plateau, so unlike the lush landscape of the rest of the peninsula.

Rose was about to doze off when Evgenij suddenly braked.

«I hope he doesn't need to pee again!», she thought.

«Come!» he invited them, surprising her. «This is really worth seeing», he said jumping out of the van.

He led them to the edge of a sheer cliff. Down below lay a valley crossed by a lazy river. All around were dozens of geysers, underground springs which surfaced to blow out sudden gushes of water and steam. They puffed, one after the other, taking turns in perfect rhythm, like the instruments in an orchestra conducted by a genial maestro.

«This is the Earth breathing...» said Evgenij.

The slanting rays of the sun lit up each droplet of water, each particle of steam. A rainbow arced timidly above the valley.

«Oh, God! It's extraordinary!» Mikael kept repeating, his eyes moist with the deep feelings this sight had aroused in him.

«How can we ever thank you enough?» whispered Rose, as she herself breathed to the rhythm of the Earth.

31

Petropavlovsk, 21 June 1992

Rose and Mikael reached the hospital well before eight am.

They had met in the hotel foyer, restless, almost holding their breaths. They had not even bothered with breakfast; they rushed straight out to Evgenij's waiting van. They feared there might be a long queue at the hospital, but once had got there they found that, on that particular Sunday morning, the place was practically deserted. So, they just sat waiting outside of the office they had been directed to, in front of the door on which hung a handwritten tag in capital letters: ARKHIV. Rose was perspiring; her white polo-necked sweater was too warm for the heat that had suddenly broken out all over the area.

«Did you sleep well?» asked Mikael

«Yes, thanks, and you?»

«I slept like a baby», he too lied, shrugging.

Neither of them had shut an eye all night.

Rose had been in the clutches of one of her usual panic attacks; she had done her best to calm down by eating the two chocolates the chamber maid had left on her pillow, as she did every afternoon when she remade her bed and tied out the room. Overcome by anguish, she had tried calling Arthur, allowing the phone to ring three times before putting the receiver down again without speaking. She had remained sitting on her bed for quite some time, just staring into space, and had then called home, thinking that was the right thing to do.

«Hi Hagop, it's me», she had mumbled.

«My love, I was beginning to worry. I was going to call you myself.»

«Worry? Why?»

«I haven't heard from you since Thursday.»

«If you were truly concerned you'd be right here by my side, my dear», she had snapped as her husband listened, speechless. «Moreover, I don't even want to try to tell you about the fear, the dismay that have gripped me this evening.»

«You're too hard on me, I don't deserve this»

Rose had found the strength to laugh.

«I'm looking for my brother on the other side of the world, I'm shattered, tomorrow I might find out that I've been chasing a ghost, someone who's been dead for forty years…», and she broke off not wanting her husband to hear her sobs.

«Rose?…»

«And do you know who's consoling me? A brother I don't even know, a total stranger I only met a few months ago, and, and… this is the beauty of it», she tittered sarcastically, «a driver, some kind of a fishmonger acting as a makeshift tour guide. And you think I'm hard? Huh?» She had rubbed it in, in a gushing outburst of venom.

«If you'd asked me I'd be there, with you.»

«I didn't want to, I fooled myself that you'd do so of your own accord.»

«Someone had to stay with the children.»

«Bollocks», Rose had cut him short, «let's try to be sincere with each other at least, no?»

In the hall, the lift opened to the sound of a sharp trill and two nurses emerged pushing a man on a stretcher.

«I spoke to Tommaso last night.» said Mikael, his eyes fixed on the scene.

«You managed to phone him?»

«Yeah. When I told him that we might find something definitive out about Gabriel today, he said something that really heartened me.»

The stretcher rolled straight past them: the patient lay there motionless, his face ashen.

«He said, among many other wonderful things, that whatever way it goes, this experience will prove beneficial to me.»

Rose gave him an intensely eloquent look.

«'You've managed to overcome your inertia, your fear, papà. Were it only for this, it'll have been well worthwhile', he told me. At times I think I am a very lucky man.»

She looked at him baffled.

«To have a son like Tommaso», he added with the hint of a smile.

The door of the office was thrown open from the inside. The siblings jolted and looked up; a lady with distinct Asian features was taking a seat behind the information desk. Neither of them moved, despite the fact they had been waiting impatiently for someone to turn up.

Mikael stood up first with a deep sigh. «I think we'd better go in.»

His sister nodded, held onto the back of the chair to rise, but failed. Mikael helped her up, took her by the arm and, together, they walked over to the office.

«You talk», Rose entreated, forgetting how poor his Russian was.

«My name is Mikael Gazarian», he began in English, using his brand-new surname.

On hearing this name on Mikael's lips, Rose felt she did not have to face this terrible ordeal alone. She was with her brother now; and it mattered little that fate had permitted them to meet only very recently.

«Madam, a young man was admitted to this hospital on the 25th of May 1953», she began, recovering her usual firm, confident tone. «We'd like to know whether he was called Gabriel Gazarian.»

«Twenty-fifth of May… of when?…» asked the woman with an incredulous little smile.

«Nineteen hundred and fifty-three.»

«And you are?…»

«His siblings.»

The woman took up some forms from the desk.

«You need to fill these in, providing the names and surnames of the patient and your own. Meanwhile, I'll begin to look», she said and went into the back of the office where there were shelves full of folders, binders and files.

Rose and Mikael waited on their feet, their eyes staring blankly on the objects around them: a photocopy machine, a telephone which kept on ringing, a telex which spewed out yards and yards of messages. Unlike earlier on, Rose was now feeling terribly cold and she drew her cotton sweater tightly around her shoulders. «Are you ok? You look awfully pale.» inquired Mikael, who stood right beside her, gasping for breath, as if some gigantic hand were trying to throttle him. He rummaged in his pockets for his pillbox and swallowed a pair of tablets.

After some time, which seemed interminable, the woman reappeared with a small folder in her hand.

«Yes», she said, «that evening a boy was admitted urgently to A&E.»

«A survivor from the Linka? His face badly burnt?» asked Rose as her face started flushing.

«That's right, it says here that he arrived at the hospital in critical conditions. That he was dying.»

«It was a boy, wasn't it? About sixteen?»

«It doesn't give his age.»

Mikael came over to his sister and clasped her arm.

«May I see your applications?» asked the woman.

«Here you are.»

She took up the forms and asked to see their ID's.

«But you're not his brother», she said looking at Mikael with the air of an inquisitor.

«Don't jump into conclusions judging by the names», retorted Rose, «but, please, tell us something more.»

The woman assumed an air of stiff formality.

«Well, if this is the name of the person you're looking for», she said indicating their applications, «I'm sorry.»

«You mean, it wasn't Gabriel Gazarian?» asked Mikael anxiously.

The woman shook her head.

«But you said, that evening, a boy was brought here who'd been saved from the wreck!» exclaimed Rose. «a survivor from the burnt ship», she emphasized, her cheeks all hot and red.

«Exactly.»

«It wasn't Gabriel Gazarian?»

«No.»

«Who was it, then?»

«I'm afraid we cannot disclose that information.» the clerk answered, challenging them with her adamantine gaze, without the least compassion for their dismay. She probably presumed that her words could not cause much pain, not after so many years.

She could not have been more wrong.

«Madam, please check again», Mikael implored her, as Rose turned her back, her body racked with sobs.

The clerk stiffened, jutted out her chin as if seeking to underline the efficiency with which she conducted her work, but she did not soften, not even a little. Nor did she allow them to read the name of the survivor registered in the file. «Is there anything else I can do for you?» she asked starkly, as she raised the receiver to answer a call.

«No, thanks…» said Mikael, as he took Rose by the hand and led her into the hall.

Evgenij was waiting for them outside the hospital beside his double-parked van. As soon as he saw them he realized that things had gone badly, and his face darkened too.

«My dear friend, we've been led astray», began Mikael, «unfortunately, the boy Batjushka fished out of the sea was not our brother.»

Evgenij lowered his gaze and stared at the ground.

«I was so naïve to think I might find my own dear Gabriel after all these years. I'm so stupid, I always cling to false hopes and end up hurting myself.» said Rose bursting into tears. «I have to admit my brother is dead… dead… You were right», she whispered addressing Evgenij, «there comes a time when we must face up to the reality.»

Evgenij suddenly looked up and their eyes met. He would have liked to say a word of comfort, make a gesture to express his compassion, but his courage failed him. He just looked at her with regret and understanding.

«I, too, had begun to believe», murmured Mikael, «that today's answer would give us the strength to go on searching.» He smiled bitterly. «I was already imagining the scene where I would embrace my twin again, at last.»

Evghenij cleared his throat. «You know, today's the longest day of the year», he said, out of the blue, looking up at the sky. His words were drowned out by the wail of a siren as an ambulance skidded to a stop and four nurses rushed out, throwing its doors wide open.

«Enough, let's get out of here», sighed Rose.

All three of them boarded the van, uncertain of what to do next. The midday sun beat on the tin roof of the vehicle and the whiff of stale fish stung their nostrils, once again.

«Now, where shall we go?» asked Mikael.

Rose shrugged.

«I want to leave, go back home», she burst out at last, suddenly aware of the absurdity of the adventure in which she had become entangled. «I miss my sons, my home…» she murmured.

She wondered if this urge to find Gabriel had been nothing more but the fruit of her own egotism, of the presumption to challenge common sense, even fate itself. She had behaved like a spoilt brat decided on rewriting the past, just to suit her own childish whim.

«Is there a travel agency somewhere near?» asked Mikael. «We need to book a flight.»

«No worries, they can do that for you at the hotel» Evgenij reassured them, as he switched on the engine and slowly wound his way into the line of traffic. «What do you want to do later?» he asked as they approached the hotel.

«Pack our bags.»

«Don't you want a bite to eat?»

«I'm not hungry», pouted Rose.

«I'd love to see the bay!» exclaimed Mikael.

«Great! We can do that later on. I was thinking…» Embarrassed, Evgenij was blushing with shyness «… if you've nothing better to do, I might cook you something at my place.»

«Your place?» Rose looked at him in amazement.

«Yes, well …I thought it would be more welcoming than a restaurant, plus, there's a splendid view.»

The siblings glanced at each other.

«We'd love to, thanks! But first we'll have to arrange our flight and pack», Mikael pointed out, as they drew up alongside the hotel.

«No problem. I'll wait out here as long as it takes»

«Sorry if we're late.»

«I've just got back myself», said Evgenij, as he loaded the shopping bags he was carrying into the back of the van. «I hope you like fish.»

«But why did you go to so much trouble?» asked Rose. «You shouldn't have.»

«It's a pleasure, believe me; I wanted you to taste my salmon *en papillote.*»

«But where did you find salmon on a Sunday?»

«I have my contacts», he responded with a smile.

They all climbed on board and rolled down the windows as the temperature had risen considerably, reaching twenty-four degrees, a record for those latitudes.

«Did you find a flight?» asked Evgenij, holding his lighted cigarette out the window.

«Yes, we leave for Moscow tomorrow morning at eleven.»

They drove up a secondary road into the foothills and soon left the noisy city behind them.

Rose looked out at the panorama and caught sight of a stretch of the bay. It looked like a postcard. She found the city to be very changeable; a lot depended on the point of view, but also on the mood of the beholder.

«We're nearly there», Evgenij announced as he rounded a hairpin bend.

A small wooden house stood amid a grove of verdant trees. Its bright blue shutters had been painted recently and above them, along the edge of the roof, ran a border of wooden openwork.

«This is my *izba!*» exclaimed Evgenij with a touch of pride.

He stopped the van and took out the shopping bags.

«Can I give you a hand?» Mikael offered.

«Thanks! That's where we were yesterday» he said, indicating the volcano.

«How long have you been living here?» asked Rose, looking around in amazement at the fence painted blue like the shutters, the freshly mown lawn, the roses in bloom.

«Two years; the city was not my cup of tea.» mumbled Evgenij as he opened the door with one foot.

As soon as they entered the hallway, the guests winced at the bright light that filled the place.

«You two enjoy the view», he proposed, going to the windows overlooking the bay and throwing them open. «You may stay out here, if you like, while I get something ready.»

Rose and Mikael stepped onto the small terrace to admire the view. Avacha bay stretched out at their feet like a circular lake, in perfect chromatic accordance with the blue of the shutters. Further south, a long narrow fjord connected the bay with the grey, vast ocean. The city of Petropavlovsk seemed so far away, even though it was only at a distance of a handful of kilometers.

«I've just uncorked a bottle of Armenian wine, I hope you like it», Evgenij announced putting three goblets down on the little table of the terrace.

«Arenì?» exclaimed Rose. «I haven't drunk it for ages.»

«And these are walnuts from Georgia», he added setting a dish down next to the bottle.

«Come on, let's make a toast», proposed Rose. «I've suffered too long for Gabriel, I have to resign myself to reality, I've done all I could to trace him. Now, all I can do is carry with me all those tender memories that bind him to me.»

All three gave a toast to health but also to their newly-born friendship.

Rose brought her goblet to her lips and inhaled the aroma: a heart-breaking fragrance from the past.

After Evgenij had gone back into the kitchen, the siblings wandered around the house examining the furniture, ornaments and nick-knacks: the divan with the colorful kilim thrown over the back, the embalmed deer head hanging above the stove, the pitch pine table with its painted legs. Mikael was attracted by a little wooden statue on the sideboard.

«What's this?»

Evgenij turned around, pan in hand. «It's a kind of relic of the Chukotka, the tribe who lived here before the Russian invasion. It's an ancient pagan divinity, Mother Earth.»

«May I look at it?» asked Rose, intrigued.

As she drew closer to the sideboard another object caught her eye. It was a wedding ring on a little glass plate which, by some strange coincidence, reminded her of the one Satèn had once worn... the ring she'd discarded, disowned, sending it to her husband in a sealed envelope.

Impulsively, she felt like taking it up and looking to see what was inscribed on the inside, but Evgenij's voice calling from the kitchen, «It's ready!», prevented her from doing so.

«What a goose you are, Rose», she told herself as she spun around, «all wedding rings look alike».

They ate out on the little terrace around a tiny fold-up table, somewhat worn out by the wind and the rain.

Evgenij had cooked barely scalded, lobster claws, drowned in melted butter, along with salmon fillet *en papillote*, which smacked of the northern seas.

«It's delicious, how do you prepare it?» asked Mikael, who liked to cook.

«Oh, it's a recipe I learnt from my mother.»

«What did your parents do?» Rose asked, laying her cutlery down on her plate.

«Simple folk, papa was a postman, mamma worked in a factory; the typical Soviet family.»

«There are no photos anywhere in the house», observed Mikael, who was mad about family memorabilia.

Evgenij shook his head. «Well, as I was telling you, everything was destroyed in the fire. We weren't able to save anything.»

The siblings lowered their eyes, looking at the empty shells and fish-bones on their plates.

«What about yours?» asked Evgenij to resume the conversation after that embarrassing silence.

«If you ask me about my parents, we need to ask which», jested Mikael with a smile. «You see, I was adopted.»

«Ah, so that's why your surnames are different...»

«Exactly», nodded Rose.

«And you and Gabriel were twins?...»

«Identical.»

«My mother used to say that not even our father could tell them apart», Rose pointed out. «She had a very difficult delivery; you can imagine giving birth in a refugee camp, in a city like Patras. It seems that the firstborn was strangling the second with his umbilical cord. I've looked into the question recently, it seems it happens rather frequently with monozygotic twins.»

«Do you believe all they say about twins? That they share feelings even if separated?» Evgenij looked from Rose to Mikael.

«If you think of it, we're talking about genetically identical organisms», said Rose before anyone else could speak, «there must be a very strong bond between them.»

Mikael stared, enthralled, at the bay that was beginning to look like molten gold. «Yes, I believe there is», he murmured as a shaft of light filtered through the wisps of cloud scurrying across the sky.

«This evening there is going to be a fantastic sunset» said Evgenij following his gaze. «A long, magnificent one», he added.

«Oh, how I'd love to spend this last evening there.» Rose jumped up, clasped the railing of the balcony and indicating the bay exclaimed: «Could you tell us where the ship sank exactly?»

Evgenij frowned. «The *Linka*?... Right there», he answered pointing at a spot in the distance, «...just beyond those three reefs.»

«Could you bring us down to the beach? To the point closest to where the disaster took place? I'd like to pay homage to our brother», said Rose, her voice full of emotion. «What do you think, Mikael?»

When she turned around, both men were looking at her with tears in their eyes.

Rose was shocked to find that there was a strong resemblance between the two faces.

«It must be the sweet fragrance of the wine», she justified herself for the absurd idea that had crossed her mind.

They left the house at dusk; the sun was playing amid the leaves of the birches throwing a lace-like shadow on the rose garden and the gravel walk.

«Take these, it'll be a bit chilly later on», said Evgenij handing them a heavy fisherman sweater each; a grey one for Rose, a blue for Mikael.

They reached the seashore in the twinkling of an eye given that the streets were free of traffic, as they always were on Sunday evenings. They drove past the port and the fish market, the moored boats and the neatly folded nets, the commissariat with its lovely blue façade before taking the road that ran along the northern edge of the bay and through an immense stretch of green meadows resembling an endless golf course.

«The tourists love it here, they say it reminds them of the Scottish Highlands», said Evgenij.

«Hmm, that's true.»

«How long have you worked as a guide?» inquired Rose.

«Since 1985, since they closed down the gulag where I used to work... I moved here and invented a job, two actually; in the winter I deliver fish, in the summer, when the opportunity arises, I work with tourists.»

He veered right onto a steep little track leading down to the beach. The van bumped and jolted over the rough surface leaving a cloud of dust in its wake like a bride's train.

«Are you sure you can drive us down there?» asked Mikael, somewhat worried, his eyes fixed on the sea that shone like a gigantic scaly reptile.

«Maybe it wasn't such a great idea, after all», commented Rose, gripping the door with all her might.

Evgenij smiled. «No need to worry, we're almost there.» he said as he parked the van beside a big bush. «Five minutes on foot now», he added as he pulled the handbrake.

They walked down to the beach in perfect Indian file. The summer breeze carried the scent of the ocean, a breath laden with seaweed and brine.

«This sea smells quite unlike the Mediterranean», remarked Mikael rubbing his nose.

Evgenij burst out laughing. «That, by comparison, is only a tiny lake», he said adjusting the rucksack on his back where he had packed a flagon of water, a handful of Georgian walnuts and a blanket lest they wanted to sit down on the sand.

They continued to descend the steps, some cut into the rocks, and soon reached an emerald clearing speckled with fuchsia-colored flowers.

«How lovely!» exclaimed Rose bending down to take a closer look at them. They looked like little flames burning into the green meadow.

Evghenij knelt down beside her. «They are called *flox*. When the wind blows they all change color, forming a shimmering wave», he said with a sinuous movement of his arms.

They walked closer to the edge and could already glimpse the shore below. They went around a bend and, all of a sudden, the whole beach opened up and spread out right in front of them. The first thing which caught their eye were the three huge reefs emerging from the water, standing upright like cyclops guarding the bay. Flocks of seagulls flew above them squawking stridently as an eagle circled on high ready to swoop down on its prey.

«Are these the rocks Batjushka spoke about?» asked Mikael gaping in amazement.

«Yes.»

«So, the *Linka* sank there?» asked Rose pointing at the spot with a trembling finger.

Evgenij sighed and drew the back of his hand over his forehead. For a moment he seemed to have lost his usual composure. He took a step forward and stared out at the ocean, roaring in the distance.

«Look», he cried, calling the two siblings over to him, «can you see that white crest out there?»

They reached his side, the image of a ship in flames in their minds.

Rose strained her eyes. «You mean that half-submerged reef?» she asked in uncertain tones.

«Yes…the fire broke out…»

The painful screech of a gull rent the air, interrupting Evgenij's story.

Rose shuddered and clung to the man standing next to her, thinking of her brother.

«What does love mean?»

Gabriel smiled.

«Please tell me, what is love?» Novàrt asked.

«Mamma is fond of you and that is love, but so does papa.»

«And do *you* love me?»

«Of course I do.»

«How can I tell?»

Gabriel kissed her dark curls.

«Love is measured in deeds, do you understand?»

Novàrt shook her head.

«You cannot really love anyone unless you are prepared for sacrifice.»

The little girl looked at him wide-eyed, trying to grasp his meaning.

«Papa works every day; he gets up in the cold and goes to the factory.

Why do you think he does that?» Gabriel asked her.

«To buy us things to eat.»

«That's right, now that's proof of love.»

«Yes! Because he is fond of us.»

«That's right!»

«And you give me your bread even when you're hungry»

«Because I love you too, little sis.»

Novàrt wrinkled up her nose trying to store her brother's words inside her little head.

«And does love never end?»

«If it's true love, it never does.»

«And when mamma goes to heaven, will she still love me?»

«Always.»

«And I? Will I be able to love her too?»

«Yes.»

«How can I love someone who isn't here?»

Gabriel looked into her eyes.

«You'll carry him in here, in a secret corner... all for him.», and he struck her breast where her little heart was.

Two light beats... like the wings of a butterfly.

«I've been here before», murmured Mikael out of the blue.

Rose and Evgenij looked at him in amazement.

«I have been here, yes, I remember. It's strange, because this is the first time I've ever set foot here... yet the beach, the reefs, those flowers, everything's so familiar...». He seemed to be suspended somewhere in another dimension. «Even the way the wind smelled as we came down the slope...»

He halted suddenly as if afraid to expose the side of himself which had always frightened him, the side which made him feel as if he were hovering on the brink between the imaginary and the real. He sat down on the grass studded with reddish pebbles that bordered the beach.

«When I discovered I had a twin», he continued, gazing out to sea at the crest of white foam which broke the calm surface of the sea, «I began to find some explanation for my tormented, anguished adolescence. I read many essays on that special, almost transcendental bond that links twins, but... but...», he stuttered staring at Rose and Evgenij, «what happened to me was different, I felt like the victim of some cruel spell. I had the sensation that I was actually living the life of another boy, identical to myself. Somehow I knew his thoughts and, above all, I felt what he felt... I was convinced that if he died I would die with him!»

Evgenij sprung around and turned his back on the siblings. Then he strode off in the direction of the cliff at the back of the beach.

«Where's he off to?» asked Rose.

She heard him coughing as he walked away. It was not the usual hacking noise he made, it sounded more like an attempt to clear a lump in his throat.

The sky above the bay resembled a painting by some prodigious Renaissance artist: against a pale background, brushstrokes of blue, gold, green and orange were creating an extraordinary chromatic mélange...

«I'd love to bring Gabriel some flowers», said Rose as if imagining a birthday and that her brother was still alive. «Let's pick a bunch to throw into the sea. Are you coming?»

Mikael jumped up and shook out his trousers.

She linked arms with her only remaining brother and they wandered through the field, looking at the flowers, uncertain as to which ones to pluck. They had to be the most beautiful, the brightest.

«These here are lovely» Rose cried out as she bent down to pick some.

«Please don't pull them» Evghenij pleaded from behind, as his hand touched hers softly.

She obeyed without objection.

They walked back to the shore all together, they wanted to enjoy the last few moments of daylight that remained.

«Those over there, do you know what they're called?» asked Evgenij indicating the dark outlines of the three rocks.

Mikael and Rose shrugged.

«*Tri Brata*, three brothers». Evgenij stressed each of the words, as if passionately desiring to reveal a heart-rending secret, but Rose grumbled something about the cold and he stopped.

«Put it on, it'll keep you warm» he said instead, indicating the grey sweater he had lent her.

«I'd forgotten about this» replied Rose donning the heavy jumper she carried on her shoulders, which almost reached her knees.

«Are you ready to go, then?»

«Give me two more minutes, if you don't mind...» Mikael entreated them and advanced to the point where the water lapped his feet. He bent down and picked up a smooth flat stone, rubbed it clean and launched it over the waves, as far away as he could. The stone skipped on the water, once, twice, then glided over and sank below the waves.

Rose looked over at her brother with a touch of childish mirth. She too picked up a stone and tried to skim it on the surface of the sea like he had done.

They both thought of Gabriel, believing that this gesture might reawaken his soul down in the depths of the ocean.

«We're here for you, dear Gabriel», they whispered.

They were not weeping, only their hearts were beating faster as they took leave of their brother.

Evgenij was trembling, his head bent down...

A star twinkled timidly somewhere behind the reefs.

Little by little, darkness swallowed up the vast ocean.

One stubborn wave, way out on the deep, continued to reflect the last ray of sunlight.

32

Petropavlovsk, 21 Dekabrija 1992

Moi dorogoi *Tommaso,*
   Today, Anjushka, a person I was terribly fond of, died. They found her lifeless body slumped in her wheelchair this morning.
   Excuse me if I begin this letter on such a sad note. After all, you don't even know who I am, so, I should have introduced myself first. Everyone knows me by the name of Evgenij Koslov and, as you can see from the heading, I live in Petropavlovsk, in far-off Siberia. I don't know if, by any chance, my name means anything to you, if your father mentioned meeting me here when he came to look for his twin, Gabriel. I acted as his guide last summer when he and your aunt Rose visited offices, hospitals and other places in hopes of unearthing information and possible testimonies regarding the fate of their long-lost brother. I fraternized with them more than I should have, much more than I usually do. I can guarantee you, I broke all the rules concerning the treatment of tourists who, since permission to visit has become much easier, flock to our peninsula. As soon as I learnt that you spoke Russian well, I used a rather lame excuse to induce your father to give me your address, although when he gave it to me, I wasn't sure whether I'd ever use it or not.
   You're certainly wondering why a total stranger living at the ends of the earth wants to write to you, so I beg you, dorogoi *Tommaso, to forgive and bear with me. You'll understand shortly, but, first of all, I have a story to tell you.*
   I've lived in Petropavlovsk since 1953.
   I'm sure you know the history of this country, so I'll be brief when outlining the political context of the times. Stalin was dead only a few

months and many deceived themselves believing that the vise of the red terror would slacken, that a more democratic and open regime would reign in the Soviet Union. They were wrong: in actual fact nothing really changed, nothing that would truly improve the living conditions of millions of people. Fortunately, this town had always been more like paradise than many other parts of Siberia full of prison camps, the notorious gulags of which you have undoubtedly heard. Petropavlovsk was never tainted with this dishonor, even if, given its strategic position, it hosted Russian nuclear submarines for many years. All this, just to give you some idea of how matters stood when I first arrived here.

And to tell you that it was by sheer coincidence that I did.

Coincidence is the crucial element in the tale I am about to tell, the silent weaver of a long, heart-breaking story, a tragedy which overwhelmed my life, and not only mine. When I think of my life, I imagine it in two stages, a «before» and an «after», as in cases when an extraordinary incident overturns the course of events, imposing new coordinates.

The «after» began, in fact, in Petropavlovsk, one mild evening in early summer, when I woke up in a hospital bed, in the grips of a nightmare. I was howling to high heaven and crying uncontrollably. I remember the distinct feeling that I was burning, that ravenous flames were devouring my face. My head was bandaged, my face swollen and I could see from one eye only. I was thrashing about and lashing out and risked pulling out the IVs and waking up all the other patients in the ward. Two nurses had rushed in to help me. «Where am I, who are you?» I mumbled as my brain wandered, oscillating between a kind of mist fogging my brain and a lacerating pain racking my jaws. In vain the nurses tried to calm me, so the stronger of the two held me down while the other tied my wrists and ankles to the bed post. «Evgenij, stay still, otherwise, I may have to hurt you», he warned me. They called me Evgenij, but that name meant nothing to me, did not belong to me. «Where am I, who are you?» I kept on repeating, like a kind of litany. Suddenly, a doctor in a white coat appeared, holding a file which he consulted briefly. «Comrade Evgenij, welcome back», he said, staring at me as if I were some kind of Lazarus risen from the dead. «You've been here in this hospital for over two weeks now. You've been in a coma. But, luckily, you've come through. We actually feared the worst.» This news took my breath away; and I forced myself to recall what had happened, but my memory was a total blank, it contained nothing that could take me back in time. I was about to scream in the throes of utter panic, fear of the unknown, when I felt a needle prick me somewhere in the arm; then a kind of torpor overpowered me and forced my eyes to close. When I woke up again the following day there was an army officer in uniform standing before me. The peak of his hat seemed so long, probably due to some strange optical illusion, it almost brushed my face.

«Good morning, comrade», he said to me, «you're a lucky man.»

I was looking at him through my half-closed eyelids trying to get him into focus but, as he was sitting with his back to the light, I couldn't see him properly.

«What do you want?» I grumbled unable to move, seeing that I was still tied to the bed.

«This is comrade Igor Bergovich», the major continued, introducing another man sitting beside him in silence and whom I had not noticed before. He was very thin and wore a sailor's uniform.

«Untie me immediately», I began to howl and felt a terrible ache in my jaws and throat.

«Later. For the moment, I need you to listen to me carefully», the officer cautioned me severely. «The good news is, obviously, that you are alive; the only survivor of the fire which broke out on board the Linka while it was taking you and many other convicts to the northern mines. None of the prisoners or the crew were saved; only you, comrade Evgenij. Comrade Igor is your savior», he explained, patting the sailor on the back, «isn't that so, comrade? Now», he added with an affected sigh, «the bad news is that you have not come through this tragedy unscathed. You have suffered concussion which has caused temporary amnesia and, worse still, the fire has burnt part of your face. The doctors did all they could to save your left eye but, unfortunately, there was nothing they could do.»

He nodded and a doctor approached to explain the situation.

«On the left side of your face there were second — and third — degree burns, so we had to operate immediately to remove the charred tissue. For the moment we're unable to tell you how deformed your face will remain, but one thing is certain, you won't have the same looks as before».

He spoke without interruption and as tonelessly as if reading the weather report and with the air of a person in a hurry to get it all over with as soon as possible, paying no heed to my wheezing, to the horror I felt on hearing this awful news. Only Igor showed the least compassion. He kept his head bowed and did not even dare look into the only eye I had left. To give you some idea of my despair, I can tell you I felt like a new-

born infant, endowed, however, with awareness and understanding, being ushered into this world only to be informed that he would remain one-eyed and deformed for the rest of his life.

«Thank you, thank you», the officer said dismissing the doctor. «Now, comrade Igor, tell us how you rescued him.»

«I was out in my little boat, fishing-rod in hand, when I heard a series of explosions...» Igor began, a tremor in his voice.

Meanwhile, as I turned my head on the pillow with a painful effort, I saw there was another soldier, an NCO, standing behind him taking notes, writing down, verbatim, every word Igor said.

«When the ship exploded the smoke shrouded everything, because of the easterly wind blowing inland from the sea. Soon the Linka *sank and the trawlers in the area struck out in that direction in hopes of finding survivors in the water.»*

«Continue, comrade, these things we already know, tell us, instead, how you rescued Evgenij.»

The sailor nodded. «I was sailing back into the bay, my heart in my mouth from fear, horrified by the disaster, when near the Tri Bra...*»*

«The three reefs?»

«Yes. I saw a body on the surface of the water, being washed back and forth by the waves breaking against one of the reefs.»

At this point, the major glanced knowingly at the NCO who nodded.

«I pulled him on board, which required an enormous effort, and immediately tried to resuscitate him; he was stiff, his skin already livid because of the ice-cold water. I managed to get him lying on one side and hit him on the back until he vomited, coughed and began to breathe.»

«Then?»

«I tried to talk to him, find out the conditions he was in; the wound on his face was absolutely horrendous.» Igor grimaced, but did not dwell on details; he was a kind, sensitive man. «It was clear, anyway, that he was very young, sixteen, eighteen at most. 'Can you hear me, can you hear me?' I asked him, but he said nothing, remained motionless; his slow breathing the only sign that he was still alive.»

As Igor spoke, I could hear his voice quaver, the shock still affected him.

«What had he on his person?» asked the major.

«Well, he was wearing only long underpants and a vest, nothing else, except a ring on one finger — a wedding band in old red gold — then a

medal on a chain around his neck, the dog tags camp personnel wear with their names and numbers on them.»

«Are these the items?» asked the major pulling two objects out of a little bag and handing them to Igor. The sailor examined them attentively.

«Yes», he ratified. «This wedding ring with the inscription S-S 1935, and the dog tag saying Evgenij M. Koslov, n. 9211145; I remember the three ones in the middle.»

«Comrade Koslov, do you remember anything about the facts comrade Igor has just reported?» the major asked me shortly afterwards.

I shook my head. I could remember nothing.

«It's in your best interests to get your memory back as soon as possible», muttered the officer between clenched teeth, «this is a Christian wedding ring... very strange, is it not Evgenij? Because your papers say that your family is of the Islamic faith. Therefore, either you are not Evgenij, or you stole the ring; in either case you owe us a convincing explanation.»

He rose, red in the face with anger, and stalked out of the room with the NCO and Igor in tow.

During the days that followed they dosed me constantly with sedatives and anxiolytics. Then they untied me as I had become innocuous. I remained in bed all the time sleeping or vegetating in a stupor. No bad news could disturb me further, yet nobody could cheer me up either: I was in a state of complete abulia. When they removed my bandages, they obliged me to look at myself in the mirror to get acquainted with my new face.

I examined the scar like a gigantic mushroom that disfigured my face, I ran my fingers over it, feeling the rough skin on the surface, the slack damaged tissue below.

«Evgenij Koslov, you're as ugly as a toad», I told myself in the end with a sarcastic grin.

The major came back often to interrogate me, every time more and more suspicious, convinced as he was that I was hiding some terrible secret from him. One day they had me take a series of X-rays, insisting in particular on my neck and head. It was then I had my first flash. As I stood naked up against the cold metal plate and the machine hummed, an image darted into my mind, one of two bodies grappling in a furious fight, no holds barred. I was immediately overcome by disgust and hatred while my heart began to race so fast that the doctor had to ask me to keep still; otherwise he would have had to take the X-rays all over again. This scene acted as a lifeline onto which I clung attempting to emerge from the turbid well of amnesia into which I had fallen. During my few moments of lucidity, I forced myself to recall who I really was and try to discern between reality and dreams, nightmares I should say. I forced myself to dwell for hours and hours on those flashes, those visual fragments which now and then troubled me and struggled to recompose the puzzle of my life with the few pieces I had at my disposal: a name, a ring and a metal tag. I would often curl up in some corner like a stray dog, wherever I happened to be, and burst into tears under the astonished gaze of the others.

One morning, the usual officer brought me a file containing a short biography of Evgenij along with a copy of his ID photo.

«Read it, who knows, maybe it will help you remember who you are.»

Here is what I found out:

Evgenij Mateev Koslov was born in Tula, Russia, in 1933. His mother died when he was nine and his father soon married again obliging him to live with a stepmother he detested. Cohabitation proved disastrous, especially after the birth of his step-brother, because the woman discriminated against and abused Evgenij shamefully. One day when his father was absent, Evgenij brutally attacked and beat up his stepmother, then went off and handed himself over to the police. During the interrogation that followed, sixteen-year-old Evgenij held that the quarrel had broken out because the woman had bitterly criticized the Party and that he, faithful cardholder and militant, had felt the urgency to teach that insolent traitor a lesson. Nobody believed him, of course, but instead of sending him to prison they offered him work with Dostroi, the Siberian construction company which also managed the fleet responsible for the transfer of convicts. In short, he became a screw aboard those floating prisons. Evgenij, strong and stout, was particularly notorious for irascibility and uncontainable violence, attributes which earned him the nickname of Lev, that is, Lion.

One final detail, though by no means unimportant, was that, in 1953, the «Lion» was to be married to a girl called Silvija and that the date of the wedding had been fixed for the second Sunday in July of that year.

I continued to scrutinize the black and white ID photograph and ask myself what I could possibly have in common with the man with whom destiny sought to identity me. I racked my brain looking for even the smallest fragment of memory regarding my life, but my memory was silent and obstinately refused to comply, as if my rebel brain, deprived of its primary functions, wished to bar my way to memories of any kind.

I spent over four months in the hospital in Petropavlovsk. I left it one day in autumn as the year's first snow began to fall. They accompanied me to the entrance and then to a car waiting to take me to my new abode: an army barracks. They shoved me into the car while I was endeavoring to inhale my first mouthful of fresh air after so much time indoors.

«Get in there!» they ordered me while I kept watching the flakes, as they tossed and spiraled silently in the air, enthralled.

They took me to the military base on the southern side of the bay, where I was held in a regime of semi-detention. They could not release me until their investigations had been completed. They took several photos of my face from various angles, then they recorded my voice on tape, as I read a love letter to Silvija, which they had obliged me to write. That fact flattered me. Suddenly I felt quite important, to some extent, a boy on whom considerable attention was being focused.

The snaps and bobbins were sealed and sent off to Moscow for analysis: my features, my voice, my handwriting, everything; even the words I had chosen to write the letter. The photos were shown to Silvija too and, later on, I was told that the girl was so distraught when she saw my ravaged face that she burst out crying. The officials had showed her the letter in my illegible handwriting and faulty syntax.

«Well, is he Evgenij Koslov?» they had asked her.

«I entreat you, don't torment me, how can I know?» the girl had answered. «He never wrote me a love letter before.» However, she had found comfort in my recorded voice. Although somewhat changed due to damage to the vocal cords, she sustained that the sweetness had remained unaltered.

Silvija had no doubts: the voice on the tape was that of her beloved Evgenij.

Major Piotr Bogdanov, the officer in charge of investigations, decided to submit me to a truly particular experiment in an attempt to reawaken my memory, a test strongly recommended by certain psychiatrists and neurologists. It consisted in having me wear a special cap attached to electrodes and close me into a little theatre with a huge screen onto which

they projected a montage of highly contrasting scenes, a rapid sequence
of frames alternating between scenes of love and tenderness and others of
violence and hatred. I sat there in the half-darkness for whole afternoons on
end, watching people being massacred and then mothers tenderly hugging
and kissing their babies; I cried and laughed simultaneously. Meanwhile,
the medical team monitored the electrical activity in my brain as it was
stimulated by these scenes.

«Who are you? Have you remembered anything?» Bogdanov used to
ask me when the lights went back on but I only stared blankly back at him.

One afternoon, however, they screened a terrible sequence showing a
sweet girl being raped by a gang of men. They had tied her down to the bed
and taken turns at raping her. The camera focused on the girl's face, an
angelic face, as she thrashed powerlessly under the weight of their bodies.

«Stop, stop!» I yelled at a certain point, springing to my feet and
rushing up to attack the screen which I would have torn to pieces had the
wire of the electrodes not held me back.

«Good, maybe we've managed to come up with something», said
Bogdanov with enormous satisfaction entering the room, waving a copy of
my EEG and pointing at the spike my reaction had triggered.

I, instead, continued to remain silent, my heart beating like a drum
making my eye pulse beneath its black eyepatch ...

Tommaso dorogoi, I cannot as yet describe what I felt on seeing that
rape on the screen. It was as if I had been torn apart. The anger, the pain
and the consternation bore through me like a flow of lava.

«Now you must speak», said Bogdanov assailing me and shoving
the EEG in my face, «science does not lie! You have had some kind of
revelation.» And it was true.

The «before» part of my life had overwhelmingly surfaced again when
I saw that girl's face and heard her cries. The bastion erected around my
memory had collapsed under this violent attack. Suddenly, I found myself
a convict on board a prison ship in flames. All around me detonations,
desperate screams and cries for help. Strangely enough, I was not trying
to save myself in the midst of all this turmoil. I was on the deck wrestling
furiously with another man, driven by hatred and an unquenchable thirst
for revenge. I would never have found peace had I not sated myself with
his blood. I was digging my teeth into his throat like a predator, to drain
him of his vital sap, to empty him of every last drop of life-giving liquid.
When I drew back from him, he was staring at me in utter astonishment,

amazed at my strength; he was still moving his lips but couldn't make even a squeak. He only managed — I swear it — a feeble sarcastic grin of contempt which made me lose my head completely. I pounced on him again, digging my teeth into his flesh with all the might in my body.

«Die, die, you bag of shit», I yelled as I bit off a piece of his flesh and spat it into the fire as the flames began to lick my body.

I took his head and bashed it over and over again on the deck until I saw his clouded eyes surrender to death. Then, I just dropped down exhausted, paralyzed by the sense of guilt that nauseated me. My murderous frenzy had suddenly abated to become unbearable remorse: I just wanted to die beside the man I'd just killed.

Dear Tommaso, I was still a child, only sixteen, and I felt like Cain, crushed by my own heinous sin.

'A fugitive and a vagabond shalt thou be on earth!', I said to myself as I begged God for pardon and cried unconsolably. And yet, unexpectedly, something triggered inside me: some kind of divine strength came to my aid; maybe it was only the instinct of survival that prompted me to act, to move.

'Get up, get up now!' it urged me.

I took the wedding ring he was wearing from his little finger. It belonged to my mother and I had made a gift of it to my darling Nina, a young convict like myself, a sweet angel raped and killed by him and four other louts. I tore it off his finger with such force that I heard the phalanges crack. I put it on my own finger and went to the parapet ready to jump overboard. But then, I turned around again and went back to carry out one last task. Around his neck my victim wore an iron chain with a medal bearing his name, surname and number. I tore it from his body, and having cleaned the blood from it, tied it around my own neck. Just then a terrible explosion shook the ship and the flames struck me straight in the face and I felt myself burn like the wick of a candle.

I threw myself into the water seconds before the Linka broke in two and sank in a billow of black smoke.

Finally I knew who I was, but that awareness had rekindled one of my most destructive sentiments: hatred. With the impetus of a tidal wave that overpowers and drowns you, so did hatred pervade every fiber of my being.

Destruction and self-destruction were the only concepts in which I now believed...

«*You are not Evgenij Koslov*», Bogdanov insisted, «*the results of our tests have come back: there are some major discrepancies, above all your dental arch: your mouth contains two molars more than Evgenij's.*»

He gripped me by the shoulders and stared straight into my face.

«*Come now, confess, tell us who you really are! Who are you?*» he roared and slapped me soundly across the face.

«*I don't know, I swear I don't!*» And I shook my head with all the vehement conviction I could muster.

Bogdanov wagged his admonishing finger in my face. He was short and thin and often had to get up on his toes to speak to me, hoping to appear more imposing.

«*You're a man without a name, a nothing, a nobody.* Nikto, nikto!*»*, he used to say his lips curling with scorn.

They shut me up in a cell, deprived me of the semi-liberty I had enjoyed until then, giving me only a bowl of soup and a chunk of bread to eat every day. Now and then, they let me come out but only to interrogate me all over again, asking me the same questions about my true identity.

But I intended to reveal it only to whomsoever I chose and when I deemed it opportune.

During the endless hours spent in solitude I tried in vain to quell the hatred I felt swelling up inside me. Unfortunately, it was the only feeling that helped me carry on, made my heart beat, my blood circulate, in short, live. And so, day after day, I plotted my revenge against the whole world.

The months went by and nobody managed to make me say anything at all about my past. I had learnt to play the part of the amnesiac to perfection. After all, I needed only to go on behaving the way I had in the beginning: stare into empty space, shuffle about slowly and unsteadily, slur my words. I wasn't sure whether Bogdanov and his team had actually fallen for my ruse but one day during one of the interrogation sessions, Bogdanov suddenly announced: «*You can't stay here no longer. It's immoral that a young man like you live off the fatherland like a parasite. We need active people, efficient, productive men and women so that our Union may excel in the world*».

Then he sprung to his feet and came over to me. I was sitting there with a dribble of saliva on my chin, the latest invention to pass myself off as a poor idiot.

«*You have a choice, mister Nikto*», he said, «*either you accept our conditions or you're done for... we'll take you out to sea again, to where we found you to start with, isn't that so, lads?», he said turning to his men. «We'll simply dump you into the ocean. What's the temperature of the water today? Minus 15? Nobody will notice you've gone, nobody will miss you and do you know why? Because you are a Nikto, a nobody!»*

I opened my eyes wide at this intimidation. «The conditions…?», I murmured at last.

They all roared with laughter, obviously finding my pragmatism amusing.

«Clever boy, isn't he?», Bogdanov quipped sarcastically turning to his minions.

They put me back behind bars again but instead of leaving me shut up to idle and languish, they filled my days with myriad activities. First of all, P.E., entire mornings spent in the gym under the guidance of a skilled instructor. I had to run, lift weights, swim in the pool doing up to seventy lengths a day. My diet was now balanced and nourishing. I ate at the army mess, where there were poultry, red meat, fruit, vegetables and desserts. The benefits soon became apparent: I built up muscle, grew stouter and fitter and resumed a normal coloring. When I looked in the mirror, I congratulated myself on this metamorphosis. I wanted to look as little like my old self as I could, and I was getting there.

The afternoons were devoted to study and mental exercise. I attended the course designed for young recruits, a group of hand-picked men and women; I was made to sit at the back of the classroom without being allowed to interrupt or disturb the lessons in any way. If I had questions I was only allowed to pose them to the teachers when classes were over. However, the directors were struck by my extraordinary learning skills and my first semester report was extremely positive; my marks were up to class average, a remarkable result in a school as prestigious as the military academy. I had worked really hard. I had always enjoyed studying and discovering the world through books. I came tops in English and German and even began to study the languages of some of the Soviet Republics, like Azerbaijan and Georgia. I had a special bent for history, philosophy and literature although I was also keen on maths and science. I spent hours on homework in my cell and studied late until lights-out every night.

I was educating myself, making up for lost time.

My academic success did not fail to arouse the antipathy and envy of my classmates, who scornfully referred to me as «the founding». They repeatedly jeered and mocked me, not only because I had no family but also because of my eye. My resentment grew and erupted in violent rows, sudden scuffles; all it took to detonate them was a malicious glance, a nasty comment or an allusive grin.

«Hey, Foundling, watch where you put your feet!» said Fyodor, the son of a high-ranking bureaucrat, as he bumped into me on purpose in a corridor one day.

«Rather than a foundling he's a one-eyed clown», jeered Antonin, his young blond friend. In his smart uniform he looked me over with an air of smugness, negatively appraising the grey flannel tracksuit I had on, the one I'd taken with me from the hospital.

The blood rushing to my head, I pounced on him, threw him to the ground and began punching him with all the angry, pent-up energy in my body.

«Say that again, and they'll be the very last words your pretty little lips will ever utter!» I yelled at him. «And remember, I am the lion, you the gazelle!»

This was how my life went on for the following three years. I never went out anywhere; when all came to all, the military base was a world unto itself, a microcosm which could offer everything a young man might desire. Little by little, I recovered a taste for life; at weekends the barracks sprang to life, vodka flowed like water, beer and wine too, and the comings-and-goings of prostitutes were tolerated by the officers who closed an eye, even two! I soon had my first sexual experiences too…

At the end of the course I came second, and that only because of my social status, otherwise, I would have been first. My dissertation was on Soviet propagandist filmography and its greatest directors: Ejzenstein, Pudovkin, Vertov, a topic which Bogdanov, a passionate lover of cinema, appreciated particularly. Later, he admitted that he had been ignorant of certain facts I had included in my work, such as the substitution of the Potemkin *with her sister ship* The Twelve Apostles, *during the shooting of Sergej Ejzenstein's* Battleship Potemkin.

«Your paper was truly enlightening», he told me as he clasped my hand warmly. He considered me his creature, and whatever one might say of him, he had always remained the perfect gentleman capable of acknowledging the merits of others.

A few days later, they invited me to a meeting attended by many of the big brass.

«*Comrades, here is the ugly duckling we've transformed into a swan, our very own Evgenij Koslov*», Bogdanov began introducing me to the pluri-decorated assembly using the name he knew perfectly well was not really mine.

I had washed and combed my hair with the utmost care and donned the brown uniform they had loaned me for the occasion; the hat was too small, so tight, in fact, that it gave me a terrible headache.

During the buffet that followed, they introduced me to admiral Tuchevsky. We spoke at length about the Great Soviet Union and its glorious future but also about my amnesia.

«*This lack of memory frees you from tiresome bonds*», Bogdanov, who had been standing to one side listening to us, volunteered at a certain point.

«*Let's send him to Magadan, the KGB can surely do with a brain like his*», suggested the admiral with a smile.

I replied with a slight bow of the head, a gesture they must have taken for consent, because a few months later I was transferred to a barracks in the Kolyma capital.

No longer as a prisoner but as a free man with a name and an ID.

In Magadan I learnt the subtle, occult art of spying.

Spying: 'clandestine activity aimed at gleaning information of a political, military and economic nature', a definition you will find in any dictionary. Inside the district HQ of the KGB, a cement building with a mastodontic statue of Lenin in front of it, I spent an entire year, learning the martial arts, the use of firearms, even attending acting and disguise classes. The model they imposed resembled, to some extent, the Ninja, the famous mediaeval Japanese spies. I soon discovered they did not want me to become a spy as such. I was trained to unmask other spies who infiltrated the Soviet Union posing as tourists, entrepreneurs or faithful communists. Our dossiers were soon full of accounts of incredible facts that surpass fiction by a long shot.

By the end of my training I had become an excellent sniper: I could hit anything, a sitting or a moving target, be it a bear or a hare; I was skilled in hand-to-hand combat, using my bare hands or a blade: a dagger, a sword, a sabre. It was a real pleasure to watch me in action, also because, dear Tommaso, I was practically blind in one eye. I kept it covered with a black patch which I donned reluctantly, though I soon learned to accept it as it was the only way I had of hiding my maimed face.

At the end of that year's training, I returned to Petropavlovsk. Besides its fisheries and the activity inside the nuclear submarine base, Petropavlovsk was a rather dull place. Nevertheless, I had a lot of work to do trying to capture countless spies, especially from the western countries who tried to infiltrate the territory. They arrived by sea or plane only, because there were no decent roads connecting the peninsula with the rest of the country. They immediately assigned me a house and a job, both quite modest because nothing was supposed to arouse the curiosity or suspicions of the locals regarding me, this new inhabitant who had arrived out of nowhere: Evgenij Koslov the secret under-cover agent.

I began working at the port — where better to survey foreigners arriving by boat or ship? I delivered crates of fish all over the city and throughout the hinterland, supplying state canteens, hospitals, the airport and even the military base itself. Everywhere I went I sniffed the air like a bloodhound and sifted all the information which, for one reason or another, aroused my suspicions. I flew regularly to Magadan, to the KGB HQ to receive instructions regarding my next mission. I entered the airport dressed as a fishmonger in my sou'wester gear, then changed and boarded planes dressed up to the nines, in elegant suits and silk ties, posing as a rich businessman.

Ruthlessness was the first rule I learned. «All for the fatherland and the Russian people», was a passage from the oath I swore the day I received my license. In the name of this principle I carried out numerous crimes. Here are a few of them:

– 1956: a French couple, Jean-Léon and Béatrice, entered the USSR posing as Polish zoologists called Ivan and Marja, declaring their intention to carry out research into the walruses that populated the seas of Siberia. In authenticity they had come to take photographs in a top-secret military zone. They were found burnt to a cinder in the car which had overturned at a bend on the coast road.

– 1958: an American Chris Metsikos, who had landed in Moscow pretending to be a Cypriot businessman called Metsovopoulos. The reason for his visit was to clinch a deal with the Siberian Tecnodrev pine and larch wood company. Instead, he tried to steal an important document from the firm's offices: a precious formula for the conversion of wood shavings into fuel. Once his cover was blown, he was shot dead in a club in Magadan.

– 1961. The Mc Abbey case: an entire English family, father, mother and their two children aged four and seven, were drowned during a

boating excursion off the coast in Avacha bay. Mc Abbey, a right-wing
extremist was planning a massacre at Petropavlovsk and would have used
the members of his family as human shields.

I carried out these murders with the impassibility of an automaton. I
considered it merely a job that needed doing. Besides, the unhappiness I
caused seemed to relieve my own, acting in some way, as a balm to the deep
wounds I carried inside me. I had become a monster and I'm convinced I
would have remained such had I not come across Anjushka on my way...

Evgenij was uncertain about how to continue his letter. He had
arrived at a point where he was afraid to go on and open up his heart.
He lifted his gaze and saw the rag doll with its straw plait, sitting
on his desk, its back against the wall. Next to it stood a photograph,
which he took up and examined at close quarters. In the snap,
against the backdrop of an amazing red sunset, were Mikael and
himself with Rose between them, a faint smile on her lips. That was
the day he had taken the siblings up to Yarkaija Avacha. They had
just left the nursing home when Mikael had asked a passer-by to
take a photo of the three of them with his Kodak Instamatic.

With the picture clutched tightly to his heart, Evgenij shifted his
gaze over to the window from which, beyond the little terrace, he
could look out on the bay.

The snow had covered everything with a candid white blanket,
muffling the sounds of the city now in the grips of winter ice.

When he took up his pen Evgenij now knew what to write next.
His hand flew swiftly over the paper without paying too much
attention to the calligraphy: he just had to get that letter finished
before he changed his mind.

Anjushka, the person I have just mentioned, came into my life back in
1962.

I was doing my usual morning rounds driving to the places on my list.
It was May, I recall, and though it was still rather cold, the days had begun
to lengthen and there was a vague promise of spring in the air. I could feel
the sap of life penetrate the birches, the bulbs of the lilies underground, the
water of the rushing rivers and streams gurgling merrily.

Nature was like a newly hatched chicken emerging from its shell.

I was wandering through the corridors of a nursing home where I had just delivered some fish when, suddenly, I saw the shape of a person seated in a wheelchair. As I drew nearer, I saw it was a young woman who had lifted her head up as if she'd just awoken up from some reverie she was condemned to dream. Don't ask me why I did it, but I went over to her as if drawn by a magnet.

She was extremely thin, her match-stick legs beneath her skirt were placed on the footrest of her chair. She had shiny blond hair woven in a long plait and her pale gaunt face made her huge green eyes look bigger, like emeralds in an ancient tiara from the Orient. When she turned them in my direction, I almost stumbled, like a dog when his master suddenly pulls on the lead. I addressed her but soon realized she was unable to speak. Anjushka was lost in a world of petrified speechlessness. She whined like some dumb animal, waving her hands about trying to make herself understood, but her trunk and legs remained motionless, as if entombed in marble. She was smiling at me, calling me over to her, believing, maybe, that she might succeed at last in giving utterance to the words trapped in her mind. Bewitched, I knelt down before this princess on her throne, and examined her at more closely, so close that I could count the shiny golden flecks in her splendid green eyes. She began to caress the band on my face, the only person ever to do so, the only person I have ever allowed do so. We stayed like that, for how long I cannot say, until something extraordinary happened. Her disarming innocence pierced me through and through, overwhelming me with a purity I thought could not exist and, that ever if it had, it had exhausted its supply to the human heart centuries before. I burst out crying; suddenly aware, by way of comparison, of the abominable ugliness which had long meandered its way into my soul, like a poisonous deceitful reptile, turning me into the repugnant being I was. Meanwhile, she continued to offer me her strange yet reassuring smile, almost as if satisfied, happy with the effect our closeness was having on me.

«Forgive me, whoever you may be», I murmured as a nurse swooped down on us providing me, despite her brusque manners, with the name of my princess.

«Anjushka, what are you doing?» she rebuked her charge.

I fled like a thief, unable to face the nurse who glared after me. But, as I hurried along the corridor, I was already promising myself that I would soon return. I absolutely needed to see that gentle Madonna who had miraculously appeared to me in the gloom of a bleak nursing home, inviting me to mend my ways and review my useless existence.

From then on, I found the means of sneaking down the corridor leading to her room, and visited her almost every day. It was really easy: years of training had taught me how to make myself invisible. I studied the timetable and knew when Anjushka was alone. I found ways of visiting the clinic to see her wherever my rounds took me to that district and even went so far as to change my delivery schedule to find time to be with her. I was overjoyed at the mere sight of her smile; that was enough for me, dear Tommaso. I always brought her some small gift or other, nothing important, just an insignificant something: a bun, a piroshky, at times a bracelet or some other trinket that didn't cost much. When Anjushka opened her eyes wide and the sadness that usually clouded them turned into happiness, I too was in paradise, and glowed with a joy that invaded my entire being.

Those meetings, I admit, did me more good than her. At last, I had found someone capable of filling the sterile recesses of my heart. The funny thing is that I didn't even know what Anjushka really meant to me. At times I thought of her as a sister, at others as a fiancée, however, the more I thought of it the more I realized how absurd it was to try to label feelings at all costs. I was fond of Anjushka and it didn't matter what kind of love mine was. Once I raided the nursing home offices and got my hands on her case history and learnt a lot about her.

Anjushka was born in 1943. She had just turned four when her parents were told she was suffering from a grave form of muscular dystrophy. Later, her father, a naval officer, abandoned the family and went to live elsewhere, though he did continue to provide for her. When her mother died, Anjushka, then aged twelve, was left all alone and as she was not self-sufficient, was admitted to a care home in town.

After a while, I found a way of getting her transferred to Yarkaia Avacha, where Batjuska, that is, my savior Igor Bergovich, was also an inmate. These were the only two people in the whole world who mattered to me: Igor who had retrieved my body, Anjushka who had retrieved my soul... and I wanted to spend all my spare time with them.

I'm sure you'll agree with me that true love does not give a hoot about social restrictions, about what is allowed and what is not. It springs into existence for no particular, plausible reason; the laws of love are written in a tongue that reason is not equipped to decipher. I insist on this point so that you may be able to understand how, despite the distance between our worlds, during the fleeting moments spent with Anjushka, I felt cared *for and cherished, as if I had finally come back home. Her little room had become my confessional. I dared tell her things I'd never have revealed to anyone else even under torture. In front of Anjushka I unburdened my soul of the unbearable weigh that was crushing my conscience; on bended knee, as if addressing an icon of the Mother of God. She dried my tears with her slender hands which she then dried on her inseparable rag doll, and, smiling at me, told me in her own special way not to worry, that she would take care of everything and relieve my heart.*

As time went by, I became less ruthless at my job. Love was thawing the ice beneath which I had hibernated my true nature for so many years. Hatred gave way to pity and indulgence. I no longer wanted to kill, even cause pain. I rediscovered my original sensitivity which I had voluntarily exiled as a result of the cruel blows fate had dealt me.

«Anjushka, you are healing me», I whispered one day, «I'm becoming once more what I used to be.»

She embraced me with her eyes, aware that the moment of truth had dawned.

I drew closer to her, rested my chin on her knees and found the courage to narrate the story of my life: the tale of "before".

I was born, moi dorogoi *Tommaso, in Patras, in Greece. My parents were Armenian refugees who had escaped from the genocide perpetrated by the Turks from 1915 on. I came into this world in the company of another little infant, my twin brother, about whom I knew absolutely nothing until my father told me everything the evening before he took his own life.*

I spent my childhood in Patras and I still have very fond memories of that place. Our home was in a shack in the Armenian refugee camp, where, despite living in extreme poverty, I was happy. I can still remember the aroma of thyme that filled the air by day, the jasmine that inebriated me by night. The winters were not cold, the summers rather temperate thanks to the sea breeze.

I was quite a vivacious child. I was always outside playing with the other children in the camp and often came back home covered in mud because of the scuffles into which I would throw myself headlong. I had a bit of a temper, you see, and could flare up at the drop of a hat. Furthermore, I was awfully proud. Yet, I felt terribly lonely and every night used to dream I had a brother lying there by my side.

My parents were too busy to notice my sadness or my need for affection. When I think of my family as it was at the time, I remember the silence that reigned in the house even during the most festive of occasions. It was as if mamma and papa had nothing left to say to each other, and that, if they had once shared something, it was now a thing of the distant past. Mamma and I slept together in the one big bed in the house, while papa lay down on a roll-up mattress on the floor, which was pushed, every morning, under the table. As a child, I didn't really notice the leaden atmosphere that reigned in our home. It was only as I grew older that I noticed the sorrow in my mother's eyes. I remember asking her more than once why she was so sad, but she never gave me a satisfactory answer. As to papa, he was taciturn and there was no way of getting a word out of him. He always had the air of a man who bore the weight of the whole world on his shoulders. He worked very hard and often travelled to nearby villages and towns selling the slippers he and mamma made together.

In 1941, when the Second World War broke out, Greece was invaded by the Italians, and Patras, due to its geographical position, was targeted. First the fascists landed to be joined all too soon by the Führer's men who trundled down into the city in their tanks from the north. Papa, who was a member of the Greek Communist Party, joined the partisans and took to the nearby Panachaikos mountains leaving the two of us all alone. With the war came hunger, and famine caused numerous deaths. Adults and children fell by the wayside like flies and Patras was full of corpses, their abdomens incredibly swollen. However, mamma, who was strong, resolute and ingenious, did not let anything get her down or frighten her and so, she began to work as a tailor making jackets and jerkins for the Greek army on the Singer sewing machine, the one she had used before that to stitch the slippers they sold. She bartered her work for a little bread, a much-prized commodity, more sought-after at the time than any other foodstuff. She even managed to get her hands on the odd bag of flour and when she did, she used to make delicious pancakes with thyme honey for me. The aroma and the taste still make my mouth water. As to papa, when — secretly and at great personal risk — he came down from the mountains, he always brought us whatever he was able to get from the peasants: a bottle of oil, a piece of cheese or a chicken.

One evening I saw my parents toasting with moschùdi, *the typical wine of Patras. Things between them seemed to have improved, also because they were celebrating a memorable event: the end of the war.*

Papa expressed the wish to spend the night at home and mamma unrolled the little mattress for him as usual. «I'll sleep there», I dared suggest in a sincere impetus of affection as I got into my pajamas. I was almost seven, in good health and it did not seem right or respectful that my poor father should sleep practically on the ground. That was the first time I remember ever seeing my parents sleep in the same bed.

As I grew up, I discovered the sheer pleasure of reading. I attended the local community school where they taught me Armenian and Greek, but English too. The teachers all complimented mamma, saying I was a particularly gifted child and that, if I continued like that, they even hoped to send me to a prestigious college like the Mekhitarists in Venice or the Melkonian in Cyprus.

My favorite teacher was Lucy, an English lady my mother was particularly fond of. It was she who taught me the Latin alphabet and make me a present of a little English-Greek vocabulary. In only a few months I learnt to read and translate entire paragraphs of a book of short stories, **The Daring Young Man on the Flying Trapeze** *by William Saroyan, an Armenian-American author with whom you are undoubtedly familiar. Lucy, however, soon returned to London to be married and from there she wrote long letters which mamma read aloud to me. These were some of the rare moments when I saw her beam with happiness.*

One day, papa announced with great solemnity that we were going to be repatriated, that is, that we would be going back to our beloved homeland, Armenia. It was 1947, the war had been over for two years and there was a general sense of uncontainable optimism in the air; those who had survived exile, famine and war made plans for the future, in an effort to look forward. A gigantic propaganda campaign was launched to attract Europe's Armenian communities, in particular those of Greece. It had been promoted by Stalin himself, with the imprimatur of the Church and the AGBU, the association for the preservation of Armenian identity and culture in the world, founded by the powerful US Armenian community. The dream which papa had entertained for years was about to come true at last. «Life is offering us one more chance», he told mamma. We had just finished lunch and the whole tiny house was full of the smell of pancakes. Mamma shook her head as she washed the dishes wondering whether it was worth their while to leave the little they had managed to build up in Greece and move to Armenia.

That night I woke up and heard papa, in bed, whispering to mamma, «Let's leave all of this behind us, this hovel, the desolation of the camp and the sadness that has accompanied us for so many years. I'm sure everything will change for the better in the homeland. I want to make you a gift of the happiness I have been unable to give you in this country. Satèn, my love, forgive me», he whispered, sobbing, as my mother embraced him again at last.

On the 22nd of June 1947 our caravan left Patras for the port of Piraeus, Athens, from where a Soviet ship was supposed to take us back to our homeland. Papa had sold the sewing machine to rake up money to pay for our tickets, but in order to have enough he also had to sell his wedding ring. That evening he returned home utterly distraught, telling us that he'd also gone to the cemetery to say goodbye to his father Toròs-agà and to Lussià-Dudù, the midwife who had helped mamma deliver me. Leaving the camp was heart-breaking, more than I could ever have imagined. I had no idea what to bring with me to Armenia and what to leave behind. In the end, I took only the little book by Saroyan, certain it would keep me company during the journey. Mamma, on the other hand, managed to pack everything we owned into two cardboard suitcases, amazed at how the contents of a lifetime and of an entire house could fit into such a small space. When she looked around the place to see if she'd forgotten anything, she suddenly burst into tears on seeing four planks in a corner of the room that had once acted as my cradle.

«Mamma, why are you crying?» I whispered in her ear. She did not answer; she kept beating her breast, digging her nails into her flesh.

The morning of our departure, I said goodbye to the families who had decided to remain in Greece and not to return to Armenia. I hugged them all fondly, even those I didn't particularly like, suddenly realizing that they had been my brothers all those years and that I had been wrong to feel lonely.

«Write as soon as you get there», they shouted as the train drew out of the station with a clatter of steel accompanied by the sad shrill whistle of the old locomotive.

At the port of Piraeus we had to await the Soviet ship for twenty days, camped like vagrants in tents on the docks. There were over a thousand of us from all over Greece. One morning, peering through the dense fog we caught sight of the outline of a ship, the word Chukotka written on its funnel and prow, approaching the pier.

When we went on board we felt heartened and happy again; many even danced on the deck convinced that life had begun to take turn for the better.

«Hayastàn, anush hayrenìk… Armenia, my dear fatherland!» we exulted.

After sailing for a week, we landed in Batumi, Georgia. We had to line up for ages at the customs, where they meticulously scrutinized all our luggage and documents. It was forbidden to take certain things into the USSR. Many had to throw their books into the sea, my mother was obliged to separate herself from the letters she had received from aunt Miriam, papa's American cousin, and from our English friend, Lucy, my ex-teacher. Some of the more zealous, lest their photographs be deemed compromising, simply tore them up. One woman wept bitterly as they trampled on her little Bible.

«What's your name?» I was asked by the interpreter standing beside the army officer in charge.

«Gabriel.»

«Surname?»

«Gazarian.»

«What are you bringing with you from the old country?»

«Only this», I answered, taking a red marble out of my pocket.

«Nothing else?»

«No», I replied, looking the official straight in the eye.

Later on, we boarded trains taking us to Armenia. When we arrived in Yerevan, several of the people, overcome by emotion, knelt down and kissed the land of their forefathers.

Papa looked up at Mount Ararat, towering above the city, the emblematic mountain of the Armenians. «There's our guardian angel, from now on it will watch over us!» he exclaimed, solemnly.

Today, I feel very bitter when I think of how he was duped, advantage taken of his trust and naivety.

For three months we lived in a camp made of tents in a park in Yerevan, until they assigned us lodgings in the Nova Sebastia district. Ours was a tiny apartment near one of the main thoroughfares and it trembled every time the tram trundled past down below on its shiny tracks. Soon, life in the fatherland turned out to be quite different from what we had imagined. If we had fled from Patras because of the destitution and unhappiness that surrounded us there, I could not understand, for the life of me, why we had chosen to come to live in a place like Yerevan. The city was a jumble of tall cement buildings all exactly the same. The weather was frequently overcast and gloomy and in winter the temperature fell below zero, at times down to minus ten. Our fellow countrymen and women considered us, returned emigrants, as second-class citizens. Aghbèr, brother, they jeered. They did not trust us because they feared we had come to steal the bread from their mouths. Nobody ever looked you in the eye when they spoke and often, they denied an instant later what they had just said a second before.

At school I learnt Russian and Armenian; but religion, which would have interested me considerably, being forbidden, was not taught. In class there reigned a regime of rigid discipline. The Union took precedence over everything else. The individual did not exist, because each person was simply an insignificant brick in the wall comprising a great people.

At night I dreamt of my beloved native Patras, missing it with all my heart.

Papa had a job in a shoe factory, six days a week, very often at night, where he worked long, unbearably taxing shifts. Mamma, on the other hand, thanks to her recent experience in Greece as a tailor, was given a job in a local clothing factory where she remained only a few months because, no sooner had we arrived in Yerevan than she was pregnant.

I think that the joy of having a new home and her hopes for the future had given her new life, in every sense of the word. As her belly grew, day after day, her appearance too changed for the better. Once thin and pale, she now became plump and rosy-cheeked.

«You're going to have a little brother», she told me one day, «feel, feel him, in here.» She beckoned me over to her and placed my ear against her bulging abdomen. I could hear strange gurgling sounds, like someone laughing with their head under water. This was my very first contact with the creature whom my mother erroneously called my brother.

One fine day in June, Novàrt was born, the sweet rosebud of our home, my baby sister. Little Novàrt was a tiny compendium of the entire universe. When I looked into her cradle, I was amazed that she looked like an adult in miniature. She had honey-colored eyes that sparkled in the sun and shone in the dark like those of a cat. Even as a very small child she was endowed with extraordinary intelligence and an obstinacy both quite amazing for a child of her age.

In one corner of the living room papa had built a partition to create *a tiny bedroom into which two small beds could barely fit. In that small space my sister and I wove a relationship we firmly believed nothing or nobody could ever destroy. At least that's what we thought...*

Evgenij paused. He felt tired, his head was weary from writing for such a long time and his mouth was dry and cloyed. He decided to make himself some tea in the old samovar he kept in the kitchen: two pinches of black tealeaves and a clove to heighten the flavor. Then, as he sipped it, he began to write again determined to finish as quickly as possible. So he briefly described the events that followed the birth of Novàrt to go on to dwell a little more on the arrest and hard labor he and his father were sentenced to, all because of a book. He wrote about their deportation to camp 11 in Altaj and then his transfer to the uranium mines aboard the *Linka* which never reached its destination.

In a few intense lines he told the sad story of Nina, «my light darkness», he called her.

He said every form of life, even that of an ant, was the greatest gift in existence.

When he came to speak of Seròp, he tried to keep to the exact words he had heard at the time...

...We had just left the Directorate of the camp. Papa was holding the letter in which Satèn declared she was no longer his wife; he had crumbled it up into a ball with mixture of rage and pain.

«You keep this», he murmured, handing me the ring mamma had returned to him.

«No! No way!» I protested. «It belongs to you, it's yours!» I insisted and put it onto one of his fingers.

«I am worthless», he chided himself, «your mother had every right to deny me. She gave me another possibility, even another child, a little girl who will now have to grow up without a father. And yet...» and he burst out crying, «I believe I did all I could...» He faltered and staggered. I tried to support him fearing his heart might give out literally as a result of this tremendous blow. I led him over to the wooden planks resting on two rusty barrels which acted as a bench, and held him as closely as I could to myself, trying to cover his shoulders with my jacket.

He was shaking like a leaf, feeble and worn out. «Gabriel-gian, God is punishing you along with me... for something I did many, many years ago...» he whispered before clasping my hand and placing it over his heart. It was as if he were about to pronounce some solemn vow or something like that. The yellow light of the lamp mercilessly illuminated his tear-stained face. «When you were born you weren't born alone, there were two of you... you had a brother, a twin; I sold him a few months after you were born... I had no choice... otherwise... otherwise... We were destitute, we had nothing to eat, not even a piece of bread.»

I listened to him dumbfounded and looked into his eyes. I had never before seen a man in such pain and the pity I felt for him was boundless.

«I did it all behind your mother's back... she was ill, I thought she was going to die... she needed medicine. I just snatched one of you up from the cradle, ran off and sold him for a handful of Drachmas». He broke down at this point and sobbed his heart out, speared to the core by that unbearable memory.

«Are you ashamed of me?» he asked, his eyes like those of a gladiator awaiting the Emperor's death signal.

I knew all too well that my father was weak, incompetent even, but he was certainly not an evil man. The long months in the camp had taught me that men were capable of crimes far more heinous than his.

«I swear that if I could choose», I told him, holding him even tighter, «I wouldn't want any father other than you.»

His eyes, as they turned towards me, were full of gratitude.

«You are an angel, not a son», he mumbled almost inaudibly.

On an impulse, I gave him a small kiss on the cheek, something I'd never done before. «And you are my hero», I murmured in his ear.

He was shaking in my arms.

«You see, heroes are not only the strong and the invincible», I ventured, «it's also those who go on fighting and admit their mistakes that are truly heroic.»

This declaration won me a weak smile from him. We remained there together until he stopped quaking. I helped him to his feet and accompanied him to his billet. I opened the door for him, but he stood there on the threshold.

«There can be no peace for me, I am damned forever», he said, before vanishing among the other prisoners inside.

His was the voice of a man whom nobody could touch anymore.

Many years later, when I was still young and strong, I did my utmost to find out about my family. I was dying to know what had happened to my own little Novàrt, and to my dear mamma. I had forgiven them for never having tried to contact me and justified their silence and inertia with the red terror that plagued the country. I was convinced that it was I who should run the risk of tracing them, but every time I decided to do so, I had to give up because I would have had to reveal my true identity.

When, last summer, in Magadan, they assigned me to a new mission, the minute I was given the names of the people I was to spy on I realized they were my siblings.

Almost forty years after my arrest, they had come looking for me at last.

I won't hide it from you, my dear Tommaso, that I reacted very badly at first. It felt as if they were holding a revolver to my temple. I truly hoped that some terrible cataclysm might cause the whole thing to fall through. All that night, I remained awake looking for a way out of what seemed to me like one more agonizing ordeal.

The day before they arrived, I got into a boat and rowed out to sea. I wanted to drown myself, finish the work that destiny had failed to accomplish, only to discover that, over the years, I had lost my swagger, my bravado, my courage. In short, I couldn't do it...

The morning after, however, at the airport, everything seemed different. I saw my colleague speaking to two strangers in the waiting room. I found it hard to believe that that beautiful woman was my sister and that distinguished grey-haired gentleman my brother.

«Relax», I told myself, «they are only travelers looking for a long-lost relative. They'll soon return home after failing to find him.»

They remained here with me only a few days. I drove them around, all three of us cramped into my old ramshackle van. I had purposely avoided getting a rented car, because I wanted to squeeze up close to them, in that small space, to test my senses and see how far I was able to resist. I wondered if one little drop of my blood might rebel and cry out loud enough to be heard: «Look at me, I'm Gabriel, your brother!»

As I waited for some kind of miracle to occur, I asked myself what still remained of the Gabriel that Novàrt spoke about. Her angel, that sweet, protective boy who gave her courage and hope on those cold nights in Yerevan.

Those were only childhood memories from my long lost past, recollections from forty years before.

Time is inconceivable. It has neither smell nor taste, body nor substance. It travels through the universe, dictating change, altering people and things. It weaves plots behind our backs and tyrannizes over our existence. It reveals the here and now; it tells us where we've been, but not what the next stage may be. And while we fear the enemies we can see and touch, he — worse than them though invisible — steals our very lives away.

Time is a fowler that ensnares us just when we are about to take flight. I have almost reached the end of my letter, moi dorogoi Tommaso.

I want you to know that your father is an adorable person. He reminds me of Seròp, the father he never knew. He walks just like him, has that same dreamy look of a boy who does not wish to yield to time. I envy him because I too would have liked destiny to spare me certain horrible experiences. I wish the purity of heart I had as a child had remained intact. Maybe, I say, maybe, I would have plucked up the courage to tell Novàrt and Mikael that I was the brother they were looking for. But in the end, I decided not to speak; I even attended my own funeral without saying a word. I wasn't even able to shed a tear, like you do when you part from someone you love. And yet, the memory of that sweet Siberian sunset we shared together, my siblings and I, is so precious to me.

The sweaters I gave them that evening to keep them warm are still hanging in my wardrobe, unwashed. You see, I don't want to cancel the smell of a life that never was.

Today Anjushka died, and with her a part of myself. I feel an enormous void inside me. Moi syn, *my son, son of my twin, I leave the decision of how to use this letter up to you.*

I embrace you with all my heart,
Your uncle Gabriel.

Hope

«Papà?» cried Tommaso as soon as the receiver was lifted.

«Hey, hello there! How are you?»

«Fine, and you?» You could tell by his voice that he was just dying to tell him something.

«Not too bad», Mikael said. «So, what's new?»

«Oh, something really extraordinary! Listen…»

Notes

1. *aghbarik* (Armenian) brother
2. *batjushka* (Russian) granddad
3. *Dlé yamàn…*: (Armenian) Alas, the sun is rising behind mount Araràt.
4. *hayrenaghiz* (Armenian) compatriots
5. *hlebushka*: (Russian) a term of endearment for bread.
6. *"Je désapprouve…"*: (French) "I disapprove of what you say but I will defend to the death your right to say it"
7. *kasha* (Russian) dinner
8. *machorka*: (Russian) typical no filter cigarette.
9. *maloletok*: (Russian) young convict.
10. *Panaghià mou*: (Greek) Mother of God.
11. *pareluìs*: (Armenian) good morning.
12. *"Vivi missi sunt…"*: (Latin) "Both were thrown alive into an incandescent sulfur pond"
13. *Yarkaiya* (Russian) Luminous